Violet's Daybreak

Violet's Daybreak

REGENCY SILHOUETTES BOOK TWO

Sarah Baughman

a GraftedHeart book

Violet's Daybreak

REGENCY SILHOUETTES BOOK TWO

Sarah Baughman

a GraftedHeart book

Dedication

To my husband,
who believed in me even when I didn't believe in myself,
and who has supported me throughout this journey.

Acknowledgements

As always, thank you to my excellent test-readers for your insight and feedback. Thank you to Heidi, my sister in Christ and my sounding board. Thank you to Amny for the horticulture knowledge (and for being "Violet").

Thank you to those at the Stephen F. Austin State University's Native Plant Center for the lovely setting for the cover image. Thank you to Shaw Photography by Alex Shaw for once taking again the perfect photograph. Thank you to Melissa Sue Photo & Design for designing a gorgeous cover from that perfect photograph. I'm so excited about this cover!

My thanks would certainly not be complete without expressing gratitude to my wonderful family and friends. Your response at the publication of my first book, and your continued support and love, mean the world to me.

Finally, praise be to God for granting me the ability to do something I enjoy so very much. I pray my meager efforts are used mightily by Him for the growth of His Kingdom. Soli Deo Gloria.

For you save a humble people,
  but the haughty eyes you bring down.
For it is you who light my lamp;
  the LORD my God lightens my darkness.
Psalm 18:27-28

Prologue

Wyndmere, Northamptonshire

1797

HER BREATH CAME in quick gasps, heart pounding painfully within her chest. The darkness of the setting sun made it difficult for her to see. She stumbled forward blindly, crashing into a hedge. The branches scratched her face and hands. Large, hot tears squeezed out of her closed eyes. An owl screeched and she bit her lip to keep from crying out.

Her younger sister had convinced her to enter the labyrinth two hours prior, when the sun shone brightly and the night-sounds were yet a long way off. Shortly after, she had been abandoned. Now, the darkness pressed against her closed eyes, and against her skin and her mind. It felt so familiar, yet so much more intense than what she knew. She sank to the ground, dropping her face into her knees. Tears dampened the fabric of her skirt.

"Violet!"

The voice was scarcely audible, yet caused her to lift her head with a choked sob.

"Violet! Where are you?" The voice was closer this time.

"I'm here! Papa? Is that you?" she asked, wiping her face on the edge of her skirt before she stood.

"You don't know your own brother's voice?" Her heart sank unaccountably. Their father seldom left his study or bothered himself concerning her. "Call out again, Violet, so I may find you."

"I am sorry. Since you started growing taller, you sound so much like him."

"Ah. I suppose that may be," said the voice, nearer now. "He's out looking for you, too, you know."

"Is he?" Hope swelled within her.

"Yes," said her brother, quite near now. She could see a glowing lantern through the hedge to her right. "I offered to look in here, since I am familiar with the paths, and he is searching in the woods to the east."

The lantern's glow moved to the left as it neared the edge of the hedge, then emerged and advanced toward her. Soon her brother's face was visible in its yellow glow. The boyish grin framed by a newly angular jaw was a welcome sight. She sighed as she stumbled toward him. He set the lantern upon the ground as she approached, rising in time to catch her as she threw herself into his arms.

"I was so very frightened," she whispered against his coat.

He held her until the shivering ceased, then assisted her to the house. While a servant was dispatched to inform the others that she had been found, Violet was placed in a hot bath before being wrapped in warm blankets and given a warm mug to sip while sitting up in her bed. Their mother entered soon after, delivering a sound scolding for her being so foolish as to be lost. The girl endured it meekly, the anticipation of seeing her father staying her.

When he finally entered the room, his light brown hair was peppered with more grey than she recalled, and his eyes surrounded by more lines.

"I am gratified to see that you are safe and well," he began after stopping several paces from the door. He looked up from the floor to her face, and his eyes widened before closing suddenly. After swallowing, he murmured, "The very image of Marianna." With these cryptic words, he turned and left.

The hope which had burned in the girl's heart was all but snuffed out. There would be no deepening of her relationship with the man she called Father, no light of comfort from that quarter. Sitting alone in the room, the darkness in her world grew, closing upon her.

Part I

One

Bainscroft, Somerset

August 1808

LORD REYMES, EARL of Bainscroft, surveyed the crowded ballroom. Born the Right Honorable Nathaniel Peyton, Lord Reymes was the fifth member of his family to hold the title of Earl, and he did his best to behave in a manner worthy of the time-honored title. His family was given the distinction generations ago and had since retained and even expanded the holdings in the southern part of the country. Just several of miles to the west of Ilminster in Somerset, Bainscroft was certain to attract a healthy crowd to any of its events. It was quite clear that his mother's party was an unequivocal success.

Nathaniel had returned from London only two days earlier, and seeing such a large number of people in his home so soon was mildly alarming, at the least. The party was given in his honor, and so of course it would be a success, despite his apathy toward the entire affair. Indeed, he would not have been in attendance were it not for the fact that he was presently needed on the estate.

His steward, Faintree, was hired four years past, shortly after the death of the fourth earl. He had managed fairly well in Nathaniel's absence, by the use of frequent correspondence and occasional trips to Town. Nathaniel knew, though, that it was past time to assume his responsibilities, especially in light of recent developments. Unfortunately, much of Society viewed his homecoming as evidence of his having determined to start a family of his own. In truth, he had done no such thing.

"Do you not think so, my lord?" simpered a Miss Pentham as she boldly laid her gloved hand upon his forearm. She was one of the ladies in the circle of guests with whom he was supposed to have been conversing, and had he been inclined toward setting up his nursery, she should have been a very good candidate for the next Countess of Bainscroft. She was not only a reputed beauty with her dark hair and luminous eyes, but also was well-connected and bestowed with a considerable dowry. He suffered no such inclinations at present, though, and so he fixed her with a disinterested gaze.

Having no earthly idea of what agreeing with her might signify, he was cautious with his answer, "Perhaps you are right." He then glanced pointedly at her hand, before dragging his reluctant gaze back up to her wide, fluttering eyes. When he raised an eyebrow, she blushed and removed her hand.

The dark-haired beauty turned back to her friend, a lady entirely unknown to him and unmemorable in appearance. Miss Pentham's blush soon faded as she smiled and preened over his conditional agreement that the gardens at Vauxhall were indeed the most splendid display of flora in the world. *Ah, so the conversation is about that.* Nathaniel did his best to hide his disdain. *I ought to have known Miss Pentham would never ask for agreement with anything even remotely controversial. She is not enough a lady of information to uphold her side of an argument had I disagreed. And I daresay she is aware of this.*

Baron Stallingsworth, a friend of Nathaniel's from his days at Oxford, stood on the other side of Miss Pentham's friend.

"My dear Miss Pentham," said the baron, "it is without a doubt that you are correct, no *perhaps* about it. Reymes here wouldn't know a lovely flower if one was right under his very distinguished nose."

Nathaniel further furrowed his stern brows, having no patience for the man's teasing. "I can only suppose, Stally, that you speak poetically of the ladies in this room."

"Or the ladies anywhere, man. They are a fair lot here, but even you must acknowledge that a comparison between ladies in Town and these country lasses will certainly conclude more favorably for Town."

Miss Pentham and her friend tittered vapidly and Nathaniel fought to maintain a neutral manner. When she commented on the use of Stallingsworth's nickname, he was forced to cough into his hand in order to hide his grimace. *Can she be unaware that even the Prince Regent insists upon the moniker* Prinny *and it is no clever thing to refer to Stallingsworth as* Stally?

Stallingsworth was one of the few friends who had remained at Nathaniel's side during his darkest days. The man constantly tried to cheer him, though, saying that he ought to frequent the clubs more for games or drinks, or at least find himself a lady-bird to help distract him from his doldrums. Nathaniel was firm in his resolve, however, that he would not be seeking solace in a woman of ill repute, despite the common practice of the day. There was a reason for its being termed "common."

Soon boring of the conversation, Nathaniel felt his eyes wandering again, looking for more stimulating amusement. Or an excuse to depart. As he glanced over those gathered in the ballroom, he noticed his mother, the Dowager Countess of Bainscroft, surrounded by her friends. Mr. and Mrs. Doberly were close, smiling and chatting with her. During his time at university and later during his self-imposed exile, she had often written of dear Mrs. Doberly's visits, which were a great balm to her in the absence of the late Lord Reymes – a balm *he* ought to have provided, as her eldest son and heir to the title which his father had left. But Nathaniel could not immediately face her after his father's death.

Nathaniel observed Mr. Doberly lean closer to the ladies, making some comment or another with a wry expression upon his face and a vague gesture to the room. Both his wife and the Dowager broke out in giggles. Nathaniel felt his heart constrict at his mother's beautiful but aging smile. She rarely smiled near him anymore, even after he had returned to his home and sought to renew their relationship. He knew that his family would never be as close as it had been, but he hoped that he might someday be in his mother's presence without the debilitating guilt which currently was his constant companion.

At the moment that guilt grew and threatened to choke him.

In an effort to avoid the dangerous path his thoughts were taking, Nathaniel distracted himself by attempting to recall all he could about the Doberly family. It was a game, of sorts, which he had begun to play with himself. As the master of such an estate as Bainscroft, he should be familiar with the tenants and neighbors, so he did his best to stay abreast of their news.

The Doberlys were a genteel, though untitled, couple, close to his mother's age. They lived on a smaller estate than his own, to the south of Ilminster. In addition to the couple, there lived at Doberly

Mill one daughter and a handful of servants. He could not recall the daughter's name, but knew her to be nearly ten years his junior. He also knew that they were entertaining relatives at present, the wife and two daughters of Mrs. Doberly's late brother. A quick sweep of the party surrounding his mother showed that the relatives were not with them. Nathaniel vaguely wondered where the three ladies had gone. *Most likely dancing, if the mother's disgustingly obvious attempts at drawing notice to the girls gives any indication.*

Determined not to dwell upon the Doberlys' unfortunate relatives and their likely proclivity for cap-setting, Nathaniel continued looking around the room. Almost immediately he spotted one of those whom he had hoped to forget. Tucked between a column and a small cluster of females, nearly hidden in the shadows, he saw the daughter whom he believed to be the eldest. Though he could not recall her name, he did remember her face. When they were introduced earlier in the evening, he begrudgingly admitted that her earnest, grey-green eyes drew him. She carried herself with a quiet grace – so discreet, in fact, that she seemed easily missed. Her eyes were downcast as he continued staring, and he could see, even from the distance, that she was wringing her gloved hands. Slowly, her eyes raised and she seemed to glance unseeingly about the room. He wondered what she was thinking; it was clear she was not enjoying herself. Suddenly, though, he realized that she returned his gaze. Immediately he looked away, continuing in his perusal of the room. While his opinion of her mother and sister did not extend to her, neither did he desire to give false hope. That would indeed not do. At best, he would break her heart. At worst, he would find himself married to a woman whom he did not desire.

And I have nothing to offer a bride, save my title and wealth. Paltry offerings they are. If only... But he pushed that thought away.

Miss Pentham relentlessly claimed his attention once again and he was almost grateful for the distraction. "My lord Reymes, I have not seen you dance but thrice. And at your own ball!"

"Indeed, Miss Pentham?" Nathaniel disinterestedly took out his snuff-box, running his thumb along the ridge of the lid, but did not open it. The top had an intricately-painted image of his home; it had belonged to his father. On a sigh, he slipped it back into his waistcoat pocket and said, "I had not been counting."

"But you must dance more – set the example!" cried she, fluttering her fan and batting her eyelashes. He imagined her to be crying *Dance with me!* in her mind.

"I shall make every endeavor to dance more later in the evening, but first I must ensure that all is proceeding as it should be." Seeing an opportunity to excuse himself for a bit, he continued, "In fact, I must speak with my housekeeper now. Good evening." And he bowed, before hastily making his escape.

Nathaniel easily determined that his staff was more than competent and there was no need for him to do more than greet his guests. Standing partially hidden in a doorway where he had stopped Mrs. Baker to ask about the food for dinner, he paused, wondering whether he would be missed should he choose not return to the ballroom. Surveying the large room once again, taking in the glimmering candles which offered light, and the colorful dresses of the ladies contrasted with the dark, formal coats of the gentlemen, he glimpsed a figure clad in pale green slip through the door to one of the balconies. *That I might slip away so easily.* Still trying to muster the will to walk back into the ballroom, for he knew he would soon be missed, he stalled for several minutes. Suddenly, he spied a familiar figure – one whom he had not expected or desired to be present that evening – follow the young lady out to the balcony. He paused only briefly before his sense of honor compelled his feet forward to ensure that his suddenly-returned rake of a brother would not sully the reputation of yet another young lady, Nathaniel's uncertain opinion of her notwithstanding.

Miss Violet Wyndham had striven to remain in the ballroom for as long as she could – in an attempt to please her mama – but it fast became unbearable. At the first opportunity, she drifted through the crowds of people from her ineffective hiding place beside a large column and out onto the balcony she had spied while walking earlier with her sister Rose. The balcony afforded a brief respite – the air was marginally cooler than inside the ballroom – but it was the lack of people which made it infinitely better than the crowded ballroom. *I suppose I have the most eligible Earl to thank for the number of people,* she thought. *Only such a sought-after member of the peerage could attract so many to a country ball.*

The stone balustrade, which edged the balcony, framed the view of the garden in the fading twilight. The outlines of various bushes and trees were barely visible, but fragrances from the gardens below told of what the descending darkness hid from Violet's eyes. She discerned the earthiness of damp soil, the sweetness of blooms, the wholesomeness of green leaves, and there was a faint sweet crispness to the air, almost lost in the heavy humidity, that hinted at the presence of orchards nearby. Several birds called back and forth to one another, and Violet was certain she heard the water of a fountain somewhere below her. In the near distance, the glassy waters of a pond or small lake reflected the light of the quarter-moon that was rising. *If only this had been a garden-party rather than a ball. Cousin*

Charlotte would have been permitted to attend and I am convinced we would have had a grand time wandering about the grounds, enjoying the lovely gardens. She wished she might see it in the daylight, but could not fathom the idea that she would ever have the opportunity.

It was into this newly-found quiet that the sound of the opening door and a spike in the music from within the ballroom alerted Violet to the intrusion of another person into her solitude. Turning from the balustrade, she saw a man closing the door behind him. When he turned toward her, he did not seem surprised to see that she was there. Violet stood still, hoping against hope that the intruder would simply turn around and leave.

It was not to be. She stood against the balustrade, fear curling in her belly, her heart racing and her hands trembling. Darkness, deeper than that left by the nearly-set sun, began to creep upon her. The man stood between her and the door, blocking her only escape.

He has done nothing, she attempted to assure herself. *Perhaps he needs a breath of fresh air, as did I.*

"Good evening, Miss—?" The man's voice had a familiar cadence and timbre, but the pitch and raspy quality were unknown to Violet. Her heart picked up its pace.

"Wyndham." Her voice was scarcely more than a whisper, thick with her trepidation. She could not meet his eyes, even with his features bathed in shadow as they were, so she settled her gaze somewhere over his left shoulder and prayed that he could not see her fear.

"I beg your pardon." He bowed deeply, almost mockingly, and she managed a quick dip into a curtsy as the fear already coiled in her belly tightened further. "Are you quite alone out here, Miss Wyndham?"

Violet scarcely had time to process the implication of his question before his steps propelled him toward her. Suddenly, he was much too close, backing her against the balustrade, causing her stomach to erupt in nervous fluttering and her every thought to scatter.

"I-I am not *entirely* alone, sir," whispered she, praying that he would understand her meaning. *I am not without connections, without friends. I am no loose woman with whom you may satisfy yourself.* But to her horror, Violet's tongue would not form the words; her throat would not unlock her voice.

"But your party is not present *here*, is it, Miss Wyndham? On this...secluded little balcony?" His voice dripped with his own meaning, his own significance. He spoke her name as a threat. When he raised a hand to toy with a curl on the side of her face, his other creeping up to rest beside her on the balustrade, Violet felt numbing panic sweep over her.

"Well, aren't you a tempting armful," he said, his voice laced with something she could not identify, could not understand, but which nonetheless filled her with a frantic desire to flee.

Violet' heart pounded heavily in her chest and her breath grew labored. She could just make out the sight of a grin cross his face as the sound of her fearful breaths reached his ears. She opened her mouth once, attempting to speak, but failed. She could still hear the sound of the fountain below her and the music in the ballroom, but both seemed impossibly far away, as though coming through a tunnel. The humidity in the air had become terribly oppressive.

Suddenly all of that was forgotten, though, as his hands grabbed roughly at her – one at her waist and one at the side of her head, his fingers forking painfully into her hair, and his face closed in on her own. She could not move, could not react. A dark fog crept in on her vision, and her ears began to ring, though a few things from her environment still broke through. He tasted of strong drink, his hands were unkind and demanding, his body solid and heavy against hers. When his hands began to roam and he attempted to deepen the forced kiss, Violet's mind finally awakened and she began to struggle.

Turning her head, she managed to hold back her rising sobs long enough to whisper, "Please, I do not wish—"

"Oh, do you not?" he laughed. "I can be rather persuasive, Miss Wyndham."

Violet turned her head back and forth, attempting to avoid his persistent mouth, and managed to cry, "No, I do not wish to be persuaded! I wish to be left alone. Please!"

And in the next instant, he was gone. Violet collapsed onto the ground near the balustrade, breathing shallowly as she drew her knees to her chest and buried her face in the fabric of her gown, attempting to calm her crying. She was vaguely aware of the sounds of a scuffle of feet, several grunts – satisfied and pained in turn – and finally some whispered threats before the door creaked once more as someone returned to the ballroom. The sound of the water below sounded more natural now and the aroma of damp earth and sweet flora floating on the air once again reached her.

"You are safe now," came a gentle, masculine voice. With one last shudder, Violet managed to tamp down her sobs and force her breaths to come at a more even pace. Still, however, she could not bear to meet the eyes of her rescuer.

"Miss, er– Wyndham, was it?" the man's voice asked, a voice similar in cadence and timbre to that of her attacker, but with gentler, richer tones. "Are you–"

"Please," she blurted, "please just leave me be!"

"I will," said he, his voice closer than it was previously, "but first may I ask if you are harmed?"

Violet could not help but be grateful that he phrased his inquiry as he did. She was not well, but neither was she truly harmed, so she was able to offer an honest answer. "I am not."

"Will you look at me?" he asked, very near now, if his voice was any indication.

Violet did not wish to look at him, but felt that she could not reasonably deny the man's request. *Such a simple matter, Violet,* she chided herself. *Truly, Mama would be shocked to see how childish, how missish you are being.* And so, with a shaky breath, Violet raised her head.

The light through the door to the ballroom afforded little visibility, but as he crouched beside her, rather than between her and the door, Violet was able to see enough of his features to recognize him.

"My lord Reymes!" she cried, allowing her gaze to again drop. She immediately began to gather her skirts in order to stand, but his hand gently placed upon her forearm stayed her. She shyly peeked up into his face.

"Miss Wyndham," he began, inclining his head slightly. "Please do not trouble yourself. These are not the polite but inane words exchanged in a ballroom or during a morning call. I want you to be certain that you are well enough before you attempt to stand, and we must discuss, a little bit at least, what has transpired just now. And what's to be done about it."

She blushed, but nodded slightly before settling again where she was. As she arranged her gown more tidily about her, Violet realized that it was difficult for her to believe that it was actually Lord Reymes who was speaking to her.

The man was rumored to be rather haughty, as many men in his position were expected to be – young, handsome, titled, and unmarried. There was a dim memory that she carried, though, of a dance shared with him a couple of years past. During the dance, she had no misapprehension of his feeling anything more for her than a vague apathy. However, he had been polite, and offered no pointless conversation. Her heart had been pained with sympathy for him, and perhaps something else which she did not understand. Something she had kept to herself when she later discussed the dance with her friend. At the time, Violet had thought that he carried a deep sorrow.

That memory had faded in her mind, especially as life with her mother and sister continued after her brother's marriage. She had all but forgotten their brief encounter. But when she again saw Lord Reymes earlier this evening, nearly two years after the shared dance, the memory began to resurface. During their introduction at the door of his house, she had forced herself to look at his eyes and saw that same sadness she had discerned when they danced. Her sister and her mama, of course, did not see anything save his handsome face, well-tailored coat, and the expensive yet tasteful embellishments to his ensemble: one fob, a signet ring, and a snuff-box which seemed more something with which to occupy his hands on occasion than to use.

The Earl sighed tiredly as he took out said snuff-box and then spoke again, bringing Violet's attention back to the present. "My brother has long disregarded the requirements and strictures which Polite Society places on him had he held to a more honorable code of living." Lord Reymes turned the small box over and over in his hands. Violet blushed after realizing that they were strong hands, yet still soft and not calloused by labor: the hands of a gentleman. She forced herself to concentrate on his words.

Oh! That was his brother? came the belated thought.

"His behavior toward you this evening was reprehensible, to say the least. If there is anything I may do to make restitution, please do not hesitate to name it. Unfortunately, he is unable to offer the protection of his name, being recently married, but I certainly can offer any assistance within my capability – confirmation of your innocence, refutation of rumors, monetary assistance – if you have a suitor who may need some incentive in the form of an increased dowry, or if there is anything else you may think of–"

"Please, my lord, do not trouble yourself." Violet suddenly felt badly for the man before her. Clearly, he was burdened by the depravity with which his brother conducted himself and his offer suggested to Violet that he had paid previously for his brother's misdeeds. Her desire to assure the man over-rode her fear of speaking to him. "Trust me when I say that I will require nothing of you. I-I cannot imagine that my party has even missed me yet!" She managed a tremulous smile.

He returned her smile with a small one of his own.

"Are you well enough to stand now, Miss Wyndham?" he asked, offering his hand. She nodded and accepted his assistance in rising.

"Thank you, my lord," she murmured while smoothing her gown.

After a moment, Lord Reymes said conversationally, "You are in the neighborhood visiting your relatives, are you not? The Doberly family?"

She swallowed before answering, hoping her earlier bravery would remain when answering his questions. "Yes, my lord," she replied. "They are my aunt and uncle."

"They are excellent neighbors."

"Yes, the very best of people." Her eyes flitted to his face, which was again darkened in shadow. Even so, she could see that a slight smile formed at her words.

"Are you enjoying your visit?" he asked, immediately followed by a small choking sound. "That is, aside from...this current unpleasantness."

"Yes, my lord." Violet knew she ought to say more, illustrate some of the meals or perhaps excursions provided as entertainment to them, but she feared that she would bore him. She settled with, "We always enjoy our visits with one another."

"Is your home far from here?" he inquired.

"No. Mama prefers to take two days for the traveling, but when my father still lived, we would go all in one. We changed horses once, but it is not so terribly long."

"I see." Hearing amusement in his voice, she looked up again into his eyes. She could not be certain, but they seemed to crinkle at the corners with his grin. She wished to ask what he found so humorous, but did not. Before she could begin to fret, he asked, "How do you find the assembly?"

"I find it..." Violet was at a loss. She detested being there, but could not very well admit that to the host. "That is to say, it is...I, er-" Violet stopped her sputtering and decided that with her bungled attempt at an answer, there was nothing for it and she must be honest. "I do apologize, but I am not very well at my ease in such...varied company."

The man's smile expanded fully upon his face. His teeth reflected the filtered light from the ballroom. *Good teeth,* came her mama's voice in her head. "So you find it as dreadful as I, then? Miss Wyndham, I confess that I do not enjoy balls nearly as much as I ought." He laughed lightly, and Violet would have thought he felt awkward had she not known better. "However, since beginning to converse with you, I allow that my opinion of this one, at least, has risen considerably."

Violet felt her face flame and prayed that Lord Reymes would not notice, in spite of the soft light she knew illuminated her face. "It is more tolerable to know someone else shares my feelings."

A low chuckle sounded before he answered, "Indeed. I suppose there is some merit to the saying *misery loves company.*"

"I cannot say that I should go so far as to say that *misery* describes my feelings on the matter." Violet felt a small smile tugging at the corners of her lips, but did her best to repress it; she did not wish so great a man to think she was flirting with him. Her mama had mentioned just yesterday that the Earl was notorious for brushing off the misses who dared act familiarly with him. *Though he did not act in such a manner when we danced,* she could not help but think. *He was not precisely amiable, but neither was he dismissive.*

Lord Reymes drew her from her thoughts. "Then you are kinder than I."

In what regard? Violet wondered initially, until she recalled they were speaking of their opinions of balls and large crowds of near-strangers.

Following a pause that had grown nearly uncomfortable, he breathed out quickly before saying in low tones, "Miss Wyndham, forgive me, but I must inquire once more as to your well-being. I am aware that you require no monetary compensation, but are *you* well? While I myself have never been – *attacked* – beyond childish, school-boy pranks, I am given to understand that these – er, these *sort* of occurrences may very well cause a lady of delicate nature, such as yourself, to suffer. Are you possibly in shock? Not that I mean to imply that you should not be as recovered as you appear to be. I wholly hope that you are well and that there are not any lasting repercussions for you. But please, do tell me if you are unwell."

Violet was taken aback at his loquacious manner of asking if she was well in spirit. He struck her as a man of few words, but then she supposed she did not know him very well. *One dance two years in the past does not make a close acquaintance. Indeed, it seems that he does not even recall that evening.* Rather than dwelling on this, though, she hastened to assure him. "Pray, do not trouble yourself, my lord. I am well. He – he did nothing but k-kiss me." The memory of ten minutes ago pressed at her from the corners of her mind, where she had relegated it for the time being, and a tremor ran down her spine.

Lord Reymes shifted closer to her. She may have imagined it, but he seemed to furrow his brow in concern. *It is rather dark; and I cannot believe that he would be unnecessarily worried over me.* "Miss Wyndham, are you certain? You cannot convince me that your shiver was from the cold."

Must he be so attentive? She found frustration coloring her voice as she said, "I will admit that the likelihood is high that I shall weep tonight, in the privacy of my bed, but I cannot very well do it here, can I?"

"Some ladies would," was his reply.

"I grant you are right," she admitted. "Extravagant displays of emotion are rather common nowadays, but the attention which would accompany such a display is something that I could not abide."

"Do not ladies live for attention?"

"Not I."

A slight grin tugged at the corners of his mouth as he answered, "No, I suppose you would not care for that." After a brief silence, he cleared his throat and motioned toward the ballroom, taking a step back at the same time. "Do you wish to return to the assembly now?"

Violet did not wish to return at all. She was uncertain, though, as to how she felt about the Earl remaining on the small balcony. A part of her wished he would go, so that she might again enjoy her solitude and compose herself. Even more, though, Violet was surprised to realize that a part of her wished he would stay and talk more with her. Although his gaze was decidedly unnerving, she enjoyed the humor in his voice and the smooth timbre of it. She realized that her quivering and fear had all but vanished. It was odd how much this man's presence put her at ease, in a manner that only her brother had been able to do previously – especially considering what *his* brother had attempted to do to her.

Regardless of her desire to remain where she was, Violet's answer bowed to the demands of propriety. "Yes, my lord. I have been absent for too long. In fact, if I do not return soon, I might be proved wrong and my absence be noticed. As it is, they must believe me to be taking some refreshment."

"I see. In that case, let us return with all due haste. Step here, where the light will show me your appearance. It would be unwise to return if you appear at all out of countenance." Violet turned her face to the light of the ballroom, feeble though it was, and felt her cheeks warm as she sensed his close scrutiny. "Your hair is slightly mussed, but perhaps you may smooth some of those escaped strands." Her fingers trembled as she swept them over her hair, pulling the loosened strands back, even as he nodded approvingly. "Your hair is much improved – we may now return." He grinned wryly as he spoke. "To avoid any rumors if we return together, shall you return first or shall I?"

She managed to breathe, "I–I will, if that is agreeable to my lord."

"Very well," he said, smiling while he put out his hand his hand to usher her in the direction of the ballroom.

Violet moved toward the door and had just reached it when his firm hand grasped her elbow. A predilection for preservation stiffened her body, fear racing through her like icy pin-pricks.

"Miss Wyndham, your dress." Lord Reymes' cautionary voice reached her. Her confusion at his words dispelled the alarm which had descended upon her and she quickly spun to see what he meant. Doing so easily broke his hold on her arm and her comfort with him returned. He was much closer than she expected, though, and Violet's eyes widened at seeing his eyes mere inches from hers. Startled, she hurriedly took a step back. Her foot caught in the short train of her dress, and she was suddenly tipping backward.

"Oh!" Violet's arms flailed, reaching for anything behind her which might stay her fall, but she was suddenly caught in a strong arm which prevented a fall. To further steady her, his other hand reached for one of her flailing arms.

One moment she was suspended in air, the next pressed against his warm body.

For the space of several breaths, Violet's heart thudded heavily in her chest and her breath came in short gasps. His spiced scent filled her head, but she felt none of the fear she had when his brother had forced himself this close to her. Swallowing thickly, she looked up into his surprised face, knowing it reflected the same emotion as hers. His deep eyes gazed steadily back into hers, darkening minutely as his arm shifted subtly around her.

"Violet! What is the meaning of this?"

"Mama!" cried she, stepping quickly from Lord Reymes' unexpected embrace, minding her train very carefully as she did so.

Violet scurried over to her mother, who was turning around from closing the door quietly behind herself. Rose was there, as well, glaring menacingly at Violet.

"How could you do this, Vi?" the younger girl spat venomously. "Mr. Langley's father shall *never* consent to his marrying into a family whose reputation has been so tarnished! I should never have thought you capable of such cruelty as to carry on with a man you only just met, even if he is an Earl."

Violet opened her mouth to say that she would never "carry on" with anyone. But Mrs. Wyndham was speaking again.

"It is, of course, imperative that this is corrected. The fact that you are nobility can have no bearing, my lord; you simply cannot go about ruining the innocence of young women without consequence to yourself."

Lord Reymes' voice, in contrast to the previously gentle tone, now spoke with authority and incredulity. "I did no such thing."

Violet wanted to speak, to defend the man who had moments ago saved her first from the stealing of her virtue, and then again from what was sure to have been a nasty fall. Mrs. Wyndham turned, though, and shot her such a glare that she was unable to force sound from her tight throat, let alone explain the true circumstances of their embrace.

Two

⤬

NATHANIEL NEARLY CHOKED upon hearing the implication of Mrs. Wyndham's accusations.

He gritted his teeth and drew a calming breath before speaking again. "What would you have me done, instead, Madam? Allowed her to fall? And have her break her wrist as she attempted to catch herself?"

"Oh, I am convinced that is not all that transpired here this evening!" He scarcely recognized Mrs. Wyndham's voice, so altered was it from their introduction earlier in the evening. Rather than the honeyed tones she used previously, the woman's voice was positively icy.

Nathaniel cleared his throat and answered the woman in an equally frigid tone. "I assure you I have done nothing to Miss Wyndham but speak with the child and prevent her from falling."

"The child indeed! She is a woman, as you well know." Mrs. Wyndham's eyes blazed.

Searing heat coursed through Nathaniel's body as anger took hold of him. "You, madam, go too far!" He was scarcely able to ground out the words. His breathing was heavy and he nearly shook with rage. How dare this woman stand here, in his home, and accuse him of abusing the girl? He did nothing of the sort!

But then the memory of holding her in his arms overtook his thoughts, how warm and delicate she had been. An almost liquid warmth, more gentle and subtle than the hot anger, flowed from his heart, gradually overtaking the rage. Feeling calmer, he considered the situation for a moment.

When examining his actions closely, he was forced to admit that they were not entirely above reproach. Certainly, he had not truly compromised her, but he ought to have released her the second she had regained her balance. He had not. Nathaniel recalled being entranced by her eyes, so near to him and reflecting the glow from the ballroom. Her eyes were not static in their appearance as were so many ladies' of his acquaintance, but showed every range of emotion she felt. As he held her, they had shifted between grey and green, reminding him of the sky after a storm.

He glanced over at Miss Wyndham, cowering beside her Mama, and raised his brows, hoping she would receive his silent message and speak up. She opened her mouth, closed it, and opened it again.

"Mama, I–"

"No, Violet!" said Mrs. Wyndham. "I will not allow you to defend this cad."

Nathaniel, seeing that the girl did not again attempt to speak, did so himself. "You cannot suggest that I have wronged her! In catching her from falling?" *In holding her for a breath longer than necessary.* His fraudulent honor seemed ever to mock him.

"Ah, but Lord Reymes, my witness claims that he saw you in a most amorous embrace, against the edge of the balcony. Do you not see?" Mrs. Wyndham turned Violet bodily around – rather forcefully, he noticed indignantly. "Besides her mussed hair and flushed face," and here Mrs. Wyndham paused for dramatic effect before finishing triumphantly, "there is dirt on her gown!"

"She stood against the railing when I came through the door."

"Oh, and what gammon have you to pitch regarding her hair? The breeze is too slight for it to be blamed."

"I have told no lies. As for her hair, I cannot say." It seemed her hair had not been as tamed as he had thought. He fairly liked the wispy looseness of its present style, but perhaps it was not how her mama had directed it to be styled for this evening's outing. Nathaniel knew that his thoughts were inane and skirting the point. He attempted to regain his focus with the question, "Who is this witness?"

"Rose, go and fetch him," ordered Mrs. Wyndham imperiously. The young lady hurried away, back into the ballroom. "He said that he would be ready should I need his corroboration."

Miss Wyndham took an audible breath, then said quietly, "What he says is true, Mama. He was merely trying to help."

She speaks at last.

The girl's affirmation of what he said, however, fell on deaf ears; Mrs. Wyndham whispered a barbed, "Oh hush, child. All he did was to help himself to your charms. You are incapable of discerning the difference." The girl's face flamed red and she lowered her head, pressing her lips between her teeth. It was then that Miss Rose returned. Nathaniel tensed when he saw who swaggered onto the balcony behind her. He did not miss the manner in which Miss Wyndham cowered when the other man entered the space, either.

Mrs. Wyndham spoke again. "Mr. John Peyton has informed me that you suggested to him earlier this evening that you planned to make my daughter your next conquest." She was entirely oblivious to her daughter's distress, but Nathaniel easily saw her eyes widen, hands began fidgeting, and her shoulders tensed. Nathaniel noticed, though.

A glance at his brother told him all he needed to know. The man scarcely held his smug grin. *Would he truly seek revenge for my having stopped him?*

Mrs. Wyndham continued. "Oh, yes, he has told us all about how he often cleans up your messes. We can't have an Earl sullying his name, now can we? I *demand* to know what you intend to do about this situation."

Nathaniel was outraged. Never before in his life had his honor been questioned, . Certainly never by some vulgar country harridan, who lacked even the slightest credibility in his eyes. Furthermore, the woman was making demands on him!

"Do? What will I do? I will do nothing, for I did nothing. We spoke briefly, I caught her from falling, and that is all. Surely you cannot expect me to – to marry the girl!" Nathaniel saw Miss Wyndham stagger backward. He instinctively moved forward to offer his arm, which seemed to clench the deal for the enterprising Mrs. Wyndham. He wished he had not allowed his words to run away from him.

"Yes!" Mrs. Wyndham cried triumphantly. "*That* is what's to be done!"

Nathaniel felt his heart leap into his throat as his eyes went to Miss Wyndham. The picture she presented was not promising – light brown hair still mussed, gown rumpled, eyes wide with shock and fear that he would have found insulting had he not been experiencing similar emotions. He redirected his gaze toward Mrs. Wyndham.

"That will not be possible." With a covert glance at Miss Wyndham, he saw relief flood her face. Inexplicably, his heart gave a slight lurch. *Does she truly find me so repugnant? I had rather enjoyed our conversation.* He knew he should be relieved that she was no more desirous of the match than he, but still his heart thudded rather painfully.

He did not pause to ponder the disappointment he felt. "My brother and I will leave you that you may aid Miss Wyndham in recovering, as best you can. A maid will be out shortly with something to help with the dirt and her hair." He turned and bowed separately to each, finality in his voice when he spoke. "Mrs. Wyndham. Miss Wyndham. Miss Rose. Good evening." Taking John's arm firmly, Nathaniel propelled him through the door into the ballroom and away from the balcony, planning to give him a severe dressing-down, if not horse-whip the insolent fool. His plans were derailed, though, as Lord Stallingsworth approached.

"Where've you been, man?" he asked, clapping Nathaniel on the shoulder.

"Getting myself into a fine Hubble, is what." He glanced about and decided to move to the hall, away from prying eyes. Stallingsworth followed easily and John followed as Nathaniel's hand on his arm forced him into compliance. Once out of the ballroom, he quickly hailed one of the housemaids who happened to be carrying an empty platter toward the kitchen. After hastily explaining what he wished for her to do for the ladies, he dispatched her and returned to where he had left his friend standing guard over his wayward brother.

"Do you recall my neighbors, the Doberly family?" he asked Stallingsworth. When his friend nodded, Nathaniel continued. "Their relatives the Wyndhams are visiting, and the eldest daughter was accosted by John here." He gave his brother's arm, back in his grasp, a rather violent shake.

"Aye, and I sent the chit's mama to the balcony to find them. Worked better than I could've planned," chortled John. "The little thing had tripped, and my dear brother, being the thoughtful dandy he is, caught her. The mama found them in a rather close embrace, if tis true what the girl's sister told me when she fetched me for corroboration."

"Enough of that, John," gritted out Nathaniel through clenched teeth. It was all he could do to refrain from dealing violently with his brother. *I should very much have liked to draw his cork right there, but I suppose that the sight of blood in the ballroom would rather ruin the assembly.* "The short of it, Stally, is that the girl's mama wants me to marry her!"

"And this is disagreeable?" asked Stallingsworth.

"You, of all people, know my reluctance to be bracketed just yet," he muttered under his breath.

"But she's of a respectable family?" pressed his friend.

"Aside from her demanding mama, I believe so. Her Doberly relations are certainly good *ton*," he admitted, referring to their good standing in London Society. "More importantly, they have proven faithful friends to my mother, most especially during her bereavement."

"Is the girl altogether unfortunate-looking, then?" asked Stallingsworth, still searching for a reason that his old friend would not simply marry the girl and be done with it.

Nathaniel paused, feeling his face warm. *Excellent. It seems I have caught the girl's propensity for coloring up.* Before he could find his voice, though, his brother broke in.

"She doesn't shine down everyone else, but she is a pretty bit o' muslin."

Nathaniel felt his ire rise yet again. Hailing a footman he spied against a wall, he ground out, "Watch yourself, John. If you wish to continue to enjoy the hospitality of Bainscroft, you will take yourself to your room and remain there the rest of the evening. If any of the servants spies you about, I shall have you immediately removed, and you will not be welcome here for some time." With a few quick words from Nathaniel to the footman, John was stalking off to his rooms with the footman following closely behind. Nathaniel turned back to his friend and said, "She is a lovely girl, but too green and fearful by far. And you know how I feel about bringing a wife into my life at this time. Furthermore, when I do, she must be a strong, capable woman. Managing a household of this magnitude is quite a responsibility. Miss Wyndham had not an ounce of steel in her when speaking to her mama. The woman silenced her with a glance!"

Throughout Nathaniel's diatribe, Stallingsworth's face had grown amused and after, he asked, "Did you speak with the girl? Before you were found?"

"I did."

"And was she weak-willed when you spoke with her?"

"I do not know, Stally!" Nathaniel could not comprehend where his friend's line of questioning was going. *What does it matter how she acted when we were alone if she could not speak up when it mattered?* "The first time I saw her – apart from when we were first introduced, though she did seem familiar however I cannot say why, and then again from across the ballroom – she was being accosted by my own brother! The man with whom I grew from infancy through childhood and my school-days and–"

"Do forgive me for the interruption, Reymes," interjected Stallingsworth, "but did you say that you met her at the beginning of the evening? And saw her again, before this unfortunate incident?"

"Yes, were you not attending?"

"I was. The real question, Reymes, is whether you were."

"Were what?"

"Attending your own words." Nathaniel had no notion of what the other man was saying and supposed his face reflected that, for he elaborated. "You said that you met her earlier."

"That does not signify. I greeted all of the guests as they entered the assembly."

"And she was able to leave such an impression that you remembered who she was," he pressed.

Nathaniel now began to see where his friend was leading, and he promptly attempted to correct his friend's misapprehension. "I did not recall her name right away."

"Oh, did you not?" Stallingsworth seemed to sag a bit in disappointment.

"Indeed not!" cried Nathaniel, jumping at the chance to discount his friend's theories. "I remembered her face, and was mildly impressed at her refusal to play the coquette, though her mama certainly that she ought to. For all appearances, it pained her to speak at all. But she did, and further, displayed sense and remarkable good-humor considering all she endured tonight."

"So she would be well able to endure your moods with grace and patience?" Stallingsworth grinned.

"What? No! That was not my meaning at all." He had again allowed his words to run away from him.

"Perhaps not, but it is true nonetheless. You say she hasn't an ounce of steel, but she certainly displayed a great deal of pluck in overcoming her unfortunate encounter. Perhaps she simply knows when to bend and when to stand fast."

Nathaniel had no immediate reply. His mind was a whirlwind of thoughts. His frustration with the situation, added to the annoyance he felt with his brother's actions, still left a bitter taste in his mouth. Nathaniel had fought for years to minimize the damage caused by his brother, and he was weary of suffering from it. Over all this hovered the guilt he felt regarding Miss Wyndham. He knew she was innocent in this. But was it *his* responsibility to rectify this situation?

"Why don't you marry her?" The question was almost expected, and yet Nathaniel could not answer. "Her family seems to be a respectable one, not near as high-up as yours or even mine, but still respectable. And you ought to marry soon, man, or the estate and title might just fall to your brother's son, assuming he does not outlive you and inherit the place himself. Imagine how quickly he will ruin the place with so much ready at hand!"

"I am not so far gone yet, Stallingsworth, as to have lost hope of finding a wife if it is not Miss Wyndham."

"Oh-ho! I must've got your back up, for you to call me 'Stallingsworth'." The man chuckled before continuing with, "Your brooding persona will only be mysterious and attractive to the ladies of the *ton* for so long, my friend. There will come a day when either they have forgotten about you entirely, or you shall be so stricken in years that even if you should convince a lady to have you, you'll be unable to give her any children."

"I'll thank you to mind your own affairs and leave mine alone. Miss Wyndham assured me earlier this evening, after my brother's indiscretion, that she was well, that there was nothing she wished from me in compensation for what transpired – or even from what almost transpired."

"Did she assure you in like manner *after* her mother's tirade?"

"There was not opportunity, though she did attempt to tell her mama that there was no reason to marry, as she was not compromised."

"Aside from what your brother did?"

Nathaniel paused, chagrined. "We, er...we did not mention that portion of the evening."

"You perjured yourselves?"

He paused, again. "We omitted."

Stallingsworth's laughter pealed out. "I am all astonishment, Reymes. You, who holds honor so dear, cutting shams to avoid –"

"As I said before, *Stallingsworth*," said Nathaniel pointedly, "I did not lie. Telling of my brother's part in this would do nothing to help Miss Wyndham. No satisfaction could be made by him, and it would make her ruin all the more bitter. As it is, only conjecture taints her, and that will likely wear off. This is only a small country ball; if no one learns of what happened, she ought to escape unscathed."

Even as he spoke the words, they rang false. There was in attendance a good deal of the *ton*, especially for a small country ball, located as Bainscroft was nearby two sizeable towns and only several hours by carriage from London. There was no guarantee that the story would not be bandied about Town, even with its population scarce in the absence of the Season.

"Will her mama keep quiet about it?" asked Stallingsworth, hitting upon the very thing which had been lurking at the recesses of Nathaniel's conscience. *Would that woman keep quiet?* He could not answer with confidence. *Sadly, she seems just the sort to cry rope on a person, even her own daughter, if it might be of benefit to her.*

Heaving a great sigh, Nathaniel conceded, "There are no guarantees in that quarter. I would not be surprised at all to find that the woman would very well ruin her own daughter if it served her interests."

"Indeed?" Stallingsworth mused. "Mayhap she would easily fit into the *bonne ton*, then, if she is not above manipulation."

"You must have very little faith in the honor of the peerage and Society in general if you believe manipulation to be so very common among them."

"Did you learn nothing during these years spent in Town, Reymes?" laughed Stallingsworth. "Good Society is determined by breeding and fashion, not by honor."

"And should we therefore abandon honor?"

Stallingsworth observed him for a moment, amusement fading. "Tell me, Reymes," said his friend at length as he nodded toward something behind him. "Does your honor stand clear before *that*?"

Nathaniel turned and what he saw caused a hard knot to form in his gut. Mrs. Wyndham entered from the balcony, looking to the uninformed observer as if she was the Dowager Countess herself. Miss Wyndham followed, hair only marginally improved, head lowered, face flushed. *I suppose a dark, humid balcony does not offer sufficient means of composing oneself.* After the Wyndham party had made their way to a small opening in the crowds of people near the walls of the ballroom, they stopped and stood close together. Upon closer observance, it seemed the mother was speaking closely to the eldest daughter, while the younger watched with a gleeful smile upon her lips. Observing the harsh movements of the mother's hands and the scowl upon her face, her address could only be described as a dressing down of the girl, and Nathaniel felt his ire rise again. *Surely she does not blame the girl for tonight's events.*

"In all seriousness, Reymes." Stallingsworth's voice was sincere. "She seems a good girl. Why not settle down? You know t'would please your mama. Besides, Miss Wyndham seems to have need of escape."

Nathaniel stood surreptitiously watching, lost in his thoughts of Miss Wyndham. *Quiet strength, unbelievable timidity, a complete lack of guile in her eyes while simultaneously seeming to know more than she would say...* After a moment, Nathaniel turned to speak to his friend, only to find that he had disappeared. Glancing about the room, Nathaniel saw that the guests continued to dance, socialize, and partake of the refreshments as though nothing had happened. Miraculously, no one seemed to have noticed anything was amiss.

He felt a stab of regret that the young lady looked so burdened. Annoyance battled sympathy, and Nathaniel found his feet moving forward even as his thoughts ran contrary to his actions. *What a bother my conscience can be. Why must I be so bound by duty, by a wrong committed long ago? Other men of import and influence have no qualms with leaving a lady to brave the repercussions of such an encounter – even more intimate than the one which we shared! Or better, why did I not leave the balcony the instant she assured me she was well? This entire mess would have been avoided.* A sigh issued from his lips as he realized that he was praying, something he had not done in some time. *I know I've no right, Lord, but I beg, give me some direction! What am I to do?*

But he knew what he would do, for he was already speaking to the conductor of the orchestra, informed him that an announcement would be made at the conclusion of the next set. With that arranged, he strode over to the Wyndham party.

Violet looked up to see Lord Reymes making his way toward her. She could not truthfully say that he was coming to see her family due to the fact that his eyes were trained quite intently on her face through his journey across the floor. Her face and hands grew clammy and her heart beat faster with each of his long strides, all while her thoughts raced through her head. *So Mama still wants him to offer for me. She certainly went on about it for quite a while on the balcony after he and his – brother – left. I still can scarcely believe that the two men are related, much less brothers! And I cannot comprehend why Mama is in such an uproar; it is not at all the Earl's fault that I am clumsy. Lord God, why is this of such great importance to Mama? If only she would simply forget this evening. I certainly wish to! Had I begged off with a headache, Charlotte and I would be settled quite cozily with books and perhaps some cards or other entertainment. No indignant Earl or rake of a brother to make my heart tremble.* A brief shudder overtook her. *My words to Mama should have been stronger. I should have tried harder to exonerate Lord Reymes.*

Upon reaching their party, he bowed briefly to all of them. Violet heard her mother greet him coldly before the tall, handsome man asked if they would please join him in a more private setting. He ushered them to the hall, and then Violet alone to a room situated off of the hall with its ornate furnishings and impressive frescos. The room appeared to be his personal study; there were no other people present and the furniture was dark and masculine. Pausing before following Violet into the room, he invited the other two ladies to be seated just outside the open door.

"Miss Wyndham, will you sit?" he asked politely. Feeling the cushion dip beside her, Violet glanced up to see him perched beside her. His posture spoke of a closer acquaintance than they could claim, angled as he was toward her, close enough that his knee brushed her skirt. Violet's eyes went to that point of contact, wanting to look anywhere but his face. She observed his black evening breeches which came just below his knees, the waistcoat peeking from beneath his overcoat, his cravat below his jaw. When she reluctantly allowed her eyes to reach his face, she saw that one side of his lips were quirked up in apparent amusement at her perusal of his attire.

Her thoughts descended into a whirl of panic as heat scorched her face. *Oh, how I wish he would stop looking at me as he is. I feel exposed already, but to have such a man's eyes regarding me so, what am I to do? How am I to think? How shall I...*

When she somehow realized that he was speaking, Violet finally drew air into her lungs and did her best to direct her attention toward the words issuing from his mouth. Try as she might, though, she could not force her muddled brain to make sense of what he was saying; the loud rush of her own blood pumping deafened her. A glance at the door revealed her mother and sister eavesdropping and none too discreetly at that. Her mother's face began to take on an ethereal glow while her sister's showed a great deal of amusement. *What on earth is happening?*

Finally, her mother's almost-sharp words cut through from the doorway. "Well, Violet, please do not keep the gentleman waiting. Will you not give him an answer?"

He must have apologized again for what happened on the balcony and then asked me to dance. What else can it be? It was clear on the balcony that he does not intend to acquiesce to marriage, as Mama wishes. And yet a dance would lend credibility to my person; an Earl would certainly not dance with a fallen woman, as Mama seems to think I now am. He is lending his aid in as much as he can, given the circumstances. Seeing all eyes trained expectantly on her, not the least of which were Lord Reymes', Violet blinked, took a shuddering breath, and whispered, "Yes, my lord, I am honored."

The smiles on everyone's faces told Violet that she must have answered correctly. She took Lord Reymes' proffered arm gently, carefully, and followed as he led her back to the ballroom.

When they reached the room, couples were just finishing a *contredanse.* Lord Reymes proceeded to move toward the orchestra. She would have preferred a more inconspicuous position in the line, but she supposed a man of his importance was accustomed to a place that everyone could see. And a more prominent place would allow more eyes to see that he was not holding her in contempt, but had asked her to dance. *Perhaps all is not lost.*

When he did not stop on the floor, but ascended the steps, she was greatly surprised and could do naught but numbly follow. He turned to face the assembly as the orchestra finished their song, and everyone quieted, turning to look at them. Lord Reymes seemed to pause as he took a great breath and opened his mouth to speak. What he said was brief and to the point, and it nearly caused Violet to faint dead away.

"Thank you for coming, friends and acquaintances. I shall claim only a moment of your time before the dinner dance commences. Miss Wyndham and I are pleased to announce tonight that we are engaged to be married."

Three

VIOLET'S SHOCK WAS like none she had ever experienced before. More than the time Ashbridge dropped a frog down the back of her dress when they were children. Greater than learning that Rose had kissed – *kissed!* – the eldest Potter boy from the village three years before their come-out. No, this was something in an entirely different realm.

She followed numbly as Lord Reymes led her down the few steps to the dance floor. The orchestra began the strains of a hauntingly beautiful minuet, one of her favorites. They danced, and as they did, Violet was absently pleased to discover that her feet and arms were able to perform the motions and steps with her mind otherwise occupied. Her thoughts and emotions rolled and churned inside of her, creating quite a contrast to the ordered movements of the dance.

Had the Earl truly caved to the pressure of her mama's demands? *I cannot believe he truly desires this union. I do not desire it, even in the face of Mama's disappointment in my refusing the only other offer of marriage made me.*

They went down the line, performing turns and dips, skips and steps with one another and with some of the other dancers in turn.

I doubt the possibility of her allowing me to cry off – and Lord Reymes certainly will not be able to, now that a public announcement has been made. He may as well have read the bans himself.

When they had a break in their dancing and other couples maneuvered the steps, she hazarded a glance across the floor at her partner. His intense eyes were fastened on her, and it was in the meeting of their eyes that the numbness left her. Throat suddenly dry, Violet could scarcely breathe. She averted her eyes once again as panic rose, threatening to drown her. Her distress of earlier in the evening had been great, but this was something altogether different. The threat was mild, but permanent in nature.

They began to dance again, circling and stepping, dipping and turning. As the other dancing couples conversed in hushed tones, she could do nothing but mind her steps, occasionally glancing at her intended. Each time she did, she saw that his gaze remained on her face, even as his hands and feet performed their required dance movements.

Violet determined to do the only thing she could; she began to pray. There was nothing in her prayer that formed coherent sentences, but her heart cried out to her God. Before long, prayer and music soothed her soul, and her anxiety subsided. She recalled His promise to always be near His own, to strengthen those who would follow Him. Violet felt peace begin to seep into her soul. Whatever the future brought, the Lord would be with her.

As the final strains of the music faded, Violet found her strength renewed. A smile graced her face as she curtsied to her dancing partner and then applauded for the orchestra with everyone else. Lord Reymes came immediately to her side and, taking her gently by the elbow, led her across the room. As they walked, he mentioned that it must be something of a shock to his mother, but he was certain that no one in the room should be more pleased than she to congratulate them on their engagement.

"No one, except perhaps *my* mama," Violet said wryly. She then clamped her gloved hand over her mouth, startled that she had spoken aloud.

Lord Reymes glanced at her, clearly surprised. Laughter suddenly burst from his mouth.

"I confess I had entertained the same thought," he began, smiling engagingly and about to continue when they were approached by her aunt and uncle.

"We wish to offer our congratulations, Lord Reymes, Violet," said Uncle Doberly.

Violet smiled shyly as her aunt wrapped her in a warm hug.

"Thank you," grinned Lord Reymes as he bowed to the couple. "I am delighted to expand my family to include you. My mother speaks most affectionately of you both."

"Your mother is a gem among women," said Aunt Doberly sincerely. "And Violet, it will be lovely having you live so near us."

She had not even considered the joy that living nearer her Doberly relations would provide. Hope bloomed in her heart.

After the two couples parted ways, Lord Reymes asked, "Forgive me, Miss Wyndham, but I must ask. Why is your mother so determined to believe my brother rather than me?"

Violet did not wish to speak further, for she already had admitted more than she wished to the Earl. In spite of her intentions, though, she found herself saying, "My sister Rose is awaiting my betrothal before she may marry her love, in accordance with his father's wishes; he is rather old-fashioned, I suppose, not wishing to have his son marry into a family with an elder sister unmarried but not yet on the shelf. Mama is quite eager to have this accomplished. She would have been happy to marry me off to the village cobbler, were he to ask."

"Surely not someone in trade?"

"A cobbler's work is invaluable, my lord. We would none of us have shoes were it not for his efforts." Violet surprised herself by how freely she spoke.

"I agree, Miss Wyndham. But you know that among polite society, the idea of *work* is rather vulgar. Your father was a gentleman, was he not? You should be wed to someone who can provide a similar position for you. While I would agree that a cobbler's work is invaluable, it does not follow that we must *marry* him." He halted in their progress and looked closely at her. Violet did her best not to squirm under his inspection. "Have you developed a *tendre* for your village cobbler, perchance?"

"Certainly not! He is a widower of seven and sixty; most assuredly in his dotage." Violet lowered her voice, feeling rather awkward at her sudden and uncharacteristic outburst. "A kinder man I've never known."

"I see. I should not have wished to take you away from a suitor whom you find more desirable. Even if you did not cherish tender feelings for the young swain you rejected, there may be another."

Violet heard the question he did not ask and did her best to assure him. "You have taken me from no one, save my family."

"And this is agreeable to you?"

"I am growing accustomed to the idea." Violet offered a shy smile. She knew her mother was pleased, but also knew that the woman was still cross with her for not accepting the offer of marriage from Mr. Barrett, the son of Lord Melton, two years ago during her Season. He was to inherit the title of Marquess, and while Violet found him to be an agreeable gentleman, she was hesitant to allow any acquaintance to progress into a more familiar territory. After her brother Ashbridge eloped with Miss Drayton, and seeing Mr. Barrett's interest end in the face of Violet's polite yet firm refusal of his offers, the three Wyndham ladies had removed from town and returned to their home at Wyndmere. "I daresay, Mama will say that I have made a far more excellent match than she *ever* hoped."

Their conversation was interrupted by several well-wishers who approached to congratulate the couple. Violet felt the assessing gazes of two young ladies among their number, and feared that they found her lacking. Her gown, which she had re-fashioned from one of her mama's older ones, was decidedly deficient in trim, and she feared they would see that it had not been created by a London *modiste*. *Perhaps Penny is wrong that my dresses are as fashionable as Madame Bélanger's.* Nothing was said by them, though, and Lord Reymes accepted the congratulatory remarks for the both of them. Soon, they continued their progress across the room.

"And what have you to say to the match?" he asked, continuing their conversation.

Violet was required to refocus her thoughts before she could answer. "I say that you have been very generous and kind in your dealing with me." She paused, unsure of what more to say. She spoke quietly and carefully. "You have seen for yourself how poorly I converse with new acquaintances. I suppose that very few years more, and I should have been secured in spinsterhood."

"What is your age?" asked he.

"I am twenty years old," she answered. "And you?"

"Eight and twenty."

Violet nodded before continuing, "It is true, then that you are likely a most sought-after gentleman: handsome, well-situated, and old enough to soon settle down. I had thought my mama exaggerated."

"She spoke of me?"

Violet felt heat suffuse her face. "You must understand, my lord, that she feared Mr. Wyndham, my elder brother, should be required to support me. And he gladly would, for we spoke of it when we were younger. He is married now, though, and I would have disliked very much to impose upon him and his wife."

"Could you not have continued with your mama and sister? Especially if her man's father should relent and allow them to marry, I should think your mama very glad to have a daughter to care for her in her advancing years."

"As my mama does not find my company agreeable, she had planned to hire a companion and ship me off to care for my brother's offspring. His wife will very soon deliver him a child."

"Your mama does not enjoy your company?" he scoffed. "I must wonder at her sense. I have found yours to be the only tolerable company in this room."

"Oh, pray do not judge her harshly," murmured Violet, discounting his compliment of her as an exaggeration designed to slight her mama and perhaps the more aggressive of the husband-seeking misses present that evening. "I am not a great conversationalist, and find myself tongue-tied when making new acquaintances."

"But you are conversing very well with me now, and have been for some time."

"I cannot account for it at all. It has long been my practice to limit my conversation with gentlemen to their sport and their animals, for I am then only required to touch upon those subjects and they will then carry the conversation. But I've asked you of neither. Perhaps because it is only two of us in conversation? I've never been allowed to develop an acquaintance without the watchful eye of a chaperone, or without being part of a larger party." She offered a small smile as she said without thinking, "Or perhaps it is simply you with whom I am able to converse, and no other."

The moment the words left her mouth, Violet could not believe that she had spoken so boldly.

He is to be your husband, interjected a small, comforting voice in her head. *Bold words to another are not necessarily bold when spoken to him.*

Lord Reymes paused, studying her for a moment. She wished desperately that he would speak and ease the tension she felt growing within her. At length, he did. "I should prefer to think that it is I. Does wonders for my confidence, as the shock on your face when I announced our engagement had left me rather bereft." She blushed when he raised a finger to touch one of the curls at her temple. The grin on his face faded then, and he said, "In all solemnity, I do not know the reason, I am glad of it, though whatever it may be."

Violet responded lightly, "As am I. It should be dreadful to marry someone with whom I cannot speak." She smiled when he chuckled again.

Lord Reymes continued walking, and they soon reached a woman dressed in a lovely gown of deep plum, striped with a slightly lighter shade, an ostrich plume dyed to match adorning her silver hair. Soft brown eyes met Violet's.

"I look forward to welcoming you to our family, my dear," were the woman's first words, spoken through a soft smile. She gently kissed Violet's cheek before turning her brown eyes to Lord Reymes. "My son, I pray that you may have the same felicity in your marriage that your dear father and I enjoyed in ours."

He smiled fondly at his mother, demonstrating the affection between them. Violet was surprised to see a shadow pass over his face after a moment. She was unable to consider the change in his expression for long, though, as dinner was announced shortly after.

She was not certain how she survived the remainder of the evening, but Violet managed to smile through the interview with the Dowager Lady Reymes, as well as other words of congratulations from nearly every guest present. She even voiced her thanks for each well-wisher's kindness and blessings.

When she at last was following her family to the Doberly carriage, she accepted her fiancé's escort, as well as the light kiss that he brushed over her gloved fingers. He handed her into the carriage before returning to his house.

During the drive to the Doberly estate, Violet attempted to speak up and tell her mother once again that Lord Reymes was a perfect gentleman in his behavior toward her, but Mrs. Wyndham would not hear her. Uncle and Aunt Doberly spoke to one another in hushed tones, and her mama and sister in rather boisterous voices. Before long, Violet simply settled back in the seat as her mama and Rose chattered on about what an advantageous turn of events this was.

A heavy weight descended on her heart. While she had been able, by much prayer, to keep it at bay throughout the evening, she was now forced to face the fact: she was to marry a stranger. Granted, she was more at ease with him than with any other gentleman of her acquaintance, but she still knew very little what he was truly like. After they returned to Uncle and Aunt Doberly's home, sequestered in her room, Violet buried her face in the pillow of her bed and cried.

Nathaniel woke the next morning uncertain as to whether he had dreamt the occurrences of the previous evening or not. He was inclined to believe that he had. However, when Mr. Garand, his butler, appeared during his morning ablutions, the man reminded him of an appointment with the Wyndham ladies that morning. Thinking quickly, Nathaniel directed Mr. Garand to see to the hiring of a coach to convey John back to his home. It was several hours' ride, and Nathaniel admittedly relished the fact that his brother would feel none too well during the journey after his excesses of the previous evening. Regardless of whether the journey would be uncomfortable for John, it certainly would not do for the scoundrel to be skulking about when Miss Wyndham arrived.

Nathaniel finished dressing, taking but little time with his cravat, to the dismay of his valet Griffin. Nathaniel suppressed the urge to laugh. The gentleman's gentleman would never change. *I wonder what he would say had I forgone using a starched cravat in favor of an unstarched one? He might very well swoon!* But Nathaniel knew better than to test his man's sensibilities; a good valet was known as such because of the minute attention to detail he paid to his master's attire and appearance, and Griffin was likely on par with the valet of that epitome of fashion, Beau Brummel – or at the least, quite close.

Once dressed, Nathaniel descended the stairs at a jog to ensure he had time to eat and compose himself before the meeting. He certainly wished his mother might have been in attendance, but she was now of an age that she was not so easily recovered from the excitement of such large parties; the Dowager was likely to remain in her chambers until supper that evening.

As he sat down with his plate of eggs, fruits and some cold meats, Nathaniel began to mentally make plans necessary before the wedding could take place. The bans must be read, but he supposed that the girl's family would see to that. The marriage license must be procured, a ring commissioned, rooms prepared, a wedding-tour planned. Recalling how her dress had been well-constructed, but of a rather dated material, Nathaniel sincerely hoped that her mama outfitted her with a suitable wedding trousseau. It would not do to have her wearing anything that would bring ridicule from fashionable Society. *It is doubtful that her delicate temperament could withstand the snubs which would certainly come if she is not considered fashionable enough by the ladies she will meet.* Perhaps it would be best if he planned to supplement her wardrobe immediately; Mrs. Baker could very well take Miss Wyndham's measurements this morning. Finally, his mother had also mentioned before retiring after the ball removing to the Dower-house on the edge of the property, that the newlyweds might have some privacy. While not believing that to be necessary, Nathaniel humored her and said he would begin immediately whatever renovations she desired.

He was quite pleased with the list he had mentally constructed by the time he rose from the breakfast table.

When the Wyndham ladies arrived precisely at ten o'clock, Nathaniel received them cordially in the morning room. The room's walls were of a pale yellow, with white molding and trim. The furniture was upholstered in soft shades of greens and blues, and gauzy fabric hung over the windows, filtering the morning light. Nathaniel noticed Miss Wyndham's eyes skimming down the hall as she stepped into the room; he guessed what she might be searching for, and stepped nearer to reassure her.

"My brother left for his home early this morning," he leaned near her to say. Her wide eyes glanced up to meet his briefly before lowering again as color spread across her face. She nodded, but remained silent as he ushered her to a seat.

He sat in a chair opposite them once all three ladies were seated.

"I do hope that you passed a restful evening," he said.

"Oh *indeed*, my lord Reymes," crowed Mrs. Wyndham. "To have one of my girls so comfortably settled – well, about to be settled – but then, the engagement is a promise of the wedding to come, so I suppose it is acceptable to say that she is already settled – it is certain to make any mother to have pleasant sleep."

"And you, Miss Wyndham?" he asked the young lady directly. *Is she to have haunting dreams of John's infraction, as I have had dreams of that night two years ago?* he wondered briefly before collecting himself and pushing the dark memories further into the recesses of his mind.

"As well as can be expected, after so much excitement," was her quiet reply, to which she received a sharp elbow in the ribs from her mama.

Nathaniel pretended that he did not see, though his annoyance began to simmer. Rather than comment, he forged ahead in the conversation, going straight for the point of the visit. "Tomorrow, I plan to look into procuring the marriage license. I trust, Mrs. Wyndham, that you will see to the reading of the banns in your parish? I've just an hour ago dispatched a message to the vicar who resides near my estate."

"Oh, most *certainly* I will, my lord," smiled the woman. Nathaniel scarcely kept from curling his lip in disgust at how quickly the woman's opinion of him had changed. *If I believed that a man had forced his attentions upon my daughter without her consent, I should not be so eager to see her bound to him.* Mrs. Wyndham continued, "The wedding will be in our parish, and the breakfast in our family home. Shall I inquire of my neighbors whether one of them would be willing to host you until the wedding?"

"Thank you, no. The nearest inn will suffice." Nathaniel took the slight pause in the conversation to ring for tea, then made an attempt to steer the conversation to include the young lady whom he would be marrying.

"Miss Wyndham, you may requisition whatever changes you desire in the house. My mother has intended to make some updates for some time, but unfortunate circumstances prevented her."

"I am sorry to hear that," began Miss Wyndham. She paused, drawing her lips between her teeth. When she opened her mouth to continue, Nathaniel leaned forward in his chair, surprised to find himself eager to hear what she may say.

"Oh, Violet! How delightful," spoke Mrs. Wyndham, clearly oblivious to her daughter's now-lost words. "I am certain that my lord shall spare no expense. Think of the moldings and draperies and chairs you may order! This room is...*nice*, I suppose, but think of how *grand* it might be! And new plate for the dining room, I'm sure, and silver and crystal and upholstery and carpets! I will, of course, be here to guide you, my dear."

Rather shocked at Mrs. Wyndham's presumption, Nathaniel intoned, "I had not been informed, Madam, that you were to reside here, as well."

He was gratified to see the woman's eyes grow wide and her mouth thin as her lips pressed together. Her apparently unintentional insult of his ancestral home had not escaped Nathaniel's notice. When he glanced her way, he saw that Miss Wyndham's eyes were wide as well, but with embarrassment.

Just as Nathaniel was about to offer a change in the conversation, Mrs. Baker knocked on the door and delivered the tea service. In an attempt to subtly remind Mrs. Wyndham that her daughter – and not herself – would soon be mistress of his home, Nathaniel asked

Miss Wyndham if she would like to pour. Followed by a brief hesitation, she acquiesced. She poured for her mama and sister first, as they had already each chosen a biscuit from the platter on the tray.

"Did you enjoy the ball, Miss Wyndham?" he asked as her slightly trembling hands at last passed a cup to him. *I know she did not, but at least the topic is rather innocuous on the surface.*

"The room was lovely," came her quiet reply. Her eyes remained on her hand as she lifted the last cup for herself.

"Oh yes, indeed!" cried Mrs. Wyndham, selecting another biscuit. "So many chandeliers! –and the food was so much more than we expected at a *country* ball! What splendid parties you shall host, Violet!"

"Yes," added Rose. "I can already imagine visiting throughout the year, parties and balls when we visit, and our children playing and growing together."

Miss Wyndham paled at this. She fumbled with the cup she was pouring and some tea spilled on the tray.

"Violet," Mrs. Wyndham's voice rose in pitch and while friendly on the surface, there was a definitive bite in the undertones which soured the overall sound. "I should have thought you learned to pour out tea by now. You are certainly of an age that you should."

"Yes, Mama." Miss Wyndham's voice trembled as her hands, and she did not meet his eyes, even when she spoke to him. "I apologize, my lord."

The visit seemed to be sinking beyond his control. The appalling words of Mrs. Wyndham, the gloating smile of Miss Rose, and the worst, the timid uncertainty of Miss Wyndham all conspired against the visit being a chance to further acquaint himself with his bride. While the situation rankled, Nathaniel decided to maintain his silence and said nothing as Miss Wyndham hastily found a napkin to clean her mess. He supposed she should have fainted had she known the cost of the fabric in her hand, now stained by the tea. The price of things was not part of polite conversation, and neither did he wish to further her distress, so he smiled and stayed her hand while saying, "Please do not trouble yourself, Miss Wyndham. Mrs. Baker will send a housemaid to clear the spill."

Miss Wyndham's face colored up – yet again – and she nodded while slowly withdrawing her hand from his. She still would not meet his eyes. *Where is the young woman from last night?* he wondered.

"This is excellent tea, my lord Reymes," simpered Miss Rose.

"Thank you." He adopted a haughty tone. "My mother spent many years to come to this particular blend."

"Indeed? Why not leave it to your cook? Or butler?" Mrs. Wyndham chose her third biscuit.

"There are certain things the mistress of the house enjoys doing. My mother never saw fit to spend her days in idleness."

"Lawks! Then she and Violet shall get on splendidly!" cried Rose.

"Always flitting nervously about, that girl," muttered Mrs. Wyndham. "Being given the tasks of caring for a house should do very well for settling her down."

I've had quite enough, thought Nathaniel, scarcely able to keep his thoughts to himself.

"Have you finished, Miss Wyndham?" he asked, rising to his feet. "Perhaps we might survey the rooms of the house, while your mother and sister finish their tea; Mrs. Baker will guide them on a tour of the estate once they have finished."

Miss Wyndham's brows rose almost imperceptibly, but she nodded before standing. "Yes, I thank you, my lord. I should very much enjoy that."

Violet urgently desired to apologize to Lord Reymes for her mother's behavior. He had been so kind, and was so very observant to see her discomfort over the possibility of seeing his brother again, and hastily assured her of his absence. During the visit, he made every effort to include her in conversation, and she was terribly sorry for the things her mama had said. *I fear making an apology shall be more easily desired than done,* she thought wryly as he guided her into yet another room. Between his near-constant descriptions of which ancestor had made which changes, improvements, and additions in room after room, together with the unsettled, fluttering feeling which came over her once she placed her hand on his proffered arm, she was unable to gather the courage to speak. And still, the desire to do so burned within her.

"My mother had already moved to another chamber when I returned to Bainscroft three weeks past, so this is the room which we shall share." She had been working up the courage to offer her apology, and merely sprinkling a hum or nod throughout his monologue. It was a startling realization to see what room he was presently showing her. Lord Reymes continued speaking, but Violet heard nothing more. She stepped away from him several paces, suddenly overcome with the realization that she and Lord Reymes would be husband and wife, in every sense of the word.

She could scarcely speak to the man. How would she share a room?

A bed? So lost was Violet in her thoughts that when his voice broke through once again, he was very nearly shouting.

"Miss Wyndham!" he cried. "Are you unwell?"

"I do beg your pardon," she murmured, doing her utmost to push aside her swirling and panicked thoughts. She was finally able to force air into her lungs when he stepped nearer. "I fear...my mind wandered."

"You are rather pale." His hand found her elbow and Violet's heart thundered, making it once again difficult to breathe. "Would you like to rest a moment? There is a private sitting room through that door."

Violet could only nod. Lord Reymes shifted his large hand to her upper arm and guided her gently through the bedchamber.

"As I was saying, I have already had some of my clothing moved into my father's old – er, that is *my* dressing room, and before you leave today, Mrs. Baker will measure you for some new dresses. I assume your mother will see to a suitable wedding trousseau, but there are a great many things for which an Earl's wife must be prepared to dress." He paused for a moment and Violet did her best to keep pace with his words. "The bedchamber is rather bare, as I still am sleeping in my old room; there are new bed-curtains and covers already ordered. If you disapprove, however, you may certainly choose something else. What do you think of the woodwork? And the draperies? I had not got that far yet."

"They seem adequate," she managed, overwhelmed by all he said. *New dresses already? His mother being displaced? Making changes to his home, when I have not known him more than a day? I cannot imagine being so bold.*

They passed into in a quaint room, small and cozy, outfitted with two wing-chairs and a small settee. It was to one of the chairs which Lord Reymes led her, allowing her to sit before he took the other himself. The seating clustered about the small fireplace to the right of the room, and empty bookshelves lined the wall opposite. The side of the room facing the bedchamber held a second door, this one glass-paned with windows on either side. Violet looked through to see a balcony with a sweeping view of the grounds, but from a higher vantage than that of last night.

"I was right, there is a fountain," she whispered to herself.

"You want a fountain in the bedroom?" asked Lord Reymes, light humor coloring his voice.

"Beg pardon? Er- No!" Violet felt her face burn. *I had not intended to speak aloud.* "I-I, er, heard the water last evening, before – you came, my lord, and thought there might be a fountain in the gardens. It is lovely. The entire estate is. As though from a dream."

She glanced over to see Lord Reymes smile, the first time it seemed to reach his eyes since he greeted her that morning. "I have a great many fond memories of growing up here. I am gratified that you see the beauty of this place."

Violet had seen the stiffening of Lord Reymes' shoulders and the muscle working in his jaw after her mother spoke of all the changes she believed Violet should make to the man's home. She was ashamed of her mama. She drew a deep breath for courage, truly hoping that the smile might remain on his face. *Now or never.*

"Lord Reymes, I-I apologize for my mama. She ought not to have spoken about your home in such a way. I find it quite lovely. The room in which you received us – I would change nothing."

"Oh indeed?" One brow rose slightly as a smile ghosted about his lips. "And what of our chambers?"

"I do not have much opinion either way. Honestly, I was greatly distracted when I first saw it and cannot remember much at all about the colors or finishes." Violet glanced about the sitting room, then through the open door to peek at the barren bed. "I do fear, though, that the bedcovers should not be sufficient once winter arrives."

Lord Reymes chuckled as he stood, offering her his hand once again. "You are likely correct. I suppose that we must find something a bit more substantial before then." His gentle chuckle sounded once again and Violet decided that she liked it very much. She sincerely hoped she might learn to bring it from him more readily after they became better acquainted.

All at once it dawned on her that the fear and nervousness had all but disappeared. Lord Reymes' easy manner dispelled her hesitance. She realized that it was similar to their short conversation on the balcony between the incident with his brother and the row with her mother, and again as they went about the ballroom after their dance. While she noticed then that she was conversing easily with him, she was still too in shock to fully appreciate the full implication of the ease of her interaction with him. They continued their tour of the house, and Violet was quickly enamored.

Of the house. I am quite enamored of this house. Not of its master, Violet told herself. *It is much too early for that.*

The sitting, drawing and dining rooms were lovely, in Violet's opinion, and she was pleased to learn that there were few rooms she truly disliked. A bedchamber in the back of the home, covered in dust and with dark, dreary fabric sent shivers running down her spine. The library was also rather dark and lacking in comfortable seating. She was glad, though, that Lord Reymes expressed a dislike of those rooms before she even had time to react, and so she felt confident that in time, she would be comfortable ordering several things to make the rooms more inviting.

Lord Reymes' ease of manner continued to soothe her as they passed each room, conversation flowing smoothly between them. He suggested they pass through the kitchen at the last, expounding upon the excellence of the food made by Peche, the cook.

By the time they returned to the morning room, Violet found herself laughing lightly at a quip he had made about his fastidious valet and what the man would think if he knew that Lord Reymes would on occasion sneak down to the kitchen in his stocking feet for a biscuit or piece of a cake.

"He was utterly mortified when he discovered a hole in my left stocking, but had no idea when it had happened." Lord Reymes led her to a settee.

"And you snagged it on your way to the kitchen?" Violet asked as she sat.

"I did." Lord Reymes sat in an adjacent chair before continuing. "But you must understand, Miss Wyndham, Peche's cakes are certainly worth a dozen snagged stockings."

Violet was shocked that she giggled at that. "Are they indeed?"

"Certainly!" Lord Reymes' lips quirked into a lop-sided grin. "Well, they are worth it to me. I am uncertain as to whether Griffin would concur."

"And Griffin is your valet?"

"Yes. He is a good man, but he struggles with chastising me when I do not allow him a full hour for my dressing. Or leave mysterious holes in my clothing."

"An hour?" Violet felt her face warm. *How did we go from discussing the food to his dressing habits?* "I fear that I have a great deal to learn, then, my lord. My own morning routine is quite finished by the time half-an-hour has passed."

"Is that so?"

"Yes. Mama and Rose think it quite shameful, but I cannot warrant taking so much time on my dress and hair when much of my morning is spent outdoors. I wear a bonnet over my hair, and who is to see my dress but the gardeners? I do take a bit more time dressing for dinner, most days, but even then, it is not a great deal of time. I do often choose gowns with fewer buttons and some which I can fasten myself."

When she paused for a breath and looked up from where she had been pleating the fabric of her skirt between her fingers, she saw that Lord Reymes was gazing at her quite unabashedly.

"Well, in a few weeks' time, you will now have a husband who will see your dress. Not that I wish you to go to any pains to alter your appearance for my sake; I find it quite lovely as it is."

Her breath caught in her throat and she was unable to immediately offer a reply.

Nathaniel wondered where the shy girl whom he had welcomed earlier that morning had gone. She seemed to have slipped off somewhere during the course of their tour, and this vibrant young woman – the one whose company he had so enjoyed the previous evening – had come to take her place. Miss Wyndham blossomed before his eyes, becoming much more a woman with whom he could envision himself spending his life, with whom he could fall in love. She had stopped speaking, though, and her eyes were trained on her hands, with an occasional flicker up to his face.

"Is something the matter, Lord Reymes?" she finally ventured. Some of the timidity had seeped back into her voice.

"No. Indeed not, Miss Wyndham." Nathaniel considered how much he should say before continuing. "I find that I am unable to understand you, though. You did not flirt when we first met."

Her eyes widened and her face flushed a becoming shade of pink. He shook his head both to clear it of the affects her blush seemed to have on him and in an effort to diffuse her alarm. *Indeed, I have made a blunder of explaining my thoughts, but who knew how becoming her blush could be?* Nathaniel rose and went to sit beside her. "I am not lamenting your lack of coquetry. In fact, it is likely the only thing which caused me to remember you last evening at the ball."

"But you did not. You heard your—" and she paused to draw a quick breath before continuing, "brother speak my name, and even then you asked for confirmation."

"While it is true that I did not recall your name, I did remember you." At her skeptical gaze, he said, "I mentioned your relatives before you did, do you not recall?"

"You did," she conceded with a nod.

"You were without the vanity and attention-seeking practices of many young ladies with whom I am acquainted."

Again, she colored up. *Will she ever stop blushing in my presence?* Nathaniel found that a small part of him hoped she would not.

"I am not very practiced at the more – intricate – particulars of the feminine social graces." Miss Wyndham's voice was subdued.

"Am I to understand you are displeased with this?"

She hesitated before answering. She lowered her head, hiding her eyes from his view. "Mama often asks that I assert myself more as a potential marriage match."

"By acting in a way with which you are uncomfortable?"

"She believes that gentlemen will not notice me if I am so quiet."

"Perhaps. But would you be happy married to a man who fell in love with someone you were pretending to be, and not with you?"

Miss Wyndham pressed her lips together for a moment before shaking her head and answering, though her voice was soft and Nathaniel wondered if she knew she spoke aloud; she did not look at him as she spoke. "Regardless of all this, it seems I am to marry a man who does not love me, so it matters little now."

Nathaniel wanted to protest, but had no grounds upon which to do so, for she spoke the truth. And neither did she love him. "Even so, to the entire world, we are a love match. You must know that word will get around that we were caught in a compromising position, even if it did not last night."

"I am sorry, Lord Reymes, for my family's intrusion into your life." Miss Wyndham shook her head, blinking away tears as she continued in a watery voice, "I know that you have only recently begun to recover from mourning your father and that you were likely not planning to take a wife for some time."

"I am surprised you would say that," he admitted. "It seems you are the only one with that opinion. Even my closest friend, Lord Stallingsworth, was of the opinion that I should marry you."

Miss Wyndham glanced briefly at him before returning her gaze to her hands. "Mama heard about you before the ball; I mentioned last evening that she had already spoken of you. All the ladies of our party – and my cousin Charlotte, too – were visiting with a neighbor and you were quite the popular topic of conversation." She began to make small folds in the fabric of her skirt, as she had earlier.

"Oh? And what is being said about me in the neighborhood?" he asked. Nathaniel suspected he knew, but wished for confirmation or correction of his supposition.

"Most believe that you have returned to establish your own family."

Nathaniel found little gratification in the knowledge that he was right. "And you, Miss Wyndham? What is it that you believe?"

"I cannot pretend to understand your mind or your heart, my lord," she began.

"But if you were required to guess?"

"*Are* you requiring me to guess?"

Some of the teasing was back in her voice, and Nathaniel found himself grinning, be it ever so slightly. "I suppose I am. You did already state your belief that I was not looking for a wife at this time."

After a brief moment's contemplation, she answered. "In that case, I should say that you quit Bainscroft immediately following your father's passing. You had only been finished with school for three or four months at the time, is that right?" Nathaniel nodded in answer, wondering belatedly whether he should have asked what he did. "Not many things would induce an eldest son to leave his newly inherited estate. Your actions last evening prove that your sense of duty is too deeply engrained to abandon your responsibilities without cause – not that I hold any claim on your responsibilities. You were not at fault last evening! However, back to your *requirement* of my hazarding a guess: I believe that your grief at the death of your father must have been very great indeed."

Through a throat thick with emotion, Nathaniel asked, "So you have me all made out?"

"No, my lord. Please, forgive me. I ought not to have spoken in so forward a manner."

"Ah, but I asked." He grinned wryly, and then leaned very close to her. "And you are correct. On most points, at any rate. Perhaps someday I shall reveal all."

"Is it terribly difficult to be here?" she asked, her voice scarcely above a whisper.

Nathaniel battled back the swell of emotion. Slowly, he opened his eyes, and they stung and felt too dry. "Yes," he managed to choke around the rock lodged in his throat. He wished, more than anything else at that moment, to rest his aching forehead against hers, and wrap his arms about her slender frame. He longed to soak some of her gentle warmth into his cold heart.

Just then, Mrs. Wyndham sailed through the open door, followed by Miss Rose. Nathaniel swallowed thickly before straightening his posture again and turning from his bride-to-be. He stood and bowed stiffly.

"You have a very good house, Lord Reymes," Mrs. Wyndham said immediately upon seating herself where he had been seconds before, beside her eldest daughter. Miss Rose chose one of the chairs. "Certainly there are parts of it which are dreadfully old, but with my guidance, Violet shall be able to outfit it quite nicely. The gardens are fashionable, though, the grounds well kept, and the rooms, while largely outdated, are all of excellent quality."

"Indeed," said Nathaniel drily as he seated himself in a nearby chair. He was easily able to regain the composure Miss Wyndham's gently-asked question had threatened to steal. Exposure to females such as Mrs. Wyndham proved profoundly effective in putting him back on his guard. It was an even simpler matter to angle his face toward the mother while keeping his eyes on the daughter. Even in the midst of his own simmering emotions, he observed that the instant that her mother entered the room, Miss Wyndham shrank into herself and the timid girl of earlier suddenly resurfaced. Her shoulders drooped, her chin tucked into her chest, and her fingers were working furiously at the fabric of her skirts.

"Yes, of course, Reymes," said Mrs. Wyndham. It was all he could do to prevent the cutting words on his tongue at the woman's familiar form of address. Not even his fiancé had taken such liberty! "Your ancestral home has never lacked the funds to see to its upkeep. How soon can work begin on the improvements I have in mind?"

Nathaniel's eyes disbelievingly snapped to Mrs. Wyndham. Had Miss Wyndham not recently allowed that she found his home charming? It seemed that *she* was in no hurry to change anything. He looked back to the girl's bowed head and her fiddling fingers.

"Violet? Do you desire that work begin immediately?"

She flushed the instant her name passed his lips. *I cannot very well allow her mama liberties with my name while taking none of my own with my bride's,* he reasoned with himself. He certainly did not feel his heart quicken at saying her name. Not at all.

"I-I am not, er, th-that is, I believe—"

"Stop muttering, child, and speak up!" snapped Mrs. Wyndham.

Drawing a calming breath, Nathaniel made an immediate decision. Standing suddenly, he offered his hand to his fiancé and said, "I only this moment realized when your mother mentioned the grounds, Violet, that I failed to show you the gardens. As you expressed interest in them during our conversation, would you care to view them now?"

The young lady's eyes widened, clouded with uncertainty. Nathaniel was gratified to see the light of interest attempting to break through those clouds. "I, er– I should like that very much, Lord Reymes."

As she stood, Nathaniel addressed the other two ladies. "As you have already viewed them, and it is a rather warm day, we will leave you here. It shan't take more than half-an-hour, at the most. Please, feel free to use any of the books about the room, or if you prefer, you may call for Mrs. Baker to bring refreshment." He offered Violet his arm and led her from the room.

When they entered the hall, Nathaniel motioned for the nearest footman. "Matthew, please fetch Miss Wyndham's things, as well as my own."

"Yes, m'lord." The man bowed, hurrying to do his master's bidding.

Nathaniel led Violet along the hall and at the end, they found the butler. "Mr. Garand," he said to the man, fixing his gaze sternly with the intent of conveying the reasoning behind his request. "Miss Wyndham and I plan to take a turn about the garden. Would you please pop in on Mrs. Wyndham and her daughter, to...ensure their comfort? We shall return shortly."

Mr. Garand nodded knowingly. "Certainly, my lord. They are to remain in the morning room, are they?" He glanced at Violet before adding, "So that I may know where to find them."

Nathaniel smiled. "Yes, Mr. Garand. Thank you."

The butler bowed and Nathaniel looked over at Violet in time to see her smile timidly at the man. They fetched their things from Smith near the door to the gardens and made their way down the grand stone steps in the back of the house.

"Do you like Mr. Garand? I saw your smile."

Violet looked up from where her eyes had been observing the gravel pathway under their feet, surprise evident in her eyes. "Did you? I did not know I smiled."

"Yes. He has been in service to my family since I was a boy."

"Is that so?" Her smile was mildly amused, and Nathaniel wished she would tell him why.

"Yes." He grinned lightly. "He is a trusted servant."

"I would imagine so, for him to have been in your service for so very long."

Nathaniel led her down a lane into the orchard. With the enthusiasm she had expressed for the gardens previously, he hoped she would enjoy seeing the wide variety Bainscroft had to offer in the way of flora.

"Indeed. He was first footman when I was young, and slowly worked his way up."

"I see," said Violet, glancing around at the various fruit trees, heavy with their bounty. "Mr. Garand is quite...discreet."

Nathaniel smiled, remembering the brief conversation they exchanged. "He is; the mark of a good staff. Is not your own staff discreet?"

Violet paused, gazing up at a ripe apple on the tree before them. "They are, to a point," she began. While she again hesitated, Nathaniel reached up and with a slight twist of his wrist, the apple was in his hand, being offered to Violet. She accepted it, smiling briefly before continuing. "My mother, as I am certain you have noticed, is rather..."

At this third pause, Nathaniel found his patience fading. "Indiscreet?"

Violet laughed. The word had slipped from his tongue before he could stop it, and he was glad she did not take offense. *I usually am much more the master of my words. I shall have to guard what I say all the more carefully,* he cautioned himself. He did not choose to dwell on why the extra caution was needed.

"I likely would have said something more along the lines of 'vocal', my lord, but your choice is apt, as well." She shook her head slightly, then raised the apple to her lips. Nathaniel cleared his throat and looked away, confused.

I expected that I might learn to care for her, and develop a certain level of...attraction. Perhaps even love someday. But for it to begin already?

"Mama has difficulty...containing her enthusiasm." Violet was speaking again and had already begun to stroll down the lane. Nathaniel hurried to close the two paces between them, walking beside her with his hands clasped behind him. "Her reactions are often leaning toward the dramatic."

"Yes," he agreed, relieved to find that his breath was once again easy to draw. "I observed as much last evening."

"I am sorry, Lord Reymes." Violet's face flushed. "I–I tried to explain to her, after we left, that nothing improper had happened – with you, that is – that we spoke, then I tripped, as I seem to do quite often. Papa used to say that I needed to grow into my limbs, but I've ceased to grow and am no more graceful than when I was a child. She would not listen, though, and I fear that I cannot procure an escape for you. I do apologize, my lord."

"Why must you apologize? It was my brother who imposed himself upon you, and set into motion the entirety of what has happened," Nathaniel began. He was prevented from continuing, though, by a boy of about ten running down the lane. When he reached the couple, he skidded to a halt, causing tiny stones and bits of dirt to spray up on the elder two's ankles. Nathaniel recognized him as one of the tenant's children, who was often given a few coins to deliver messages or small packages. Nathaniel could not account for it at all, but most of the tenant families had treated him rather coldly after his return from London. This boy was one of the few who still treated him with the same cordial openness he had enjoyed prior to the late earl's death.

"What is it, young Matthew?"

"Me lor', Peche asks if he should order some special foods if the ladies is stayin' to supper," he said.

"I see, Matthew. I am afraid they are not, so please tell Peche that whatever not-special fare he had planned shall do quite nicely."

"Ver' good, me lor'." The lad bowed, turned, and was off running again.

"He is a very spirited child, is he not?" asked Violet, amusement coloring her voice.

"That he is." Nathaniel began walking once again.

"It seems," said Violet, "we have often been interrupted today during what may be considered important conversations."

Nathaniel considered this. He also measured her apparent need to apologize. Grasping the hand which did not hold her apple, Nathaniel planted his booted feet on the ground and gently turned Violet to face him.

"Yes, we have been interrupted quite a bit recently," Nathaniel agreed. "Allow me to speak once more, and then we shall think no more of these frightfully grave subjects." He waited until she met his eyes, and finally spoke when he held her gaze. "You have nothing for which to apologize. My brother is a scoundrel, and your mother did fly up a bit when she found us on the balcony. However, I am not entirely free of blame, either. I ought to have released you the second I felt that your balance was restored. And so I find that *I* must apologize to *you*, Miss Wyndham. I hope you will forgive me and allow me the privilege of addressing you by your given name, as I have rather come to enjoy it these last few times I did."

Miss Wyndham smiled softly. "I confess that I am not quite used to hearing my name from anyone besides my family. However, as we are to be married, I suppose I must grow used to it. And you have no more for which to apologize than you claim I do."

"Perhaps for my brother?"

She shook her head. "You are not your brother, my lord."

"Might you call me by a more familiar name?" Nathaniel asked.

After a pause, she asked uncertainly, "Perhaps after we are wed?"

He grinned at her uncertain manner. "I suppose if that is the best you can manage for now, I have no choice but to be satisfied. But please know that it is my sincere hope to someday hear you call me by my Christian name, Nathaniel."

Miss Wyndham responded softly, "Perhaps someday."

They continued on their way, viewing a deliberate and orderly garden with well-trimmed topiaries to their left, between them and the house, and a lovely wilderness to their right, with an authentic ruin adorning the edge. Nathaniel was gratified when Violet's eyes shone at his admission that it had not been constructed to add to the *picturesque* view, but that it was in fact an old chapel from even before his great-grandfather's time. When he offered, Violet readily agreed that she would enjoy in the future going to explore the remains of the old chapel. Soon their path led them back to the house, passing the stable and the kitchen garden. As the pair finally mounted the steps to the house, the door opened and Mrs. Baker emerged onto the terrace.

"My lord," she said as she curtsied first for him and then again for the young lady. "Miss Wyndham."

"Yes?" asked Nathaniel after a greeting nod. The three made their way into the house.

"Might I borrow your bride, my lord?" said the housekeeper. "I must measure her for the dresses you intended to order; I even managed to secure the *modiste* for the occasion, that she might see what shades and fabrics will best suit her."

"Certainly." Nathaniel turned and bowed to his intended. "I shall rejoin your mother and sister. Mrs. Baker will bring you to join us when she is finished."

He watched the young lady follow his housekeeper up the back set of stairs to a dressing room he knew the matronly woman had prepared as a temporary fitting room for several dresses and other items of clothing, about which Nathaniel knew very little. He supposed that he ought to learn, so as to surprise his wife with occasional gifts. As he made his way back to the morning room where her relatives awaited him, the thought occurred to him that she likely would care little for such fripperies. *Perhaps a new variety of rose or tree would better endear me to her.*

At the door to the morning room, he waved away the footman who prepared to open the door for him and paused to school his face into a disinterested mask. Mrs. Wyndham was certainly trying his nerves, even after she had secured his offer for her daughter. *P'haps even more so now.*

Just as he placed his hand upon the door-handle, a giggle reached his ears, followed by a girlish voice he could only assume to belonged to Miss Rose.

"Do you suppose he suspects?" asked she.

"Do you suppose it signifies?" came Mrs. Wyndham's acidic tone. "He has offered, she has accepted. He is bound now, both by honor and by the law."

"Unless Vi is found to be unfaithful."

"Oh pshaw! Girl, how can you be so dull? Your sister can scarcely converse with a man, gentleman, or nobleman, neveryoumind seducing one."

"And yet she has managed to ensnare one in marriage."

There was a pause, during which Nathaniel pressed his ear nearer the door, his frown deepening as he tried to catch any sound from the room at all.

Finally the silence was broken by the mother's indifferent voice. "It appears she has." Another pause, then a chuckle and, "Indeed, I should never have suspected her quiet and demure front would lure, much less catch, a husband. She played her part well, better than I should have hoped."

The ladies' conversation drifted to other, more innocuous subjects, such as the popular neckline during the past Season, and whether the sleeves would lengthen or shorten on the most fashionable dresses in the next Season.

Nathaniel found he was oddly detached from the simmering cauldron of emotion in his heart. His mind seemed caught on the oddity of a matron who put herself forward as fashionable and quite beyond the common, and yet using terms related to *fishing*, of all things. *Odd that a female would use a fishing example. Perhaps her late husband fished frequently and spoke to her of his activities? Perfectly plausible explanation,* he reasoned with himself.

While his mind remained caught in the odd, hazy paradox of Mrs. Wyndham's words, his heart was undergoing a great deal of stress. First, it had been calmed and drawn to a woman who seemed very different from the uncertain mouse of a girl to whom he had become engaged the previous evening. She did not fully blossom until they were walking together about his house. Then, his poor heart was very nearly laid bare to the same woman, one whom he scarcely knew. And by a simple question related to the loss of his father! Finally, his warming, vulnerable heart had been quickened by the same woman, by her artless appeal. He felt, for the first time in many, many months, true stirrings of attraction. And now to hear such speech against her?

A small commotion behind him caught his attention, effectively pulling him from the anger, the frustration, and even the more tender feelings occupying him. When he turned, there stood Violet with Mrs. Baker beside her. Violet curtsied, a small grin quirking her lips. He could not bow.

"I fear, Lord Reymes, that I have none of the expertise in bespeaking gowns of such elegance as it seems you are prepared to purchase for me," she began. "The *modiste's* questions left me quite unsure. Would it be too much of an imposition for you, or Mrs. Baker, or *anyone* else to make these decisions until I have gained the necessary experience to make my own decisions in a wise manner?"

It seemed her shyness had not yet returned. *I do hope she does not catch wind of what her family thinks of her, for I fear she will not soon recover. Even when not burdened by the uncertainty her family brings about, she does not even have enough confidence to choose clothing that she likes.*

"Is...something the matter, my lord?" she asked, uncertainty clouding her voice.

Forcing his clenched jaw to open, Nathaniel managed to say, "It shall all be seen to. It may be best if, for now, we refrain from ordering anything. After we are married, we shall make a trip to London. Perhaps on our honeymoon."

"Very well, my lord, if that is what you wish. Truly, though, I do not need a great deal in the way of my wardrobe. I am rather used to fashioning much of my own clothing, and even your *modiste* said that my gown is rather well-made and fashionable."

She met his eyes as she spoke, and a small measure of pride shone from her own when she spoke of the blue gown she wore, but Nathaniel could see that Violet was concerned. *Likely she can hear the annoyance in my voice and is afraid she has done something to displease me. I am uncertain as to whether I can see her family again today, though. I fear that I shall lose all semblance of propriety and ring a fine peal over the both of them, much worse than what Mrs. Wyndham attempted with me. That she would speak of her own daughter in such a way...* "Please accept my apologies, but I have urgent business to attend; I will be leaving for Town within the hour. Mrs. Baker will see you out. Good day, Violet."

He managed a stiff bow to the wide-eyed girl, before he turned on his heel and hastily removed to his study. After he slammed the door behind him, he leaned heavily upon it with his eyes closed. And he still saw her eyes, just before he stalked away from her – full of hurt and uncertainty. But not nearly as full as his heart.

Four

VIOLET COULD NOT at all account for Lord Reymes' abrupt farewell. She had the impression that he was beginning to like her – or, failing that, to *accept* her. Likewise, some of her reserve began to fade as she grew accustomed to his deep voice and his fixed eyes.

But now, she had not the slightest indication of how she would be received when she returned to his home as his wife in several weeks.

The evening after the tour of Bainscroft and Lord Reymes' farewell (if such an icy departure could indeed be called a farewell), Violet sat with the other females of the house in her Aunt Doberly's drawing room, listening to her mother babble on about the grand house, and how much pin money she suspected Violet would have, and what fine parties she would hold – both at Bainscroft and in Town. Rose sat beside their mother, smiling and adding her agreement to all that the woman said. In spite of the seemingly cheerful conversation, there was an underlying tension apparent to the careful observer. Their hostess, Mrs. Doberly, was a most careful observer.

It was not until Mrs. Wyndham and Rose had retired for the evening, claiming the excitement of the past two days as having fatigued them both, that Mrs. Doberly gave voice to her observations. She remained in the drawing room, together with her daughter Charlotte and her niece Violet.

"Did you enjoy your tour as much as your mama and sister did?" she queried, though she suspected she knew the answer already.

Violet's face told her aunt far more than the simple words she murmured. "Yes, Aunt, I did."

"Do you suppose, Violet, that we met Lord Reymes all those years ago when we were used to walking about the countryside? I remember very little of him from when I was a child, and have not seen him in years. Is he as handsome as he is rumored to be?" asked Charlotte pointedly.

"And where have you been hearing rumors, Charlotte?" asked the girl's mama.

"Oh, you know how girls talk when we visit," she replied. "Sunday last, before we left the churchyard, Miss Haberthy and Miss Lyndon both said they saw him in the village the week before and both insisted that he is very handsome."

"Charlotte, I should hope that you know better than to take part in idle gossip."

"But Mama, they were simply stating a fact! I chose to leave their company and greet Miss Brown when they started talking about his Papa's passing, and why he left, and how his brother still carries on in spite of his marriage to that girl from the North."

"How then, daughter, did you hear so much of their conversation? It seems quite impossible that they should jump to so many topics in the short time it would take for you to walk across the churchyard to speak to Miss Brown."

Charlotte's looked down at her book. "I left as soon as I could politely do so. I am sorry, Mama. I shall do my best to move along more quickly in the future."

"I am exceedingly glad, child, that even when I subject you to close scrutiny, you are found to be so full of goodness and quality. Come, Charlotte, allow me to give you a kiss."

The younger girl immediately perked up, stood, and crossed the small space to offer her cheek to her mother. Violet smiled wistfully at the exchange, wishing fervently that she might have had some similar encounters with her own mama. As Charlotte returned to her place on the settee beside Violet, Mrs. Doberly looked up to see the wistfulness on her niece's face.

"Charlotte, dear, you had best hurry along to bed. Miss Graham will be here early tomorrow for your music lesson, and you know how she dislikes to be kept waiting."

"Yes, Mama. Goodnight." She dropped a curtsy before adding, "Goodnight, Cousin Violet."

"Goodnight, Charlotte. Have pleasant dreams." Violet stood and began to say, "Aunt, I am afraid that I am rather exhausted—"

"Oh, but I had hoped to have a *tête-à-tête* with you, dear, cozily settled as we are; with the breeze from the window, it is quite pleasant in here, is it not?"

Violet was rather surprised, but remained quiet as she moved closer to her aunt.

The other woman, only fifteen years or so Violet's senior, asked, "Much has changed in a very short time."

Violet nodded. "It has."

"While it is rather sudden, and brought about rather...speedily...I must admit that I am gratified that I shall have you so near to me. I've always been grateful for your influence over Charlotte."

Violet was startled into responding without thought. "But Charlotte is such a good girl! Why she should need the influence of anyone is beyond me!"

"Charlotte is a good girl – an exceedingly good girl. But she is prone to occasional bouts of silliness; I sometimes fear that the influence of some of her friends is too strong. She has a good heart, and finds great joy in helping whomever she is able, but that generosity may be cause for an unscrupulous person to prey upon her as she grows."

"But how would I influence her for the better, Aunt?" asked Violet. "You know I am quiet and she usually guides our activities when we are together."

"Yes, my dear, but there is a tempered quality to her behavior when she is in your presence. I believe that your reserve reins in some of Charlotte's enthusiasm. But that is not the topic I wished to speak with you about."

"It is not?"

"Oh no, dear. I supposed that your influence upon her should naturally happen with this closer proximity. What I wished to discuss with you was your marriage."

"Oh," she murmured unenthusiastically.

"Goodness, child! We are not speaking of some punishment or sentence to a life of drudgery! Lord Reymes is a good man, if a bit standoffish. He has, while living a life of privilege, also been subject to a great deal of sadness and difficulty of late. I cannot blame him for his churlishness."

Violet could not help but interrupt. "Forgive me, Aunt, but you are mistaken. Lord Reymes is not...churlish. He has been kind and generous in his dealing with me and with my family. And he is a kind master; I am certain that he is fond of his staff, and they of him.

Why, when we were out walking in the gardens, a boy from the house ran out to ask him a question, and the grin he had for the child was certainly doting."

"Then what is the source of your distress? Your mama has been quite outspoken concerning her intention of finding you a match as soon as possible; she has talked of little else since your arrival. I daresay this was much more efficiently accomplished than even she could have dreamed. Even so, you cannot tell me that you are surprised it has happened."

Violet's stomach turned in protest. *I had not wanted to believe that Mama would contrive to have me matched by such means.* Aloud, though, she simply said to her aunt, "I am aware that she has since my come-out been looking for a marriage for me, but please believe me, Aunt, that Lord Reymes and I – all we did on that balcony was speak to one another – and then when I nearly fell, he caught me. That is when Mama stepped onto the balcony."

"And I can easily imagine how that interview went, regardless of what story your Mama is bandying about concerning it. Still, this is not what I wished to discuss." Violet's aunt reached across the space between them to take her hand and give it a gentle squeeze. "Are *you* happy with the match, dear?"

She thought of the darkness that seemed to be her frequent companion, but which appeared to have faded some during her time with Lord Reymes. She could not account for it at all, and was unsure if she even desired to make an attempt. The darkness had not left her entirely, but she knew that it was not as pressing as it had been that morning when she rose. Upon glancing up at her aunt's expectant face, Violet attempted to collect her thoughts quickly.

"I find that I am not precisely *unhappy*, but I truly cannot say. This morning, while Lord Reymes showed me his house, he seemed to grow to enjoy my company more and more. And I found that I was growing comfortable with him, as I rarely am after such a brief acquaintance." She paused. "He even used my Christian name several times, and when we were walking in the gardens, he invited me to call him Nathaniel."

"Your tour of his gardens seems to have featured prominently in your time there. Mayhap it was a time full of meaning or at the least, enjoyment." When Violet remained quiet, she continued. "Then you must know that you will enjoy at least that aspect of your married life." Despite the rather innocuous words, Mrs. Doberly had an understanding smile upon her lips.

Violet decided not to question her aunt about the incongruity between her words and her smile, and commented only on what the elder woman had said. "Yes. His gardens are magnificent. Everything I could have ever hoped for in my own. But when we returned to the house we parted because his housekeeper was directed to have me measured for some gowns."

"Is not your mama to supply you with a trousseau?"

"She is. But I believe that Lord Reymes wished for me to be outfitted properly. I suppose I am to be a Countess, after all."

"You suppose! Are you not certain?"

"I am not *un*certain. But it still seems rather unbelievable at present. Ash and Penny still do not know, and..." Violet drew a deep breath before continuing. "My parting with Lord Reymes has rather unsettled me."

"Here we come to the crux of the matter," said her aunt. "I wondered when we should. Tell me, dear. What happened?"

"My fittings went well. The *modiste* even complimented me on my gown."

"Did she?"

"Yes. It was one which I had fashioned from an old gown of Mama's which she deemed too last-century for any respectable party, and the colors did not suite Rose's complexion."

"You've always been a talented seamstress," smiled her aunt.

Violet brushed by the compliment and continued speaking. "Regardless, the time at Bainscroft was pleasantly spent for the most part. Mrs. Baker is a motherly sort of woman, whose manner immediately put me at ease. Her voice is soft, and her eyes kind. The tour of the house consisted mostly of the history of the place, and some discussion of renovations to be made to help keep the house up with the modern trends of our time. But Mrs. Baker told me of my duties as mistress of such a place, and of the tenants, and servants and stable workers and gardeners. It is quite a formidable task."

"Which you shall carry out with aplomb," inserted Mrs. Doberly.

Violet again disregarded the compliment. "It was not until we had returned that Lord Reymes seemed to...have changed. He was not nearly so warm in his speech when we returned, and did not look at me for very long when he spoke his farewell."

"And he was looking directly at you previously?"

"Oh yes, even before the...er, engagement. When we were introduced upon our arrival, it felt as though his gaze was burning holes in to my face. And when we spoke on the balcony, and danced after the announcement of our engagement, I was rather uneasy with how fixed his eyes were." Here Violet paused briefly, thinking about how she had been growing more comfortable with Lord Reymes. "However, as we spoke throughout the course of the morning, I felt that I was becoming accustomed to it. At least in part. Though I cannot account for the warmth I felt often when we spoke. To be sure, it was a warm day, but this warmth seemed to come from inside me."

"The man who can loose your tongue, Violet, is certainly a prize."

"Oh, I am chattering on so! Please forgive me, Aunt."

"No such thing! It is a joy to hear you speak so freely. It is indeed rare that I am given such a deep look into your mind and your heart." Mrs. Doberly affectionately patted her niece's hand. "But please, you were discussing Lord Reymes' short farewell. He ushered you out hastily?"

"Not at all! He left his own house!"

"He has left the neighborhood?"

"Temporarily. He muttered something about business calling him away, gave a hasty good-bye, and nothing else. He was gone."

"Very odd indeed. And you can think of nothing which might explain this behavior?"

"Nothing at all." She swallowed thickly before saying, "I fear he is again as unhappy as on the balcony, when Mama first suggested marriage as the remedy to this mess. Only this time, I fear his ire is directed at me."

"She *suggested* marriage? Demanded, more like. I dearly loved your father, my brother, but his sense had gone begging when he decided to allow your mama as much latitude as he did. When they first married, she was a spoiled creature. Now, she expects entirely too much from the rest of the world, because he was unable to withhold anything from her."

Violet wished she could protest her aunt's words, but she could not in good conscience do so, for they were all true. Still, she felt she must try. "Aunt, are your words not rather harsh?"

"Harsh they may be, but sometimes the truth is not pretty. Though I am sorry, child, for maligning your mama's name in your presence."

"No, I know her manners are...lacking, and I am afraid that my own thoughts toward her are less than charitable at times. But I do try my best to think of her better qualities."

"Yes, that is a good practice."

"She is quite devoted to the task of securing her daughters' futures."

"That she is," smiled Mrs. Doberly before adding in a more cynical tone, "to a fault."

"Aunt!"

"I am sorry, Violet." Mrs. Doberly shook her head as she chuckled to herself. "But you know it to be true."

"Perhaps," she allowed.

"But no more of this talk. What of your Earl?"

"Oh pray do not call him that." Violet did her best to cool her cheeks with her hands upon them. "He is not mine. And he would not be anything to me were it not for the meddling of my mother."

"Ah, even you cannot keep from stating the ugly truth, can you Violet?"

"You asked about Lord Reymes," Violet reminded the elder lady. "I cannot account for the quick change in his temperament. But what is to be done?"

"Is there anything to be done, Violet, aside from making your preparations?"

Violet paused to consider this. She truly had no recourse. She could not cry off, for if she broke the engagement, she would be deemed a ridiculous woman: either wanton, behaving inappropriately with the Earl and thinking nothing of her virtue to the point of rejecting his hand, or foolish, to have turned away from such a profitable match. While she knew neither to be the case, Society would surely scorn her and she should be left to find some occupation for which she had no training and no ability. Or live in shame with Ash and Penny. *I could not bring such shame to their house.*

"No, aunt, I suppose there is not." Violet found she could speak no more and quietly excused herself to retire for the evening.

Once in her room, the reality of her situation descended upon Violet like heavy chains, rendering her unable to do aught but lie upon the bed and try to breathe through the oppressive weight on her chest. After some time, she managed to ring for the maid, who helped her unfasten the buttons on the back of her gown, and then her stays. She excused the maid then, choosing to slip into her nightgown by herself, and finally she crawled beneath the bedclothes.

Just this afternoon, I had joked with him about the bedclothes in our room. I've never managed to say anything humorous to a man before in my life, apart from Ash, and scarcely even then. Dear God, why must this opportunity to be married to a man I might learn to love and who might learn to love me, be snatched away so suddenly? What am I to do? I suppose I ought to console myself with the fact that I shall have my dear Uncle, Aunt, and Cousin so near. But I cannot. To marry a man I do not love, and who I fear shall never love me. Who – even more – very likely despises me! When he looked upon my face that last time, before leaving so abruptly, his eyes held all the contempt and scorn with which he beheld my mother. Whatever shall I do?

Five

NATHANIEL TRAVELED TO London immediately after he left Violet standing in the hallway at Bainscroft. He felt badly leaving her in such a manner, but he had been quite overcome by such distress that he truly doubted his ability to behave civilly toward Mrs. Wyndham and her youngest daughter. He chose to ride the entire way there, pushing the physical limits of both his stallion and himself.

Once arrived in London, he quickly bathed and dressed before going out again. He visited his solicitor to make the necessary arrangements for Violet's allowances, pin-money, and the like. He also procured the license before returning to the house to plan their honeymoon tour. As soon as that had been settled, Nathaniel wrote to Violet. His letter was brief, but he found himself worried for her, and hoped that she was faring well with her mother and sister in the time between their parting and the wedding. He made some excuse of asking if she knew of a suitable abigail to serve her, but sincerely hoped that she would see his concern for her happiness as his true reason for writing. He admittedly suspected that she would answer that she was doing well, regardless of her true situation, and so when he was struck with the idea that a visit would be much more telling than a letter, he eagerly added a line to the short missive to include the request for permission.

Once the letter was dispatched, he scrawled a note to Lord Stallingsworth, asking for the honor of his presence at supper. The man had traveled to Bainscroft for the ball alone, and had returned to his London home in the wee hours of the following morning. And so it was that later that evening, the men were situated in Nathaniel's study after having shared a light meal. They were in their shirtsleeves, for the weather was unseasonably warm, and neither saw a need to stand on formalities with no-one present save the two close friends.

Nathaniel handed Stallingsworth a glass of brandy, then poured his own. As he did so, he attempted to explain to his friend how he was worried for his fiancé, that he feared her mama and sister might be mistreating her at that very moment. The other man listened, alternately taking a sip of his brandy and scrubbing the hand not holding his drink over his mouth as he unsuccessfully tried to hide his chuckles. After several guffaws from his friend, Nathaniel had quite enough.

"I do not understand what you find so very amusing about the abuse my future wife might be suffering in her childhood home," he grumbled after he saw that Stallingsworth would not be made to understand the urgency and anxiety he felt on the matter. He sipped from his glass as he waited to see what the other man would answer.

"No, no, Reymes," chuckled Stallingsworth, removing his hand from his face, setting down his glass on the nearest table, and carefully folding his hands upon his crossed legs, "you misunderstand me. I do not laugh at her predicament, but at your reaction to it."

With a frustrated grunt, Nathaniel asked, "Are you not indignant at their treatment of her?"

"Oh, to be sure I am," he replied. "Allow me to offer this reassurance, though, which has aided me immeasurably." Nathaniel nodded warily. He suspected his friend to be mocking him. "Tell me, has she endured this all her life?"

"I fear she has, and that is no reassurance!" Nathaniel took an angry gulp from his glass.

"And she has managed to survive it to this point?" his friend pressed farther.

"Yes." Another gulp. "She is a remarkable woman to show such forbearance and patience with them."

"Then you've nothing to fear." Stallingsworth raised his drink with a satisfied lift of his brow and quirk of his lips. *The man clearly believes he is about to make some great philosophical point.* "I am sure that if she has persevered through her formative years, your lovely bride shall certainly endure another month until you marry her and take her away from that place."

"You mean from that woman," Nathaniel spat. It seemed the brandy had loosed his tongue, so he bit it for a moment to prevent a verbose diatribe on the unfortunate parentage of his bride. "I must admit that she spoke rather fondly of her brother, if I am not mistaken. So not *all* of her family has treated her in this manner."

Perhaps I ought to pay him a visit.

"Might I make an observation?" Stallingsworth asked nonchalantly as he drew his snuff-box from his pocket.

"If you must." Nathaniel stood abruptly from his chair and began to pace to and fro before the dark fireplace, certain he would not care for his friend's observation. It seemed the man was determined to speak in riddles. *Infuriating gabster.*

Stallingsworth flipped the lid back from his box with an elegant movement of his wrist. "You are rather fond of the girl, are you not?"

"I suppose, but does that signify?" Nathaniel exhaled a ragged sigh as his feet stopped their pacing and he leaned heavily upon the fireplace mantle.

Stallingsworth took a pinch of his snuff, immediately closing the ornate box and slipping it once again into his pocket. "It might. Let us return to my observation about your reaction to Miss Wyndham's family." He dusted off his fingers, several tiny specks falling from them.

Nathaniel sighed tiredly. "And what was your observation?"

"You are rather fond of the girl."

"Yes. We have established this. But we are to be married, and I therefore fail to see your point." Nathaniel scoffed at his friend, incredulous that he had believed Stallingsworth to be about to impart some valuable insight. "Would you prefer that I had taken a disgust of her, rather than a liking?"

"No, but it seems to me that perhaps you've taken *more* than a liking to her."

"Impossible." Nathaniel stood upright again.

"Why impossible?"

"We've known one another for less than a week and in that time have only seen one another twice!" Nathaniel scoffed at his friend's illogical supposition. "I offered for her because honor demanded it, not due to some instant, ardent admiration."

"Oh, I thought it was her mama who demanded it," dead-panned Stallingsworth.

"No." Nathaniel began pacing again. "I compromised her by being on that balcony with her for such a length of time, unchaperoned. Not that anything questionable took place, but I could not allow Society to believe ill of her."

"So you sought to protect her. And you worry excessively for her, as is evidenced by the manner in which you make a fuss about her mama," grinned Stallingsworth.

"Not excessively. Her mama and sister abuse her horridly, without regard for the company present. Most vulgar women."

"I do not doubt the mother is of a commonplace mind, but do you not find your reaction rather extreme?"

"Extreme!" Nathaniel cried, restlessly pacing again. "I suppose to a man who does not really know her, who is not soon to be her husband, it may seem extreme."

"A man who is not half-way fallen in love with her already?"

"Precisely!" cried he, caught up in the moment and warm from both the brandy and the emotions churning within. Nathaniel quickly and somewhat clumsily attempted to smooth over his perceived error, though. "That is to say, no, not at all. Yes, I am fond of the girl. It seems you are not above manipulation; you have tricked me into admitting more than is true."

"Have I now?" Stallingsworth pressed his lips together for a time while looking thoughtfully at his friend for the space of several moments before he spoke again. "Tell me, Reymes. Do you believe in love at first sight?"

"What a schoolgirl notion. I am hardly in my salad-days, Stally, and certainly not suffering from some calf-love!" Nathaniel scowled, doing his best to discount whatever foolish notions his friend was so interested in sharing. He returned to his chair. "I scarcely remembered her when we first met, she hardly left an impression."

"Oh, did she not?" The other man shook his head, staring down into his drink with a sardonic smile as he swirled the red liquid round and round. "Well, never mind then. I still have your admission that you are, quote: fond of the girl."

"Well," he began uncomfortably, "come to think of it, I allow that I *am* fond of the girl. I did offer for her, did I not?"

"I thought that was a matter of honor and duty and whatnot," laughed Stallingsworth as he finished off his drink and rose to help himself to half a glass more.

"It was," agreed Nathaniel, "But I did – I do! – enjoy speaking with her."

"You spoke on the balcony, and then again this morning?"

"And briefly when we met."

"But you claimed that she left no impression," Stallingsworth reminded him, returning to his chair.

"I said that she *hardly* left an impression. I allow she did leave a small one," Nathaniel admitted. "There is something vaguely familiar about her, but I've yet to place it. Her looks are rather common to many ladies so perhaps that is all. I was certainly not struck with some mythical love-arrow of Cupid's."

Stallingsworth laughed outright.

"Enough! You've talked me in circles and I'll have no more of it."

His friend nodded but said, "Very well, if you'll but answer me once more."

Reymes resisted the urge to roll his eyes.

"You've admitted to being fond of her, yet seem annoyed with the admission. Why is that?"

Reymes was taken aback. *Why do I not embrace the fact that I enjoy the presence of the woman who is to be my wife?*

"She is too timid; even last evening when her mama stormed onto the balcony with us. The girl could scarcely speak. It was most aggravating, that she would not speak up in my defense – or even her own! As we have spent time together, though, apart from her mama, she seems to be emerging from her shell."

"Rather insightful observations you've made of a lady of whom you claim to be merely *fond*." Stallingsworth's voice still held an element of levity which grated on Nathaniel's nerves. "Regardless, she's quite the tempting armful. Is she not?"

"Watch yourself, Stally," warned Nathaniel in low tones, rising to his feet and taking a step toward the other man.

"Easy! I mean no insult!" he insisted. When Nathaniel withdrew to his chair, Stallingsworth continued in a jovial tone, "You looked ready to sport your canvas, man."

"I was not looking to fight! And over so trivial a statement," huffed Nathaniel, though he knew it to be merely a half-truth. He wasn't ready to challenge his friend for what he had said, but it echoed too closely his brother's words.

"I see," grinned Stallingsworth.

"What ought I do, though? Since we parted ways this morning, I have been unable to think of little but her having to live with those two harpies. I am considering procuring a special license, that I may take her away sooner," he admitted.

"Oh-ho, Reymes! Why do you not simply go to her house and spirit her away during the night? Young ladies find elopements terribly romantic and all, do they not? Or perhaps visit and ask to walk with her in the gardens, but have a carriage waiting to carry you to Gretna Green. Ladies adore that sort of scheme."

It seems that the brandy has effected Stally as well, though the idea of taking Miss Wyndham away immediately does have some merit. But I cannot elope with her. I suppose her mama would fly up into the boughs over that, and poor Violet would never hear the end of it. Mrs. Wyndham certainly does not seem the sort to forgive easily.

"That is not an option, Stally, I will not rob my bride of a respectable start to our marriage."

"You've already robbed her of that when you compromised her on the balcony," countered his friend.

"I will say it one more time, Stallingsworth: I did not compromise Miss Wyndham. I found her with my brother attempting to do so and stopped him."

Nathaniel steered their conversation away from Miss Wyndham after that, and without the entertaining topic of conversation, Stallingsworth soon bored of his company and bade his "love-struck" friend *adieu*.

After the idea was planted in Nathaniel's mind to go and visit the brother, he found he could think of little else. After Stallingsworth took his leave, he strode to his desk to retrieve a paper and pen. Uncapping the ink-bottle, he quickly inspected the quill before hastily dipping it into the ink.

> *Reymes House*
> *Hanover Square, London*
> *22 August 1808*
> *To Mr. Wyndham:*
> *You are as-yet unacquainted with me, but as I will soon call you "brother," it is my hope that you will receive me tomorrow morning. Perhaps your mother has already written to you, but there was an unfortunate accident which resulted in the necessity of an engagement. I would speak with you regarding the particulars of my marriage to your sister Miss Wyndham.*
> *Your servant,*
> *Lord Reymes, Earl of Bainscroft*

After blotting and sealing it, Nathaniel called for a footman to deliver the letter. It was rather late in the evening, but he supposed that the import of the letter excused the lateness of the hour. After he readied for bed with the assistance of his valet, and lay in bed staring unseeingly at the draped fabric of his bed-curtains, images of soft brown hair and green-grey eyes danced in his vision.

Mr. Ashbridge Wyndham kissed his wife's forehead and gently touched her rounded belly for just a moment before he took his leave of the private sitting room. It connected his and his wife's chambers, and while they had yet to use both simultaneously, he suspected that an extra room in such close proximity to the one they usually shared might prove helpful in the very near future.

Ash followed the hall to the stairs until he began descending them. The card, handed him by the butler as he announced the presence of a visitor in the morning room, bore the name of the man whose brief missive he had received last night, and whose name had been so effusively praised in a rare letter from the elder Mrs. Wyndham.

And briefly mentioned in a short note from his sister, informing him of her engagement to said gentleman. *At least she wrote well of him.*

Entering the room, he saw Lord Reymes perched upon the edge of his chair, one knee bouncing rapidly. *Nervous?* Ash wondered. *Suppose I might be nervous meeting the brother of a woman I'd compromised, if Mrs. Wyndham's letter is to be believed.* As soon as Lord Reymes spied him, he hastened to his feet and Ash could not hide the amusement he felt.

Grinning broadly, Ash bowed deeply and said, "Welcome, my lord, I am pleased to receive you – and pardon my wife's absence, as she is indisposed at this time." He motioned for Lord Reymes to sit, then followed suit himself. "In most circumstances, I am loathe to welcome into my home someone who has won the affection of Mrs. Wyndham with such ease, but it seems that you also had the good sense to have won Violet's, so you cannot be lacking in *all* good judgment!"

Lord Reymes conceded to his assessment with a nod, but hastened to say, "I thank you, but am compelled to tell you first that your sister and I scarcely know one another."

Ash felt his stomach drop instantly, and could not help the suspicion that crept in on him. "Indeed?" he intoned coldly. Ash felt his heart clench at the ideas forming of what the letter he had received just a day ago might mean. "Mrs. Wyndham wrote that you and my sister were most violently amorous toward one another."

"Not at all! That is, I do not dislike her, but we've scarce been given a chance to become acquainted." Lord Reymes drew an audible breath and when he spoke, he almost seemed to stumble over some of his words. "I assisted her with some trouble, but then she tripped. I caught her, and Mrs. Wyndham spied us before I could release her. We did nothing disgraceful, and yet your mother insisted that she had been compromised."

Ash felt the tension leave him in a rush. "Ah. I was rather curious at how Violet had managed to speak to you enough for you to take notice of her, much less fall in love with her. Terribly shy, my sister – almost annoyingly so."

"So her behavior is not meant for me alone?" Lord Reymes' eyes widened and his face reddened the moment the words had left his mouth.

Ash could not help but snigger a bit. Drily, he assured the other man, "Not at all. Now that I know how this engagement came about, I must admit to a great eagerness to see how your marriage shall go on, her not being able to speak to you."

Shifting slightly in his chair, Lord Reymes said, "She did quite well when we were absent from Mrs. Wyndham."

"Did she now? Most interesting," mused Mr. Wyndham. More than the man's words, the tone of defensiveness peaked Ash's interest. *A man who will look to Violet's interests and come to her defense when she does not for herself...* "Come to think of it, I cannot say that I've seen her in company with a man apart from that woman, with the exception of her Season two years past." In the interest of helping Lord Reymes to better understand Violet's character better, Ash added, "But I fear she has changed since then."

"In what manner?" asked Lord Reymes.

"Before I met my wife, Violet was to stay with me, and keep house. Much easier in my mind to tolerate a timid sister than a troublesome wife. But of course, the Lord had other plans. When Penelope – that is my wife – and I married somewhat unexpectedly, Violet decided that I would rather not have her hanging off my sleeve—her words, mind you, not mine. Of course *my* Mrs. Wyndham would have been more than happy to have her stay with us, but Violet can be stubborn concerning some things." The memories of this unexpected separation, and the months of worry over his sister's wellbeing, made Ash most uncomfortable. He stood and moved to gaze out the window; looking out over the activity of the street was much easier than allowing a near-stranger to see his pain. even if that stranger would soon be family. "Violet has always lived up to her name. She is shy and timid, and very rarely speaks in her own defense. It has grown worse since my wedding – not due to

Sarah Baughman

the marriage itself, but because I have not been present. With the lack of true affection and encouragement, she has retreated even further into herself." He shook his head and looked back to Lord Reymes. "Am I correct in assuming you have come for my blessing, my lord?"

"Yes, Mr. Wyndham," replied the man. His face was troubled. "I can see that you care deeply for your sister. It is my sincere promise that I will do my utmost to be worthy of your sister. She is a most valuable woman."

"As to my blessing, I cannot very well withhold it, given the circumstances. I am compelled to tell you, though, that she is most adamant that God's Word is the source of authority in her life, and will not bow to any attempt to influence her otherwise. She will do it humbly and respectfully, but she will fight it. Indeed, it seems to be the only thing for which she will fight." Lord Reymes again shifted in his chair, but this time he seemed to be discomfited by Ash's words than defensive of Violet. Even so, Ash pushed onward. "Just over two years past, I was of the opinion that only I would determine my own actions and decisions, that no one else need be consulted. Violet never supported that ideal, but was gentle in her reprimands. She often hinted, if not outright said, that I was operating under a grave misapprehension."

"And now?"

"I came to realize that I had dreadfully mangled my attempts at ordering my own life. I had a scheming widow in Mrs. Wyndham, a simpering, silly young girl in Rose, a shy and unappreciated Violet...and worst of all, worse than being unable to manage my family – to prevent Mrs. Wyndham's absurdity, to teach my sisters either restraint or self-assurance – I could not even choose whom my heart would love. Nothing that I previously thought within my influence was proceeding as I had planned. Indeed, I had no intention of being riveted until absolutely necessary, but as I said, it seemed that the Lord had other plans."

"Are you saying that you believe this is God's design, that Violet be compromised and forced to marry me?" Lord Reymes sounded truly appalled.

"Not at all. Only that He can certainly bring good from that which is bad."

Lord Reymes opened his mouth to respond, but closed it after a moment, seemingly unsure what to say.

"I say this not to lower myself in your esteem, Reymes," said Ash thoughtfully, "But to demonstrate that I cannot allow Violet to wed someone who will stand against her faith."

"I will not claim to have as lofty a faith as Violet's," Lord Reymes began. Ash raised his brows, both in reaction to the other man's candor and to his use of his sister's given name. When he did not comment, though, Lord Reymes continued. "Never, though, will I tell Violet that something her conscience demands is wrong. She has demonstrated herself to be a kind, compassionate, and *good* woman, and I cannot believe her to ever be convinced of anything contrary to that."

Ash considered Lord Reymes for a time, measuring the man's steady gaze for honesty and his swallowing throat for possible nerves. *Good; he ought not be too assured of his worthiness of my sister.* At length, Ash answered, "My sister deserves a husband who will match her in faith. However, the Lord has a way of working through her quiet words and sincere care. And as you've given your word not to oppose the Scriptures by not opposing her in that matter, I shall give my blessing. And who knows? She may yet win you over."

"I am pleased to give her the opportunity."

Ash could not keep a sardonic smile from his lips. It seemed the man was a fair way to being enamored of Violet already. Deciding not to comment upon that particular observation, he said instead, "That's right; you'd mentioned her beginning to speak more freely with you. Last winter, Lord Ashbridge invited me, as well as my family, to visit him at Linsdon for the Christmas season. We took Violet with us, and remained above a month. The poor girl was terrified to meet such a high-ranking man as Lord Ashbridge, but she eventually found her tongue. Of course, I daresay the absence of Mrs. Wyndham – not mine, mind you – greatly helped with her feeling free to speak."

"Was she happier away from her mama?" Lord Reymes seemed to perk up at the possibility of gaining intelligence on his bride.

"Indeed. Once *my* Mrs. Wyndham's babe arrives, and my family moves to take up permanent residence at Linsdon, it had been my hope to persuade Violet to come with us, for a visit if nothing else. Now, I extend an invitation to the both of you."

Lord Reymes nodded and then asked, "You are to inherit the Marquess' title, are you not?"

"I am."

"Is it a familial relation?"

"I fear I am not at liberty to say. It is a legitimate inheritance, of course, or else it would not be taking place. The old Marquess, however, has begged me not to make it public at this time."

"I see."

"You received your title...was it four years past?"

"Yes." Lord Reymes offered no more, looking uncomfortable. He rose from his chair and extended a hand toward Ash with an almost abrupt manner. "I thank you for your blessing. I have not had a great deal of time to become well acquainted with your sister, but she smiles more when she speaks of you than of anything else; I can see that your opinion and blessing mean a great deal to her."

Ash stood and shook his hand before sitting once again. "As we are to be brothers, why do you not call me Wyndham?"

Lord Reymes nodded and offered the same familiarity before saying, "I must admit to being most gratified to see that Violet's entire family does not treat her in the same manner as do her mother and sister."

"You are an astute man, Reymes." Ash shook his head. "Her letters, while not directly expressing unhappiness, certainly have a much more melancholic tone of late."

"I am sorry to hear that," murmured Reymes, strolling over to the unlit fireplace. "May I ask – has she written of me?"

Ash was glad for evidence of the man's interest in what she might have written of him. He said, "Yes, as a matter of fact. She enclosed a brief letter with Mrs. Wyndham's. She said that you were a terribly imposing figure upon first acquaintance, but that once she came to know you more, she has reason to hope that she will learn to have a felicitous marriage – or at the least, a content one."

"Indeed?" Reymes seemed unsure whether or not to hear these words as encouragement.

"Don't take it too hard, Reymes. She is cautious when it comes to her own hope of happiness. I found it most telling that she even included the word *felicitous*. Under the circumstances, the best I'd have expected was *comfortable*, or *well-provided-for*."

The rest of their conversation was filled with those civil pleasantries used by first-time acquaintances. Ash looked forward to seeing how their marriage would be. After Lord Reymes took his leave, Ash returned to his wife and found her resting upon a settee, reclined against some cushions.

"Not many more weeks now, Pen," he said with a hand to her abdomen. He felt a gentle *bump* against his palm and smiled broadly.

Penny opened her sapphire eyes and gazed up at him. "You just met Violet's betrothed and this is what you say to me?"

Ash laughed. "Oh very well, but please allow me to sit." He lifted her feet and slid onto the settee beneath where they were. Taking them into his lap, he slowly removed her slippers and placed them on the floor.

"Lord Reymes is indeed an imposing man," he began while moving his hands over her feet. "He spoke with adequate humility and seemed sincere in his desire to care for her."

"Does he not love her?" asked Penny, a frown creasing her brow. She began to attempt to sit up, but was unable to do more than prop herself up on her elbows.

"Are you not supposed to be resting?" Ash shook his head at her in mock frustration. With a firmer pressure, he began kneading the pads and arches of his wife's feet. When she rested against the cushions once more, he continued, "Neither of them loves the other. They were found in an innocent but misconstrued circumstance, and forced to marry."

He could see that Penny nearly attempted to sit up once again, but did not. "Indeed?" she cried instead. "I cannot believe anyone would think ill of Violet."

"It was Mrs. Wyndham who found them."

"Oh, I see." Penny's face fell. "Everything is changing. With Cornelius doing who-may-know-what in Canada, Mr. and Mrs. Pelter selling artists' supplies in my old studio, your friend Spence finally taking his duties to his estate and family to heart, and MacDougal purchasing a commission in the Royal Navy—I cannot bear for Violet, too, to be torn from us!"

"Do not fear, wife," he paused and allowed the grin to spread across his face before continuing, never tiring of calling her that. "All will be well. You know as well as I that the Lord has a way of working these things out."

Nathaniel found himself impatient to leave London, as his desire to return to Violet had intensified after his conversation with her brother. He was glad of the man's approbation and blessing, but worried all the more for his bride. While the warning as to Violet's religious tendencies left him with an almost-unidentifiable twinge in his heart, the more pressing matter in Nathaniel's mind was that of her welfare.

After Nathaniel took his leave of the Wyndham household, he immediately went to purchase a wedding ring for his bride – a single pearl affixed to a simple band. After this was finished, he heartily attacked the remainder of his business in Town and within two days, rather than the four he had anticipated, he was finished. This left him with little to do but sitting and stewing and worrying over his bride.

When on the third day he received a letter from Mrs. Wyndham, rather than her daughter, he was all the more determined to assure himself that Violet was well. As Mrs. Wyndham wrote in response to his request to visit that he would be welcome at any time, Nathaniel prepared to travel to their home at the time he had suggested, a fortnight before the wedding was to take place.

Violet winced at the sharp prick on her shoulder. She was surrounded by a seamstress and two of the Wyndham housemaids, all of whom were fitting a wedding gown to her willowy frame. Her mother and her sister sat together on her bed, poring over fashion plates in magazines as they chose what Violet would have for her wedding trousseau.

"This riding habit is glorious," Rose commented.

"Yes, indeed, my dear. So fashionable," returned Mrs. Wyndham.

"But rather *too* fashionable, don't you think, for our little Violet? She has not the airs to wear it convincingly."

Their mother was quick to agree. "And she does not ride overly much."

All the while, Violet did her best to ignore them. Her cheeks burned with shame that they should say such a thing in the presence of a stranger and the maids. *Very soon and I shall no longer be required to bespeak clothing with Mama and Rose, but may do so myself, and for myself alone.*

Rose continued. "Mama, may *I* have a riding habit in this style for part of *my* trousseau? I think in a burgundy velvet, it would be *divine*! And I do so *adore* this trimming. Of course, I must travel to London, for I should never be able to find a suitable velvet here."

Mrs. Wyndham agreed once again and they discussed whether Violet really *needed* a new riding habit – she rarely rode, as it was – before the conversation moved on to day dresses. It was decided that Violet certainly needed a new day dress, so as to not send her off too shabbily, but beyond that, well, the girl *was* marrying into money. And a title!

Rose was in raptures thinking how glad her dear Mr. Langley was upon receiving word of this new connection. Violet had certainly done right by her family. But Mrs. Wyndham wondered, Rose dear, whether you might now be able to make a more famous match. Rose maintained her devotion to her *dear Mr. Langley* – for he was of the first circles in Society, even if a mere second son, and rather a favorite with the Prince Regent – and the two ladies continued to peruse the fashions.

As they did so, not once consulting the one whose clothes they were discussing, Violet allowed her mind to be distracted. The seamstress, Madam Levasseur, asked Violet to raise her arms. The young woman complied, and then allowed her thoughts to wander.

The morning after their poorly-ended visit to Lord Reymes, the Wyndham party quit Doberly House and returned to their home. There was talk before their departure of traveling to London for the benefit of the best modistes and mantua-makers, but Mrs. Wyndham decided against it, claiming that they must hurry with preparations for the wedding, which would be upon them in a short time.

Four weeks after the engagement was announced so unexpectedly at the ball. Time enough for a wedding gown and a modest wedding trousseau to be sewn, the banns read, a breakfast to be planned – and then the wedding would take place.

Their last meeting with Lord Reymes was already a fortnight past – only two more weeks until Violet would become Mrs. Reymes. *No,* Violet corrected herself mentally, *Lady Reymes, Countess of Bainscroft.* Violet still could not fully comprehend that she was to marry an Earl. A part of her could. And an Earl who did not love her, and who quite possibly despised her. Violet's tired mind had concocted all manner of possible offense he had taken of her – she did not praise his excellent home enough, he was displeased with her manner of comporting herself, or any number of other things. While she knew on some level that she was being a goose, Violet could not help herself. Thankfully, it would be another fortnight before she would be required to see him again. *But then we shall be wed.*

Violet did her best to trust that God was with her and was guiding her life. Her faith held her in secure belief that despite the unpleasant aspect before her, and the uncertainty and even fear she felt regarding her future with the Earl, she would also be with her Lord. He would not leave her. Her mind settled into a tense but somewhat static state of prayerfulness.

Mrs. Wyndham's voice drew Violet from her reverie. "That's settled, then. Violet, I'll expect you and Rose for dinner in one hour."

"Settled? But I have not chosen any dresses beyond this one." Violet's mind struggled to grasp what had happened.

Mrs. Wyndham gave a long-suffering sigh. "Rose and I have seen to everything. Now, if you'll excuse me, I must speak to Cook about which pastries to serve at the wedding breakfast."

Perhaps I should not allow my mind to wander so, thought Violet. *First an engagement occurs without my knowledge and then an entire trousseau bespoken! What will happen next?*

Mrs. Wyndham exited, and was soon followed by Mrs. Levasseur. Elsie and Jane, the housemaids, helped Violet out of the basted gown before taking their leave. Mrs. Levasseur would complete the sewing during the coming two weeks and add any embellishments that Mrs. Wyndham and Rose deemed necessary.

The moment the door closed behind the other ladies, a loud and decidedly unladylike exclamation from Rose startled Violet. "Oh! I am in *raptures!*" Violet stared at her sister, uncertain what precipitated this outburst. "Dearest Violet, I cannot thank you *enough* for securing this marriage!"

"Rose, you must understand that it was unwanted by both Lord Reymes and me. Neither of us had any idea of marrying, let alone a near-stranger, before that night."

"Oh Violet, you silly thing. That is of no import whatsoever. Gentleman and Ladies marry those with whom they are only slightly acquainted quite often." Violet shook her head, wondering how her sister could be so unfeeling. "The point is, my dear Mr. Langley and I can publicly announce our engagement, since you are now to be married! Thomas will be so happy!" Rose jumped from the bed, clasped Violet's hands, and began to dance about the room with her.

Violet pulled her hands free, frowning. "Rose! I must insist that you please stop." Violet reached for her day dress, which was laid across the foot of the bed, and began to step into it. She knew that her fear pushed anger to the fore, yet she could do nothing to stem the emotion. "I am truly glad for you, Rose, but I cannot claim happiness for myself. Please do not expect the same fierceness of emotion from me as you so enjoy to exhibit."

"Oh Vi, you worry overmuch. Lord Reymes is *devastatingly* handsome, do you not agree?" Rose giggled. "He shall certainly be a nice one to have around. If I had not yet met my Thomas...well, but I have and so Lord Reymes is yours. So stately and tall, even your lanky frame might seem feminine." Rose threw herself onto the bed with a giggle.

Violet pulled the dress over her arms, the hem of the sleeve settling just above her elbow. The fabric was a pale color somewhere between orange and pink, with a deeper shaded ribbon tied just beneath the bodice.

"You will remember us after you are married, won't you?" came Rose's voice, uncharacteristically quiet and small.

"Rose?" Violet turned as she finished tying the ribbon.

"After all, you shall be a grand *Countess* and Mama and I shall still be ordinary Misses and Miss. Though I shan't be a Miss for long."

"Oh, Rose, of course I shall never forget you." Violet moved to sit on the bed beside her sister, working on the buttons that she could reach on the back of her gown. "I figured that it would be as you'd said: visiting one another and writing letters and the like."

Rose sniffed a bit, then straightened her head and cocked it to the side loftily. "Yes, well. You shall certainly be able to afford to be generous to your poor sister and mama, with all that you shall have."

Violet sighed and wanted to shake her head, but thought better of it. Choosing not to respond, she instead said, "Would you please help me with these last three buttons? I can never seem to reach them." Violet turned her back to her sister, waiting for her to fasten the small buttons.

Rather than helping, Rose moved from her place on the bed and rang the bell for a housemaid. Before long, Jane entered and curtsied.

"Miss?"

"Violet needs her dress fastened." Rose was again lounging on the bed, studying her neatly trimmed fingernails.

Jane hastened to oblige.

"Thank you, Jane," said Violet. Suddenly she remembered something that Lord Reymes had mentioned in the one letter he had sent. In addition to inquiring after her well-being and asking permission to call on her – she could not quite recall when, as her mama had taken the missive before Violet could commit the date to memory – he asked if she would prefer to bring her own ladies' maid. "Jane, would you be willing to leave Mrs. Wyndham's employ and accompany me to Bainscroft after the wedding takes place?"

"Bainscroft?"

"Yes, Jane. Bainscroft is Lord Reymes' family home."

"Why, yes, Miss." Jane, having finished with the buttons, quickly straightened several of Violet's curls and curtsied again, as she said, "Thank you, Miss." She then took her leave.

"Violet! Mama will be in an uproar! You know how hard it is to find good help!"

"Rose, Mama agreed when Lord Reymes wrote and asked if I would bring one of our housemaids to attend to me, as he had no one who would be appropriate. As you will be married soon, Mama hasn't as much need of so many members of the staff."

"But Elsie is simply *dreadful* at arranging my hair! Whatever shall I do?"

"Elsie does a tolerable job, as she has learned a great deal since she first came to our employ; and you'll be married soon, and then your husband may hire an abigail to attend you."

"But—" Rose began, but was interrupted by a knock and Violet could not be more grateful. She was not accustomed to standing up to her sister, and the effort had left her tired. Jane entered and announced that Mrs. Wyndham awaited them in the dining room. Violet hoped that the discussion would be permanently finished, for she hoped to have Jane with her; seeing one familiar face after her marriage would be a great comfort.

Upon arriving at Wyndmere, Nathaniel was welcomed warmly by Mrs. Wyndham. Rather than the usual practice of being received in a parlor, he was ushered directly into the dining room.

"Should we not await the ladies in a parlor?" he asked his hostess uncertainly.

"You are practically family!" cried Mrs. Wyndham. "We do not stand on formality with one another. My daughters shall be down directly. I've ordered a larger meal for us for the mid-day, as you mentioned in your letter that you will not remain long enough for a dinner to be served at the common time."

He nodded and rather uncomfortably followed her example by sitting at the table. The room was well-appointed, but dated, and lacked the refinement afforded by a truly masterful worker applying his craft to the finishes. Still, the room was by no means shabby.

Nathaniel rose from the table when he saw the Misses Wyndham enter the room. Miss Rose led the way – most unconventional as she was the younger. Violet was dressed in a stylishly cut gown, her hair in slight disarray. *Is it ever styled impeccably?* Rather than finding the thought distasteful, he rather fancied the imperfection. He could not help but admit that his bride was lovely to behold. He looked forward to the following few hours in her company with unexpected eagerness.

It seemed, however, that he was not part of Violet's expectation for the evening. She immediately dropped a curtsy upon sighting him, but her face betrayed her unease. Nathaniel was concerned for her sake. *Did Mrs. Wyndham fail to inform her that I would be a guest today?*

He moved around the table to hold the chair for Violet as she sat, then returned to his own place once the other ladies were both seated. Although he had enough footmen at his own residence to seat each person at the table simultaneously, he often dined with friends who did not. He in actuality preferred the less formal settings, but there were certain expectations that a guest had when dining with an earl, which Nathaniel felt obligated to meet. He looked forward to informal dinners with Violet.

As the party dined on venison, potatoes, and a variety of other fine foods, Nathaniel did his best to engage Miss Wyndham in conversation. He asked how her day had been, if she had been well in the past fortnight since he had seen her, whether she preferred venison or hens. Her answers were the definition of succinct. He determined after the meal to ask of her mother whether he might have a private audience with his intended.

Once they had all settled in the drawing room after the rather extravagant luncheon and the request made, Mrs. Wyndham gave her hearty consent. Nathaniel bore her enthusiastic response with impressive equanimity before approaching his object, who was perched on the settee with her sister, sewing some garment or other.

"Violet, might I trouble you to show me your gardens? As I drove up, I saw your labyrinth and have been contemplating adding one to the grounds at Bainscroft. I should very much like to view yours at a closer distance."

Miss Rose spoke up quickly. "Oh, I *adore* them particularly, Lord Reymes. Violet is not overly fond of the labyrinth – she once was lost in it for three whole hours, you see – but it would be my *delight* to show you." As he stared at her with distaste for her boldness, she actually batted her eyes at him! "Ours is a difficult one, indeed, and I would be *loathe* to see you become lost in it." She gazed up at him with a coy smile on her pretty face.

Nathaniel was rather shocked. He looked pointedly at Miss Wyndham, who was still working intently at her sewing. *What game is she playing at? And will Violet not defend her place as the eldest? Or even as my bride?*

Choosing to ignore Miss Rose, Nathaniel squatted down on his haunches before his intended – rather undignified, but it was imperative that he see Miss Wyndham's face. He gently removed the white fabric from her hands, placed it in the basket from which she had taken it, and clasped her hands in his own. "Please do me the honor," he whispered, "of accompanying me."

After a brief pause, she nodded and rose from her place beside her sister. He tucked her hand into the crook of his arm and led her from the room. He could not resist a backward glance at Miss Wyndham's sister. Miss Rose's face was odd, not necessarily disappointed, but certainly annoyed. It seemed she was not accustomed to being denied.

As they wove through the rooms to the back of the house, Nathaniel made light conversation with Miss Wyndham. They paused at the door while she donned her bonnet, gloves and a shawl, and he his own gloves and beaver hat. Finally, they left the house and began to follow a long, straight lane which led them to the labyrinth. The way was lined with many kinds of flowers, both wild flowers allowed to grow where they chose, as well as several planned groupings of roses.

When they came to a rosebush still boasting several late-summer yellow blooms, Nathaniel paused, asking "May I?" and then took his pen-knife from his pocket. He carefully cut a single flower, just barely begun to bloom. Handing it to her, he said, "For my bride."

Miss Wyndham nodded her thanks as she accepted the rose, a light blush dusting her face.

"I should like it very much, *Violet*, if someday we might come to a point at which we may converse freely without your feeling so embarrassed," murmured Nathaniel with a small grin.

Her blush, of course, intensified, but she bravely said, "I am not precisely embarrassed, but I do find it rather intimidating speaking with you."

Nathaniel was surprised. "Intimidating? How so?"

"You do have a reputation of being somewhat taciturn and...well, intimidating," Violet replied. She ducked her head as soon as he turned from their path to look at her.

"Oh, yes," grinned he. "It is a reputation cultivated by months of carefully raised eyebrows and bored sighs. And we must not forget to credit the declination of invitations from all but the *crème* of Society and even the occasional *cut direct* given to several of the more forward contenders for the position of being my wife."

Nathaniel was gratified when Violet laughed lightly before answering, "Oh yes, I never supposed that you were truly as cruel and haughty as some of the more enthusiastic gossip-mongers claimed, but all that aside – you are still a terribly handsome earl. That in and of itself is quite intimidating."

Choosing to walk on at this point, hoping to alleviate some of Violet's discomfort, Nathaniel turned again toward the path. He walked several steps with his hands linked loosely behind him, Violet easily keeping pace. "What did you say I was?" he asked then, suppressing a smile. *Well, perhaps I should not alleviate all of her discomfort.*

A lovely blush bloomed on Violet's face. "An.. An earl?" she said quietly.

"Yes, but what was it you said just before then? What *sort* of an earl?"

She answered innocently, "A terrible one?"

Laughing, he said, "Ah yes, being married to a *terrible* earl is an intimidating prospect indeed." He nudged her shoulder lightly with his own, enjoying as her face once again colored up, and he decided that it did his masculine pride no harm that he was so easily able to evoke such a response from her. As they continued on, he again put her hand on his arm, leaving his other hand upon her fingers.

"You must understand, Violet, that the reputation which I cultivated was born largely of necessity," he mentioned as they made their way through an open lawn.

"Oh indeed?" was her reply.

"Yes. I unsuccessfully attempted to gently dissuade the more tenacious of my admirers before resorting to alienating most of Society."

"You seem to have a very high opinion of your appeal to the feminine sensibility," Violet assessed.

At her words, Nathaniel realized that his statement did sound rather conceited. He felt heat rush to his face and lowered his head to study the toes of his black Hessians. "I did not mean to imply–" he began, but stopped when he felt her slight shoulder jostle against his arm lightly.

"I am *teasing* you, my lord," she said. "I know that you are a desirable match for any woman."

Nathaniel looked up at her to see a small smile ghosting her lips, and felt one of his own break forth. "I see, Violet. You wish to make sport of me."

"Indeed not, though I must own that I feel a freedom in your presence which I have rarely felt with another person, especially a – a man," she said. "I cannot converse comfortably with most acquaintances, and I often find myself questioning that my words are really the best manner in which to express my thoughts, or that if I do attempt to tease or even have a light-hearted conversation with someone, that he or she would not appreciate my humor or remarks."

"What do you suppose is it about me that allows you such freedom? Especially in light of your confession that I am rather intimidating?" Nathaniel found that he hoped for a great deal in her answer – certainly not a profession of love, but at the least that she felt some measure of connection and comfort with him.

Several minutes passed before she answered, and Nathaniel did his utmost to await that answer patiently. "I believe," said she, "that I have no fear of appearing foolish; you've already seen me so."

"When did I see you behaving in a foolish manner?" asked Nathaniel, truly perplexed.

"Perhaps not *behaving* foolishly, but you have seen the manner in which my mama and sister speak to me. In addition to that, the first time we spoke, aside from our introduction, you *did* rescue me." She ducked her head and blushed, but bravely raised her eyes to meet his and offered a weak smile.

"So you feel gratitude toward me?" he asked.

"Of course I do," she said. His heart inexplicably fell. "Truly, my lord, I cannot bear to think what should have occurred if you had not intervened – both with your brother and later with my mother. She would have been crushed with the certainty of my downfall."

"I see."

"In our brief acquaintance," she continued, warming his heart with her words, "I've come to see that you are honorable, you have never been anything but kind and thoughtful toward me. I am honored to become your wife. I know that while our union is not founded on romantic love, I hold great respect for you and hope that I may be equal to the task of being the wife of such a man."

Nathaniel could not hide his grin, though he certainly tried before it broke forth upon his face. "So you do not yet love me, but you believe with time, you might?"

Violet's blush was immediate. "I-I believe so."

"This is excellent news, my dear, as I fear I already am making considerable progress in that direction myself."

He heard her breath catch before a wry grin turned up the corners of her mouth. "You are half-way in love with yourself? Really, Lord Reymes."

"You tease me!" he accused.

"I do," she agreed with a cheeky grin.

They were approaching the labyrinth, and he cast a sidelong glance her way. "I own I do not mind being teased by you, Violet."

"Is that so? Then I must make every effort to ensure that I do so with frequency."

Nathaniel felt his heart swell with – something. Violet stood before him, her bonnet and curls framing her face prettily, and her eyes twinkled in the sunlight. He shook his head as he raised a hand to gently stroke her cheek with the pads of his fingers. "I attempt to share my burgeoning feelings, Violet, and you deflect it with a jest. I fear that I have not been blessed with many happy emotions in the past several years, and I should like very much to revel in these."

Violet's voice was thin and uncertain when she spoke, "I do apologize. I find it easier to ignore rather than revel in unfamiliar emotions. I should not have allowed my discomfort to push aside your sincere confession."

Nathaniel shook his head and took a purposeful step nearer her. "Do not apologize. I understand that you are facing more upheaval than I. For I shall keep my home, my name, and my daily routine. You will not."

She nodded, but did not look down or step away. He took it as a sign that she did not mind entirely the changes about to take place. It called to his mind the driving purpose behind his visit, dousing his growing ardor as surely as a bucket of cold water over his head should have. He began walking once again, offering his arm as he continued to lead her on their path.

"Are you well, Violet?" he began again, hoping to bring up the subject around which they had already skirted. "I have seen enough of your interaction with your mother and sister to know that you rather suppress your spirit when in their presence. And I see your blush, but please believe me when I say you have nothing to blush for. I cannot abide how they speak so unfeelingly to you, how–"

"Pray do not fret on my account, Lord Reymes," she boldly interrupted him, bringing her free hand up to clasp his arm, while compelling him to once again halt his steps. He doubted he would have tolerated an interruption with such grace were it from any other person. "I have borne it these twenty years. I daresay I shall endure for another fortnight."

"You are a remarkable woman," he murmured, shuffling carefully closer, feeling her soft breath touch his face as she blinked up at him.

"No," she whispered, turning away from him, "please do not say such things. I am not. I...I cannot stand up to my mother, despite how often I imagine what words I might use. I still cannot speak easily to other gentlemen –"

"I find I do not mind this so very greatly," Nathaniel said, glad he was the only one she teased and the only one for whom her eyes sparkled. Violet's gentle laughter rang in his ears and in his heart, and warmth flooded him.

"Then – would you say that I have given you no cause for offense?" she asked, her brow slightly furrowed and her eyes not quite meeting his.

"Indeed you have not." Nathaniel was confounded. "Whatever could have given rise to such a question?"

She whispered, "You were so very short with me when we parted at Bainscroft. I feared that I might have offended you."

Nathaniel's first inclination was to deny what she said, but he paused to consider before he answered. He had been upset with what he heard her family say about her, and he realized that his frustration did color his manner of expression. "I am sorry to have caused you concern, Violet. I...received some unpleasant news just prior. It did not occur to me at the time that you might see my frustration and consider yourself to be the cause. Please believe me when I say that you were not."

Throughout his explanation, Nathaniel observed Violet trying to meet his gaze, but not succeeding until the end of his words. Finally, she met his gaze hesitantly as she said, "Very well, then. I was deeply troubled when I believed your displeasure to have stemmed from our interactions. You have been so kind to me, in spite of all that has occurred, and it should be dreadfully ungrateful of me to do anything which might be objectionable to you."

Again back to her feeling grateful. Nathaniel chose not to dwell on his reaction to this. Instead, he resumed their path.

Before long, they reached the entrance to the labyrinth. It was flanked by two stone benches, each of which was surrounded by urns overflowing with ferns and a few pale flowers sprinkled haphazardly among the greenery.

"Would you care to rest before proceeding?" he asked.

Violet demurred, and they continued into the labyrinth. In the shade from the pruned hedges, the air felt cooler. Nathaniel was glad that she had thought to bring her shawl. *Although, keeping her warm myself might be more enjoyable.* He almost tripped at the unbidden thought. *We are not yet wed. Best keep those thoughts for later.* To redirect himself, Nathaniel commented on the landscape.

"Your family's garden seems to be a blend of the old style and what has become increasingly popular in recent years."

"Oh?" They came to a dead-end and turned around.

"Surely you must know that it is fashionable nowadays to plan your garden very carefully, as before, but now the end result is for it to look *unplanned*." He paused, wondering if they should go straight, right, or left.

Violet smiled. "Yes, I do recall a similar conversation about your own gardens. It is rather *picturesque*, I daresay."

"Oh yes, 'the picturesque' is all the rage." Nathaniel smiled down at her. Her eyes seemed darker, deeper in the shadows. "Which direction shall we go?"

Violet looked about her and said, "I have no earthly idea. Shall we proceed straight?"

"It seems as good a route as any," he laughed. As they continued meandering through the twists and turns, frequently retracing their steps, a comfortable quiet descended.

The crisp aroma of the hedges, the richness of the soil beneath their feet, and the delicate perfume of her lavender-water combined to a wonderful aroma which sent waves of peace and calm over him. It seemed that Violet was having similar feelings, for at length she sighed and said, "While it is true that I became lost in here as a child, I have since learned to remember where I have come from and find my way out again, as well as appreciate the solitude this place offers. Nothing so remote, I'm sure, as your estate might afford, but the hedges muffle sounds, and my sister and mother prefer to remain on the terrace or the yard closer to the house."

Nathaniel smiled in understanding, and placed his hand over her fingers where they rested upon his arm, but said nothing. After a moment, she spoke again. "I've found that whenever my spirit is troubled, I may spend some time out here, in prayer or contemplation of the Holy Scriptures, and I am much restored."

He felt his smile grow stale. He knew he oughtn't be surprised; her brother had warned him, had he not? Even so, her words touched a painful place within him. After the passing of his father, Nathaniel found it increasingly difficult to spend time in earnest prayer. He was not hostile toward the Lord, but he certainly did not have any urgent desire to learn or study the Scriptures or to even be mindful of God's working. His duties associated with his estate and the tenants, the business of caring for the various holdings and investments consumed his attention and energy. He allowed no time for anything else.

Nathaniel found himself asking, "I know that you and she are quite different people, but are you close with your sister?" He did not know for certain whether he was trying to change the subject, or if the words just came out of his mouth of their own volition. He feared it was the latter.

Miss Wyndham immediately looked up into his face and he saw what almost looked like anguish pass through her eyes before she lowered her head. "We have constantly been in one another's company. I am only two years her senior. Mama even allowed her coming-out to be at the same time as mine."

"The same time?" Nathaniel felt his eyes widen as his brows rose, all without his permission. *At least I've managed to keep my mouth from gaping.*

"Yes." Violet offered a small smile at his astonishment. "I know it was somewhat irregular, but Rose was quite insistent. There *are* only two years that separate us. It was Mama's hope that we would both secure a match in our first season, as financing a second was unlikely. And I didn't mind, truly. Our first ball was nearly too much for me as it was, even with Rose claiming most of the gentlemen's attention."

Nathaniel stilled his steps and turned to face her. They had come to another dead-end. "It seems we can go no further."

She nodded and peeked up from beneath her bonnet. "Perhaps we should retrace our steps and try another route."

Nathaniel nodded, though he felt disinclined to walk just then. "Perhaps. Or perhaps..." As though under a spell, he found himself lowering his head, gently grasping her elbows with his hands. A light brush with his lips was all he intended to do, all he would allow himself. But before his lips found hers, Violet tensed. Nathaniel immediately thought she might be offended, but when he leaned his head back slightly, it was fear that he saw on her face.

Nathaniel greatly desired to gather her into his arms, soothe away her misgivings, but he suspected that it would not help her to feel better. Instead, he took a deliberate step back, released her arms, and gently took one of her gloved hands.

"Forgive me; I cannot say what came over me," he said while his brain screamed, *Liar! You do know!* But he ignored the thoughts and said instead, "It seems I have frightened you."

Violet answered in an uncertain and breathless voice, "No – er, *I* am sorry. I-I do not, that is – I cannot," and her words failed. Drawing a breath, she strove to compose herself. Glancing up shyly at him for a brief moment while color flooded her face, she added, "I fear that I have not put what occurred on the balcony before you came as far behind me as I would have liked."

He deeply regretted hearing her words, but chose not to comment. Instead, he placed a chaste kiss on the back of her hand and offered his arm. "Shall we find our way out of here and rejoin your family? I fear that I return to Bainscroft this evening. I must meet with my steward to ensure that all will be seen to when I am gone, as well as ensure that my mother will be well while we are away for our wedding tour." Was it his imagination, or did Violet seem to sag with...disappointment? Or was it relief? *I wish that it was disappointment. I am uncertain as to how we shall manage a true marriage if she cannot even bear my embrace, on account of my wretched brother.*

Nathaniel felt his heart give several painful thuds, before it settled into a strong, if slightly fast, rhythm. He would deal appropriately with his brother, and see to it that the man was punished accordingly for the many sins of which he was guilty – not the least of which were those against Nathaniel and his soon-to-be-wife.

Late in the afternoon, Violet was asked by Lord Reymes to accompany him to his carriage. When Rose proposed that she accompany them as well, he cleverly pointed out that her gauze and satin dress was much too thin to be worn outside. Lord Reymes placed Violet's hand on his arm, much as he had in the garden. Just the reminder of their time in the garden brought heat to Violet's face, but she had little time to dwell on it as he signaled to the footman and whisked her out the open door.

Outside, the sun was sinking low in the sky and the air had grown chilly. The couple emerged from the house onto the small front terrace. Violet shivered as they walked along, and Lord Reymes disentangled their arms before wrapping one arm about her, tugging her alongside his warm body.

"I fear I shall not see you again until the wedding," he said, drawing to a halt several paces from his waiting carriage.

Violet's mouth felt dry when he turned the full force of his gaze upon her. *We spoke so easily in the garden; how am I so shy of him now?* But she bolstered her courage and said, "May God keep us both until we are united once again."

Lord Reymes took both her hands in his and gently pulled her around to face him until she felt her feet bump into something. Glancing down, she saw that the toes of her slippers were touching his highly polished black Hessians.

He used a finger under her chin to bring her eyes to his.

"Until that time, Violet, you shall remain constantly in my thoughts."

Violet felt her face warm for about the ninetieth time that day, and she murmured, "I thank you, Lord Reymes. You shall also be in my thoughts, as well as in my prayers. Pray, do be safe on your journey."

He placed a lingering kiss on the back of her hand, his eyes fixed on hers, and then he was gone.

Part II

Six

Wyndmere, Northamptonshire
September 1808

IN ADDITION TO flurried preparations which filled the fortnight between the earl's visit and the wedding, Violet also endured constant remonstrance from Mrs. Wyndham on how her behavior should to be adapted to fit what was expected in an earl's wife and innumerable exclamations from Rose as to what a *famous* match her elder sister had managed to make. These both Violet could have born with ease were it not for the battle she fought within herself regarding the monumental undertaking of being the wife of Lord Reymes, and Violet felt unequal to the task. The tension growing in her during those two weeks made for a heavy load to bear.

She attempted to pray and leave it in God's hands, but worries that she would never be adequate as the wife of such an important man crowded her mind. In addition to this, she found herself thinking back to their time in the gardens and how she had believed that he might kiss her. She had instinctually tensed in fear when he stepped so close to her, secluded as they were in the labyrinth. In an instant she had been back on that balcony at Bainscroft, powerless to stop Mr. Peyton. But Lord Reymes never demanded more than she was willing to give, nor had he teased or belittled her for being missish when she balked so obviously at such a simple gesture as a kiss from her betrothed. She had no choice but to add *patient* to the list of his attributes. She only wished she might be found worthy of this man.

By the time the wedding drew near, Violet was suffering many doubts regarding their match; his position seemed so far above hers. Headaches and an ill appetite were the only clues which might have alerted her family she was unhappy, had they observed her enough to take notice. Both her mother and her sister were too consumed with overseeing the various and frantic work of the staff as they prepared for the upcoming nuptials.

Cook began preparing food a week prior, storing up cakes and biscuits, ordering meats which would be served cold, ensuring that fruit would be available to be served, the tea and coffee and punch plentiful. Mrs. Wyndham instructed that the wedding cake be ordered from the baker in the nearby town; it would not be as grand as one from London, but she could not have a daughter of hers married without doing the job creditably.

The housemaids were busy scouring every inch of the house: woodwork was to be polished, the floors scrubbed, the draperies and carpets beaten to remove every speck of dust. The grates in the fireplaces were scraped and scrubbed and polished with blackening, though it was unlikely that they would be in use at the wedding breakfast, as the September weather was still warm during the days. Plates and crystal and silver were all prepared and set out for the close inspection of the housekeeper, who was managing her own extensive list of tasks. While only family and close friends would be in

attendance at the ceremony, Mrs. Wyndham contrived to have it spread about the community that all would be welcome at the breakfast to wish happy her daughter and soon-to-be son.

Violet's gown arrived three days prior to the ceremony. As she stood for the final fitting, Rose also in her own dress, Violet saw that it was surprisingly well-suited to her – indeed, nearly all that she had dared to hope she would find in her wedding-dress. The gown itself was made of a soft white satin, fitted closely in front, the neckline dipping a bit lower than she would have preferred, but still keeping her modesty intact. The capped sleeves were short, but with the one new pair of gloves Mrs. Wyndham had deigned to order, Violet's arms would be covered. She was somewhat chagrined that the gown did not have long sleeves – the law dictated that all wedding ceremonies take place in the morning, and so long sleeves would be more appropriate. There was nothing for it, however; the gloves would have to do.

Along the hem of the sleeves and the neckline were tiny rosettes of the same fabric as the gown, closely grouped and with a few tiny seed beads scattered amongst them. As Violet turned before the looking-glass, she saw that the back of the gown was heavily gathered, in keeping with the current style. The lovely fabric fell to a short train in the back and would float over the ground as she walked. A small smile crept onto Violet's lips, despite the turmoil inside of her. She decided that even if she fell short, her gown at least did the earl no disservice.

"Vi," Rose simpered while nudging her out of the way to preen into the looking-glass herself, "I cannot comprehend for anything why you *insisted* on such a plain gown. I am rather overdone in mine, as a mere bridesmaid." The younger sister's voice held no hint of regret, as might have been expected from her words.

Violet could not help but think, *I did no such thing. You and Mama chose everything!* Aloud, she merely said, "You look lovely, Rose, and no one will fault you for that gown. It is of the first fashion."

Rose wore a gown of pink satin, overlaid with a white gauze pelisse. Jewels and ruffles trimmed the daring neckline, as well as the waist, and the sleeves of the gauze pelisse came down to the wrist. The colors of the gown complemented Rose's golden hair and blue eyes, the latter of which sparkled at the finery she wore.

"You are correct, of course, Vi. I will be wearing Mama's diamond collar, and you will wear the pearls." She cast a mildly reproving glance at Violet, as though the pearls were a punishment. Heaving a sigh, Rose reached up to remove the fichu which had been draped about her neck and tucked into her dress, concealing her décolletage. "Such a silly thing that what we may bear in the evening must be covered in daylight."

Violet listened half-heartedly to her sister prattle on about her dress and the newer fashions coming from Paris, growing ever more daring. It at least distracted her mind from the dreary thoughts, ever lingering at the back of her mind like a cloud. With a sigh, she nodded at Jane, who was ready to assist her from her gown. While her newly-appointed abigail's deft fingers worked at the satin-covered buttons down the back of her gown, Violet turned to prayer, as she had many times before.

*Lord, help me, please, to endure this wedding – this marriage! It is alarming enough that I shall be under the scrutiny of everyone for an entire morning; but for the rest of my life, I shall be attached to a man whom I scarcely know! That we shall spend our lives together, that I shall bear his—*Violet's face flushed at the direction her thoughts had taken.

"Are you well, miss?" asked Jane. "Your face has gone red. Need you to lie down?"

"No, Jane, but thank you." Violet ducked her head and welcomed the distraction of raising her arms for the gown to be lifted over her head.

Once left alone, dressed in her pale blue day dress which she had made from an old gown of her mama's and trimmed with a lace from the local millinery, Violet sat upon her bed, drawing deep breaths. "Oh, Lord," she whispered. "I fear so much that I shall prove nothing but a disappointment to him. I am growing fond of the man, but I fear so much that he shall live to regret that he has committed himself to me, to a woman who has so very little to offer to this union. I've no notion of fashion as Rose has, but am more than content in refashioned gowns like this one, and I cannot imagine how I shall abide being under such scrutiny as there is sure to be when we are required to go to Town. And dealing with the tenants, and new neighbors, and..." But she could not continue her prayer as well as retain her composure.

Violet rose and made her way to where her Bible lay upon the small table beside her bed. She grasped it in her hands, but did not open it. The memory of his kind eyes as they bid one another good-bye the last time came to her mind. "But I know him to be a kind man, who will certainly care for his wife and – and family." She ignored the heat rising to her cheeks and continued. "He loves his mama dearly, and I believe he should prove a faithful and caring husband, if only I can manage to trust him without reserve. Lord, please be with Lord Reymes and keep him in Your care. I commit him, our marriage, and myself into Your hands."

The next moment, Mrs. Wyndham and Rose burst into Violet's room, chattering excitedly about the new responses to invitations which had been received that day. It seemed a duke had consented to attend, as well as several other members of the peerage.

Somehow – by the grace of God alone – Violet survived the following three days. She was swept along like a leaf by the gusts of her mother and sister's enthusiasm. The one bright spot to those days was the arrival of her brother. Ash was received into the household with joy by Violet, with forced politeness by Mrs. Wyndham, and with indifference by Rose. Penny, unfortunately, was much too close to her time to travel even a short distance. She sent a lovely likeness of Wyndmere, done from her memory of the two times she had visited there, and assisted by Ash with some of the particulars which escaped her recollection. When Violet removed the protective paper wrapping, she struggled to conceal the welling of emotions in her heart, which threatened to leak from her eyes.

The evening before the wedding was a succession of oils and ointments purported to bring a youthful glow to Violet's skin, soften her hands, and coax a sheen from her locks that was not usually present. When the morning of her wedding dawned, she arose and obediently went out to pick her wedding-bouquet from the gardens, as well as a small posy for her sister. Her brother accompanied her.

"Are you pleased with this match, Violet?" Ash asked as she plucked a daisy.

Violet did not care to lie, but she could not share her concerns with her brother. She feared that if he had any idea, he would compel her to cry off. After considering for a moment, she answered, "I will not pretend greater affection for Lord Reymes than I have. However, I believe that he is a kind man, generous and caring."

Ash nodded, but said nothing. Once she had finished the posy, he held it while she gathered more for her own bouquet. The time outdoors, with her sympathetically silent brother, helped to restore a measure of peace to Violet's spirit. Soon, she had finished and returned to the house and bound the flowers with ribbons. After a very modest breakfast, she returned to her bedchamber to prepare for the ceremony.

Jane arranged Violet's hair which she had wrapped in curling rags the previous evening. The girl showed herself to be adept as a ladies' maid, coaxing Violet's hair into a splendid cascade of curls and wisps at the epitome of the current fashion. When Violet commented, the maid shyly admitted that after Violet invited her to Bainscroft as a ladies' maid, she had been studying the fashion plates from London and practicing on Elsie's hair in their spare time. Strands of beads were woven through the glorious mass of Violet's shining brown hair; later, Jane would complete the effect with a simple yet elegant veiled bonnet. She aided Violet in removing her robe and settling the wedding gown over her slender frame. Once she was ready, Violet scarcely paused before the looking-glass to take in her appearance before hurrying down the stairs to the waiting carriage.

Violet's ride to the church was filled with her family's chatter, which she ignored in order to concentrate on prayer. All too soon, they arrived in front of the church. At the back of the sanctuary, Violet waited for Rose to go before her down the aisle. She peeked timidly up at her husband-to-be, and saw that his visage was serious and his face neutral. Scarcely before she had time to realize it had started, Violet was marched down the aisle, the ceremony performed, and the wedding registry signed by the couple. Through all this, Violet could not bring herself more than once or twice to hazard a glance at Lord Reymes' face. Each time, his expression was stoic. *Not exactly telling,* she could not help but think, but then immediately regretted her sardonic thoughts. She scarcely knew him and could not in good conscience pass judgement on what he was thinking or feeling. She did her best to keep her mind on the service, on the words of the vicar, and to not worry over what was – or was not – to come. Before she knew it, though, everything had been accomplished, and Violet was a wife.

Nathaniel's first sighting of Miss Wyndham at the ball had been very nearly forgettable. He doubted, in all honesty, that he would have pursued an acquaintance with her had the circumstances not required it. Seeing her now, walking slowly down the aisle on her brother's arm, prepared as a bride for her husband – for him – Nathaniel's heart quickened and he knew the moment would be engrained in his memory for years to come. He was glad that nothing was required of him at that moment, as he would have been unable to perform even the simplest task. Thankful for years of practice in keeping a tight rein on his feelings, he schooled his features into an impassive expression and concentrated on the ceremony. As he promised solemnly to be her husband, he knew that he would do his best to love and care for her.

After the conclusion of the service, he drove the Wyndham's phaeton, pulled by a fair piece of horseflesh, back to Wyndmere. On the way, the couple did not speak, except for Violet occasionally pointing out which way he should turn the cart. Nathaniel was unsure what to say and feeling rather overwhelmed by the way his heart responded to every brush of her shoulder against his at the phaeton's jostling. During his visit a fortnight ago, he had wanted to kiss her. Although he refrained, the desire was still present, but he in no way expected this intensity of feeling upon seeing her again. It rather confused him. *Have I not only recently discovered that I have tender feelings for her? Why should passions plague me so soon?*

Upon arriving at the house, he offered his hand to help her descend from the seat. Immediately, warmth spread from where her gloved hand clasped his and traveled up his arm, exploding in his heart, and finally spreading outward. After handing the reins of the horse to the waiting groom, Nathaniel offered his arm to his bride as they made their way into the house. A quick glance at the sky hurried him along, as it threatened rain.

Violet's mood was as grey as the sky above. For the duration of the ride from the church to the house, Lord Reymes spoke not one word to her. Her directions to turn left or right were met with a mere nod. She could feel her heart sinking with each step the brown horse took. Like the sky that had yet to shed a drop of rain, Violet kept a tight hold on her emotions and prepared to play the part of the happy bride as best she could.

I know he was affected by our nearness in the labyrinth, but he acts almost indifferently toward me now, she thought as they disembarked from the carriage. *Not that I expect or even desire anything from him. But I should like very much to know that he has not taken a disgust of me, or come to regret our union so soon!* She knew she was being irrational, looking for significance in the innocuous, but could not seem to stop herself. She timidly took his arm as they climbed the steps to enter the house.

Circling the parlor with her husband, she greeted the guests and thanked them for attending. Her husband's demeanor through the entire affair was as it should be. He smiled, spoke with grace and gentility, and generally behaved as a gentleman of his station ought, notwithstanding the detachedness which seemed to color much of his interaction. She could not reconcile this detached yet proper man with the one who had been so amiable giving her a tour of his estate and later walked with her in the labyrinth.

At one point only did her husband's action seem driven by genuine, deep-seated emotion. The newlyweds had found a quiet moment in the corner of a room and were sipping some punch. Lord Reymes suddenly set down his punch cup and moved close to Violet. Her heart began to beat more quickly when she felt the warmth from where his hand rested possessively on the small of her back. When she raised her eyes to follow his cold glare, her heart nearly stopped.

Mr. John Peyton approached, a lovely woman on his arm. Her red-brown hair gleamed and as they drew near, her hazel eyes sparked.

Violet had hoped that there would be more time before she was required to face this particular trial, but it was evident that she would not. If she must face Mr. Peyton again, though, Violet was glad of her husband's presence. Had he not been there, she was certain she should have fainted dead away.

"Violet," spoke Lord Reymes lowly, "you remember my brother, and may I present his wife, Mrs. Frances Peyton. John and Fanny, my wife – Lady Reymes, Countess of Bainscroft."

The couples bowed civilly to one another before exchanging pleasantries. Violet did not speak, but rather listened to the conversation, smiling shakily at Mr. and Mrs. Peyton's felicitations. She was bolstered by her husband's strong presence beside her, and the protective arm which at some point had slipped from its place upon her back to encircle her waist. Violet attempted to smile at her new sister. The woman's reaction was rather chilly.

Mrs. Peyton returned the silent greeting with a nod and a lift of the eyebrow. Violet could not understand such a reaction until she felt her husband shift minutely. When she glanced at him, curious of the cause, she saw him glaring at his brother. The other man was grinning rakishly at Violet, his eyes lingering where they should not. Violet felt her face grow hot – *Even with all the mischief he has wrought, that man still dares let his eyes wander!* Almost suddenly, Lord Reymes curtly thanked the other couple for their well-wishes before he begged their pardon rather coolly, making the excuse that they had yet to greet the Doberly family.

As she was led away, Violet glanced up again at her husband and was overcome with gratitude. No, she had not married a man with whom she was entirely comfortable, nor had she been given time to be courted and wooed properly. She was married, though, to a good and honorable man. She was certain that he would always treat her with kindness and patience, if not love.

True to his word, Lord Reymes escorted Violet over to greet her Doberly relations. She was thrilled to spend a few moments speaking with her cousin. Their visit at the Doberly house had been cut short by the unexpected engagement, and Violet had scarcely any time to discuss all that led up to it with Charlotte; she was used to their visits consisting of hours upon hours spent walking, talking, reading, and enjoying one another's company. With a promise to write as soon as she was able, Violet bade her uncle, aunt, and cousin *adieu*, then went with her husband to greet more of the guests.

The entire affair felt rather fabricated and almost ridiculous to Violet; she had never enjoyed visiting among large crowds of people, and meeting strangers always left her fatigued and uncertain as to the impression she made. Regardless of her knowledge that she had been wed to a kind and good man, she felt her apprehension grow as the wedding breakfast ended, the cake was eaten, and the time came for the bride and groom to depart. All too soon, she had changed into her traveling-dress and Lord and Lady Reymes were bidding their guests good-bye.

Knowing that Jane would be joining them the following morning was a small comfort to the young bride, but not enough to put a halt to the more nerve-inspiring thoughts which occupied her mind. Once they were both seated opposite one another in the carriage, Violet could not help but wonder, *How will the façade endure now that there are no guests to entertain? Will we behave as husband and wife, or even acquaintances, or shall we behave as we did in the phaeton? After all, we are little more than strangers.*

As these thoughts tromped through her consciousness, the footman closed the door behind them and the grey sky opened, pouring cold water over everything. Violet peered through the small carriage window, striving to fix on something to occupy her mind and prevent her from releasing the torrents inside her as the sky had done. Lord Reymes had told her it would be a three-hour journey in a northerly direction until they stopped for a brief respite, and then onward they would travel toward the Lake District for a couple of weeks before heading south again. *How shall I ever maintain my composure?* The window was no friend, however, as the only view it offered was of the rivulets of rain on its outside, chasing one another in downward motion. A gentle touch on her hand bade her turn back to the carriage interior.

"Are you well, Violet?" He leaned forward on his seat. "You look pale."

Violet shifted uneasily under his scrutiny. "I-I am quite well, I thank you." *I was so grateful for his presence at the breakfast, but now I wish he might be just a bit less attentive.*

Grasping about for something to say, Violet found herself returning the question. "Are *you* well, my lord?"

"Quite, I thank you." The quiet grew once again, allowing Violet to explore the new course her thoughts were taking.

The memory of their wedding, mere hours ago, came to her. Violet felt the fluttering begin again that had filled her midsection as he spoke the words: *I, Nathaniel Fredrick Reymes take thee, Violet Adele Wyndham to my wedded Wife, to have and to hold from this day forward.* Unable to stop the thought, she wondered, *Would I indeed welcome such an intimate moment as him holding me?*

Her cheeks burned hotter than before with shame as she strove to move her thoughts to a more appropriate venue. This was not the sort of thing a young lady ought to be pondering. Still, she found her mind returning to the way his hand had moved possessively around her back as they encountered Mr. Peyton and his wife at the wedding banquet.

It saddened her to see such tension between brothers. *I cannot imagine that such discord is the result of only Mr. Peyton's trespass against me. Lord Reymes seemed entirely unsurprised to find his brother in such a state – disapproving, but also unsurprised. Is there nothing to be done to aid in the mending of their affection? Certainly, two brothers so close in age should at one time have been the best of friends. But then how close of friends are Rose and myself?* Violet resolved to dedicate time of earnest prayer to the matter.

With a new, much more constructive and selfless course of thoughts to occupy her mind, Violet felt a weight lift from her heart. Perhaps there was nothing she herself could do to help the brothers, but she was convinced beyond a doubt that the Lord could heal whatever rift had been driven between them.

Seven

NATHANIEL SAT IN the carriage, watching his new bride from his seat across from her. She had an understated elegance, lovely in its simplicity, but it seemed that the more he looked at her, the more he found to appreciate. The few curls which peeked from beneath her bonnet filled the spectrum between gold and honey and he was certain it would be soft to his touch. Her face was smooth and while her looks were by no means extraordinary, they were decidedly pleasing. Her eyes, however, drew his attention. More grey than green at the moment, they were trained on the window beside her. Foggy and rain-spattered as it was, he was certain she could not in actuality see through it. *I wonder what thoughts could be occupying her so as to cause such serious contemplation.*

Studying her profile as she fixated on the paths of rainwater on the window, Nathaniel searched his mind for a topic to engage her in conversation. Suddenly, though, she started slightly and glanced above her.

"Is something amiss?" he asked immediately. Her face showed surprise, perhaps that he should notice so subtle a movement.

"I–I believe that I felt a drop of water."

He peered at the roof of the carriage and saw that there was indeed a leak. "Please, come and sit beside me; it is quite dry here." Once she was settled beside him on the cushioned bench of the carriage, Nathaniel continued. "What an embarrassment to have my new wife see evidence that I keep my property in poor repair, which I can assure you is not the case." He knew it would not be a pleasant conversation that he would have with his coachman after they arrived at Chesterfield for the evening.

"Certainly it is not," Violet smiled kindly.

Nathaniel offered a sheepish grin as he was unable to think of anything to say at the moment, having found that he enjoyed being so snugly positioned with his wife. At length, he decided to push for an answer to his earlier curiosity. "Forgive me, but when I saw you flinch from the water, I had been watching you and trying to decipher whether you were happy or not."

Violet said nothing for a moment, eyes lowered and a rosy glow darkening her cheeks before she looked up and answered, "Why should I be unhappy?"

"Your face," he began in a quiet voice and gently touched her smooth cheek, "seemed rather contemplative. I was not certain that you were pleased with our circumstances."

His wife straightened and offered, "I am glad to be settled so well."

"Oh indeed?" He responded. "And did your mama give you those words?"

A surprised laugh erupted from Violet's lips at that. "Indeed not! I daresay I *am* settled well; I've a kind, honorable husband who offered me the protection of his name when he had no such responsibility to do so. How can I say I am anything but well-settled?" She sighed then, almost dramatically if he was not mistaken, and said, "Although I fear that I know as much of my husband as you know of your wife. You very likely know more, as you have considerable spheres of influence and greater ability to attain information."

"That is true," he conceded. "Tell me, then. What would you like to know?"

"I do not know." Violet suppressed a laugh at the idea that they would simply trade information of their lives. "Is not becoming acquainted something that must be done over time, as two people converse and learn about one another?"

Nathaniel's heart soared that she seemed to be shedding her reticence and opening to him again as she had previously. "Most assuredly. And we are talking. What would you like to know about me?" he repeated.

"Very well, I shall humor you." She paused while thinking and then asked, "What is your primary residence?"

"*Our* primary residence shall be Bainscroft, though there is of course also a house in Town. We do have various other holdings, but few of which with accommodations suitable for a lady. I hope you will not mind staying for the greater part of the year at Bainscroft?"

"Not at all."

"I understand you are quite close with your relations the Doberlys?"

"Yes, my late father's sister is married to Mr. Doberly. I love them dearly."

"Yes, I believe we discussed that briefly on the balcony, did we not?" He felt his heart drop as she colored up and lowered her eyes. "I am sorry to have mentioned that. I–"

"No, my lord." Violet turned toward him and reached hesitantly for his hand. "I do not wish this to be a place of unease with us."

A smile crept across his face and he murmured, "It is very good of you to say that."

Violet blushed fresh as she replied equally softly, "Tis sensible, nothing more."

Nathaniel he once again reached up to gently stroke one finger down the smooth skin of her face. "You have a lovely blush. Perhaps I shall make it my mission to see it as often as I can." Again, her face grew red and he retracted his hand, shaking his head slightly. "Very well, I shall no longer tease you. For the time being. Let us return to the subject that we were discussing previously: I must admit that your aunt and uncle are my favorite neighbors."

Violet's relief in the change of topic was evident in her voice. "I am glad. We have been in the habit of spending much time together throughout my life. In fact, I believe my mama would send me to them on occasion when she grew weary of me." Nathaniel wondered if she intended to say all that she did and so chose to ignore her self-deprecating speech.

"And your cousin's birthday was celebrated during this most recent visit?"

"Yes – Charlotte; she is their only child." Nathaniel had heard from his mother that Mrs. Doberly had been unable to bear any more children and the doctor had said that the daughter's life nearly was the end of the mother's.

"I see."

Violet gazed at her clasped hands for a moment before offering, "I do love Charlotte a great deal. Although she is several years my junior, we have many similar interests."

"Such as?"

"Well, for one, we love being in our gardens, playing the pianoforte, and sewing, to name a few."

"Do you prefer whitework embroidery or tapestries?"

Violet said, "I can do both, but what Charlotte and I spend the majority of our time sewing is shirts and dresses and other items of clothing for the poor."

Nathaniel was impressed. To do something tangible for the poor and needy, rather than merely make occasional donations so that one's name would be mentioned in thanks, was noble indeed. Giving her gloved hand a gentle squeeze, he said, "You are to be admired."

Violet's discomfort was evident. "Oh, no, my lord. I do no more than anyone else."

Nathaniel kept to himself his disagreement with her claim and asked instead, "And you also enjoy gardens?"

"Immensely."

"Then I am happy to offer to you the entirety of our gardens at Bainscroft. If you recall, they are quite extensive. Perhaps your cousin would like to come and visit you there."

Nathaniel was rewarded with Violet looking up at him and beaming. "Yes, thank you! Charlotte will be most pleased to receive an invitation."

"I am glad. I failed to mention when I visited earlier that I called on your brother when I was in Town. It is my hope to invite him and his wife to visit after their child is born."

Violet's face glowed with happiness at this news. "He did mention your visit to me when he arrived at Wyndmere several days past. Thank you, Lord Reymes. Ash and I are very close." After several seconds of silence during which he observed her fidgeting again with the gloves, she ventured to ask, "Will your, um, brother reside at Bainscroft as well?" The query was made hesitantly, almost as though she did not wish to make it. And when she did, Nathaniel himself wished she had not. It served to dampen his mood severely.

"No, he most certainly will *not*," Nathaniel said darkly. A glance at her face revealed that she had been frightened or at the least, disturbed, by his tone. Clearing his throat, he forced his voice into more pleasant modulations, even if his heart did not feel pleasant at the moment. "He and his wife *were* there, but now that I am free of my obligations in London, I shall preside at the seat of my title. John and Frances have already moved to another piece of land our family owns, Fairfield. It was our mother's wedding gift to him and Frances. And the dowager will be moving to the dower house on the Bainscroft estate."

"Oh dear! All to accommodate my arrival? Your mother really needn't relocate. And to a cottage! What a degradation of status."

Nathaniel's heart softened at Violet's kind and humble words; the ire toward his brother dissolved in the face of more tender feelings for his wife which he felt emerging. "Please do not worry. My mother nearly cried tears of joy when she knew I would be married. She sees this as a great blessing to her; the cottage is much less to manage."

"If you are certain..."

"Yes. And this brings to mind a question I had wanted to ask you." He waited for Violet's polite nod. "Have you been taught to manage a household?"

Nathaniel observed Violet toy once again with her gloves before she said, "I have not been *taught* precisely, but I have observed a great deal at our home. My *hope* is that I will be a capable mistress."

At her look of uncertainty, Nathaniel hastened to assure her. "I am sure that you shall have no difficulties. Your gentle mode of speech and your kindness will instantly endear you to the staff. And the housekeeper you have met already. Mrs. Baker is a kind woman who will be happy to assist you in any way you need until you feel settled. She is eager for your arrival at Bainscroft after our honeymoon tour."

"Are you certain that you can spare two whole months for this trip?"

"I plan to take only one honeymoon tour in my life, and I have no intention of doing it in half-measures." Nathaniel smiled warmly. "Besides, I have been engrossed in business for far too long. Two months dedicated largely to pleasure will certainly be a blessing."

Violet attempted to suppress the sense of alarm that grew at his words. *Pleasure? I had just put that from my mind...* She quickly terminated the thought, knowing that nothing would be expected of her at this time in the carriage. Or at the least, she hoped not. *Better to let tomorrow worry about tomorrow. Or tonight about tonight.*

In an effort to move her thoughts toward a less intimidating direction, Violet found herself asking, "Please, will you tell me about Bainscroft? I enjoyed the tour you offered me, but it told me very little of the *feel* of the place." This last part she added quickly and quietly and wished as soon as she said it that she had not. She felt her face warm at the fanciful thought.

She needn't have worried, though, for Lord Reymes smiled and began speaking almost immediately. "Bainscroft holds many fond memories for me, but also some more recent ones that I would as soon forget. My father's decline is likely the worst." His voice was low, gruff as he spoke. "Not only was it difficult to lose a parent, but there was other unpleasantness involved. I shall tell you more than this, at some time. But it is still rather – painful – at present."

"I understand," she murmured. In a moment of daring, she reached for his hand again. Upon feeling her touch, he turned his hand over, lacing their fingers.

"The main house is the original building. Wings have been added in years past, and various changes as times and fashions progress. But my ancestors managed to preserve the integrity of the place while making those changes. I dearly hope that any changes I may make will do their work justice."

Violet squeezed his hand and smiled as she offered, "I am certain that you will." She found the more she acted boldly, the further her shyness retreated.

Some time later, they stopped for a brief meal and so that the coachman might water and rest the horses. The small town in which they found themselves was charming, despite having very few diversions within its borders.

Across the road was a small vegetable garden heavy with late-summer produce. Violet was content to observe the garden as she waited for her husband to finish speaking to his coachman. She remained under the eaves of the coaching house, trying to avoid getting her hem damp in the rain, and noticed a small corner of flowers in the garden, the last blooms bravely standing against the rain in spite of the weather that threatened to turn even colder in a very few weeks' time.

Lord Reymes approached her just as the rain eased and offered her his arm. "Shall we take a turn about the block? A short walk will afford us a bit of exercise before we return to the carriage."

Violet glanced at the sky, still dark with clouds. "Do you believe it will rain again?"

"We shan't go far."

Violet nodded and timidly rested her hand on his arm. In spite of having now clasped his hand twice, Violet was still shy of holding onto him. She was soon distracted from any unease though, as they ambled up the street. More cottages with vegetable gardens came into view, and Violet delighted in seeing the fruit of the earth displayed in each plot.

"This is a lovely little village, is it not?" observed Violet. She moved ahead of Lord Reymes to better see the plants. "I hope that this family can harvest the peas before the first frost."

"So this is what peas look like when they are growing?"

Violet turned toward him in surprise. "Surely you must recognize a pea plant."

"I fear that I am much too ignorant of the flora, even on my own estate, to have deserved as knowledgeable a wife as you." Her husband softened his teasing words with a smile. "And so of course I do not recognize a pea plant. What are those?" as he pointed to another plant growing beside the peas.

"Potatoes, Reymes." Her voice dropped to a low murmur on the last word.

"Or Nathaniel."

"Perhaps some day, but not when I have known you only a month and spent far less time than that in your presence."

"Very well, my dear." She heard her husband say on a sigh. "I do wish that it had been within my power to remedy this for you with a less life-altering method."

Violet said nothing, but her heart beat steadily in the knowledge that though she expected to face no severe hardship, the Lord God would certainly see her through whatever difficulties might arise – becoming accustomed to a new home, a new role as wife and mistress of the home. *I know that I can do whatever He asks of me, as He is my Strength. Even now, He shows me yet again that my husband is a caring and thoughtful gentleman.*

Lord Reymes cleared his throat. "Come along, let us continue on our stroll." He took her hand and drew it through his arm, effectively fastening her to his side as they made their way back to the waiting carriage. He led her carefully, avoiding what puddles he could and helping her cross the others with minimal damage to her gown.

Just before they reached the carriage, however, the sky opened once again, pouring cold rain upon them. Violet began to run (a difficult task given her dainty slippers) to keep up with his quick pace. She felt terribly unladylike, but it was not to be helped. By the time they reached the carriage, they were both damp and giggling.

Seating themselves on the leaking side of the coach – Lord Reymes suggested they leave the dry cushion for once they were dry themselves – the couple realized that they were quite a bit more soaked than they had previously thought.

Lord Reymes quickly shrugged out of his coat before the rain soaked through to his white shirt and waistcoat beneath. His pantaloons were only slightly damp.

Violet had no such luck. With only a bonnet and light spencer designed more for fashion than protection from the elements, her dress was drenched; already she had begun to shiver. Her husband glanced over at her, dismay evident upon his face.

"I am sorry that I allowed you to be exposed to the elements. Speaks terribly of me," he said. Before Violet could refute his words, he stated, "We should get you out of that dress."

Heat suffused Violet's face and she was unable to look at him. When uncontrollable shivers overtook her, though, she knew he was correct in his assertion. *But where might I change my gown? And I cannot reach all of the buttons!* A gentle touch at her back stilled Violet's thoughts. Her thoughts quieted as his fingers worked at the buttons.

As his hands moved from the middle of her shoulders down to the small of her back, Violet felt her gown slowly loosen. Her cheeks flamed, but she found herself saying, "I have a spare dress in my portmanteau, as well as some half-boots. I had planned on wearing them tomorrow."

He busied himself with removing the bag from beneath the seat while she scrambled out of the wet dress. Violet was glad to discover that her underpinnings were still comparatively dry, but she felt chilled all the same. As she struggled to pull the dry dress onto her body in the unaccommodating space in the carriage, she stole a glance at her husband. His eyes were averted, gazing out the window. Thankful, she hurriedly pushed her arms through the sleeves and brought the gown up and over her shoulders.

Violet would have started working on the buttons, but again Lord Reymes came to her assistance. While she was uncomfortable with the intimate action, she owned she was grateful as well, for fatigue suddenly overtook her. Her husband brought her over to sit beside him on the dry cushion, wrapping an arm about her shoulders and tucking a blanket over her lap. At his urging, she allowed her head to rest against his strong shoulder.

The remainder of their journey to Chesterton passed without incident. Violet found herself dozing and was awakened by Lord Reymes' gentle nudge, telling her that their rooms and a meal had been arranged. He had returned his coat to its place on his tall frame, as well as retrieved a cloak for her from one of the trunks. Once settled in their rooms at the Nettlecomb, the best inn Chesterton had to offer, Violet sat in a chair beside the small fireplace to rest, still shivering slightly, while Lord Reymes went down to inquire as to what time the evening meal would be served. In addition to the chair in which she sat, there was a table and a second chair, as well as a bed and washstand.

Her unease was increasing greatly. The close quarters of the room seemed to shrink before her eyes. She would be sleeping in this room with her husband this very night! The difficulty of the day, coupled with the weakness which was now claiming Violet's body proved too much for the young woman. She suddenly felt very much alone and very fatigued.

Violet spent her time resting in the chair, and somewhere between sleep and wakefulness, she remembered that the Lord was indeed her strength, always with her to lend whatever aid might be needed. She woke suddenly when Lord Reymes arrived back in the room, her spirit more at peace. That peace was momentarily disturbed upon seeing her husband, a fine specimen of a man, remove his jacket and place it on the back of the chair at the small table in the room.

After telling her that they could go to eat in half an hour, Lord Reymes drew out his writing box and began to pen a letter. Violet wished that she had brought her own writing materials, rather than packing them in her trunk. Unfortunately, she was left with her thoughts only, which were at the moment causing no small amount of heat to suffuse her face.

"Would you care to write to anyone? I've plenty of paper and ink, as well as an extra pen."

She nodded with a small smile. "Thank you."

Violet accepted the paper and extra pen that her husband handed to her. She began to scribe a letter to Penny, dipping her pen into the inkwell he placed on the table between them. She expressed her sincere thanks for the lovely painting before she detailed the events of the past month. After that letter was finished and set aside to dry (Violet did not care to trouble her husband for the sand), she began another letter, this one to Charlotte. She attempted to describe all that she did not have time to tell her during their brief conversation earlier that day at the wedding-breakfast, but by the time she was nearing the end, her hand trembled so that she was scarcely able to move the pen as precisely as she wished.

Once her letter was completed, Violet retrieved her Bible from her portmanteau and returned to her chair. She knew she needed the help that could be found only in God's Holy Word. She was vaguely aware, as she seated herself, of Lord Reymes sealing his own letter. Before she had read more than two verses, he spoke.

"Aside from our adventure in the rain, our journey has been rather easy thus far, has it not?"

"Yes, I daresay it has." Violet's eyes remained trained on the words she was reading.

"How do you find our rooms?"

"Quite comfortable, thank you." *Is he teasing me?*

"You are most welcome." Here he paused, but only for a moment. "And I don't suppose you feel like conversing."

Violet felt a small twinge of guilt, but remained steadfast. "I suppose I am a bit fatigued."

"Ah, yes. I suppose you would be." After another brief pause, "Are you reading the Psalms or from the book of the Proverbs?"

"Proverbs." Violet kept her eyes on the page still.

"You might inquire as to how I knew what you read."

With a small sigh, Violet returned, "How did you know?"

"I am decidedly clever." His face was amused when she looked up at him in astonishment, clearly delighted with her reaction to his unexpected answer. "Finally. It is much better to see your face when speaking with you. Care to know how I really knew what you are reading?" At her small grin and nod, he admitted, "You opened to the middle of the book; a psalm or a proverb was the most likely choice." After a bit of a pause, he asked, "Would you mind reading aloud?"

Violet glanced back down, took a breath, and began to read.

There had been a time that Nathaniel was quite faithful in his own Scripture-reading, even if he had time for only a few verses in the morning. The tutor whom his father had employed for him had been a German man, whose family had taught him to read the Word of God voraciously, and part of his teaching had included encouragement of Nathaniel to do so himself. With the difficulties in his life of late, he had fallen from that habit. He had not intended to ask her to read aloud, but the draw he saw in her to the book lying in her lap had spoken to something inside of him. He did not particularly wish to delve into what that thing was, so he instead asked her to read.

The proverb that Violet had chosen was something of a surprise for Nathaniel.

In a quiet, gentle voice, she read, "Who can find a virtuous woman? For her price is far above rubies. The heart of her husband doth safely trust in her, so that he shall have no need of spoil. She will do him good and not evil all the days of her life."

As Violet read on, a thought occurred to Nathaniel. *Does she fear she may not be a good wife?* It was comforting to him to observe his bride paying heed to her wedding vows. *Have my actions suggested that I intend to do the same?* he wondered. Nathaniel was certainly frustrated with the manner in which their union came to be, but he did not wish for the beginning to define the remainder of their lives together. He would need to ensure that he communicated his own intention to honor their marriage to the best of his ability.

When Violet came to the end of the Proverbs passage, Nathaniel smiled and said, "What a timely reading." At her hesitant smile, he stood with a grin and offered his arm. "Now, *Wife*, shall we ask them to deliver supper? I have it on good authority that the food here is splendid. I also reserved a private parlor for our comfort."

She stood and took his offered arm. The feel of her hand upon his arm was becoming quite familiar, which he rather enjoyed. Now, however, her hold was decidedly weak. Previously, her hesitance was clearly the cause of her butterfly-like touch. Now, though, a pale face and shoulders which still shook on occasion suggested that she was not well.

Nathaniel felt his heart give a couple of nervous thuds before he added, "The first course, I am told, consists of soup; it should help to warm you."

As they waited for their food to be brought, Nathaniel tried to keep the conversation moving along, but Violet seemed even less inclined to talk than usual. He watched her intently as she ate. After they began, she had spooned the soup into her mouth with a touch of eagerness. Gradually, though, she slowed, until she was merely pushing the spoon around in her bowl, and not even half of it had been consumed.

"Are you unwell, my dear?" he asked quietly.

"I suppose I am rather tired from the journey."

"Yes, you said that earlier."

Her eyes had taken on a glassy appearance. "Would you mind if I retired early?"

"Certainly not." He stood and moved to assist her. "Please, allow me to assist you to the room. I shall return here and finish my meal while you dress for the night."

Nodding, Violet began to stand, but staggered and nearly lost her balance. Nathaniel felt alarm rise within as he caught her and pulled her close to himself. "You are unwell. Come, let's get you to bed."

With one arm wrapped around her for support, he saw her to their room, assisted her in laying out her night clothes and unbuttoning her gown, and withdrew from the room. Back in the dining room, concern for his bride drove him to eat so quickly that he scarcely tasted the food and burned his tongue more than once. When he reached their rooms once again, he entered after knocking quietly.

A lump under the bedclothes told him that she was abed. He quickly shrugged out of his outer clothing, washed his face and neck, and crawled under the covers. When he rested his hand on her head, she stirred slightly, turning toward him. Her face was pale, and warm against his palm. Nathaniel snuggled her up against himself, wanting to offer some sort of comfort, even if she was unaware of it.

His mind drifted toward prayer. He felt uneasy approaching the Lord, but three words floated across his consciousness as he drifted into sleep: *Please help her.*

Eight

❧

THE STAFF AT Bainscroft performed admirably in preparing the house
for the unexpected arrival of Lord and Lady Reymes. An early-
morning express informed Mr. Garand and Mrs. Baker of the change
of plans.

Violet had awakened the morning after their wedding, still
plagued with the headache which had come upon her at supper the
previous evening, and still feeling chilled and slightly queasy. When
she turned in the bed, not even noticing that the bedclothes on the
other side had been in use, she saw her husband sitting in the same
chair from which she read yesterday, regarding her gravely.

He announced that he intended to return to Bainscroft that very
morning and Violet wanted to protest. She even began to rise from
the bed, but her strength suddenly failed her. *When I feel weak
before even leaving my bed, how can I argue with him?* Once seeing
the determined manner with which he helped her from the bed,
assisted her with putting on a dress, and then fastening her half-
boots himself, she knew that even had she been well, she could not

argue with this man. He told her that word had been sent to the servants to make ready for their arrival. Jane had been conveyed to Bainscroft rather than meet them in Chesterton. Violet resigned herself to assuming the role of Countess of Bainscroft immediately.

Lord Reymes helped her into the waiting carriage, then re-entered the establishment briefly to settle with the inn keeper. After he was seated beside her behind the closed door of the carriage, he pulled out two blankets which had been stored inconspicuously beneath the seat, settling them snugly over her person. Lord Reymes then pulled her into the crook of his arm, and spoke soothingly into her ear, bidding her to sleep.

For three days following their arrival at Bainscroft, Violet was confined to her bed. Lord Reymes thoughtfully arranged for her to sleep in the room adjoining his own. For the first two days, she did indeed sleep – for the majority of the day as well as the night, but by the third day, she was feeling much more the thing and wished the doctor would be sent for to proclaim her well.

When he finally arrived, Dr. Curteys agreed that some time spent in the morning room should be entirely acceptable. The family morning room – separate from the one in which Lord Reymes received Violet and her family prior to their marriage – was comfortably appointed while still maintaining the elegance that the entire house exuded. Its many windows, well-cushioned chairs and settees, and small pianoforte in the corner created a comfortable retreat. If the style was a bit of the previous generation, Violet did not notice, nor would it have signified if she had. She was quite pleased with this room and, upon the information from her husband that it was tradition for each new bride to begin her time as Mistress of Bainscroft by updating the room, Violet was uncertain as to how she might improve upon the current finishes and furnishings. She determined to give it no more thought until the time came for the changes to be made; no one would require her to begin during her convalescence.

Lord Reymes spent a great deal of time with her in the room. She feared that his absence from his regular duties would be felt by the estate, but he reminded her that he had prepared for an extended absence for their honeymoon, and so he was presently at his leisure. They played cards, read both silently and aloud to one another, and discussed the house and household. Violet was also mildly surprised when during their evenings spent quietly in her bedchamber, Lord Reymes asked almost shyly from his chair near the window if she would care to read aloud from her Bible. He never asked to discuss what was read, and sometimes she wondered if he even heard the words she spoke, as she often glanced up to see him gazing into the fire or out the window into the dark night sky.

One week and several days after she was first allowed to spend time out of her room, the doctor returned for the last time and pronounced that his lady Reymes was indeed well. Violet thrilled at this news, for she had a beautiful view of the gardens from her bedchamber and wished to spend time out there, as well as assume some of her duties as mistress.

Lord Reymes seemed eager to more closely acquaint her with his home, as well, for he asked her during breakfast the next day, "Would you care to tour the house again today? I am certain that you cannot yet know how to find your way to all the rooms."

"Can you spare the time?" asked Violet hesitantly.

"Certainly, if the idea is agreeable to you." He smiled at her over his cup of coffee. "Would you care to start once you've finished your meal?"

Violet smiled and nodded her head. After a few more bites of toast, she swallowed the rest of her tea. "I am ready."

"Surely you want more than a crust of bread and some tea, dear?" asked Lord Reymes. "Are you still feeling unwell?"

"I fear that my appetite for breakfast is not great." She smiled across the long table at him. "But I am pleased to wait until you have had enough, my lord."

A mock scowl came upon his handsome face then and he said playfully as he rose from the table, "I have made my feelings known regarding your use of 'my lord' and yet you still persist in using it. Shall I give you more incentive to use my name?"

"No, my lord. Er, that is – Reymes."

"Nathaniel."

Violet could not suppress her smile at his teasingly stern face, so she ducked her head and took his arm, allowing him to lead her from the breakfast room.

As they strolled through the house, Violet's arm tucked inside his own, Nathaniel felt at peace. At one time, he might have preferred a lady more assured of herself. Now he reveled in the calming effect her quiet spirit had upon him, and how her kind words and gentle smile soothed his heart. As they walked about the house, he did not remember half of what he said regarding the furnishings, tapestries, or paintings, the moldings or floors; he likely said it all during her first tour of the place. She bore any repetition with grace, though. Of course, he reiterated his offer to Violet of the funds and his blessing to remake any rooms of the house that she wished.

"It all seems very comfortable to me," she said as she cast her eyes about the formal parlor, taking in all that she saw. "I cannot see how I might improve upon this house. It seems to be the very picture of hospitality and good taste." Nathaniel wondered if she realized she spoke more than the first sentence aloud, so intent was her observation of the room.

All the curtains were drawn, awaiting the time company arrived and they would be opened to allow sunshine to flood the room. The furniture was finer than that in the family's sitting room, still comfortable, but not in the well-loved manner that the less formal of the rooms could claim. Nathaniel gazed at her expressive eyes, which looked very deep in the dim light of the room. Those eyes came to rest on the large pianoforte in the corner of the room, a much costlier instrument than the small one situated in the less formal family sitting room. He was loathe to give her up, but felt he must as she removed her hand from his arm and moved toward the instrument.

"Oh, it is beautiful," she breathed.

Tempted to reply with "She certainly is," as he had been thinking, Nathaniel decided that to give her such a compliment would certainly break the reverent mood into which she had fallen. Besides this, he had discovered that whenever he offered a personal compliment to his wife, she became flustered and sometimes went as far to deny what he had asserted. While he found her reactions rather adorable, he did not wish to spoil the excitement she demonstrated at seeing the fine instrument.

Instead, he offered simply, "Yes. Would you care play?"

This query seemed to break the spell sure as a compliment would have. She immediately turned her gaze from the pianoforte and shook her head. "Oh, no, but I thank you all the same."

"Beg pardon? Did you not tell me in the carriage as we traveled to Chesterton that you enjoyed playing?"

She hesitantly admitted, "I do play. But only when I am alone."

"What ever for?" Nathaniel was rather confused.

Violet seemed to weigh whether she ought to tell him, then rushed to say, "At home, Mama insisted that Rose and I practice often. When they were trimming bonnets or discussing something, I had no difficulty. But as soon as their discussion ceased and they turned their ears to the music, my fingers fumbled and I could not make them do as I wished. Before strangers, it is worse."

"I am sorry, my dear, to hear that." He came up behind her, wrapped his arms about her waist and rested his chin on the top of her head. "You do enjoy playing, though?"

"I do." Her voice sounded a bit thin, as though she were unable to take in a full breath. *I am not holding her that tightly, am I?*

"Then allow me to instruct the servants to leave this room alone for – what, would you care for an hour? Two? – each day, so that you may continue your music." He shifted his head downward ever so slightly, until his nose touched the soft hair piled high upon her head. He inhaled, enjoying the scent of lavender.

Violet turned in his arms, attempting to pull away, but Nathaniel held her fast. He felt slightly guilty for forcing his attentions on her in this way, but he could not seem to help himself. She knew he had read and spent time with her in the sitting room, but what she did not know was that he had sat by her bedside nearly constantly during the first two days and nights of her illness. He even attempted to pray. Her pale face and fever-glazed eyes had been quite imprinted upon his memory. The sight of her in the sickbed reminded him too strongly of his father during his last days.

Now that she was well again and far removed from danger, he found himself desiring to touch her hand as they walked, to hold her in his arms as he did now. Indeed, it seemed his heart was now influencing other parts of his body. Currently, he could not seem to impress upon his arms that they ought to relinquish their hold on her. Looking down into her upturned face, Nathaniel realized he was in a fair way to fall in love. Slowly, he began to lower his head. When his wife's eyes fluttered closed, he—

A knock on the door brought his head up abruptly. He might have released his hold on Violet, but when she attempted immediately to move away from him, his heart demanded that he keep her close.

Mr. Garand, the butler, entered the room. His brows rose almost imperceptibly at the sight of his master embracing his new mistress, but quickly his face regained an impartial, bland expression.

"The carriage is ready, my lord."

He bowed and left the room, closing the door silently behind him.

When Nathaniel turned his gaze to Violet again, her eyes were lowered and a rosy glow covered her face. He decided to spare her further discomfort and stepped back, releasing her.

"I thought we might take a quick driving tour of the grounds, in addition to our walking tour of the house." Nathaniel grinned at the small smile making its way to her rosy lips. Offering his arm, he asked, "Would that be agreeable to you?"

"Oh yes, I should enjoy that above all things!" She took his arm and they began walking to the door.

Raising his eyebrows, Nathaniel could not help but add under his breath, "*All* things? I can think of one or two activities which *I* would find more enjoyable."

Once the couple was seated comfortably in the two-seat curricle, a groom riding tiger on the back, Violet warmly bundled into several layers, the horses began to make their way down the long drive away from the house. Nathaniel pointed out things of interest as they went: the gates at the beginning of the drive which were made of iron three generations back, the tenant farmers in the fields who were scrambling to finish harvest before the colder weather set in, the small village situated a short distance from the end of his property. As they drove through the village, which was called Horton, he pointed out the milliners', the shop where their mail could be picked up (Mrs. Baker usually took care of that when she sent a girl to the village for food items), and one mantua-maker. Lord Reymes sent the groom to fetch the post. There was a letter from Penny, which Violet determined to read soon. As they headed back out of Horton, Lord Reymes gestured toward the dressmaker's shop again.

"It is not so grand as the shops in London, but she does keep current fashion plates on hand, delivered weekly from Ilminster."

"I am sure her dresses are fine," murmured Violet, suddenly embarrassed at her trousseau, or lack thereof. Fresh shame burned her insides that her mama and Rose had bespoken not even half of the dresses which would have been appropriate for her to have. She did not mind for her own sake, but she worried that the wife of such an important individual ought to have finer clothing than her family had seen fit to provide. She knew that Lord Reymes had mentioned before their marriage his plan to order more gowns for her when they were next in London, but she knew that her illness had prevented their traveling there. Unsure how to broach the subject with her husband, Violet determined to stretch her clothing as far as she could. If she could purchase some fabric, she certainly could sew some dresses of her own.

Once the tour had been completed, Lord Reymes admitted that he must travel to London for a fortnight to attend to some business. He had planned to deal with the matter while they traveled through during their honeymoon tour, and delayed his trip for the duration of her illness. His hope was that he would not be away for long, but his business depended on another man's ability to procure a document and he would not know until he was there how long that might take. Violet wished that she might have been bold enough to request that she might accompany him, but the words stuck in her throat, and she could do naught but swallow them.

Shortly before he was scheduled to depart the following day, Lord Reymes summoned Violet to his bedchamber. He had just instructed his valet as to which clothing should be packed when his bride entered. After the valet left, her husband pulled Violet into his arms and held her for a moment. Her heartbeat accelerated rapidly as it did every time he held her. He placed a kiss on her hair, then her forehead, but stopped when he came to her mouth. She feared her heart would beat out of her chest in its thunderous thumping. Instead of kissing her lips, he merely raised her hand and pressed his final kiss to that appendage, to Violet's disappointment.

Disappointment? Violet did not realize she had been anticipating his kiss. *But surely it does not signify. He is my husband, and a kind man, and I believe only a blind person would be able to deny that he is very handsome.* She blinked in an attempt to turn her errant thoughts elsewhere, and noticed that her heart had calmed itself. *And kisses, as Rose has informed me on several occasions, are not necessarily accompanied by tender feelings.* Having thus rationalized away the fluttering in her midsection at the man's nearness (or if not rationalized away, then made a valiant attempt at it), Violet accompanied him to the front of the house where his horses and carriage awaited him, and shyly bade him good-bye and Godspeed.

Violet's first feeling when he took his leave of her was that of relief. He had been quite attentive during her illness, as well as after. Though kind, he was still quite imposing and Violet's nerves were strained thin being near him so constantly. She soon discovered, though, that there was a prominent part of her heart that missed his presence. He had become a fixture in her life quite quickly, and his absence was felt much more acutely than she would have supposed.

Grasping for something with which to occupy her confused thoughts, Violet searched out the letter from Penelope, where she had left it in the pocket of her spencer.

22 Grosvenor Square
London
Dearest Violet,
I am remiss in not writing to you sooner; do forgive me! Thank you for your kind letter, and I am most pleased that you appreciate the painting I made for you. I signed it with my own name, so please do not allow anyone to examine it too closely, or my secret may be revealed! Until recently, I have enjoyed painting at my leisure so very much. I am so glad that God has seen fit to bless me with a loving husband; and with him, a position in which I may paint for my enjoyment and not for my support.
The baby has arrived. I wished to name him for your brother, but he refused. Said that he disliked being saddled with such a name as Ashbridge, and would not do the same

to his child. So, Andrew Charles it is. Andrew, for the name Ash wishes he'd been given, and Charles for your father. And for mine. Did I ever tell you his name? I cannot recall. I am slowly learning to release the poorer of my memories of him in favor of the happy ones. I do not excuse his poor behavior toward the end of his life, but I see now that there was a time that he cared for his family, for me. Forgive me! I had no intention of rambling on so morosely.

I've had word from my brother. He arrived safely in Canada more than a year ago, but lacked the funds to post a letter. He found that he was rather gifted at wood-carving, so he apprenticed himself to a carpenter and is now learning the trade. Odd to think that my brother is applying his hand to a trade! He has promised that once he is able, he will send something or other which he has carved. At present, the post is too costly for something like that. Ash and I have discussed going to visit him at some point, once I am recovered from the birth, and the babe is old enough to be left with a relative. Perhaps you would like to practice your mothering skills?

I chuckle as I write this. I know with certainty that you will blush when you read the part about you being a mother. Truly, though, Violet, when a woman finds a man who loves her, and she him, there is little to rival the joy found in their union. So do not fret, dearest, but enjoy your marriage!

I must close this letter. See how I've crossed it, and am still running out of space to write?

I remain,

Your devoted sister,

Penelope Wyndham

Violet enjoyed the letter and was glad that Ash and Penny were so happy. The letter also served to amplify her feeling of being alone, though. She was truly thankful to be away from the unkindness of her mother and sister, but Wyndmere was the only home she had ever known.

During the following days, Violet occupied herself as best she could. Now able to do more than sit sedately reading or sewing, she was eager to form a closer acquaintance with Mrs. Baker and learn the duties of managing the household. The day following Lord Reymes' departure, the two women met in the housekeeper's room. It was small, but furnished with a comfortable simplicity that Violet liked very much. Mrs. Baker had set out a modest tea, and proved every bit as kind and helpful as Lord Reymes had promised she would.

"He is a most generous master." The woman, nearing her elder years, smiled slightly as she spoke. "If I may be so bold, my lady is most blessed to be his wife."

Violet smiled, saying, "Indeed. Since our arrival, he has been nothing but kindness itself to me." This elevated the new mistress in the housekeeper's estimation a great deal. Surely a woman who knew the great value of being the master's wife must be at least sensible. Violet felt an instant connection to the matronly woman and nearly asked Mrs. Baker to address her by her Christian name, but fortunately remembered at the last moment that such a thing would not only be highly irregular, but make Mrs. Baker uncomfortable.

For the next several hours, Mrs. Baker went over menus, cleaning schedules, and countless other things that Violet had no previous idea were part of the smooth running of so great a home. She complimented Mrs. Baker on her administrative skills, immediately gaining the woman's full approval, if it had been at all lacking before.

That afternoon, Violet sat at the pianoforte in the parlor and played for two hours. Even in his absence, Lord Reymes was true to his word, and no servant entered the room during that time. What Violet failed to realize, however, was that within a matter of minutes, it was spread about the house that the new mistress played beautifully, the emotions which she did her best to keep to herself throughout the day pouring out through her fingers and into the music. The servants, while keeping from the interior of the room, did pause on occasion to listen at the door. Smiling to themselves, they continued with their tasks, humming the lovely tunes drifting through the door.

Nathaniel hopped from the carriage without waiting for the footman to lower the steps. He hurried into the London townhouse in Grosvenor Square, which had been his dwelling until his recent return to Bainscroft. The footman never even had a chance to receive his hat. Taking the steps two at a time, Nathaniel hurried into the parlor, tossing hat and gloves onto a table. His secretary Fredrick Ganley was there, awaiting his arrival.

After the other man's quick, obligatory bow, Nathaniel asked, "What news, Ganley?"

The two men discussed the intelligence gathered regarding the finances of Nathaniel's disreputable brother. He had for some time been suspicious of John supplementing his income by some ill-gotten means, but he was at a loss as to what that means might be. He had been working to solve this mystery, but his unexpected nuptials caused a temporary halt in his efforts.

Mr. Ganley reported that John had indeed been spending more on clothing and other accoutrements than his allowance should have permitted. Further, he often placed wagers in the gaming halls that exceeded what a man with twice his income would have been prudent to make – and losing those wagers, more often than not. As he heard the report, Nathaniel considered what could be done. One of the footmen, Ezekiel Harris, had been entrusted with discreetly following John when he was in London. Ezekiel was, of course, not to wear his livery during his reconnaissance, but was given a suit of clothes and enough blunt to credibly pass for a country gentleman visiting London. Nathaniel had secured him a membership at Boodle's, White's and several other clubs he believed his brother to be frequenting.

After learning very little from Mr. Ganley, Nathaniel called Ezekiel Harris into the parlor, hearing the same from him that the secretary had divulged.

"What halls does he frequent most, Ezekiel?" Nathaniel asked his footman.

"He jumps about, my lord, but lately I've seen him at Boodle's quite a bit."

"A bit high for a man without means, eh?"

"Yes, my lord," said the younger man. "My thoughts exactly. Shall I go now to watch him?"

"I shall go there directly, myself." Nathaniel stood, securely placing his hat on his head and drawing on the gloves that he had laid across his knee. At the other man's nearly-hidden disappointment, Nathaniel added, "Come to the club in thirty minutes. We will not know one another, but if he gives me the slip, you may follow him more easily than I."

"Yes, my lord," said the young man. "Very good, my lord." His eyes had taken on the glint of a man about to embark on a most exciting adventure.

At the door, Nathaniel turned and looked back at his footman. "May it be safe to assume, Ezekiel, that if I need similar services in the future, you would be willing to oblige me?"

"Oh yes, my lord! Don't mean to boast, but I can fit into any company of folks without them so much as batting an eye. And I usually sniff out the havey-cavey right quick! Most willing and happy to oblige!"

"As I thought." Hiding his amusement, Nathaniel moved down the stairs to his waiting carriage.

Violet received a call three days after her husband's departure for London. She was in the sitting room sewing a shirt as a gift for his return when Mr. Garand opened the door and announced the Dowager Countess of Bainscroft, Lady Eunice Reymes. Violet, quite disturbed and startled, quickly put aside her sewing and moved to greet her mother-in-law.

The woman was dressed in a gown composed of a rich blue trimmed with purple ribbon along the hem and lovely jewels draped round her neck. A plumed turban over her grey hair completed the ensemble. Violet felt downright dowdy in her yellow lawn gown, devoid of embellishment save a thin row of lace at the neckline.

After they were both seated, Violet folded her hands neatly in her lap to prevent them from fidgeting.

"I thank you for calling on me, my lady," she said with a discernible tremor in her voice.

"Think nothing of it, my dear. I am most happy to supply some sort of company while my son is away. What detestable gammon, leaving you alone mere weeks after your wedding!"

"Oh, no, my lady." Violet did not in any way want Lady Reymes to think she thought ill of her husband. He was, after all, the woman's son. "His business in London was most urgent. I wonder that he waited until I was well to attend to it."

"Any son of mine ought to have waited!" cried the dowager. "If he is treating you ill, my girl, I desire you should tell me at once."

"Nathaniel? Treating me ill?" Violet almost could not believe her ears and scarcely recognized her slip in using his Christian name.

"Ah, so I see that he is devoted to your happiness, then." The elder woman's smile was satisfied indeed and her brown eyes had taken on a glow of reminiscence. "I realize that your marriage did not begin as a love match – Natty did not give me the particulars, but I gathered it had something to do with John – but neither did mine with the late Lord Reymes, rest his soul. It was arranged by our parents." She paused, seeming to offer Violet the chance to comment, but all the girl could manage was a nod of her head. The woman's frankness was rather intimidating.

The dowager seemed satisfied with her nod and was about to continue, but a gentle tapping on the door announced Mr. Garand's return. He placed a tray with tea service on it before the ladies, complete with some cakes and fruits. He bowed out of the room, glancing surreptitiously to ascertain whether his new mistress was faring well with the dowager. Assured that she was doing as well as might be expected, he quietly shut the door behind him.

As Violet poured tea, the dowager continued what she had been about to say before Mr. Garand's interruption. "Now *I* had the benefit of knowing that my in-law's approval was secured, since they had been integral in procuring the match. You, my dear, need feel no more anxiety than did I. You certainly do have my approval."

"Th-thank you, my lady," Violet murmured as she handed the dowager a cup of tea. She was unequal to saying more.

"Oh, I suppose Natty was required to employ some ill-gotten means to have you use his Christian name. You *are* addressing him by his Christian name, are you not? You did say it to me, just now." Violet's rosy face was the only answer she could give. "I will do no such thing as stoop to bribery or threats, however I do wish that you would call me Mama. I never had a daughter. Though I suppose as your own dear mama is still living, it would be rather poor to do so, think you not? I'll settle, then, for your addressing me as Eunice, or if you are more inclined, Lady Eunice."

Violet said quietly, "I believe I could manage Lady Eunice."

"Oh, very well." The dowager smiled cheekily at Violet before helping herself to a cake. "And how do you enjoy your new home? Getting on well, are you?"

"I-I cannot imagine that I could not, Lady Eunice," replied Violet. "It is all very lovely."

"It should be. I decorated each room here, excepting the billiard room and the conservatory. When my dear husband – rest his soul – and I came here after our marriage, his mother told me that it is customary in the family for the new bride to always remake this room upon her arrival. That is all I dared do at first, mind you, but in time I became more comfortable and felt equal to the task of updating nearly all the rooms in a more modish manner."

Violet nodded politely, wondering as she did how this woman could ever contrive to feel *uncomfortable*.

"And so, I have come to inform you that you may do the same."

"But this room is fine as it is. I cannot think of a thing to change."

"Oh, moonshine!" cried the dowager. "Even I, the authoress of this room, can see that the furniture is now outdated, however the crème of style it was at the time. The colors are too dark for current fashion, and the woodworking is in need of a good polish at the least."

"But—"

"Stuff and nonsense! I will send my man over to you on the morrow with some excellent books and the names of several designers and tradesmen to help you." Lady Eunice helped herself to several of the fruits, as well as another small cake. After eating quietly for a moment, she sighed heavily. "I do not know, my dear, where I went wrong with my boy."

"M'lady?" asked Violet, unsure as to the direction Lady Eunice's thoughts had taken.

"John. I raised him the same as I did Natty. Pray, where did I err?"

Violet's tongue remained still, but her mind whirled. *What does she know of her son? How much do I truly know?* She was spared from being required to make a reply when Lady Eunice continued.

"Of course, Natty was always held to a higher standard, being the eldest. The future of our family – and that of the people living on our land – rests on his shoulders. I might have been too lenient with John. He was a sweet boy, but perhaps I indulged him too much. Yes, I am convinced that I did." Her hand trembling lightly, Lady Eunice sipped her tea. "Dreadful, odious boy he has become." She shook her head sadly.

"I-I am praying, Lady Eunice, that the Lord might touch his heart."

The woman raised her head, looking tearfully at her daughter-in-law. "Now, aren't you a gem of the first water? I know how awful it must be for you, away from all that is familiar. I promise, my girl, that Natty *will* come to be a comfort to you, rather than a source of difficulty."

"Is my discomfiture so very apparent, Lady Eunice?"

"You are a new bride, with no illusions of romance or visions of having made a grand conquest, though that must be how all the people see it. I can see that you are of a genuine quality and will bear up well as the Countess of Bainscroft. You'll see, my girl. All will be well."

The rest of the conversation kept to safe topics, but Violet was determined to tuck away this bit of encouragement from Lady Eunice to be recalled in times that she was not feeling up to the task before her.

Finishing off the last of the cake several moments later, Lady Eunice delicately brushed off her fingertips over the plate and swallowed the rest of her tea.

"La! What a gabster am I," said she, "going on so for this age, not allowing you to get in more than a few words."

"I've enjoyed our conversation immensely, ma'am," Violet hastened to assure her. "Please, do visit whenever you have the slightest inclination."

"You are a dear girl," said the elder woman, reaching across to clasp her hand and smiling warmly. "Natty is quite blessed to have happened on such an excellent wife."

At this, Lady Eunice rose to take her leave. The visit was ended in much the same manner it had begun.

After informing Mr. Garand that they were finished with the tea service, Violet decided to take a turn about the garden. As she walked along a rambling lane beyond the roses, she recalled that Lord Reymes had never said anything again about the labyrinth that he had considered adding. *Perhaps it was simply an excuse to go walking with me,* she thought, wondering even as the idea flitted through her head whether it could possibly be true. *He did not desire this marriage any more than I did. I cannot expect him to feel any affection for me. Indeed, I am quite surprised that he seems to feel no contempt or resentment, as he was nearly as forced into it as I was.*

Violet realized that her course had taken her to the back edge of the garden. It was a lovely area, with a good amount of open space which would be lovely for a picnic when the weather turned warmer. Perhaps she could arrange a small party and invite her aunt, uncle, and cousin Charlotte. The sun was high in the sky, indicating that luncheon would soon be served. Violet did not look forward to dining alone in that large room but did not wish to disrupt the servant's plans. Resigned, she turned her steps homeward.

When Nathaniel arrived at Boodle's, he nodded in greeting to several gentlemen seated at the card-tables, then sent a cursory glance about the room. He located John easily. He was watching the card at his table darkly, and Nathaniel guessed that his brother was not in the midst of a winning streak.

"If he would only understand," muttered Nathaniel under his breath as he made his way across the room toward the table where John sat, "that it is not luck that governs life, but honor and dedication to fulfilling one's duties."

While he was still about ten paces from the table, John suddenly stood and cried out, "Gammon! You're cheating!"

"No such thing!" scowled the dealer, standing himself. "You're ape-drunk, man!"

Nathaniel closed the space between himself and his brother and took John by the arm. "What does he owe?"

John whirled on him. "You!"

"Leave this establishment now," Nathaniel ordered. "I will settle for you, but you will no longer be permitted on these premises."

John scoffed. "Oh, the great Lord Reymes, ordering his miscreant of a brother to leave polite company." He scowled and turned, nearly shoving someone out of the way as he moved toward the exit.

"I say, he did not pay his vowels!" came the dealer's voice. Nathaniel's head snapped around as he realized the room was silent. Slowly, voices swelled as the men resumed their games, discussions, and, he thought with chagrin, undoubtedly some talk about the scene, however short, that he and John had just provided for them. *Hopefully it will not be interesting enough to be counted among the* on-dit *circulating in the city.*

Nathaniel turned to the man who had dealt and asked what John owed.

"Nearly nine hundred pounds, my lord," came the reply.

He suppressed a scowl and told the man to go see his secretary the following day for a bank-draft. With as much dignity as he could muster, Nathaniel walked to the door and then out to the street.

"You'd be well-advised to watch yourself," a smooth voice hissed in Nathaniel's ear. He turned and saw that John had been waiting for him. "Watch your innocent little wife, too; wouldn't want her to be tainted by me, or by what you really are."

"And what is that?" asked Nathaniel, his own voice belying the swirl of emotion in his chest.

John's eyes seemed unable to focus entirely, though he kept his speech clear. Nathaniel suspected the dealer's accusation of John being rather far into his cups must have some validity. When John spoke, though, all musings as to whether or not his brother was foxed fled Nathaniel's mind. "You know what you've done. And what you've neglected. You aren't as innocent as you claim to be, as immune to pain as you pretend you are."

Nathaniel's reaction to John's words was instant, but he hid it well and spoke with a deadly calm. "No, I am not. I will not, however, stoop to the sort of behavior you do in an attempt to escape that pain or that guilt." He turned to face his brother fully. Glaring down at the younger man, he continued. "You are my brother, much as it may revolt me to admit at times. I do, however, care about your well-being." He paused, hoping that his words might sink through the alcohol-induced cloud that no doubt surrounded John's mind. Continuing very slowly and deliberately, he finally allowed some of the anger brewing in him to seep into his voice. "I am compelled to warn you, though, that if you lay so much as a finger on my wife, you will wish you had never set *eyes* on her. Do not mistake me!"

John's enraged face glared for the space of a breath or two before he turned on his heal. He nearly collided with a young man just approaching Boodle's. The other man touched his hat, nodding toward John and receiving only an annoyed grunt for his trouble. John crossed the street and disappeared down a shadowy alleyway. The young man, who turned out to be Ezekiel Harris, glanced over at Nathaniel before sidling up to him.

"Shall I follow?" he asked quietly.

Nathaniel gave an almost imperceptible nod. Ezekiel straightened his jacket and crossed the street at a lope. He had turned down the same alleyway before Nathaniel strode over to where his carriage waited. With a quick word to his driver, he climbed into the equipage before the footman had a chance to open the door.

Riding back to his house, Nathaniel contemplated what John had said. *Would he truly wish to hurt my wife? I suppose I can easily believe that he'd seek some revenge on me, but Violet?* Suddenly the two-day journey from London to Bainscroft seemed enormously long; and he could not even leave immediately, for there was business which demanded his attention.

For the next three days, Nathaniel remained in his house. Even without the full staff to which he was accustomed, all of his needs were met, with one exception. He found that he missed his wife. They had been married such a short time, and yet he acutely felt the absence of her company. Certainly, Violet did not chatter away as some females, but her quiet presence, her example of reading Scripture frequently, her blushes and shy voice when he paid her compliments – all these filled his thoughts when he was not otherwise employed. And sometimes when he was.

Violet received a second visit two days after that of Lady Eunice. Thursday morning her cousin, Miss Charlotte Doberly, called. Violet happily received her, both girls exclaiming that they had no idea of seeing one another again so soon.

During the course of their visit, they discussed the letter from Violet which Charlotte had received three days past, the new pond Uncle Doberly was planning to have put in, and finally their talk turned to how Violet was faring in her new marriage.

"I daresay Lord Reymes is a kind husband. He is most solicitous of my comfort and even put off a trip to London until I had recovered from a cold." Violet offered a small smile to Charlotte. "Do you know him well?"

"La, no, indeed not. That is, my mama and papa know his family better than I do. I'm not even out in Society yet. He was away at school before I was old enough to know what Society was."

"I see." Violet suppressed a sigh. "I suppose I had hoped that you could offer some insight. I want to be a pleasing wife, but I do not know him well."

"Just be yourself, Violet. He married you, did he not? Does he not love you?"

Violet felt her heart stop. Did Charlotte not know the way their marriage had come about? *Oh, Lord, I am convinced I cannot tell her. Ought I though? If her mama and papa did not tell her, neither should I. Right?*

Violet found herself saying, "I-I think we have not known one another long enough for a *true* love to have developed."

"Oh." Charlotte seemed slightly deflated. Perking back up rather quickly though, she exclaimed, "What a wonderful blessing this marriage is for you!"

Violet could not help but smile at her young cousin's enthusiasm. "How is that, Charlotte?"

"Think of all the people you can help, now! With the funds now at your disposal, you can do more than simply sewing clothes for the poor or offering food to the destitute."

"I had not thought of that," said Violet. She now began to see a new realm of possibilities, a new purpose opening to her. "But I do not know that Lord Reymes will feel the same way."

"Even if he doesn't, you can still be of assistance to the people near you, can you not?" Violet did not see where Charlotte's ideas had leapt and gave her a questioning look. "Violet, you are used to a certain amount of economy. Your pin money will certainly be generous, if Lord Reymes' income is any indication. If you continue to exercise economy, you will be able to put aside some of that pin money for charitable endeavors."

"How clever you are, Charlotte." Violet felt eagerness for opportunities to help others rise within her. "I ought to meet some of the tenants and determine what need there might be."

"Yes!" cried Charlotte. "You know, Violet, my papa's estate is entailed away to – to – oh, I don't remember who, but someone. I have been considering going to live at a poorhouse in Town, if I am unable to secure a match once I come out next year. Oh! Don't look so shocked! My circumstances certainly will not be so dire that I'll be *required* to go there. Mama had some money put aside for me. No, I'll go there to *help* and serve the Lord's poor."

The girl's excitement was equal to some Society girl's who was telling of a trip to Bath or some other enjoyable locale. Violet knew that her cousin had been forced to part with a dear friend some seven or so years past, when the girl's family was unable to pay some debt accrued and was forced to leave the tenant farm they had rented previously. Knowing Charlotte's misery at her friend leaving, and the resulting urge to help those in need, Violet felt her heart swell. *It is prodigiously good to live so near Charlotte. I do so enjoy her company.*

"As tea is usually not delivered until a bit later, would you care to take a turn about the gardens in the meantime?" Violet asked her cousin.

"Would I? Oh, Violet, I've been sitting here this *age*, wondering when you would invite me! Yes, let's!" Charlotte, as she spoke, had risen and picked up her shawl and gloves. Fifteen minutes later found the girls ambling through the winding lanes at the back of the property, their heads bent closely and their arms linked, discussing life and love.

At the end of Nathaniel's fourth day in London, Ezekiel reported that he had not seen John for twenty-four hours. His business completed, Nathaniel decided that it was time to return to Bainscroft. He was no closer to discovering the source of the extra funds to which it seemed John had gained access. Additionally, the words of threat which John had uttered against his wife were constantly upon Nathaniel's mind. *Where did that cur go? Did he give us the slip so he could go exact revenge on me by hurting Violet?* He could not bear to consider the possibility of her suffering on his account.

So it was that Nathaniel traveled back to Bainscroft in half the time it took to leave it, stopping only to change horses. He told the livery with which he left his own animals that his groom Hobbs would be back to pick them up in a few days' time. As the miles closed between him and his home, he found his thoughts turning darker and darker. By the time he was within an hour of the house, he could scarcely contain himself, sitting in the carriage and unable to do anything to hurry along his driver.

Nine

❦

VIOLET HAD TAKEN up the habit of walking about the estate and even ventured to Horton on occasion. Already she had visited with several tenants briefly, as she had purposed to learn their names and the size of their families, as well as any difficulties they were experiencing. While polite, no one seemed particularly welcoming or talkative. Despite the difficulty in developing a relationship with any of the tenants, the weather was pleasant, if a bit warm for the beginning of autumn, and Violet enjoyed seeing the countryside. She often picked up the mail when in the village, much to the surprise of Mrs. Baker. If that's what the mistress wished to do, though, who was she to stop her?

This particular day, there was no correspondence waiting, so Violet started back to Bainscroft empty-handed. Enjoying the lovely weather, she decided to take a different, longer route. Birds sang and the sun shone brightly. She had just crossed a field and a bridge over a small creek when she come upon a small cottage surrounded by overflowing gardens.

The cottage was indeed small, consisting of only one floor. A door sat squarely in the center of the structure, with one window on either side. When Violet came closer, she saw that there was a woman out front, harvesting peas from the garden. When she saw Violet, the woman stood and called out a greeting.

Violet was rather surprised to find the woman's belly swollen large with child. She had never seen anyone so...well, so *advanced*. Sunny curls peaked out from beneath a tattered straw bonnet with a wide brim. Her clear blue eyes were smiling along with her mouth as she waved in a friendly manner.

Violet approached the woman shyly, dropping a quick curtsy when she reached her.

"Good morning, Miss. I've not seen you around here before."

"I—uh." Violet's usual words of introduction seemed to have fled in the face of so unexpected an encounter. *Ought she to be out here in the warmth of the day in her condition?* "My uncle and aunt live nearby," Violet managed to supply. She was about to add that she was the new wife of Lord Reymes, but the woman began speaking again.

"Care to sit for a spell? I only have a bit more to collect, but it can wait."

Violet observed the woman's flushed face and then let her eyes fall once again to the bulge underneath her plain dress. "May I help you?"

"Oh, that would certainly be a blessing, but I can't ask you to do that."

"I am offering, Mrs.—"

"Tessel. But please call me Mary, Miss."

"Pleased to make your acquaintance. You may call me Violet." Violet felt sure that if she were she to admit that she was the wife of the Tessel's landlord, Mrs. Tessel might not allow her to help, so she decided to keep that information to herself for the time being. *She ought to have help with this task.*

Glad not to have worn either of her new, finer dresses that day, Violet knelt down beside the pea plants and began to pluck the pods from the vines. Her gloves quickly became soiled, but as they were not the new pair, Violet found she could muster but little concern.

"'Tis a kind thing, helpin' as ye are, miss," offered the other woman with a small smile.

"Oh, no! Please, I am glad to be useful." Violet offered a shy smile. "I have very few acquaintances here and it is so nice to find a friend."

"My husband, Hezekiah, works this strip o' land. He's yonder, beyond that stand o' trees, gettin' the grain in. Our youngest two are playing near him. When they help me with harvest, more goes into their mouths than into the basket! The rent is higher these past years than previous, so we're hopin' to get as much as we can from our garden, to be sure we have food this winter."

"He has?" Violet's surprise was great.

"Oh, t' be sure. Lord Reymes is nothin' like unto his father. He's greedy and wantin' all he can squeeze from us." The woman's ire was clear in her voice and face.

Violet was speechless. *Could the man she speaks of be the same that I married? He has been so good to me. Would he treat those of inferior circumstances with so much disdain?*

Dwelling on her concern would provide no immediate help to the situation, so Violet attempted to steer the conversation to cheerier subjects after this. She commented on the beauty of the countryside, asked when the child was expected, and whether she had enough clothes to be ready for its arrival.

Once the peas were all in the basket that Mrs. Tessel had been toting along with her, Violet carried it to the door for the tired woman. When she asked whether Violet would like to come to tea tomorrow, Violet gladly agreed before taking her leave. In addition to Mrs. Tessel's clear need for rest, Violet knew she ought to be getting back or Mrs. Baker would be certain to fret.

As she walked, she did her best to absorb the new information that Mrs. Tessel had given her. The memory surfaced of Lord Reymes asking, when they first danced after their engagement was announced, whether she were smitten with her village cobbler. *What exactly were his words? I do wish I could remember. Something about a cobbler being a "low connection." Certainly, I am not a member of the working class, but I do see that they are valuable people, that in God's eyes, all are the same. Surely a man who has been so kind to me, whose staff are so loyal to him, would not hold such people in contempt. Would he?*

Violet's thoughts chased one another in her head as she made her way back to the house. When she passed through the door into the solarium, she moved toward her rooms to change her dress and prepare for dinner. Upon reaching the foot of the stairs, however, she saw Mrs. Baker coming toward her from the direction of the sitting room in a hurried frenzy.

"Whatever is the matter, Mrs. Baker?" asked Violet, alarmed. She had never seen the woman anything but calm and collected.

"The master's returned and is none too happy that I've been allowing you to walk about the countryside each day by yourself." Her worried eyes took in Violet's appearance. "Where have you been? Dirt on your gloves and face, your dress muddied. Oh, never mind. Would you mind going in to see him, please, my lady? I fear no one will have a moment of peace until he has spoken to you!"

"Certainly, Mrs. Baker." Violet offered what she hoped was an encouraging smile as she removed her bonnet. "Surely he cannot hold you responsible for my choices."

With a dubious look upon her face, Mrs. Baker merely curtsied and said, "Thank you, my lady."

Violet patted her hair into place as best she could without the help of a looking glass, drew her soiled gloves from her hands, and smoothed her dress while Mrs. Baker attempted to wipe some of the smudges of dirt from her face. She moved into the sitting room, where her husband was standing, gazing out of the window. A soft "ahem" brought him from his reverie.

"Violet!" *Is it anger or happiness raising his voice?* She tried to offer a bright smile.

"Good afternoon, my lord."

"Nathaniel."

"Yes, well." She blushed and drew a breath. He still had not approached her, but kept his place by the window. "Was your business in Town met with success?" she asked by way of making conversation.

"As much as it can be thus far."

"Oh, I see." Violet did not see at all.

"Where have you been walking?" His words were somewhat stilted, and his voice seemed full of tension to Violet, giving it a slight tremor.

"To the village; it is a lovely walk. Oh! And I've met the wife of one of your tenants; her name is Mary Tessel."

"Ah, yes. The Tessel family has been on our land for generations. How is she faring?"

"She was harvesting peas." Violet glanced self-consciously at her rumpled gown. "I offered to help her."

"Whatever for?"

"She is—um, in the family way," and here Violet's cheeks blazed, "Quite far into it, and I could not bear to watch her working in the hot sun, so I offered my assistance."

During his journey back from London, Nathaniel had speculated agonizingly over what harm might have befallen his wife while he was away. To return only to find her gone, and unaccompanied no less, was not a pleasant experience. Violet's face, so sweet and genuine and yet uncertain at the same time, caused his heart to thud heavily in his chest. She was safe. Nathaniel felt his annoyance melt away in the face of his relief. No, he had not been annoyed. Perturbed? Perhaps. Worried? Certainly.

In point of fact, it seemed that the only trouble she had found was that of ruining her dress. Now that worry over her welfare no longer demanded his attention, he allowed his thoughts to follow his gaze.

Her dress was made of a light, delicate material and now sported smudges and streaks of dirt. He knew little of women's fashions or fabrics, but he doubted the ability of anyone to remove such stains. *Let us hope that it was not one of the new pieces of her wedding clothes,* he thought with some humor. But upon closer inspection, he saw that it was the one she had worn that day he visited her family's home, a fortnight before their wedding.

Is she wearing a morning dress as a walking dress? Does she have no idea of the requirements of fashion and what clothing a woman of her standing is expected to wear? A look at the fichu she wore about her neck and tucked into the front of the dress for modesty's sake during the daytime demonstrated that she was at the least somewhat sensible of the protocol of fashion. *Could it be she simply lacks a sufficient amount of gowns?* Nathaniel continued to inspect her, seeing that in spite of her disheveled appearance, she still cut an attractive figure. The gown set off her lovely form in the same way it had the first time he saw her wear it.

That, of course, brought to mind their walk in the shrubbery of the labyrinth, their conversation, their near-kiss...and all of their near-kisses since. At that, he quickly strode to his bride, ready to take her into his arms. When he reached her, though, he was stopped by two things.

The first and perhaps what would have been the most noticeable to a bystander was that of a slight odor surrounding her person. From a closer vantage, he saw that the gown was damp and her hair clung to the sides of her face. He almost laughed. Of course Mrs. Baker had come to her all aflutter because the master was cross with her, and would my lady please go smooth things over with him? His poor wife had not even had a chance to change from her soiled clothing, let alone have a bath and recover from her – ahem, *dewy* state.

The second thing that made him stop was the hint of fear that he saw in her face. Surely, her smooth cheeks were flushed and her eyes bright from the exercise, but there was something else there, too. An uncertainty and, yes indeed, it *was* fear! Was she still so affected by her remembrances of his brother's impropriety? *Dashed cad!*

Deciding with some difficulty not to gratify his desire to kiss her right then, he instead reached for the pull which was conveniently located on the wall behind her and rang for a servant. That accomplished, he claimed one of her hands. When Mrs. Baker appeared, he was careful to speak kindly, so as to reconcile with the woman (who received his cordial tone eagerly), and asked for a bath to be drawn for Lady Reymes.

Turning back to Violet, he raised her hand and pressed a gentle kiss to the warm skin there. "Go, my dear, have your bath and let Jane pamper you a bit. I am sure you must be fatigued from your work today. I can wait until dinner to enjoy your company. Would that be agreeable to you?"

At her slight nod, he bowed to her curtsy and then returned to his contemplation at the window. He could admit to no surprise at learning of his wife's activities. He already knew that she had a decided tenderness in her heart for those less fortunate than herself; she had shown him as much when she mentioned sewing shirts rather than tapestries. *But is it entirely proper for the lady of an estate to aid the tenants in their work?* Granted, the woman was...*how did she put it? "In the family way"* and Nathaniel found he could not help smiling. He found himself wondering how long until she would be in a similar condition.

That cannot occur, he thought, *until we—* but he clamped down ruthlessly on the thought. He knew of his own eagerness for their full union, but he refused to force the issue with his wife. Considering her difficult encounter with his brother and her life of being put upon by her family, his desire to be patient and gentle outweighed his desire for her. He knew they would come together when she was comfortable with him, but he did not know how long these things generally took. True, they had scarce been married a month, but it seemed she was, by and large, greatly self-conscious in his presence.

I ought to have taken her with me to London. The time apart has surely not been a friend to our union. For my part, the separation and subsequent reunion has only strengthened my affection for her.

Not wishing to dwell on unproductive thoughts, he moved from the window. Nathaniel was determined to remain close to her throughout the coming days, hoping to aid her in opening up to him.

After making his way to his wife's chamber, he raised his hand to knock on the door, but hesitated. In a decidedly bold action, he instead opened the door unannounced. A quick glance about the room revealed Violet seated on a comfortably padded stool, with Jane moving toward her with a brush. Nathaniel strode across the floor, held out his hand for Jane to give him the instrument, then with a smile, motioned for her to take her leave. The abigail dropped into a brief curtsy before closing the door silently.

"Jane, would you please brush my hair?" asked Violet.

Nathaniel moved over to her and began to move the brush through her damp tresses. He worried about pulling too hard and kept his hand purposely light in his work.

"You are being more gentle than usual, Jane," laughed Violet, turning around. She gasped when she saw her husband there instead of her maid, and clutched at the opening of her dressing gown. "You are not Jane," she blurted.

"No, I am not." He offered a playful grin before extending his index finger to draw a circle in the air. "Turn, if you please."

He continued to carefully pull the brush through her hair, pausing to deal with tangles every now and again. "Are you feeling more the thing, my dear?"

"I am, thank you." As she spoke, she raised her hand to discreetly rub at one shoulder.

"You were picking peas, you say?"

"Yes."

"Hmm. I suppose you are unused to such strenuous work."

"One could scarcely call it strenuous. Mrs. Tessel was doing it easily." He thought he detected a touch of obstinacy in her tone.

"But she is used to labor."

Violet sighed. "Was I wrong to offer help to her?"

"No." He paused, wanting to express his point without tramping on his wife's delicate sensibilities. "I have no qualms with your desire to be charitable. In fact, I applaud you for it. But how was it that *she* allowed you to aid her? I must admit I am mildly astounded that she did."

Violet's posture sagged in a most unladylike manner. In a small voice, she replied, "It may be that my identity as your wife never entered the conversation."

Nathaniel bit back a laugh. *Of course.* Careful to keep any trace of amusement from his voice, he intoned "Indeed?"

"She would not have allowed me to help," Violet stated in a stronger voice as she sat up a bit more, some of the obstinacy returning. Nathaniel finished with her hair, but rather than allow her to rise, he gently tossed the brush onto her bureau and rested one hand on either shoulder, looking at her reflection in the looking-glass before her.

"So you avoided that bit of information in order to help her? And worked yourself to exhaustion?"

"I am not exhausted! Not in the least!" He refrained from commenting and she turned to face him. "I fear that I heard something rather disturbing from her as we worked."

"Oh?"

He gently turned her to face the looking-glass once again before gently moving his fingers over her shoulders, easing away the tension he felt there. After a few moments, her breathing became slower and her shoulders relaxed.

Still, when she continued the conversation, it was in a quiet tone that he could not hear.

"Beg pardon?"

She stood suddenly and began pacing nervously before him. "I cannot say it."

"Come here." When she did not capitulate, Nathaniel was almost glad, for he enjoyed seeing the tenacity she was showing. But he wished for her to be stubborn for things that she felt were important, not because she was reluctant to face him with uncomfortable news. He shot out a gentle hand to grasp her forearm as she passed before him again. "Come here, my sweet. You have nothing to fear from me. Tell me what she said."

Her lips pressed together, indecision in her eyes.

He at this point sat heavily upon the stool and pulled her into his lap, leveling his gaze at her. "*Tell me.* I cannot address any problems if I am ignorant as to what they are."

Violet averted her face and it seemed that she would not speak. At length, she managed in hushed tones, "Sh-she said that you were a man d-driven by greed and – and malice."

Nathaniel felt his masculine pride swell at the slight tremor in her voice; it seemed she was as affected by their nearness as was he. *At this rate, I'll soon be turned arrogant and prideful.* But then his brain registered the content of what she said.

Careful to keep his voice even, he asked, "On what basis did she make this assertion?"

"She said that you were requiring more from them than your father before you did," whispered Violet.

Nathaniel's confusion grew. "But I have not changed the terms of the rent. Rather, I have authorized funds for repairs to our tenants' dwellings. How can she say such a thing?"

"Perhaps she was misinformed?" As Violet spoke, she raised her head to peek up at him. Nathaniel found himself transfixed by her face. Her clear grey-green eyes reflected the firelight from the lamp on her bureau, and her almost-dry hair shimmered in the same light. He raised a hand to brush aside a lock that had fallen across her cheek and heard her breath hitch. His own breathing felt oddly irregular.

Nathaniel had the realization then that he was no longer falling in love. He was already there. And he could not help but think what an odd time it was for such a revelation.

For a time, Lord Reymes said nothing, but simply gazed at her. After clearing his throat, he said, "If they are paying more than I am receiving, what happens to the excess monies?"

Violet's muddled brain scarcely made sense of what he said. She had been staring at his firm, masculine lips, wondering whether they would claim her own. His face had been moving nearer and nearer to her with every passing moment. Or so it seemed. She drew a steadying breath before attempting an answer.

"Could it be that someone else is keeping the extra funds?"

"I was just pondering the same," agreed Lord Reymes with a look of approval for her in his eyes, which she would have missed had she not ventured to steal a glance at his face. "It would have to be someone who is in authority and could require it of the tenants."

Violet felt mildly ill at the thought that one of the servants or persons of authority under Lord Reymes might be abusing the tenant farmers by underhanded means. Many of them were likely struggling to meet the needs of their families, as was the case for the Tessel household. It was a sad thing indeed.

"Who might be responsible?" she asked.

A steely glint came into her husband's eyes and he tightened his hold on her waist until it became an embrace. His face showed a hardness that she had not seen since their brief interview with Mr. and Mrs. John Peyton. She suppressed a shudder at the memory of that man. "I believe I have an idea, but I do not wish to endanger you, so I shall say no more at present."

"Endanger? But I cannot imagine that someone would..."

"Even so, I will not take the chance. Perhaps I ought not to have shared as much as I did. However, as you now know what you do—"

"Which is very little indeed," interjected Violet.

"Yes, dearest, but that is for your safety. As you now know what you do, I would ask that you remain indoors as much as possible, unless you bring a footman or even two. Please do not walk about as you did when I was in Town. I should not be able to live with myself were anything to happen to you. I *will* see that you remain safe."

"But for how long?" she asked. "I have come to treasure my time spent walking, and even have begun to make the acquaintance of some of the tenants, that I might be some small source of help should they ever be in need."

"I am deeply gratified that you are embracing your role as mistress of this estate so enthusiastically, but I must insist that you do as I ask, just for a time, until all is resolved. Trust me, and trust the upper-servants, but I must ask that you trust no one else, until such a time as I may assure you that this time of caution has passed."

Violet forced herself to look into his eyes, nervous though it made her. What she saw there, in his intense gaze, was the assurance that he asked this of her for no reason save his concern for her wellbeing. Knowing this, she could do naught but answer, "Very well, my lord. I shall do as you ask."

His face went through a transformation, the muscles about his mouth relaxing into a smile until his eyes followed suit. "Even address me as Nathaniel? Oh dear, and you cannot meet my eyes any longer, can you? Well, it is no matter. Come, let us dress you for dinner. They shall wonder what we are about."

Violet's eyes widened and panic rose within. *Does he indeed intend to help me dress? I know he aided me a bit at the inn, but only minimally, and I was not well; indeed, I scarcely remember our time there.* But she was spared further worry by a light rap at the door. She called for the person to enter as she jumped from Lord Reymes' lap.

Jane entered, dropping a quick curtsy. "I apologize for interrupting, my lord and my lady, but if I am to coax my lady's hair into something acceptable, it must be before it is fully dry. As it is, I fear too much time has passed already."

"Of course, Jane," said Violet. Her relief was immense, yet when she glanced at her husband, the disappointment she saw briefly on his face was nearly enough for her to repent her quick agreement with Jane. Nearly, but not entirely.

Ten

THE DAWN OF the following day found Nathaniel hastening from his bed – still, much to his chagrin, a separate one from his wife. He called for his valet while considering what to wear.

It was not surprising to Nathaniel that Griffin was not yet present when he rose, though the valet may very well be shocked; members of higher society were generally late to bed and late to rise. Even in the country, where those same people rose earlier, it was not this early. Indeed, any day besides this one, he would still be abed for several hours. His mind, however, would not allow him any rest until he tended to the matter which had cost him no few hours of sleep.

During dinner yesterday, Nathaniel had been in a rather contemplative mood, still unsure what course to take regarding the difficulty with the tenants. Try as he might, no inspiration came as to how he might get to the bottom of this. And so he had been quiet, allowing his wife to eat her dinner without being accosted by his charms.

My charms indeed, he thought with self-deprecation as he pulled a coat from the wardrobe. *She seems even more immune to me than she was at our reunion. She seems to have no difficulty speaking to me now, and even, on occasion, will initiate conversation.* But then he remembered her breathlessness when he held her the previous day, how very affected she did seem to be. *What do I expect, after all? That she would make a declaration? Certainly not. I am sure it falls to me to do that.* Striving to push his tumultuous thoughts from the fore, he turned when his valet entered the room.

"Yes, my lord?" the man asked, his face slightly pale and his voice betraying a trace of his surprise at seeing his master risen so early.

"I must dress, and quickly." These words sent Griffin into action. While Nathaniel pulled on his pantaloons, Griffin retrieved a bright white shirt and starched cravat from the wardrobe, as well as a discreetly embroidered waistcoat. After a few more moments, Nathaniel donned his well-fitting coat with Griffin's aid, and the valet managed to assist him in pulling on his highly-polished boots with little difficulty. Nathaniel's hair, which had a bit of natural wave to it, was easily coaxed into a mild version of the windswept fashion which had gained so much popularity of late. In under twenty minutes (perhaps a new record), he was hastening down the hall to the breakfast room. After somewhat haphazardly tossing several pieces of food onto his plate, he opted for coffee rather than tea, hoping the slightly stronger liquid might jolt him into conceiving a solution. As he ate, he reviewed what he had learned thus far.

John had indeed been garnering greater income than his living; the expenditures which Ezekiel had been able to confirm were in great excess of John's income, even than his wife's. The source of those supplementary funds, however, had remained a mystery. Until now. When Violet spoke to him of the anger the Tessels felt at being required to pay more, all appeared to fall into place.

Someone must have falsely raised the rent on several of the tenants' land. Nathaniel felt with no small amount of certainty that the Tessels were not the only family; it *would* explain the barely-hidden glares of animosity he received whenever encountering most of the tenants after his arrival from London. Even Violet, who was loved by all who met with her, noticed the cooler greetings of the tenants who learned her identity. And certainly the funds which he had intended to be distributed for repairs and upkeep of tenants' homes had not been disbursed – at least not to the tenants. And the ill-will they now harbored toward him prevented them from speaking frankly about who or what was involved.

He knew what the difficulty was. *But how to solve it?* Sending letters explaining what seemed to have happened might restore some of their good-will, and he could even offer recompense. But then the guilty parties would go free. He could involve the local magistrate, but if it happened to be a frightened under-servant whom John had coerced, what purpose would that serve? And if John caught wind of Nathaniel's suspicion, before action could be taken, he might act rashly. The situation was a delicate one. Even the slightest variances in his plan of action could cause rather significant adjustments in the outcome.

As Nathaniel further considered the matter, it became apparent that someone besides his brother must be involved. *Anyone who knows John would be suspicious of him involving himself in the workings of the estate; word would have gotten back to one of the upper-servants, at least, and they'd have cried rope. There must be a lackey.* Unless he found that person, though, the matter would never be settled.

Suddenly finding himself with an empty plate and still no real idea how to proceed, Nathaniel swallowed the last of his coffee and rose from the table. Upon exiting the dining room, he spoke to the footman beside the door, asking for his horse and greatcoat. He had always found that a morning ride helped him work through whatever problem was bothering him.

While the days were still warm, the air cooled considerably during the night. The morning air stung his face as he urged Hannibal into a gallop. They raced through a pasture, darted between the trees in a small forested area, and finally emerged into another pasture beyond the trees. Slowing slightly, Nathaniel urged his horse over a fence before again giving him his head. The sky, dotted with clouds, promised a lovely day, and he was eager to spend some of it with his wife, but first he must determine a course of action.

There is also the matter of my wife's safety. I was so eager to bring her from her family home, where she was so mistreated. I will not allow her to be harmed in my home. Nathaniel felt a helplessness that he had not experienced often in his life. The only other time he remembered feeling so powerless was roughly two years past, when his life and family began to fall to pieces. Great emotion rose in his breast, threatening to choke him. Harshly, he swallowed it down and forced his mind away from the past in order to give all his energy to the present.

The helplessness still weighing heavily upon his shoulders, Nathaniel reined in his horse, hopped off, and allowed the animal to graze on the sweet grasses at its hooves. Perching himself on a low rock barrier nearby, he leaned his elbows heavily on his knees and dropped his head, heart pounding. *What can I do? If we had made a love-match, or if Violet was more comfortable with me, we would share a room and I could simply keep her with me always. But I have no desire to cause her alarm by suddenly being with her all hours of the day and night. And even if I did keep her with me, there is by no means a guarantee that she will be safe. What if I fail to protect her? A moment is all it would take for harm to come to her.*

A breeze lifted the hair on his forehead, cooling him slightly. For the first time in years, Nathaniel wanted to pray. He wanted to trust Someone bigger than himself, to admit that he couldn't face this with his own strength. Taking a deep breath, Nathaniel began to speak quietly, lowly, knowing that the One for whom his words were intended would hear him regardless of his volume.

"There is very little which usually would induce me to change my course. You know, Lord, that only something which touches me very deeply will serve to change me. The first instance of this happening was several years past, and the second is happening now. I pray that the effects of this second change will be for the better, and also prove to be longer-lasting than the first." An urge to laugh struck Nathaniel, but the chuckle sounded hollow to his ears.

"I'd always believed that if I was in control of any given situation, the outcome would be one which was pleasing to me. I can see now how faulty was my logic. Try as I might, I am not the master of this outcome." Nathaniel stood and began pacing the edge of the meadow. Hannibal looked up at him for a moment, but seeing that he was doing nothing of interest, the horse resumed munching on the sweet grasses at his feet.

"My Father in Heaven," continued Nathaniel, "I am at a loss. Humbling myself before You in repentance is not the difficulty; I know my sins. And I am not inclined to think that I know better than You, for I cannot presume to see all that You see. Even so, I find that my fear and worry consume me. Violet so often appears to be frightened or nervous, and I've repeatedly asked myself how I might help her avoid those feelings. Now, I come to see that I am just as fearful as she. Not, perhaps, in the same matters as plague her, but those things that frighten me hold just as much sway over my heart and actions as those which frighten her. Release me from them, Lord God, that I may serve You and follow You in all that I do and say and think.

"Guide me as I seek to bring my brother to justice. Show him that the life he has chosen is not one that is pleasing to you, nor is it one which will benefit him for more than a short time; the peril to his soul is far more significant than the fleeting pleasure he has found. Even as I ache for him to return to the boy I once knew, I fight with my anger toward him for all that he has done to our mother, to our father's memory, to me and to Violet." Nathaniel halted his pacing. The memories of the past few years swirled together, demanding action on his part to set things right. At the same time, his present uncertainty and fear of proceeding incorrectly warred with that demand, urging him to retreat. Nathaniel was stymied.

"I cannot act rashly and accuse John, for I fear what he might do to avoid paying for his crimes. And he cannot be acting alone. Who else might be involved? Mr. Garand and Mrs. Baker are both loyal to a fault; I cannot believe that either of them is involved. The under-servants do not have the necessary authority. The bailiff – he might!" Mr. Faintree, as bailiff of the estate, managed much of Nathaniel's business with the tenants and would naturally be meeting with them often, collecting rent and the like.

Of course! Why had he not thought of him already? *Thank You, Lord!* That must be the place to start. Nathaniel had charged John, in a rare show of desiring his younger brother to redeem himself, with hiring a bailiff. It seemed upon retrospect that had not been a wise decision.

It would be too time-consuming and tedious to interview the staff in his household in an attempt to gather intelligence and identify with certainty John's accomplice – who may or may not be the bailiff. And if Mr. Faintree was guilty, he may hear of the interviews and run before Nathaniel had a chance to confront him. Someone who could speak with one or more of the tenants, who had garnered some level of trust with them, would be an ideal asset to his cause.

Suddenly struck with an idea, Nathaniel slapped his knee and uttered, "By Jove, that's it!" He rose and moved with purpose toward his horse. The pair was soon sprinting across the field, toward the house, a prayer of thanks in his heart. The idea was really quite simple, but he could not have conceived it without having first cleared his head of all the confusion and misery which had been clouding his thinking. His mind and heart were now sharply focused where they needed to be.

Violet had only recently risen from her bed. She finished using her tooth powder as bidden by Jane who had hurried down to the kitchen to fetch some hot water for her mistress' morning toilette; it had not yet been ready when Violet pulled the cord to summon the abigail to her chamber. Violet was in the process of removing her dressing gown from over her chemise and stays when a knock sounded at her door. Thinking it was Jane with the water, she hurried to the door to open it for her maid.

Upon unlatching it, though, she found Lord Reymes on the other side. His face was set with an intensity which she was used to observing in him, but it was a relief to see that it did not seem to be directed at her. Remembering herself, she stepped aside, quickly re-wrapping her dressing gown about her slender frame.

Lord Reymes entered the room, looking much too dashing for Violet's peace of mind. His tailored coat fit his broad shoulders snugly, as it was designed to do. His cravat, formed into a simple yet elegant knot, framed his chin and jaw most handsomely. Violet suddenly wished she had arisen earlier, so that she might be fully dressed as well for this interview. It was most disconcerting to feel so exposed. Their talk the previous evening left her feeling similar, but some of her discomfort had been softened by her fatigue at the end of the day. *He is your husband,* came a comforting voice in her head.

"Would you care to sit?" She ushered him to the upholstered bench at the foot of her bed. He took hold of her hands, pulling her along and sat closely with her on the bench. At once, she sprang up from the seat. At her husband's mildly alarmed expression, she hastened to find an excuse.

"I just now recalled that I have a gift for you." She hurried to the drawer where she had hidden the shirt. "I made this for you."

Her husband's smile as he took the fabric from her filled her with warmth. When he unfolded it and fingered the small line of embroidery stitched onto the cuffs and collar, she hastened to say, "I do hope it is to your taste, my lord."

"I wish you to call me Nathaniel," he said, leveling his gaze upon her and grasping her hand to draw her down to sit beside him on the bench yet again.

"Yes, Nathaniel," came her quiet reply. *Surely he must think me a child! Why, oh why can I not maintain my composure when he is so near?* And yet with his hands clasped warmly about hers, with the pressure of his knee beside her own, she could do little to calm herself.

"I do like this, very much, Violet. Thank you." He leaned toward her to place a light kiss upon her temple. "Today you plan to visit Mrs. Tessel again, do you not, my love?" Violet raised her eyebrows. She had not expected to hear this from him – neither the question nor the endearment.

"Yes; she invited me for tea."

"Do you think you might learn something from her? I need to know at whose command they are required to pay more for their rent. And whether the repairs I authorized were completed. I'd ask myself, but it seems whoever is behind all this has also poisoned the tenants against me."

"I shall do my best to find out," she promised. "Was that all you needed to know?"

"Yes, that will be enough to guide my next course of action." He smiled encouragingly at her and took both her hands in one of his, wrapping his now-free arm about her back.

Violet hesitated, looking down at his strong hand gently holding both of hers, before she spoke haltingly. "I had – had hoped today to apologize. To Mrs. Tessel, that is, for not revealing who I was. Would it be a problem...may I still do that?"

"Of course, darling!" At his words, she looked up to find him smiling warmly at her.

"Will she be forthcoming with me once she knows?"

"Let us pray together and hope that the Lord will move her to trust you, and by extension, me. I can certainly understand why she may not wish to."

As he petitioned the Lord on their behalf, Violet's heart warmed, and she knew beyond a doubt that the ill-treatment of the tenants was not her husband's doing. After his "Amen," she could not hide her smile.

He pulled his face further from her own, the better to see her. "Why the smile? A moment ago, you were concerned about whether Mrs. Tessel would be open with you."

Violet reminded herself that Lord Reymes had shown no sign of disdain for her, as had her mama, her sister, and even to some degree her father. She pushed away her uncertainty and spoke. "Forgive me, but I was thinking how glad I am to be your wife."

Pressing a kiss to her forehead, he said, "There is nothing to forgive on that count."

"Yes, but I when she told me yesterday of the rent, I must admit to feeling uncertain as to what was the truth."

"Concerning me?"

"Yes. I am sorry, but I did doubt you for a moment at least."

"But now?"

"Upon our first meeting, I was convinced of your integrity and good morals. Your offering for me was evidence of that, though the action was not necessary."

"We will not belabor that point; I cannot bear more discussion of your mama, my brother, or that evening. Unless it is to simply say that God works even in the most unlikely circumstances."

Violet nodded her agreement. "But when Mrs. Tessel, who struck me as a good, honest woman, began to tell me that you were corrupt," and here she could no longer hold his gaze, "I must confess to at least *wondering* whether I ought to give credence to her words."

"Oh you did, did you?" Lord Reymes gently nudged her chin until she raised her head. She was immediately struck by the light in his eyes, as though he already knew what she was about to say; indeed, his countenance suggested a man utterly confident of having his wife's approval. His thumb began to gently brush over the side of her face that he held.

Violet pressed onward. "I *hoped* that she was misinformed, but I was not certain."

"And now?" A smile flitted about his mouth as he reached to raise one of her hands to it.

Though she could not seem to draw a full breath, Violet managed to say, "I know you to be an honorable man, and that you would never mistreat a person under your care. I greatly admire you for it." Violet could scarcely believe she had spoken so freely, but had little time to wonder at herself. His lips pressed against her hand, and then he straightened her fingers and pressed a kiss upon the pads of her fingertips, as well.

Releasing her hand, he slipped both arms about her and ordered softly, "Kiss me."

"I beg your pardon?" Violet was frozen in his embrace, the room spinning then fading around her until she could see only his face.

"Kiss me." It was whispered this time and sounded like a plea.

"I, um." Violet drew a breath that she intended to be fortifying, but as she released it, she felt her fingers begin to tremble where they had fallen in her lap.

Lord Reymes tightened his arms about her, lowered his head slowly, and gently pressed his lips against her own. As his lips moved, Violet felt her heart quicken its pace, and when he deepened the kiss, her senses were quite overwhelmed. Somewhere in the back of her mind, she wondered at her husband's action.

At a sharp rap on the door, Violet attempted to jump from his embrace, but he held her fast. "What will the staff think, to find us..." She could not say it aloud, but her rosy face spoke volumes.

Lord Reymes answered, "They will think that we are a newly wed couple, very much enamored with one another. There is nothing reprehensible in that." More loudly, he called, "Enter!"

Jane pushed open the door, betraying no surprise on her round face, and bobbed a curtsy before pouring hot water from a kettle into a pitcher on Violet's washstand. Once Jane had left to return the kettle to the kitchen, Lord Reymes turned his attention back to Violet.

"While I would like nothing better than to spend the morning with you, I know I ought to allow you to dress and call on Mrs. Tessel." He released her with a quick, chaste kiss and took his leave. It was some moments before Violet roused herself, rose from the bench, and moved to the washbasin to begin her toilette.

Nathaniel supposed he ought to regret kissing Violet as he had. He was certain that she was not yet prepared for the full extent of his amorous attentions. Her blushes and often hesitant words attested to that. And yet, he could not in truth claim regret as being one of his feelings regarding his action.

He discovered that he was in love. When he entered her room, and found her so embarrassed and yet simultaneously trusting of him, he knew. He had, as a youth, entertained infatuations with various young ladies of his acquaintance, but never had he felt such a protective instinct, such a yearning within his deepest self as he did for his wife. He knew also that she was either ignorant of his feelings or she simply did not believe the hints he was attempting to send her – or perhaps both. At times, he had wondered if he ought to allow her time to grow comfortable with him or simply be a companion to her. But after his time of prayer out in the field, and now knowing his heart fully, he decided that the best course was an active pursuit of his wife.

As nothing could at this moment be done on any front (that of his wife or that of his brother – both equally pressing but in vastly different manners), Nathaniel decided to put his time to a constructive use. While Violet prepared for her call on Mrs. Tessel, he moved to his bedchamber and retrieved his copy of Scriptures from the small table beside the bed. Walking to a comfortable chair situated next to the window, he settled in for what promised to be quite a while. Since his time in the field, pouring out his heart before the Lord, he hungered for deeper knowledge and understanding of his God.

After reading a psalm, he began to pray again. He could not bring himself to explore the darker parts of his mind and heart, but instead let his mind wander over those pressing things which caused the current unrest in his soul. He prayed, placing all at the foot of the cross: the damaged relationships with the tenants, his wretched brother, his new wife. The difficulty with the tenants certainly weighed on him, but it was his wife that monopolized much of his thoughts at present. He found her artless modesty refreshing, her sweet disposition endearing, and her conversation, which was slowly becoming more frequent, indicated at a hidden yet clever wit. He hoped that in time she might grow to love him, as he loved her.

Lord, is this why You brought us together? So that we might grow together in love and in following You? I struggle with the fact that I want ours to be a marriage in every sense of the word: I want us to share our days, our love, our nights... It is my desire, though, that she approach me. Need I tell her that? Should I simply say to her that I love her? Lord, please guide my words and actions.

Although nothing was solved, Nathaniel's feelings were much more settled when he rose from the chair and moved to his office to see to several minor matters which required his attention. Once those had been attended, Nathaniel scrawled a brief missive to Ezekiel, apprising him of this latest information, and requesting that any new intelligence revealing John's location be sent by express.

Once finished in his office, and lacking anything with which to occupy his mind, Nathaniel wandered about the house. He made his way from room to room, inquiring of the staff which he encountered as to their health, their families, and their work – and generally making a nuisance of himself.

Mrs. Baker, after hearing from a third housemaid that the master was making her nervous by asking about her work – "Oh, Mrs. Baker, am I to be given the sack?" – decided she's had enough and went to approach the master. She found him in the smaller of the house's two kitchens, mere minutes after the third girl left her to return to her dusting.

"Lord Reymes, might I have a moment of your time?" she queried.

"Certainly, Mrs. Baker! What may I do for you?" His bright, almost relieved smile nearly caused the staid servant to lose her habitually businesslike demeanor and give in to an absurd urge to laugh outright. She glanced about to ensure that none of the under-servants would be eavesdropping, but the kitchen was occupied only by two kitchen maids, peeling potatoes for luncheon on the opposite side of the room.

"I am afraid," she said with a meaningful look, "that some of the girls are fearful of losing their jobs."

"Why would they fear that?" Nathaniel's blank countenance demonstrated that he had no earthly idea as to there being a problem. "Has their conduct been unbecoming?"

"Certainly not, my lord!" cried the housekeeper indignantly. "I hire only the most morally upright girls."

"What then, Mrs. Baker, is the difficulty?"

"You, my lord."

"Me?" He was incredulous. "Whatever can you mean?"

"This brown study, if you'll forgive me, my lord, into which you've fallen. I am most gratified to know that the Lord has seen fit to bless you with an ardent love for the new mistress, but the stewing, the making a nuisance of yourself while my staff is attempting to perform their duties – it will not do, my lord!" Throughout this speech, she had slowly straightened her already-ramrod posture until she had appeared to grow several inches. Her exasperation was clear, and Nathaniel knew that only extreme desperation would lead the woman to confront him in such a way. He was, in a word, speechless.

After a moment, he grinned like the lovesick fool that he was and found his voice. "I am sorry, Mrs. Baker. I did not realize that I was frightening the poor girls. Perhaps I ought to go for another ride."

"Very good, my lord, I will send a pageboy to ask the groom to ready your horse." The relief was evident in her voice.

"Do tell him that I'll go easy on Hannibal this ride; I know he will fret at my taking him out again so soon."

"Of course, my lord."

"Thank you, Mrs. Baker."

"Not at all, my lord," she murmured. "Thank *you*."

Violet sat silently praying as the carriage brought her to the Tessel home. She had dressed in the new walking dress that her mama and Rose had chosen for her. It was of a sage green, trimmed with a simple lace and tied with a green ribbon. The dress looked almost like a pelisse, worn open as it was over a white underdress. Checking nervously that her bonnet was straight on her head, Violet drew a fortifying breath and continued her prayer.

It was a short drive and soon she alighted from the steps with the help of the footman. Violet told Mr. Brown, the coachman, that she would not require his services again; she would walk home.

"Begging your pardon, m' lady, but it's the master what told me to wait for you. I'll be out back, in the barn."

Resigned, Violet nodded her assent and walked to the cottage door. When Mrs. Tessel answered her knock, her eyes widened at the carriage and its crest behind Violet. Fear and mistrust colored Mrs. Tessel's face while Violet's heart sank.

Regardless of what the other woman might be feeling, she politely, if a bit coolly, asked Violet to please come in. Once they were both seated in a modest parlor, Violet began to speak.

"Mrs. Tessel, I must confess to you – and please do not speak until I have finished, or I may lose my courage. I did not tell you who I was yesterday because I feared that you would not allow me to help you with harvesting the peas."

"And you'd be right!" cried the woman, forgetting that seconds ago she had nodded her agreement not to interrupt. "No countess should be harvesting peas."

"I am sorry for that, but I am not sorry for what I learned from you, regarding the rent you say my husband is charging."

Mrs. Tessel's face turned red; from anger, fear, or embarrassment, Violet did not know. Still, the other woman kept her peace.

"When I spoke to my husband – that is, Lord Reymes – of it, he—"

She seemed unable to contain herself. "Sure'n you did not tell him, Miss! I mean m'lady!" Her distress was evident.

"What you told me did not seem consistent with what I know and what I have learned about his character. I am glad I told him, for he claims that he never authorized a raise in the rent. And that he ordered repairs to be made to several of the tenant farms at his own expense!"

"You ca'na' think that I lied. 'pon my honor, m'lady, no repairs were done," cried Mrs. Tessel, fear lacing her words as her brogue became more pronounced.

"No, we do not think that. But Mrs. Tessel, do you happen know who told your husband that the rent was raised? Lord Reymes wishes to solve this problem and set things right with the tenants."

The other woman's face grew thoughtful. "I wish I could tell you, m'lady." She shook her head. "Mr. Tessel said three years past that the new master had raised the rent. Shall I fetch him from the field and ask?"

Violet spoke up quickly. "Oh no, Mrs. Tessel. Lord Reymes can certainly come later to talk with your husband, to see if we might get to the bottom of this. I won't have you exert yourself in that way; your child may come at any time."

"So it may." Her smile was affectionate as she rubbed her swollen mid-section. "We've still much of our first-born, Abraham's things. He an' Miriam's playin' in the back room right now. Miriam is second and this one will be our fourth; Aaron was still-born."

"Oh, I am sorry. Is there anything I might do to help when the child comes?"

She nodded appreciatively, but said, "Dearie, sure'n you know your husband is our landlord. It would be terrible if I were to ask anything of you."

"It might be irregular, but I should like to be of service to a *friend.*"

She smiled appreciatively, but shook her head. "I do thank you for the thought, but we really aren't needin' anything."

Violet kept any arguments to herself and determined to send some food and clothing for the baby once it arrived. The women's conversation turned to lighter topics – the weather, the milliner in town, the roses that grew in the gardens of Bainscroft – as they sipped tea and ate biscuits that Mrs. Tessel had set out with the modest tea service.

Finally, Violet rose to take her leave, Mrs. Tessel accompanying her to the door. Suddenly, though, the expectant mother stopped and doubled over, clutching her midsection.

"Mrs. Tessel? Are you unwell?" Violet asked, alarmed.

"Oh!" She took several deep breaths and then straightened. When she spoke, her brogue had become more pronounced. "I feared distressin' ye, m'lady. I've 'ad mild rushes all the day. But this was far worse'n the others. I fear the babe may be here before day's end."

"Oh! Good heavens! What shall I do? Go fetch Mr. Tessel?" Violet felt her heart begin to race with fear and excitement.

"I canna' ask you to do that. He's in the field, an' your pretty dress—" but she could say no more, for another wave of pain had overtaken her.

Violet rushed through the door, running round to the barn and burst through the door, startling the coachman and footman who were sitting and playing a rubber of cards on a barrel's end.

"M' lady!" the coachman cried, clearly shocked.

"Mrs. Tessel is about to have her baby. Please, go fetch Mr. Tessel from the field! And we need the midwife! Do you know where she may be found?"

"M' lady, I beg your pardon, but I canna' leave you!"

Violet drew herself up to her full height and said with as much authority and indignation as she could muster, "Mr. Brown! These are extenuating circumstances! Surely Lord Reymes would not hold you to his orders—"

"Oh yes he would," came the voice of Lord Reymes from the door she had just entered.

"Nathaniel!" Violet whirled around, never happier or more relieved to see her husband. "She's about to have the baby!"

Nathaniel turned his eyes to Mr. Brown, nodding that he should go fetch the appropriate people. The coachman quickly set about his business as Nathaniel led his wife from the barn.

"Are you well, my dear? You are flushed."

Violet curtsied, as though belatedly realizing she had not greeted her husband properly. Nathaniel stopped just before the path leading to the door of the house and took her briefly in his arms.

"I am well, I thank you, but I daresay she needs—"

"Yes, yes, Brown is fetching the midwife. Would you like to keep her company until she arrives?"

"Oh yes, Nathaniel! Thank you!" Nathaniel was surprised when Violet voluntarily used his name two times in as many minutes, but was utterly shocked when she then rose on her tiptoes to place a kiss upon his cheek. His own shock, though, was no more than Violet seemed to feel. Her eyes widened as soon as she had stepped back from him, and her cheeks took on a rosy hue. Grinning, Nathaniel contemplated drawing her back into his embrace. *I suppose now is not the time. And we are in public, even if no one is about.* Ruefully, he stepped aside, motioning her to precede him into the house.

"Oh, Mrs. Tessel! Are you well? I do apologize for leaving so suddenly. Our coachman is fetching the midwife and the footman is fetching Mr. Tessel – Oh! Are *you* Mr. Tessel?" Nathaniel was amazed and amused at how this apparent crisis had loosened his timid wife's tongue.

The poor man seemed flummoxed by the sudden onslaught of feminine flurry, and his face flushed nearly as red as his hair. Nathaniel merely stood, leaning against the doorjamb, immensely amused by another newly-revealed side of his bride. As Mr. Tessel was called upon by his wife to lay a damp cloth across her forehead, Nathaniel addressed Violet's question.

"Violet, may I present Mr. Tessel. I found him while riding today, but that does not signify at this point." Nathaniel smiled down at his wife. Her brow was creased with worry for her friend and he found himself wanting to alleviate her fears. "I do not suppose there is anything we may do to help, Mr. Tessel?"

"I fear not, m'lady." Mr. Tessel's voice, with a more pronounced brogue than his wife, seemed to have a calming effect on both the ladies. Mrs. Tessel relaxed the tension in her shoulders upon hearing her husband's reassuring voice, and Violet's brow smoothed. "Once Mrs. Little arrives, she'll know what's to be done. Me an' Mary's been through this thrice a'ready. We'll weather this'n, too."

"Very good. You have our best wishes and our prayers for Mrs. Tessel's and the baby's safety. Would you prefer we left you, then?" Nathaniel observed that Violet's fear in this situation seemed to center on the welfare of her friend. Nathaniel, however, was experiencing his own fear regarding his wife's witnessing the pains of childbirth. How might Violet's constitution endure if she was to witness too much of the woman's struggles? *While I've never myself witnessed it, all that I hear suggests that birth is rather – indelicate.*

Mr. Tessel immediately nodded gratefully and crouched by his wife's side as she sat in the chair. Nathaniel was just about to usher his own wife from the cottage when Mrs. Tessel's hand shot out, grasping Violet's wrist firmly. *Oh, no!* cried Nathaniel inwardly. *She wants Violet to stay!*

"Violet," panted the woman, "thank ye kindly for comin' today. I am terrible sorry—" and here another pain seized the woman. She drew several deep breaths, a fine sheen emerging on her forehead, and after a moment was able to continue, albeit in a panting voice. "I'm sure'n sorry for our visit to end so, and I'd count it a right blessing if you'd come again."

Violet's face broke into a soft smile as she said, "I would be delighted to call on you after your little one has been welcomed into the world. Good-bye, dear, God bless you!" She placed a brief kiss on the woman's forehead, tenderly smoothing away some dampened hair as she did so.

Mrs. Tessel was once again overcome with a pain and unable to answer, but she managed a brief smile before the agony grew more intense. It was with great relief that Nathaniel finally quit the cottage with Violet.

"Are you well, dearest?" asked Nathaniel, drawing Violet's hand through his arm. "I myself feel rather tried, having witnessed Mrs. Tessel's pain."

"Oh, yes, I feel quite well, thank you." She sighed deeply. "I wish that I could spare her the pain, but what a blessing! To be with a woman, so shortly before she brings a new life into this world. I hope someday I—" But her voice faltered as a deep blush bloomed across her face, her eyes widening.

Nathaniel felt his heart leap within his chest, but resisted the urge to respond verbally to what she had said. Instead, he observed, "Mr.

Brown has not yet returned with the carriage. I suppose our choices are to either walk or ride."

"Which horses would we ride?" Violet looked about her, but only Nathaniel's horse could be seen, tied in front of the cottage.

"We shall ride together on Hannibal."

"I believe that I would prefer to walk," she faltered. "I am not much of a horsewoman."

"I will be riding with you, so that does not signify in the least."

"None of my protestations signify, do they?" she asked with a touch of humor to her voice. At his questioning gaze, she continued, "You said in the barn that even the imminent birth of the newest Tessel was not sufficient reason to disregard your orders, even when I believed it ought to be. And now it does not signify that I am not an accomplished horsewoman."

"I see." Nathaniel led her to the side of the horse. "If you truly have strong objections to riding with me, then I will say no more and we shall walk. However, allow me to warn you that Hannibal here will not be pleased to walk sedately along the entire way home." Nathaniel chose not to include that he might easily leave the horse in the Tessel barn to be retrieved later by the groom. "And I will not tolerate your walking alone."

With a dramatic sigh, Violet teased, "I am not so selfish as to disregard your fine animal's comfort, my lord, so it seems that I have no choice but to ride with you."

Nathaniel held his grin in check until he had situated her on the horse's back and she was arranging her skirts, her face turned from his own. He mounted the horse in front of her and instructed Violet to hold him firmly about his waist. She grasped the sides of his coat, trying to maintain some sort of distance between them. *I suppose she would believe herself to be more comfortable situated in this manner,* thought Nathaniel. *Even so, it is not the surest method of remaining atop the horse.* Gently, he disentangled her fingers from the fabric of his coat and drew them about his waist.

"You will be better able to keep your seat this way," he promised, glancing over his shoulder at her.

"Yes, my lord." It seemed she had reverted to the more formal manner of addressing him.

"Nathaniel." He could not keep the grin from his face. As he nudged the horse into motion, Violet lunged backward slightly, but her hands clasped in front of him prevented a fall. Nathaniel felt her tighten her grip and enjoyed feeling her embrace.

As they rode, Violet reminded him that he had promised to tell her how it was that he came upon Mr. Tessel.

"I found myself becoming – shall we say, *impatient* while waiting for the intelligence we hoped to gain from your visit, so at Mrs. Baker's kind suggestion, I decided to take a ride. As Hannibal and I went along, we found ourselves near the Tessel farm. Mr. Tessel was in the west field, harvesting grain. I stopped to speak with him, and we began talking about the rent and who authorized it. As it turns out, it was Faintree, my bailiff, who delivered the message. Tessel was most apologetic when he learned that I had authorized no raise in the rent, and confessed that no repairs had been performed, save those he had done at his own expense."

"How unfortunate!" was Violet's response, muffled against his coat.

"Indeed," said Nathaniel. "Mr. Tessel has agreed to accompany me in going to speak with the other tenants. I had considered sending letters, but not all are able to read well."

"I shall be glad for this to be sorted. All of the tenants I met with thus far were somewhat cold in their reception of me. I feared they simply did not like me," she admitted quietly, her voice muffled against his back. "I am sure that Mr. Tessel's presence shall be a great asset, and his clear approbation of you should also aid our cause."

"You are quite right, my dear," said Nathaniel, momentarily holding Hannibal's reins in one hand that he might lay his other over her own hands, clasped in front of him. He gave them an affectionate squeeze. "It is a sad truth that not all landowners are kind to their tenants, and even with my family's long-standing reputation of fairness and honor, it is without great difficulty that seeds of suspicion and distrust are planted. When I speak to them, it is my aim to explain that it was under false authority that those changes were made, and that I fully intend to rectify the situation. I shall be collecting lists of repairs needed, and compensating them at the time that we speak, in hopes of improving relations."

"But that will be such an expense!" came her still-muffled reply.

"Perhaps," he consented, "but we cannot allow anyone to suffer on account of this."

"How *good* you are!" Violet cried, tightening her hold on him, causing warmth to bloom in his chest.

"It is my duty," Nathaniel replied simply. He began to feel uncomfortable with the course of their conversation. After all, how *good* could he be while harboring such angry thoughts against his brother? While living with the guilt from *that evening?* After several moments, he composed himself and asked, "Did you have a nice visit with Mrs. Tessel?"

"Yes, it was lovely. That is, until her pains began." Violet shifted on the horse behind him.

"Is all well?" he asked.

"Certainly. I was beginning to slip a bit, but am fine now."

"I see."

Several more minutes passed, but then it was Violet who broke the silence. "Why did you not allow the coachman to leave me at the Tessel's? It is not a long walk from their home to ours. I walked to the village all week."

They had arrived at the back of the gardens and Nathaniel dismounted before turning to assist Violet. Once her feet hit the grass, he did not release his hold on her waist, but held her firmly until she finally looked into his face.

"You did agree to remain indoors to or take someone along to ensure your safety. I had not wanted to frighten you with particulars, but perhaps an explanation would be best." Her open, trusting gaze warmed Nathaniel's heart. "John made some threats when I was in London, and the man I had tracking him has not seen him for several days. I feared that he might have come here to make good on his words."

Violet sagged and might have fallen to the ground had he not held her. Her voice trembled as she asked, "Do you...do you think he might come still?"

"I do not know, though the fact that he has not yet gives me hope that it was strong drink which spoke, and that he has no true intent to cause harm."

"Oh." Violet's eyes, which had been filled with fear a moment ago, stared up at his face for the space of several breaths before she blinked and stepped back from his embrace. "We...we ought to be going in. I intend to ask Peche to prepare soup and perhaps a hen for the Tessels, and I hope to have time to begin several gowns for the baby before dinner."

Nathaniel felt disappointment at her leaving him so suddenly, but knew that there was sense to what she said. "Very well, my dear. I'll not detain you."

As he watched her walk up the steps to the house, his heart was filled with gratitude for such a kind-hearted wife. She seemed to be entirely moved by compassion to assist the Tessels, and he was certain that as their relations with the other tenants improved, she would be similarly caring toward them. Nathaniel remembered a time when he was more concerned with his fellow man, but the anger and disappointment of the last few years had created such a fog in his head that he was unable to do much of anything beyond fulfilling his duty, and surviving. While Violet's entering into his life had helped in dissipating some of the fog, he knew there was still a great deal which needed to change in his life before he could be perfectly content and healed from what had happened those several years ago.

Eleven

VIOLET WAS QUITE fatigued from the adventures of the past two days: harvesting peas one day, and then the visit with Mrs. Tessel the next, which had such an exciting ending. Still, she managed to send soup and three gowns for the baby the following day, and a hen, a basket of vegetables, and bread the next. A short but sincere note of thanks was received the evening of the third day, expressing the family's gratitude.

Signore Peche, a rather stringent adherent of order, agreed to Violet's request that something be sent at least three times each week for the next several weeks. It certainly did not hurt that she preceded the request with an effusive praise of the healing qualities of his soups. A note from the young countess often accompanied the food, inquiring after Mrs. Tessel's health, the baby's, or the family in general. Each missive was given a reply, sometimes detailing a new thing that baby Ruth had done or some comical comment that the elder children had made. Violet herself brought the food once each week, but these visits grew increasingly disturbing.

Mrs. Tessel, while professing a happiness to see her each week, grew more and more withdrawn. Her eyes slowly lost their brilliance and her hair grew dull and flat. Her gowns seemed to become looser and looser on her frame, until it seemed they would swallow her. One month after baby Ruth was born, Violet decided to broach the subject with her husband.

As they rode to services at the church in the village one chilly morning in early October, they were discussing news of the village. One of the farmers had recently acquired a set of prized ewes, and Mrs. Green, one of the widows living in a cottage near the village, had come down with a slight fever.

After she shared that the widow's fever was falling as of yesterday afternoon, he asked, "Did my mother call on you again this week?"

"No, I went to see her after leaving Mrs. Green." Violet smiled as she spoke.

"Indeed?" She saw from the corner of her eye that he turned upon his seat a bit to face her as he spoke.

"Yes, it was most pleasant."

"To be sure," he said while claiming her gloved hand in his own. "Mama is an excellent hostess, especially when she delights so much in the company."

"In me?" Violet was surprised. Her mama had frequently told her that she was rather dull company.

Lord Reymes' smile was warm as he began to use his other hand to trace the embroidered pattern on the back of Violet's glove. "Oh yes, she has told me several times how fortunate it is that you are my wife."

All Violet could manage was a wondering "Oh." When his fingers traced the scalloped edge of her glove around to the inside of her wrist, Violet was unable to suppress a small shiver.

"Are you warm enough, darling?" he asked. "It is rather brisk today."

Violet fingered the collar of her fur-lined pelisse before replying, "I am, thank you." Lord Reymes had brought the warm coat for her from the mantua-maker in the village as an unexpected gift. He really was kind and she counted herself as blessed to have such a caring husband, who supported her in aiding her friends and others in need. Oh! She had been meaning to ask him about Mrs. Tessel! "But please, Nathaniel, you have distracted me! First morning visits and now the weather. There is a subject I have been meaning to discuss with you. I am concerned for Mrs. Tessel's health. Has it escaped your notice that she has not yet begun attending services again?"

Lord Reymes – although she attempted to do as he requested and address him as Nathaniel for part of their time together, at the least, Violet was still able to think of him only as Lord Reymes – finally ceased his attentions to her hand when he drew said hand through his arm, patting it gently as he replied, "Darling, do not worry. I daresay it is a difficult thing for a woman who has given birth, and with two little ones to see to, besides."

Violet nodded. "True, my— er, Nathaniel."

"Your Nathaniel?" he queried. She felt his eyes on her and peeked around the brim of her bonnet at his face. His lips were quirked into a playful grin that set her heart aflutter.

After several agonizing attempts, Violet found her voice. "I-I um, I didn't, that is—" It seemed her voice had slipped away from her again before she could verbalize any sort of response.

Lord Reymes, sniggering, slipped an arm about her shoulders and bent down to place a kiss upon her cheek. Violet held her breath, fearing, hoping. But he simply settled back against the cushion again, a small, contented smile upon his handsome face.

Throughout the rest of the ride to the small country parish, Violet was left to her thoughts – which had once again wandered from their original course. Her husband's attentions were disconcerting, but she found that she was much better able to recover than when he had first started. She also was surprised to discover that she was beginning to enjoy them and – what shocked her further! – that she at times desired to initiate a kiss. She of course did not, but she was amazed at her anticipation of those intimate moments. All this tumbled through her head as they rode on, but she knew that dwelling on those thoughts would be of no benefit to her state of mind. She turned to prayer for the present and gave the service her full attention once they were settled in the pew.

The vicar spoke of the faith of Abraham. Violet was glad to be reminded of God providing for the man of faith. Even when Abraham did not act with faith, God proved faithful.

At the conclusion of the service, Lord Reymes escorted Violet through the throng of people to the door. They greeted the vicar and stepped out into the chilly air, making their way to the grassy area where their carriage was waiting. Just as Lord Reymes was about to hand her into the equipage, Violet spotted Mr. Tessel.

Turning abruptly, she teetered and nearly lost her balance. Lord Reymes' steadying hand was there, however, supporting her arm until she regained her balance and the blush had cooled on her face.

"I saw Mr. Tessel over there, helping the children into his wagon," she said by way of explanation.

"And you wish to speak to him?" asked her husband.

"Yes, if you do not mind a brief delay."

Lord Reymes' smile was warm enough to chase away the chill in the air. He offered her his arm and without a word, the couple moved to greet Mr. Tessel.

"Good day, Mr. Tessel!" called Lord Reymes as the man pulled himself into the wagon. When he heard the voice, he turned his head, after settling himself into his seat.

"My lord Reymes! My lady! A pleasure," he said, half-standing and doffing his hat at the same time. "The weather certainly has taken a turn, eh?"

"Yes it has," agreed Violet. "Good morning, Abraham, Miriam." The children's red-gold hair shone in the sunlight. "Pray, how is Mrs. Tessel? I do not see her here today."

Mr. Tessel averted his eyes briefly before answering, "No, m'lady. She's feeling rather poorly of late."

"Oh dear, I had feared as much. Is there no one in either of your family who might see to the children for a time, that she may rest?" Violet's concern was evident in her face and voice, as well as in the way that her hand suddenly clutched at Lord Reymes' arm.

"No, m'lady," said he with a slow shake of his head. "She were raised by an unwilling aunt on account o' her folks perishin' when she were a wee babe. My sister's all what's left o' my family, an' her husband has taken her to Canada."

"I am sorry, Mr. Tessel," said Violet. "Do you think she will be improving within the near future?"

"I canna' say," began the man. He cleared his throat, then continued. "She's tired quite a lot, and don't sleep well." In a lower voice, he added, "And her bleedin's yet to slow."

Violet felt her heart sink within her. A quick glance at Lord Reymes' tense face and she was struck with the thought that he might be about to give the man a dressing-down for speaking thus to a lady. Violet spoke up quickly to prevent.

"And I suppose with little Abraham and Miriam, she cannot rest very much at all, can she? Never mind preserving food for winter."

"No, m'lady – and the little ones are near grown from their clothes a'ready, so she has sewing to do when she ain't workin' on the food. Sure'n I can't help her, for I have my own work to prepare the farm for winter, with the help of my hired man, o' course. My poor wife is truly in a bad way." Mr. Tessel paused, his Adam's apple bobbing several times. When he spoke again, his voice shook with emotion. "I begin to fear for her life."

"Has the doctor not been called to see her?" asked Lord Reymes.

"No, m' lor'." Mr. Tessel shook his head and lowered his eyes. "We have not the resources to pay him."

"I shall send my physician to her tomorrow, Mr. Tessel."

"Oh thank you, Nathaniel!" cried Violet, reaching for and clasping his hand. His face, alight with something Violet could not quite identify, smiled at her. After a brief moment, she turned back to the man sitting upon the wagon. "Please tell Mrs. Tessel that I shall call on her tomorrow evening, before dinner is served; I would like to hear what Dr. Curteys does for her, if it wouldn't be a problem."

"To be sure, m' lady." The children were beginning to squirm and Mr. Tessel took up the lines, nodding at the couple. "I thank you for asking after my Mary."

Violet smiled warmly and curtsied as Lord Reymes bowed. Her husband escorted her back to their carriage and after handing her up, he did not release her hand. As they rode back to Bainscroft, he continued to hold her hand, gently caressing and occasionally placing kisses on her gloved fingers. Violet began the ride by attempting to discuss with him her friend's condition, but her husband was in no mood to speak. Before long, she fell quiet for the remainder of the time, trying not to enjoy his attentions more than she felt was appropriate.

The staff was busy, making the nursery ready. There were new linens to be got, the coverings to be removed from the furniture, and everything cleaned thoroughly. Nathaniel was rather baffled as to how it happened, but the two young Tessels were coming for an extended visit. After the doctor left Mrs. Tessel, Nathaniel accompanied Violet to call on the family; what they found seemed to break his wife's tender heart.

Mrs. Tessel was reclining on a sofa in the family's small parlor, holding little Ruth. Even to Nathaniel's usually unobservant eye, the mother did seem rather sickly. Later, when Violet was lamenting her friend's state of ill-health, Mrs. Tessel's sunken eyes, sallow complexion, shrunken frame with sagging dress were all pointed out to his notice. Mr. Tessel told them that the doctor recommended rest, and Violet cried with uncharacteristic indignation, "But how *is* she to rest, with all that must be done?" Turning her lovely eyes with their thick fringe of lashes toward Nathaniel, he knew that whatever she was about to ask, he would give her without hesitation. "Might I come to help her?"

Except that. Recalling Violet's ruined dress after picking peas, the fatigue which seemed to assail her immediately after, together with her many household duties at Bainscroft, he did not wish to have her assisting in this particular manner. "Why do we not send one or two of the kitchen servants instead?" he offered.

"Oh, yes!" she answered. "They should be infinitely better helpers, as they are already knowledgeable of the tasks to be done."

The visit turned out to be of short duration, as Mrs. Tessel tired quickly. After they had taken leave of the home, just before Nathaniel was about to hand her into the carriage, Violet turned abruptly, her face mere inches from his own. "Might we offer to have little Abraham and Miriam come to stay with us, while Mrs. Tessel rests?"

Nathaniel scarcely heard her initially, though he strove valiantly to heed her words and not the way her breath flitted over his skin as he stood, his head bent downward over her upturned face. *Control, man! She has no idea of the manner in which she affects you.* With effort, he was able to force his feet to step back from her before he said, "They are too young to work, dearest."

"Oh no, of course not to work." Violet smiled. "How absurd! I meant that they should be our *guests.*"

"I see."

"And then Mrs. Tessel may have the rest she needs. Might I go directly to inquire as to whether this would be agreeable to the family?"

Nathaniel glanced quickly about to be sure no eyes were watching them. Seeing the driver waiting with the carriage had his face turned away, he placed a light kiss upon her nose and said, "Certainly. I shall await you here."

She returned from the cottage quickly, her face glowing with happiness. In the carriage, as they returned home, Violet relayed to her husband what plans had been hastily made with the Tessels. Though they both protested that they could not impose so greatly, she had assured them that it would be no difficulty, and she would bring the children frequently to see their mama. She was to retrieve the children in two days' time, and they would remain at Bainscroft for at least a month, at which time future plans would be made in accordance with how Mrs. Tessel's recovery progressed. She also managed to inform the couple politely but firmly (so as to forestall any objection which either might raise) that at least two of the

Bainscroft kitchen staff would arrive tomorrow to aid in the housework until either the food was put up or until Mrs. Tessel was quite recovered.

As she spoke, Nathaniel could see the excitement at the plan shining in his wife's eyes. He was also sensible to the demands such an endeavor would place upon her, and he felt compelled to suggest a way in which her burden might be eased.

The next morning, the house was a flurry of preparations. Nathaniel was looking for Violet to ask whether a housemaid or two might be spared to sit with Mrs. Tessel while Mr. Tessel accompanied him in speaking with the other tenants. When he finally spotted her in the upstairs hallway, though, and observed her flushed face, untidy hair, and slightly wild eyes, another question sprang to his lips.

"My love, do you think that we ought to bring on a nurse for the children? I do not wish you to overly tire yourself with their care."

She paused before answering, conflict clear upon her lovely face.

"I should like to keep the children with me as much as possible," she finally said, "but perhaps it would be beneficial to have someone who could see to their needs if I am needed elsewhere. After all, I cannot very well cease to meet with Peche about the menu and Mrs. Baker about the household, and I simply *must* continue my visits with the tenants, should there be any need of food or clothing – Mrs. Smith down by the river has nearly reached the end of *her* confinement, you know – and seeing to the updates to the house which *you* seem to desire so very much–" she offered a teasing smile here "–and it really would not do to pull the household staff from their regular duties to mind the children when I am otherwise occupied."

Nathaniel smiled at her, impressed with her sense. "I shall ask Mrs. Baker to begin looking for someone, but perhaps you would care to interview the candidates along with her?"

"Oh, yes, I should like that very much." Violet's gaze on him was soft and he found his heart quickening at the sight.

"M'lady," interrupted one of the housemaids, "Mrs. Baker sent me to ask that you come see the new curtains in the nursery; they've just been put up."

With an apologetic smile to him, Violet hurried off after the girl.

"I suppose sending for one of the maids to sit with Mrs. Tessel is out of the question," Nathaniel said to the empty hall. Deciding instead to hire two girls from the village for that purpose, he ordered his horse be readied and prepared for a long day of smoothing things over with the disgruntled populace living upon his land.

By the end of the day, he had lists of current rates of rent, old rates of rent, and repairs needed. Thankfully, the list which concerned him most – that of embittered tenants – had disappeared. Nathaniel gave the lists to his steward and asked the man to compare the rents and make necessary adjustments. As the estate was doing well and he was in no need of increased income, Nathaniel was of half a mind to lower the rents, in addition to issuing reimbursements for the falsely-charged rent. He would need to know first, though, what the totals would be, and what repairs would be funded.

With all the recent flurry of activity preparing for the arrival of the children, Nathaniel was surprised that even his valet could be spared to assist him in dressing the morning of their arrival. Once he had finished shaving, he donned a white shirt laid out by his valet – the one Violet had sewn for him, as per his request. After fastening the snug-fitting buff pantaloons, Nathaniel began tying his cravat.

As he was in the process of configuring the length of starched muslin into a deceivingly intricate design, a soft knock sounded on his door.

"Enter!" he called, without fumbling in the process of tying. All was lost, though, when he glanced in the direction of the door. Violet stood in the opening, dressed in a soft pink gown that reminded him of a rose-petal in the spring. His fingers fumbled and the knot fell apart in a limp cascade down his chest. With a sigh, he called, "Griffin! Another neck cloth, if you please." Turning to his wife he said, "Good morning, my love. Do come in."

Violet hesitated at his door before stepping over the threshold and into his dressing room. He realized that she had not been inside his bedchamber since that day he departed for London, which now seemed ages ago.

"What a lovely surprise this morning." He smiled at her as he accepted a fresh neck cloth from his valet. "Thank you, Griffin. Please, excuse us a moment."

Griffin bowed and exited, softly closing the door behind him, a mild look of alarm in his eyes at being dismissed mid-dressing.

Nathaniel smiled apologetically at his wife before back to his looking-glass to tie his cravat. As he did so, he glimpsed his wife watching him with what he thought might be admiration. He nearly ruined another neck-cloth when he saw it. Determined to finish in a timely manner, though, Nathaniel set his mind upon his task. Once the cravat was tied to his satisfaction (though perhaps not to his valet's), he hurried into a pale blue waistcoat and struggled into his coat of dark blue superfine. *Here is an instance in which I should like very much for the fashion of the day to be just a bit less fitted. I desire earnestly to attend my wife, and this blasted coat is creating the most absurd delay!*

Coat finally in place, Nathaniel slowly approached Violet. Stopping a mere foot from her, he offered a small bow, cleared his throat, and asked "How may I be of service, my lady?"

His wife's face shone with her amusement. "I wished," said she, clasping her hands behind her, "to express my heartfelt thanks for your generosity toward the children."

"I thank you, dearest, but surely you know that it is your generosity and not mine." He smiled at her with love and admiration for her compassion overflowing in his heart. "To be sure, I never should have thought to invite them to stay here."

Brow slightly furrowed, she stepped closer and raised her hands to grasp gently at the lapels of his coat. "You do not mind terribly, do you?" Violet's voice betrayed worry for a moment, which was quickly overcome. She again stepped minutely closer to him as she released and smoothed his lapels, then rested her hands lightly on his chest. "Of course you do not. You are so kind that it would never occur to you to be put out with me for asking, would it?"

Her smiling, shining eyes and prettily shaped lips also formed into a smile worked in tandem to melt any annoyance he might have secretly harbored with the arrangement. "My love, I cannot claim such virtues as you bestow upon me, but allow me to assure you that I am far from feeling put out."

Nathaniel was about to gather her into his arms when she moved a few paces away and spoke again.

"Do you recall how distraught I was last night that the interviews yesterday were not met with success? It is providential, then, that Mrs. Baker has just now mentioned to me that her cousin, Miss Stokes, is seeking a position somewhere." Violet smiled radiantly before continuing. "I believe she will be an excellent nurse for the Tessel children. She has five younger siblings, three of whom are significantly younger than she, and whom she has aided in rearing. I wished to seek your approval before asking Mrs. Baker to send for her."

"Does this Miss Stokes come with references?" asked Nathaniel.

"Yes, in addition to Mrs. Baker's own glowing recommendation. She is rather young, for a nurse, but I've read the recommendations and believe she would be an excellent choice."

"Is she aware that the position is temporary?"

"She is, but Mrs. Baker and I did discuss the possibility of keeping her on in an alternate capacity, if she should desire it. The house can certainly support an assistant to Mrs. Baker or another upper housemaid."

"Quite true."

"Besides..." When Violet did not speak right away, but stood fidgeting with her hands and blushing furiously, Nathaniel raised his brows and silently entreated her to continue. "It may be that before very long, we shall have need of Miss Stokes' services ourselves."

Nathaniel was unsure what to say. Yes, he yearned for the day that Violet would welcome him in that manner. But it seemed so far off that the idea of seeking someone to fill the position of nurse to their children had not even entered into his consideration. *Her behavior toward me certainly never has suggested that she might be desirous of that activity in the near future. It cannot be possible that she does not know how it is that a baby comes to be, can it?*

"You, ah, you do know what is necessary for us to *need* a nurse, do you not?" The words left his mouth before he could stop them.

"A baby?" said Violet, confusion creasing her features. "What else would a nurse be responsible for?"

"Of course." Nathaniel paused a moment, considering how to proceed. "I only meant what is necessary for that baby to exist."

"Oh! Oh, yes, my mama did speak with me." Nathaniel feared that his own face reflected her blush for the first time in their acquaintance. "I, er- I merely meant that I had supposed that you would want an heir sooner rather than later, and – but if not, I certainly will not object, I only meant that I expected that *you* expected, or not that you *expected* precisely, but that you *should* or *might* expect..." Violet trailed off before suddenly burying her face in her hands and lamenting, "Oh, I do not know what you or I expect, or even what I mean to say!"

Nathaniel attempted to reassure her. "I believe I understand your meaning. We've time, and have yet to visit one another's chambers for...more than talking...so there has been no opportunity for us to have any immediate need of a nurse."

"Of course," murmured Violet, shyly peeking up from her hands. After a pause, she asked in a hesitant voice, "I've been wondering...do most husbands and wives of your...*our* station – that is, I have never been a wife, and do not know – do most usually keep...separate bedchambers?" With each stumbled-over word, her face grew more and more flushed, until it was brighter than he had ever seen it. The determination about her mouth as she spoke hinted at the likelihood that she did not want to ask, but felt it necessary.

"Some do," Nathaniel answered carefully. *Is she wanting...* "Why do you ask?"

"Well, my own mama and papa shared one, and I believe that the Tessels do, and my brother and his wife, as well as Aunt and Uncle Doberly..." Her voice trailed and she lowered her eyes.

"Are you concerned that our marriage is not like other marriages?" he asked in as gentle a voice as he could muster, desperately hoping the excitement creeping into his heart had not yet found its way into his voice. *Just a moment ago, we were discussing the potential of future progeny, and while I am rather surprised that it is she who broaches this subject, this is a rather logical next step from the previous conversation.*

"Perhaps." Violet raised her head to once again meet Nathaniel's gaze. "I think, though, that I am more concerned for young Abraham and Miriam."

Was I dwelling on the glorious thought of conjugal felicity, wondered Nathaniel, *and missed a part of the conversation?* "Beg pardon?"

"You see, they are used to their mama and papa sharing a chamber."

"We are not their mama and papa." Nathaniel feared that perhaps he was shooting himself in the foot. *Does it matter why, if she wants to join me in sharing this chamber?*

Violet nodded. "Yes, you are right." He suspected she was relieved but trying to hide it.

Nathaniel wished he could retrieve the words he had spoken. In a futile attempt to retract them, he found himself saying, "You do draw my attention to another matter, though, Violet." At her questioning gaze, he continued, "I do not mind the staff knowing the nature of our relationship, for they are familiar with how this marriage came about, and are, as you earlier observed, remarkably discreet. But, as for the tenants – and the rest of the neighborhood for that matter – I would like to keep at bay any suspicion that we are not yet as *close* as most couples would be at this point in their marriage." *Perhaps I oughtn't mention that sharing a bedchamber will also allow me to know that she is safe while she sleeps.*

Understanding dawned in Violet's eyes. "You think the children might innocently reveal – I see. Shall I ask Jane to move my things into your dressing room?"

Nathaniel was rather surprised at the ease with which she agreed to share a chamber with him; he was required to pretend to consider the matter for a moment while he composed himself from his shock. At length, he said, "As my parents before me shared this chamber, there is a dressing room for your own use, on the other side of the bedchamber. Ask Jane to have your things moved; we will decorate it accordingly later."

"Certainly. Anything else, my l—er, Nathaniel?"

Nathaniel closed the short distance between them and took her hands in his, raising them to his lips. "Are you quite certain that you wish this? It is not my desire that you should feel forced into anything."

"Oh, no. I agree that we should give all appearance of being of one accord." Violet smiled up at him, then her smile faded and her eyes widened. "Forgive me! I do not mean to say that we are not. Er, I know that, well... We are, that is, I am, ah –"

Nathaniel ended her fumbling words by gently pressing his smiling lips against her own.

Preparations for the young Tessel children were being made with remarkable ease and efficiency; nearly everything had been accomplished a full day before the young Tessel's arrival, and it was after several servants were finished with their morning tasks that Violet asked for her things to be moved.

She was quite pleased with the staff and wasted no time in conveying her pleasure to Mrs. Baker. As they had taken to doing when discussing the household, Violet and Mrs. Baker sat in the housekeeper's parlor, a small room below-stairs, which was adjacent to the servant's chamber. Mrs. Baker had set out a modest tea, and the two were settled with their cups and biscuits before Violet spoke.

"I commend you, Mrs. Baker, on the excellent staff you manage. The preparations for our young visitors have been made with great efficiency and everyone is so pleasant and kind, in spite of the extra work."

"My lady must know that the entirety of the staff would gladly do anything you asked of them," Mrs. Baker answered with an affectionate smile.

"That cannot be true!" protested Violet with a laugh.

"Indeed it is," returned the housekeeper kindly. "We had all but despaired that the master would choose a bride, and we all feared if he did, she would be a demanding, unfeeling beauty, for then his heart would be in no danger if that were the case."

Violet wished desperately to ask what the elder woman meant by her words, but could not muster the courage. *Does she mean to imply that Lord Reymes is in no manner attached to me, if they expected him to marry a woman whom he could never love? But why then are his attentions so marked? And his kisses are rather ardent. Oh, I feel my face heating! I do hope that Mrs. Baker cannot guess at my thoughts; she looks at me with such serious eyes! But still a kind expression. Perhaps she means to say that Lord Reymes might, in time, learn to love me? That I am not the cold but beautiful wife they had expected him to take?*

But Mrs. Baker spoke again, pulling Violet from her confused thoughts. "Surely you know that the entirety of the staff are most pleased to be in your service, my lady."

She offered, "Then I suppose it explains why we all get on so well. I must tell you how pleased I am with your suggestion of sending for your cousin to care for the children."

"Her reply to my express arrived just a moment before you joined me. She is quite eager to come and meet the children. Due to the distance she must travel, she will not arrive until two days hence."

"That will do nicely. I am more than content to keep the children with me tomorrow and the following day until she arrives and is settled enough to commence her duties."

"That is very generous of you, my lady," said Mrs. Baker. "Would you rather that I keep the wee dears, though?"

"Oh, no, Mrs. Baker. I am quite able. And I shall enjoy it immensely. I used to care for my cousin Charlotte when our two families visited."

"If I may be so bold, my lady, how is it that your family visited Doberly House so often in your childhood, and yet never met with my lord Reymes? Of course, he was simply the Honorable Nathaniel Peyton at the time. Still, he and his brother both played in the countryside, and I should have thought that your paths had crossed at some point."

"As Miss Doberly was quite a bit younger than I was for a while, we were required to remain close to the house for quite a while. Once she was older, we did not often leave the grounds of Doberly House; she wished to, but I was fearful of reprimand."

"She is fortunate to have such a conscientious cousin."

"And I am fortunate to have such an adventurous one. I should never have done more than sit in the garden and read had it not been for her influence." Violet could not help but smile at the fond memories that filled her mind of rambles with her cousin. "We did venture beyond the grounds on occasion. On one such excursion, I recall that we encountered two young men. They were riding their horses, and stopped to help when Charlotte tripped and her boot became stuck on a fallen log."

"That sounds like what the master would have done as a youth. It may have been him and his brother, or p'haps a school friend of his."

"I fear I do not recall the name of either young man. Then, and even now, I am quite overcome by shyness when strangers speak to me, and I have difficulty attending their words."

"Mayhap Charlotte remembers? How romantic if you married the young man who came to your aid so many years ago."

Violet laughed lightly before replying, "Yes, though I never should have suspected at the time that I should one day be his wife. And we did dance at Almack's two years past, though I've yet to bring it to his recollection. I fear he will feel badly not remembering and I've no wish to cause him discomfort."

Mrs. Baker's smile grew as she said, "I did once hear him mumbling to himself about you seeming familiar. If I may be so bold, you ought to ask him if he recalls coming to the aid of two maidens when home on holiday from school."

"Perhaps." Violet declined when Mrs. Baker offered another biscuit before adding, "I am surprised, looking back now, that it was Charlotte and not I who needed aid. I was always far clumsier than she when we walked."

"Indeed?" asked Mrs. Baker.

"Oh yes. I suppose it was part of my hesitance in going for longer rambles off of my aunt and uncle's land. Come to think of it, I believe that I shall ask her to come visit soon after the children arrive. She is of an adventurous spirit, and I believe the children would greatly enjoy meeting her."

Their *tête-à-tête* was concluded soon after, and both women returned to their respective duties.

Shortly after noon, Violet took the carriage to fetch the children. There had been two sacks packed with their small clothing, along with each child's favorite toy. Abraham did his best to be the young man that he knew his mama and papa wished him to be, but once they were settled in the carriage, his small blue eyes flooded and tears began trickling down his freckled cheeks.

"I miss Mama!" he cried, as Violet put a gentle arm about the small boy. She held Miriam upon her lap with her other arm.

"Oh do not cry, dearest. We shall see your mama tomorrow! She must rest now, so that she will be ready when you go back home!" Abraham rubbed his fists into his eyes and took several shuddering gulps of air before he seemed to be better. Violet told him of all the fun they should have, the horses and the gardens and the books. By the time they reached the house, his mood was much improved. Miriam, being quite young, did not fully understand what was happening. She was relatively content to sit on the pretty lady's lap and eat a biscuit.

Violet assisted Mrs. Baker in settling the two children in the nursery and then sent for her husband. He had promised at breakfast that he would come to welcome them upon their arrival.

"How d'ye do, m'lord Reymes?" asked the young boy.

"Young Mr. Tessel. I see you have found Old Brown Horse." Lord Reymes smiled at the boy, who was holding an ancient cloth animal of dubious identity. "He was a favorite of mine when I was a boy."

"'e's a bang-up hack, m'lord!" The small boy grinned. "Me papa and mama call me by the name of Abie, an' so may you."

"Do they now? I shall endeavor to remember." Violet met Lord Reymes' smiling gaze from across the room where she sat with Miriam on the floor, playing with a small doll. "Lady Reymes, would you accompany me into the dining room for a moment? The new wallpaper has been hung."

"Certainly." After the sitting room's decoration had been completed, Lord Reymes asked her to choose new wall-coverings, draperies, and furniture for the dining hall. He claimed that the moldings and floor were still of good quality and style, but the other items were showing signs of wear. "Abie and Miriam, Mrs. Baker will wait with you until I return." Violet smiled brightly at the children.

"We'll be all right and tight, Lady Reymes. See you in a trice!" Abraham returned to Old Brown Horse and Miriam went easily into Mrs. Baker's arms. Lord Reymes offered his hand to Violet, assisting her in rising from the floor.

After the door was closed behind them, Violet said, "It seems young Abie has decided to make the best of the situation and not mourn the brief separation from his mother." Lord Reymes' answering grin was warm.

When they arrived at the dining hall, he opened the door and ushered her into the room. Violet gazed around at the lovely design on the walls, the scrolling patterns in varying shades of green giving the room an entirely different character than it had before. The previous paper had deep blue and purple stripes accented by scrolling gold patterns within each stripe, oppressive in its opulence. New drapes still were to be hung, and Lord Reymes had assisted her in choosing new furniture for the room.

A brief knock on the door announced Mr. Garand's entrance. "My lord, Lady Reymes' personal effects have been relocated to her new dressing room. Is there anything else required at present?"

When Lord Reymes deferred to her, Violet said, "Thank you, no, Mr. Garand."

"Very good, my lord, my lady." The stoic butler's voice was impassive, but the smallest of smiles on his face made Violet feel as though she had won the approval of the grandfatherly man.

After the door had closed at Mr. Garand's exit, Violet found herself admitting quite freely, "I must say, had someone informed me a year past that today I should be a countess overseeing the remaking of my husband's dining room, I doubt that I should have believed him."

Lord Reymes chuckled, but appeared to be mildly discomfited.

"Pray, is something amiss, Nathaniel?"

Taking her into his arms, he evaded her question. "I *delight* in hearing you address me by my Christian name."

"You are not answering my question," she chided him playfully.

With a sigh, he shook his head and released her. Violet was mildly alarmed; he rarely, if ever, released her from an embrace without some show of reluctance. Her concern grew as he silently led her out of the dining room, up the stairs, and into their chamber. Once there, he closed the door and turned to her before speaking.

"I am sorry, Violet, for this odd behavior." He scowled lightly and reached a hand up to grasp the back of his neck. "It is a rare occasion that I am reminded that I am an earl."

"But at balls, surely you are announced as the Earl of Bainscroft. And when someone is introduced to you, you are addressed as the same, are you not?"

"While that is true, it is seldom brought up in my house. When in company, I am able to assume the persona which others would expect of an earl – the hauteur which prevents anyone from thinking they can behave in a familiar manner – it helps prepare me for it. Here, I am unused to such references."

"But the staff always says 'my lord'."

"But nothing else." His voice had risen in volume, and his face grew red as he spoke. "In my home, I do not have to endure the simpering fools who would befriend me only due to my title!"

"I-I am sorry, Lord Reymes. Are you upset with me?" she asked, moving to stand beside the bed. She hoped he did not suspect her of caring more for his title than she did for him. "It is no matter to me, truly, that you are an earl. Indeed, I had never set my sights on anything so grand as a titled husband, and is of little import to me."

"And yet my title is at the *crux* of the matter," Lord Reymes huffed out with a frustrated breath. His hands rose, long, strong fingers combing ruthlessly through his hair. "I had not intended to *be* an earl this soon. I had not wanted to make my bride a countess in the same moment that I made her a wife."

All fell into place, and Violet saw that her husband did not mourn his title, but his father. *Is something preventing him from healing?* Hoping for understanding, she whispered tentatively, "It has been two years."

Lord Reymes looked to contemplate her words, though his furrowed brow still bore the mark of his frustration. After a time, he moved to the bed and flopped down, sprawling on his back, the heels of his hands pressing into his eyes. It was disconcerting to see her usually-stoic husband behave in such an undignified manner. After several attempts at speaking, he finally managed in a voice raw with emotion, "It should not have happened when it did."

"Was not his death preceded by a lengthy illness?" she asked tentatively, but he did not answer. Instead, his breath became ragged and she though there may have been slight dampness seeping from beneath his hands.

Uncertainty pricked at Violet's heart, and she could not think of anything that might ease his agony. Moving to sit beside him on the bed, she reached out, grasping both his hands. Violet sat quietly, clasping his hands for several moments before releasing one in order to gently thread her fingers through his hair.

"I do not believe that your grief should end after of the time of mourning has passed," her gentle voice came to his ear. "Nor do I believe that it was made easier by seeing him ease into death. I merely mention this as a means of asking why you seem to have been shocked when it occurred."

The pain bloomed in his chest at her words even as the movements of her hands were a balm, contrasting sharply with the tumult inside of him. Just before attending his duty to greet the young Tessel children, he had received the final list of what restitution needed to be made with the tenants. The expenditures he was facing were quite a bit more than he had anticipated. While they would certainly weather it without extreme difficulty, it rankled that once again John was the source of such aggravation. As Violet knew none of this, and he did not wish to concern her, he allowed himself a self-deprecating smile as he rose up on one elbow. With his face so much closer to hers than it had been before, he saw Violet's eyes widen and her cheeks take on a pinkish hue. There was a distinct shift in who controlled the situation; it was no longer her, even though she still looked down at him from her seated position. Nathaniel raised a hand to run his fingers down the side of her face in a gentle caress.

"You are a comfort to me," was all he could manage to say. Suddenly and without any conscious decision, his lips were on the corner of her jaw, in the gentlest of touches, and she shivered. He withdrew as the ever-present guilt, born on that fateful night, grew and threatened to choke him. *How can I even contemplate conjugal felicity when the past presses upon me, upon my mother? What sort of man am I, to so easily reach for happiness when I caused such sorrow?*

Forcing his thoughts to the present, he said, "I of course was not shocked at his death. That did not, unfortunately, lessen the guilt."

"The guilt?" she questioned.

"Mm-hmm." Desperate for a way to ease the memory, he surged toward her, his lips once again seeking the skin of her face, scattering light kisses along her jaw.

His pain was intense, but the pleasure derived from loving his wife in this manner was enough to numb that pain, however fleetingly. He soon lost himself, scarcely aware of what he was doing and yet painfully conscious of what he was feeling: the smoothness of her skin beneath his slightly chapped lips, the quickness of her breath, the pounding of his heart. His hands alternately caressed her face and shoulders. Soon he was shifting again, supporting himself with his arms, that he might meet her lips with his own. Eyes closed, he lowered his head to place his lips upon her own. Rather than the soft, delicate body of his wife, though, he was met with a face full of bedclothes.

Confused and disoriented from the abruptly-broken spell to which he had succumbed, Nathaniel slowly raised himself onto his elbow, looking about the room for his wife. She stood near the door, smoothing her dress and hair with quick, nervous movements. He observed her draw a deep breath before she said, with a touch of humor in her voice, "As it seems you have no desire to further pursue this conversation, and I have promised the children an excursion into the garden, I fear I must leave you now."

Nathaniel was relieved that the enjoyable activities of the past few moments had served to deliver him from his doldrums. He felt tired, but also blessedly numb to the guilt – for the time being, at any rate. In response to Violet's teasing, he scowled as he sat upright. "Must you? I was rather enjoying myself."

Violet replied primly, "I really cannot arrive in the nursery with mussed hair and a rumpled gown."

"You managed to compose yourself quite nicely the evening we met," he rejoined.

This time, Violet's blush was immediate and unstoppable. "Though I cannot be certain, I should imagine that recovering from the undesirable advances of a stranger is rather not the same as recovering from the desirable attentions of one's husband."

Her words served to dampen his nearly playful mood. He stood and closed the five steps which separated them. He quickly clasped her hands and drew her near before raising them to his lips. He spoke from behind her knuckles. "Forgive me, Violet. It was unconscionably unfeeling of me to mention that, let alone make jest regarding it. I am thoroughly ashamed."

Before he could continue, Violet turned her hands to gently cover his mouth with her fingertips. "Do not trouble yourself on my account. Your words did not harm me, and even the events of that evening are fading in my memory."

"Are they?"

"Indeed. One must learn to live with what has befallen them, both good and bad. We may rejoice in the good and grow from the bad."

Nathaniel gently kissed her fingertips before lowering them in order to draw her nearer. "You show a maturity beyond your years."

"I am not so very much younger than you."

Nathaniel merely hummed his acquiescence to her statement before shaking his head slowly. "What am I to do, then, when rather than a past occurrence which has stopped, I am plagued by a recurring offense?" Nathaniel debated with himself regarding what to say. He had no desire to overburden her with the guilt of his past, certainly, but there was also a part of him which feared her reaction if she knew the full extent of his sins, of the true cause of his pain. He knew that his brother was an unabashed cad, but he secretly held more loathing for himself than for the other man. After a moment, he cowardly followed the path with less risk. "My brother has always been an unabashed user. As a child, he stole sweets from the kitchen. As a young man, he borrowed a great deal of my own money, as well as from other people, and never bothered to keep a record so as to repay it. He has taken advantage of many women, more than I know, to be sure. And now, as an adult, he has continued in this same track."

Violet looked on him with sympathy in her eyes as he spoke, but toward the end of his summary of complaints, her eyes took on a determined glint. When he had finished, she closed those eyes briefly and drew a breath before speaking.

"And who, Nathaniel, went without a sweet? Who repaid the lenders pressuring John for their money? And now who has married a woman who was disadvantaged by his usage of her? You are attempting to redeem a man who has no interest in redemption. And one whom you *cannot* redeem!"

Nathaniel felt something cold wash over him. *My guilt is as terrible as John's. How will she ever love me when she knows?* Aloud, he asked, "Are you saying that he is beyond even God's reach?"

"I said no such thing. I said that *you* cannot redeem him."

Her words, though spoken kindly and with concern and compassion in her voice and on her face, cut Nathaniel to his heart. *Have I so forgotten that You alone, Lord, are Sovereign that I left You out of my dealings with John? With even myself?* He could not continue the way his thoughts were proceeding, for it was a great deal too painful.

Sighing heavily, he admitted, "You are right, Violet." He smiled weakly at her. "May I walk you back to the children?"

"I thank you, but no." Her gentle smile soothed the sting of rejection. "It seems that you are in need of some time to yourself. I will be in the garden with the children if you need me. And as I see you are about to ask, yes, two footmen will accompany us."

Nathaniel smiled gratefully at her as he saw her to the door of their chambers. Desperate for the comfort of it, he quickly pressed his lips to hers before closing the door behind her. Lost in thought, he moved toward the small sitting room off of their bedchamber.

I know very well that I cannot save John, but I have been behaving as though that job lay upon my shoulders alone. He entered the room and stood before the window, staring without seeing. *And how I have tried to save him! Numerous times through our younger years, I have told him that he ought to mind the state of his soul – not that I was wrong in doing so, but to be so conceited that I thought it must be by* my *words that he would be reached. And to have let myself become so utterly despondent in these past two years that I even ceased prayers...for him or for anyone. This business with my father, with allowing myself one night of irresponsibility which ultimately led to his demise, and the guilt thereafter...I cannot bear this much longer.*

Too weary to stand longer, he sank into a chair and dropped his head into his hands.

Lord, I am quite lost. I've finally realized that I cannot ignore Your moving, Your direction in my life. But I still find myself struggling with so many things. I confess my pride and conceit and arrogance in thinking that it would be I who reach John, who saves him, when I cannot even save myself. You are the Savior, the One who turns men's hearts to you. Thank You for turning my heart to You. Keep me ever mindful that it is You who saves, and that I am merely Your servant. I ask that you continue to work on me, painful though it may be, that I would be a fit husband, and a caring son and brother, that my tenants and those who rely on my leading would be able to trust and respect me. Remove my guilt. Not because I deserve it, but because You promised to do so. And please, Lord, see fit to turn John's heart, as well. In spite of everything, he is my brother and I love him.

Nathaniel struggled against a pricking sensation behind his eyelids. While many men of his time indulged in open and extravagant and perhaps even public displays of emotion, he could not bring himself to be counted among their number. Nathaniel supposed he must be rather old-fashioned in that regard.

After regaining mastery over himself again, he picked up his Bible and read a portion of the one-hundred thirty-ninth Psalm. *You do know me, Lord, you know my tendency to take more upon myself than I ought, You know where I am and what I am about. You also know where Violet is; please, watch over her. Protect her, Lord, from any evil which might seek to harm her. Let your hand be upon John, as well. I pray, Lord, that he would see the dreadful evil which he allows to reign in his life and that he would be turned to You. I worry for John. I ask that if it please You, that You would use me as You see fit, in Your plan for his life.*

Peace, not from himself, soaked into Nathaniel's soul. Feeling much better than he had in ages, he determined to go to his study to begin assigning monies for the tenants when he remembered that Violet's things should be settled into her dressing room. He decided to look in to assure himself that everything had been seen to.

Upon entering the small chamber, he was struck by the difference between the delicate gown laid out on a low chest and the decoration of the room. The wooden moldings were all quite dark and the wall colors dreary. The chests of drawers and the highboy in the corner were all of a deep mahogany and stood ominously in the shadows. He recalled visiting his mother in this room as a very small boy, but the decoration of the room had been offset by vials of perfume on the dressing table, bonnets and hats set about on stands, and gowns overflowing from the chests. With only the barest of items displayed now – a gown he supposed was set out for Violet to wear to the evening meal, a comb and perhaps some lavender water on the dressing table – the room reflected none of the soft femininity which characterized his Violet. Nathaniel rang for a servant and Jane quickly answered the summons; he instructed her to fetch Mr. Garand. She seemed to hesitate a moment, glancing around the room over which she, as the ladies' maid, had dominion. She simply curtsied, though, and turned from the room. After she left on her errand, Nathaniel turned to the chest of drawers, which was nearest him. While he knew that it was not necessarily *improper* to look at his wife's things, he experienced a fleeting sensation that he was prying.

The piece of furniture was surprisingly empty. Of the four drawers, each held just one or two dresses. Nathaniel quickly strode to the highboy, but found it too was sparingly filled, this time with female delicacies: gloves at the top, handkerchiefs and fichus in the next drawer, and on down until he had seen the entirety of his wife's underpinnings. A quick look at the cabinet set atop a chest of two drawers revealed about five bonnets, ten or so white linen caps, and several slippers, half-boots, and shoes lining the drawers. He briefly wondered if all of her clothing had indeed been brought in, but Mr. Garand would never tell him that it was finished without first ensuring that the task had indeed been completed. It had not before occurred to him, but Violet did seem to wear only a few dresses.

He moved back to the chest with her gowns for a closer inspection, and opened the top drawer to find the white gown she wore when they were married. He fingered the gown, and the fabric was cool and soft under his fingers. In the next drawer rested the pale orange dress which had been dirtied when Violet worked alongside Mrs. Tessel.

Did she not dispose of it? he wondered. *But then there are so few dresses. Perhaps the stains were removed?* When Nathaniel pulled the dress from the drawer and he saw that while the stains were not as drastic as they had been, they were by no means gone. He quickly replaced the orange gown, knowing Jane would be annoyed at having to fix his poor folding of the fabric.

Moving to the third drawer, Nathaniel spied a bit of green fabric peeking out from beneath the traveling dress Violet had worn when they left for their honeymoon tour. Pushing the heavy fabric aside, he found himself looking at the gown in which he had first seen his bride. A flood of feelings and thoughts assaulted him, most especially how she had blossomed since their first meeting. Again, that nagging sensation that perhaps it was not their first meeting poked at the back of his mind, but as he could not recall any previous encounters, he ignored it.

She had been a shy, demure little thing. He had seen her as a mere chit of a girl. But his wife, who that evening would begin sharing his bedchamber, was the very woman of his heart. She had shown kindness, determination to do what she believed to be right in helping the Tessels, as well as bravery in approaching him with the intelligence regarding the dubious finances of the rents.

Shaking himself from his thoughts, Nathaniel's attention settled on the chest of drawers once again. *Did her mother not provide her wedding clothes? I knew that she was rather ill-prepared, but this is quite poorly-done, even for them. It is a good thing we did not marry during the Season, or she would never have enough to wear to the assemblies and soirees and card-parties held in London.* Pulling a pale brown dress from the lowest of the drawers, he noticed that the sleeves were worn thin at the elbows and the hem was frayed. She had worn it just yesterday, but hid the flows well with a scarf and a gardening apron.

"Nathaniel!" Violet's voice made him jump. He hurriedly replaced the gown in his hands and turned guiltily to face his wife. Her eyes were questioning, but she did not seem to be annoyed to find him looking at her things. "The children are resting in the nursery; they grew weary after their time in the gardens."

"So soon?" he asked.

"We were out for nearly an hour."

"Oh. I had not realized so much time had passed."

"It is no matter. There was nothing pressing which needed your attention." She smiled and paused, fidgeting slightly with her sleeve cuff before speaking again. He observed that the hem of the pale blue gown was slightly lighter than the rest, likely from being often cleaned from dirt and dust, and the pattern brought to mind the gowns his mother had worn when he was a boy, rather than the fabrics being used by the dressmakers in London. "I wished to find you, Nathaniel, because I worried that my words prior to our last parting had injured you."

He immediately understood her hesitance to speak, and hastened to assure her. "My dear, your words carried nothing but the truth I dearly needed to hear. Unfortunately, not every truth is pleasant. I have recently learned yet again how much relief is gained in trusting God's leading, especially in times that I would rather determine my own way."

Violet's eyes were gentle and understanding. "I find it necessary to learn that lesson quite often." Nathaniel returned her smile gratefully, and the silence settled over them like a comfortable blanket for a few moments. After a short time, Violet spoke timidly. "I suppose, seeing the dressing room now, I would not mind terribly to have a lighter color on the walls."

"Yes, of course. I, ah, I beg your pardon, my dear, for intruding here. I simply wanted to make certain that your things were all placed where they ought to be." Even to his own ears, it seemed a poorly-constructed excuse.

"You've not intruded." Violet's hesitant smile seemed to suggest that she knew something was amiss. "

"Oh bother," he burst forth, "Violet, my love. This will not do." Nathaniel scowled and continued, frustration coloring his voice. "Have you no more dresses?"

Violet's brows rose and she was speechless for a moment, then her color changed. "I do not. Is...is this a problem?"

"Not precisely, for we can easily bespeak new gowns for you, but did not your mama fit you out with wedding clothes?"

"Pray, do not be put out with me," Violet replied. "She and Rose believed I would not need very much; they did choose several—"

"*They* chose?" Nathaniel took a step toward her. As he was not yet within reach of Violet, he chose his next words carefully, hoping she would not step away from him. "Were the clothes not your own?"

He knew her too well; she took two small steps backward as she squeaked, "Yes, I daresay they were, but—"

"You daresay, do you?"

Violet attempted another step at his words, but the dressing table was behind her. "Yes, I—"

"You have a habit of removing yourself from my presence."

"My lord?"

"Nathaniel."

"Yes, of course. Nathaniel."

"Is it so difficult?"

"Is what, my, um, Nathaniel?"

"Trusting me." Her brows raised, but she said nothing. "As your husband, I should hope that you are comfortable and have sufficient confidence that I will never mistreat you. You may come to me if you have any concerns."

"But I have none!"

"Then you ought to. Three dresses, Violet. Three dresses *alone* which are suitable! As a bride, you ought to have been given dresses enough to last for the coming year. That is what Society dictates as proper." Violet's eyes widened; Nathaniel heard as his voice rose, but it seemed as though he was watching someone else speaking to her, and not himself.. He unconsciously stepped toward her as he spoke. "Have you no steel in you? Speak up for yourself!"

"Are you certain you are not cross with me because I spoke frankly with you regarding your brother?"

"What? No, of course not." He blew out a frustrated breath. "As I already said, I am grateful that you did. I had not been handling my brother well; indeed, I had quite nearly left the Lord out of the equation. And I thank you for helping me to see that."

"I am sorry if I spoke harshly—"

"You? Speak harshly?" he interjected with a wry smile and something approaching a laugh. "Not at all!"

"—but I am glad that you are feeling better about the situation. Perhaps if you had realized it sooner, you'd have been spared this marriage."

Nathaniel frowned at her. "Spared this marriage? I will not belabor *that* point with you, besides to say that I have no regrets regarding our marriage now, save one that I hope to remedy before much more time has passed." Violet's questioning gaze tempted him to confess his love, but he did not feel that this was the appropriate time or place. "But discussion of our marriage brings me back to my initial point: your family did not provide you with the dresses necessary for a lady of your standing."

Violet's voice trembled, but she blinked away tears which had pooled in her eyes. "I thought, my lord, that the clothing was not an issue. My pin-money is sufficient to supplement my wardrobe, I am convinced, but now that I think of it, I *have* used much of it for things for the tenants who need some thing or another."

Seeing her discomfort, Nathaniel's heart softened and he lowered his voice. "You need not defend your actions. You may do what you wish with your pin-money. But I will not have my wife be stepped on. Your mama and sister, I daresay, have used you very ill indeed!"

"No, you must be mistaken!" she cried. "They were right; Rose would have more need of dresses than I. Who have I to visit, after all? Rose will be living in London after her wedding, which is fast approaching. Why, just yesterday, I received a missive requesting that I confirm our plans to attend."

"Do not change the subject," interjected Nathaniel.

"I have time to have more gowns made. In fact, I have a mind to purchase material for three gowns next week."

"I have no objection to you fashioning your own clothing, if that is your wish, but do not do it because you feel you *must*."

"I do enjoy sewing, but perhaps my time would be better spent seeing to other things," she allowed. "I suppose I will only purchase fabric for one dress, and the rest can be purchased in London."

Nathaniel smiled down at his lovely wife and decided that perhaps a change in subject would be for the best. "I look forward to sharing my chamber with you."

"You...you do?" Now it was Violet's turn to look panicked.

Nathaniel said softly, "Oh, do not fear, dearest, I have not the least intention of forcing my attentions on you. I shall follow your lead in this matter."

"Your attentions? But you already are rather determined in your attentions, indeed, especially at the outset of our marriage. Though you eased off a bit in that regard of late, I cannot imagine you as being more marked in your attentions than that." She gazed openly up at him and he was amazed at her innocence. *Could it be she does not comprehend my meaning? The meaning of a husband and wife coming together?* But then understanding dawned in her eyes and her face was overtaken by a blush. "Oh! Oh dear. I see."

Nathaniel pulled her once again snugly into his arms and tucked her head beneath his chin.

The two young Tessels were dressed in their night-clothes, hair combed and faces washed. As Miss Stokes, the nurse, would not be arriving until the the next day, Violet had decided that she would see to the children for the evening. When she attempted to tuck Miriam's bed-clothes about her small frame, the little girl's chin wobbled and she began to cry.

"Let us not have tears, sweet girl," cooed Violet, picking her up again. She cradled the head of soft curls to her heart and rocked back and forth, humming a quiet song. She smiled over Miriam's head at Abraham. He grinned back at her, waiting patiently until his sister finally dozed off.

"She's an ornery thing, eh, Lady Violet?" he whispered as Miriam was finally tucked into bed.

Violet glanced over her shoulder at him, raising her brows. "Is that what you call it? I merely thought she missed her mama."

Abraham's grin grew sheepish and he shrugged, but still he whispered, "Only babies are homesick by now."

"So you are well?" Violet asked. "No need to read a story to you before you sleep?"

Abraham's face fell. "Oh, well, come to think of it, m'lady, I do miss me mama a bit..."

Violet chuckled as she moved toward his bed, taking up a fairy-tale book on her way. She perched on the side of his bed. "Very well, Abraham, I shall read a story."

After she began reading, Violet glanced in the boy's direction and saw his increasingly heavy eyes. Upon finishing the story, she closed the book and looked at him, only to find that he was sound asleep. She prayed quietly over the children before silently leaving the room, careful to avoid a creaky floorboard she'd discovered earlier that day.

She found Lord Reymes in the family sitting room, reading some book or other, and joined him by the fireplace.

"Are they settled in their beds?" he asked.

"Yes. Little Miriam cried a bit, but she fell asleep rather quickly when I held her. After she was asleep, I read Abraham a story."

Lord Reymes murmured, "Sounds charmingly domestic." Setting aside his book, he rose from his wing-chair and casually strolled around the back of Violet's chair. Soon, she felt his fingers gently caressing the hair of which she had spoken. Her midsection felt as though butterflies had taken up residence there.

"I cannot imagine what happened to your hair," came Lord Reymes' low voice.

A slight shiver raced down Violet's spine. With difficulty, she explained, "Miriam patted my hair while she fell asleep. It was quite cozy and pleasant."

"Like this?"

"Um, I daresay similar, but her hands were much smaller, her fingers shorter, so it was *somewhat* different."

"I should *hope* that my caresses are not comparable to those of a small tot's!" sniggered her husband.

Violet began to turn round to face him, but he was no longer standing behind her. She suddenly found herself being pulled from her chair and settled firmly on his lap.

"There. This is quite cozy and pleasant, as well, is it not?" His playful grin made Violet smile as well.

"Nathaniel, there is something I wish to ask you, or rather to tell you."

Violet nearly lost her determination, for Lord Reymes chose that moment to begin removing pins from her hair.

"Your hair, my love, is a deplorable mess – no doubt due to the grubby hands of that tot who now must be sleeping most angelically."

"Yes, I suppose she is." Violet's head felt surprisingly light as he continued to pull pins from her chignon, the loosened hair spilling about her shoulders and down her back. "But that is not what I wished to say. The children need..."

Violet could scarcely speak when Lord Reymes' fingers began to carefully comb through her hair, smoothing the tangles. He raised his brows, bidding her silently to continue. *As if he is ignorant of what he is doing*, she thought. Drawing a deep breath, she plunged onward. "The children's clothes are worn, too small, and I had hoped to purchase some things for them."

Lord Reymes had ceased running his fingers through her hair and swept the locks over her far shoulder, exposing the side of her neck. "Mm," he murmured, his lips hovering next to the soft skin of her neck, just before he pressed a brief kiss on that sensitive area.

"Would...would that be acceptable to you?"

Lord Reymes had just placed another kiss upon her neck, but pulled back to look at her. "Why would it not be?"

"Oh! I do not know." Violet paused, hoping that he did not see her question as evidence that she believed him hard-hearted, so she hurriedly continued, "I merely did not wish to do so without consulting you."

"Ah, I see. Very good then." Lord Reymes resumed his attentions to her neck.

"Very good?" she questioned.

After placing another kiss on her neck, he said in a languid voice, "Excellent, even."

"Then, you do not mind—"

"Whatever amount you need."

"Thank you, Nathaniel."

"You are the one being charitable."

Violet was prevented from answering by Lord Reymes' rather distracting kiss.

Later that evening, the couple retired to their chamber. Griffin and Jane were each called to assist them in preparing for bed. After Jane left her, Violet's heart hammered as she, dressed in her high-necked, frilled nightgown, emerged from her dressing room and moved toward the bed.

It was a comfortable-looking piece of furniture, the coverlet and bed-curtains of matching chintz. Lord Reymes sat upon the coverlet, wearing his under-drawers and shirt. Violet had never seen him without a cravat and collar – save that morning as she watched him tie his cravat – and had difficulty meeting his gaze.

Lord Reymes patted the mattress beside him. "Violet, I'd like to spend some time with you in devotion to the Lord each evening."

Violet's previously-stuttering heart fill with joy at his words. "I should like that *very* much, Nathaniel."

The couple sat together on the bed, reading Scripture and praying. It had been a long day, full of both happiness and heartache. When Violet did her best to, unsuccessfully, stifle a yawn, her husband stood, pulled her to her feet, and kissed her gently.

"Good night, my love."

"Good night, Nathaniel."

Violet pulled back the coverlet and slipped beneath it as Lord Reymes did the same. She lay still upon the bed, her heart pounding in her ears. When her husband had been breathing evenly for some time, she was able finally to relax, and at length drifted off to sleep.

Twelve

⟨ ❦ ⟩

VIOLET'S EYES OPENED slowly, blinking away sleep. Nathaniel had been awake for some time, gazing across at his wife's peaceful face. As the embers in the fireplace faded during the night, and the room grew colder, she had snuggled up beside him in her sleep. When he awoke, his own arm was wrapped about her slender frame, and she was tucked securely against his side.

"Good morning, my lovely Violet," he whispered.

Violet's eyes widened. "Oh dear!"

"Is something amiss?" he asked unhurriedly, propping himself up on his elbow to see her better.

"Yes!" came her urgent whisper. "It would be dreadful to be found like this."

"Like what?" He knew it was not particularly kind of him, but Nathaniel could not help but enjoy his innocent wife's discomfiture.

"A-abed!"

"But the curtains are drawn," he offered helpfully.

Violet's body relaxed against him at this, but then she almost immediately attempted to disengage herself from his embrace. "Please, allow me to—"

"Will you not give your husband a good-morning kiss, first?"

Oddly enough, Violet did not blush as she pressed her lips into a thin line for a moment before leaning toward him and placing a tentative kiss on his cheek. Nathaniel could have shouted for joy.

Scarcely able to hide his grin, he whispered, "Thank you."

Violet offered a shy smile and said, "You are welcome."

She then hastily threw back the coverlet and retreated into her dressing room.

With a sigh, Nathaniel also rose, moving to his own dressing room to begin readying himself for the day.

Violet assisted the children in dressing and then led them out to the gardens. They wandered about for some time, trailed by matching footmen in pale blue coats and powdered wigs, eventually finding themselves in the orchard. Abraham had a wooden sword and was play-fighting imagined pirates amongst the nearly-barren trees. The leaves were changed, awaiting a stiff wind to blow the last of them from their tenuous hold on the branches. Miriam toddled about, occasionally plucking a leaf from the ground and cramming it into her mouth.

"No, no, dearest. Those are not food." Violet laughed at the face Miriam made upon tasting the dry, crunchy leaf. Carefully sweeping the child's mouth with her finger, Violet quickly found the moistened bit of nature and pulled it from between tiny teeth.

Violet looked about to assure herself that Abraham was still within sight, and then scooped the tot into her arms, dancing about the orchard with her. She sang a silly song to make the girl laugh, then broke out in giggles herself. Lord Reymes found them, snuggling together as Violet held her, leaning against the stone fence that ran the perimeter of the orchard.

"What a lovely picture!" called Lord Reymes as he strode toward them. "Is young Abraham about?"

"Yes; he is over there." Violet nodded in the direction of the tree behind which the boy was hiding. She watched as Lord Reymes strode to the tree, hunching down to converse with the young child.

"What an excellent sword!" he began.

"Yes, me papa made it for me!"

"Very good!" His smile for the boy was genuine. "And whom are you fighting?"

"Pirates!"

"But of course. May I assist you into this tree? It seems very much like the mast of a ship!"

"Oh, yes, if ye please, sir!" exclaimed the boy. Violet giggled as Lord Reymes showed Abraham how to climb onto the low branches of the apple tree. After ensuring the boy was secure in his footing, he made his way back to Violet and Miriam.

"How pleased was Abie! Did you see how his face glowed?" As she spoke, he held out his arms for Miriam; the tot went willingly to him. Violet's heart was full.

"How is it that you are so comfortable with children? My mama maintains that most men are not, and she used to warn me not to bring them up in conversation, or to allow them to draw near to any gentlemen with whom I kept company."

"And you have kept company with many gentlemen?" The question, studiously disinterested, might have caused Violet to think her husband jealous, had she not known better.

"Dear me, no. But Mama did try. She was forever inviting gentlemen to the house, especially our first Season in London."

"And when was that again?" Lord Reymes asked. Miriam began to squirm and Violet watched as her husband gently set her upon the ground. She immediately toddled off toward a small patch of tenaciously blooming wildflowers several feet from where the Earl and Countess stood. "I remember that you told me, Violet, but I am afraid that I cannot recall the answer."

With an understanding smile, she replied, "Just two years past. I believe I told you previously that we made our come-outs together, so it was decided that I should wait until Rose had become old enough; I was eighteen and she sixteen."

"I see. Could it be that we had met, then?"

"Actually, I believe that we danced together once at Almack's."

Lord Reymes simply stared back at her, as though seeing her anew. At length, he broke out in laughter. "I can scarcely believe it! I thought at the ball here, when first we were introduced, that you seemed familiar. Now and again, I have tried to place from whence I know you, but have been unsuccessful until now." He drew a bit nearer her, raised a hand to gently caress her face. "And you've remembered me all this time?"

"I'd nearly forgot," Violet said as she shifted minutely farther away from him, "but when I saw you again that evening, it came back to me."

"It is a wonder you condescended to treat me with politeness, if my recollection of that dance is at all accurate. I fear I was abysmally rude to you. I scarcely spoke."

Violet shook her head ruefully, hiding her relief that he had not stepped closer. She still had a dreadful time keeping her wits about her when he stood so close. "You were quiet, but I counted it to the recent loss of your father. I could see that your friend had nearly coerced you into asking for the dance, so I could not hold your reserve against you."

Lord Reymes was clearly amused with something, if the slight curve to his lips and the laughter in his eyes were any indication. "Astounding."

"What is?"

"Even then, you were attuned to the climate of my heart," he said fondly.

Lord Reymes glanced about briefly, and she followed his gaze to see that Abraham had climbed down the tree and was dashing about, fleeing imaginary villains, and Miriam was still occupied with the flowers which had caught her attention. Violet was still smiling at Miriam's antics with the flowers, and failed to see that her husband had closed all but several inches of the space between them.

"I've long believed there was something familiar about you, Violet, but I still feel that I've met you before that. Even when we danced, you seemed familiar – possibly another reason why I was uncomfortable when we were introduced."

"Do you think we met here?"

He looked at her with an unreadable expression before speaking. "I remember stopping to help a young girl. My friend Stally was with me, having come to stay at Bainscroft during a holiday from school. Though he was simply Ollie then. We both heard the cries of the girl who was caught and Stally reached her first. While he was helping her free her foot, I did my best to converse with the other young lady."

"I had never been the sole object of anyone's attention, and could not make words form."

"I was enchanted," he murmured, "by the quiet girl who seemed scarcely able to speak with me, yet still tried."

Violet buried her face in her hands and replied, "I was mortified at my childishness." She looked up then and said, with laughter in her voice, "But surely you are spinning tales! How could you possibly have remembered me?"

"As I suppose was typical for a young man in his early teenage years, I soon forgot about that encounter. But as you have just now brought it to my recollection," and here he leaned closer and spoke for her ears alone, "I must say that it is a pleasing coincidence that you are her, and that she is the one whom I married."

Violet laughed lightly and said, "Nathaniel, I can scarcely make any sense of your words."

Can he truly be happy? When we first met, he certainly did not want a marriage. Now, though, he seems to think quite the opposite. If only I could stop doubting his affection. For my part, not once did I expect a love so deep and— and she faltered, surprised at the course of her thoughts. *Do I love him?*

Violet's question was pushed to the recesses of her mind as Mrs. Baker could be seen, making her way to them from the house, a young woman accompanying her.

"Mrs. Baker," Lord Reymes said by way of greeting.

The housekeeper and the young woman both curtsied. "My lord and my lady, please allow me to present to you my cousin, Miss Elvira Stokes."

"Ah, yes," said Lord Reymes after nodding in greeting. "We are very glad to have you here."

Mrs. Baker spoke again. "Shall I show her to the nursery? Or does my Lady Reymes wish to?"

Glad of the excuse to gain a reprieve from her husband and the startling thoughts he was eliciting from her, Violet hastened to say, "I should be pleased to introduce the children and show you to the nursery, Miss Stokes." She smiled at the friendly-looking woman.

When Lord Reymes smiled warmly at her, Violet felt her heart give a slight flutter. *I must take time later to consider this new...development. Yes, later. When Lord Reymes...Nathaniel...is not present to so frequently confuse my thoughts.*

"Very good. I am afraid that I must excuse myself. I have business with my bailiff." After nodding politely to Mrs. Baker and Miss Stokes, the source of her confusion took Violet's hand in his own and raised it to his lips. Afterward, Violet was acutely aware of the place on her gloved hand where his lips had lingered in his kiss. "I shall see you after a short while, my love," were his parting words.

Violet smiled shyly at her husband as he took his leave of the ladies. *Dear me, I had entirely forgotten about Mr. Faintree! Lord, please guide Nathaniel in finding the truth. I know that he would not wish to accuse an innocent man, but if Mr. Faintree knew that he was prevaricating as he delivered the messages to the tenants, he cannot be allowed to escape without consequence.*

Violet turned to Miss Stokes and gestured for her to follow. They chatted amicably about the house as they went along. Miss Stokes appeared to be a lovely young woman. Her cheery disposition and bright auburn hair were like light brought into the nursery's drab, outdated atmosphere. Violet was quite comfortable leaving the children in her capable care when she was called to the parlor to receive a guest.

Charlotte was seated in a wing-chair when Violet entered the room, paging through a book that Violet had left on a nearby table the last time she was in the room.

"Charlotte!" cried Violet, rushing over to her younger cousin. "I forgot entirely that I sent word for you to come today!"

The girl laughed and said, "I wondered if that might not be the case; on most occasions, you meet me at the door before I can even announce myself to the butler! I do hope that this is a convenient time. Or shall I return at a later date?"

"Oh, please never think that your presence would not be welcome."

"Thank you," grinned Charlotte, "though I suppose I shall endeavor to refrain from arriving while you are still abed!"

Memories of the morning assailed her, but Violet pushed them away and asked, "Shall we remain here, or would you care to walk about the gardens as we visit?"

"Do let us walk, if you please," said Charlotte happily. "These gardens are quite sufficient cause for me to visit frequently, even if I did not love you so dearly, Violet!"

The two young women strolled arm-in-arm through the house and out into the gardens.

Once Nathaniel left the party in the orchard, he asked Mr. Garand to send for Mr. Faintree and bring him to his study. As he waited for the man, he prayed.

Lord, You have been with me throughout my life, and especially have I been aware of Your guiding hand recently. Please direct my thoughts and especially my words at this time. I've been so very enthralled with this deepening relationship with Violet, that I should have much preferred to forget this unpleasantness. Help me now, O Lord, to bring it to an end.

There was no more time, as the door opened and Mr. Garand announced Mr. Faintree. The man hesitated on the threshold of the room.

"Please, come in, Mr. Faintree." Nathaniel gestured toward a chair by the fire before dismissing the butler. He watched while the man took hesitant steps toward the chair indicated. His hair, tied with a ribbon at the nape of his neck, was speckled with grey. His clothing was by no means fashionable, but certainly neat, if a bit worn at the seams and elbows. As he lowered himself into the chair, Nathaniel saw that his stooped shoulders sagged a bit.

Nathaniel decided a direct and honest approach would be best. "Mr. Faintree, I shall not waste your time. It seems that the tenants were told that I instituted an increase to their rent, when I, in fact, did no such thing."

He paused for a moment, looking expectantly at Mr. Faintree. When the man said nothing, Nathaniel asked bluntly, "Do you know anything of the matter?"

The older man pressed his lips into a thin line, beads of perspiration emerging on his forehead and Nathaniel imagined beneath his neck-cloth, as well. "Me lor', I tol' John 'twas a bad idear, that you'd know of it wi' little trouble. But 'e isn't one to heed reason."

"So you knew of this. Were you the one to deliver the demand to the tenants, as well?"

The man positively drooped. "Yea, me lor'."

"So you are an accomplice. I could have you dismissed – or worse – for this."

At those words, Mr. Faintree's eyes widened and he said, "Oh, no, me lor'! Me Lolly, she's in a poor way to be sure. I canna help her if I'm outen work. Please, me lor'!"

A strong urge in Nathaniel told him to prosecute to the full extent of the law. But at the mention of Mr. Faintree's wife, his heart softened. He knew that he himself would do whatever was in his power to ensure Violet's comfort and safety. How could he fault Faintree for doing the same?

Nathaniel sighed and poured two glasses of brandy. Offering one to Faintree, he said, "Please tell me, from the beginning, what exactly happened." He moved to the chair opposite Mr. Faintree, and settled in for a long discussion.

More than an hour later, after excusing Mr. Faintree, Nathaniel went in search of his wife. When Mrs. Baker informed him that she was walking in the gardens with young Miss Charlotte, he moved in their direction.

Violet and Charlotte ambled along just outside of the rose-garden, beside a tall hedge. They had briefly discussed how the children came to be at Bainscroft before turning to news of the community. An upcoming wedding and the Smith's acquisition of a new breed of cow were all discussed before Charlotte mentioned her neighbor's eldest boy in a quiet voice.

"Stan has returned for a holiday from school."

"Stan?"

"Edward Stanhope," clarified the younger girl. "Surely you remember him; always teasing, pulling my hair, stuffing frogs down the back of my dresses when I was a girl."

"Oh yes, I recall that some of your letters mentioned him. I believe that Ash may have taught him that particular trick. Has he made any attempts this visit with a frog?"

"Gracious, no! I've not even seen him. And I certainly hope I do not, save at services on Sunday." Charlotte grinned. "His mama said that he returns to Oxford in one week."

"I see."

Violet and Charlotte continued in silence for some time. Now that Violet's attention was not claimed by the children or by her husband, she was able to more fully appreciate the beauty of nature. The weather was lovely, if a bit chilly. Both ladies were glad for their warm pelisses. The sky above, blue and clear, allowed the sun to shine brightly, showing off the splendor of the day in glorious testament to the creative power of God.

"Do you recall," asked Violet when they had stopped to admire a late-blooming rose, "the time your boot became wedged in that log?"

"I do!" cried Charlotte. "You were so very terrified that we should encounter those two young men who were riding in the field beside the woods, where we were walking."

"Oh, I had entirely forgotten about seeing them earlier!" cried Violet.

The two girls laughed together for a moment before Charlotte quieted. "I must admit to something."

"What is that, Charlotte?"

"My foot was not caught. I feigned the entire thing. I knew that you would not allow us to meet them, and I desperately wanted a bit of entertainment."

"Charlotte!" cried Violet. "I was so mortified to be found in such a foolish position, and that I could not assist you myself."

"I do apologize, Violet, but you are none the worse for it."

"Charlotte, the two young men – it was Lord Reymes and his friend Lord Stallingsworth."

Charlotte gasped, then blurted, "Surely you must be jesting!" The younger girl's laughter rang loudly – too loudly for it to be genuine.

"Indeed not. He and I spoke of it just this morning," countered Violet. "Do not fret, Charlotte – yes, I know you are not truly amused – I am not angry. I admit to being a bit shocked, to be sure; but as you said, all is well now."

"I know I am too impetuous," offered Charlotte. "Ought I apologize to Lord Reymes?"

"Oh no, do not trouble yourself," soothed Violet. "He seems pleased with our situation, as well."

"If you are certain," said Charlotte. The pair continued walking for a time before Charlotte spoke again. "You said that Lord Reymes is pleased with your situation. Are you, Violet?"

"I am, Charlotte. I must confess that I...I-I love Lord Reymes," Violet said, her voice scarcely more than a whisper. The full realization had just dawned upon her, as she and Charlotte walked along. While she had begun to suspect it while in the orchard, it was not until that very moment, in conversation with Charlotte, that Violet came to such a clear understanding.

"Why ever would you not?" asked Charlotte with surprise.

"Surely you must have suspected that our marriage was not a love-match. We have from the start shared a common respect and possibly even affection for one another, but I did not expect to experience such strong feeling so soon, if ever. Truly, I do not know what to do!"

Charlotte giggled a bit at her cousin's distress. "Violet, must you *do* anything? You love your husband. What is so extraordinary in that?"

Violet was mildly peeved that Charlotte regarded her dilemma so lightly. "I have no idea of his returning my affection, I know not how he would react were he to discover—"

"Then you do not intend to share this with him?"

"Good heavens, no!" Violet's heart beat faster and harder at the thought that he might somehow come to know.

"But why ever not? Would he mock you?" Charlotte's tone suggested that she knew he would not.

This gave Violet pause. "Of course not. I daresay he would be the last person to mock me."

"Would he spurn you?"

"Oh Charlotte, don't be ridiculous. He is my husband; he would not spurn me."

"So why would you not tell him? He would not be unkind to you. He would not mock you or be hateful or...or anything of the sort!" Charlotte regarded the elder lady with something approaching condescension. "You have nothing over which to worry."

"There is sense in what you say, Charlotte," said Violet. "I am being a goose – I know it! But it still does not help the nervous fluttering here," and she rested her hand on her stomach.

"And here?" asked Charlotte, indicating Violet's heart.

Violet's slightly doubtful gaze might have caused Charlotte to continue, but as it happened, they had reached the end of the hedge. As they stepped past it, to continue to the field beyond, a man stepped also from the other side of the hedge.

Both ladies, startled, crying out. Charlotte then burst forth in laughter while Violet felt her face burn uncontrollably. *What did he hear?* Lord Reymes stood before the two ladies, his face unreadable.

"Oh, Lord Reymes, you gave us quite a start!" sputtered Charlotte, still gurgling with laughter as she dipped into a hasty curtsey. "I suppose that I must be on my way; I really only intended to stay for a short visit. I shall take myself off directly; do send for me at a later date, when it is convenient for me to meet the children. No, don't worry about my getting home. I shall walk. The day is glorious, is it not? Good day, Cousin Violet! Good day, Lord Reymes! Or may I address you as Cousin Reymes? We *are* cousins now, after all. I shall see you again before long, I daresay." And Violet was left alone with her husband, unable to meet his gaze.

Nathaniel glanced up to see that Miss Doberly was making headway toward her home, but still not far enough to grant them privacy. He took his wife's arm at the elbow and began to lead her to the gardener's shed, located only a hundred yards from where they stood. As they went, he felt a strong sense of urgency drive him to walk faster and faster. Had Violet been wearing something more substantial than kid slippers, Nathaniel would have begun running.

Upon reaching the shed, Nathaniel ushered his wife inside, then closed the door resolutely behind them. There were gardening tools hanging on nails, a few scattered on the work-table against the far wall, and several seed-packs waiting to be planted in pots in the greenhouse. The dimly-lit interior offered an intimate setting. Facing Violet, he secured himself of her hands, clasping them with great earnestness. He saw that his wife's countenance was pale as she faced him uncertainly.

"You little goose!"

His words had an awakening effect upon Violet. "I am not a goose, sir!" she cried, as close to incensed as ever he had seen her. She continued to speak, but no coherent sentence came out. He was able to discern something about his nerve calling her such a name and the evils of eavesdropping.

"You most certainly are a goose!" Nathaniel felt a grin overtake his face as he drew Violet into his arms. "How could you possibly be uncertain of my affection, love?"

"I—"

"I've done nearly everything save declare myself, dearest. How can you doubt me?"

"Rose once told me that kisses meant nothing." Violet's voice was hushed and trembling.

"Rose? My lovely, perhaps kisses in *her* experience mean nothing, but allow me to assure you most earnestly – *my* kisses do indeed mean a great deal." Nathaniel had never been a man easily over-run by his emotions as were some of his contemporaries. Still, he found it necessary to swallow the lump lodged in his throat before he could speak again. "Violet, I love you."

As she threaded her arms about his neck, she opened her mouth to speak. Through trembling lips came the words, "Oh, Nathaniel, I – I love you"

Nathaniel crushed her to himself, kissing her passionately. His hands came up to tangle in her simple chignon, displacing many of its pins. After a moment, he broke off the kiss suddenly. *I cannot forget myself. Thank you, Lord, for giving both of us love! But help me remember to allow her to lead us into a more intimate expression of that love.*

"Shall we go see to the children?" he asked, by way of forcing himself into a situation in which he would be in no danger of forgetting his resolve.

Violet hesitated, uncertainty written on her face. After a moment of looking at their surroundings rather than at him, she spoke.

"Now that we are...mutually assured of one another's regard, may I be safe in assuming that...you will no longer be awaiting my...er, initiation of our...that is...what I mean to say..."

Nathaniel was amused at how her thought had so coincided with his own. He drew her back into his embrace. Dropping a light kiss on her nose, he said, "I most certainly *shall* await your leading."

Violet looked so crestfallen that Nathaniel could not hold back a chuckle. In a whisper, she said, "But I assure you, Nathaniel, I am...er, prepared, to welcome any attentions you desire to—"

"Any?" he asked skeptically. For a moment, he stood still, debating what to do. *I can show her that she is not ready or I can try to convince her with words.* While showing her would certainly be to Nathaniel's taste, she might be frightened of him. However, words had proved ineffective thus far. *Lord, please guide me.*

"But how can you be?" he asked.

"I...I trust you," she returned with determination.

Nathaniel raised an eyebrow at her, and then tugged her against himself, burying his face in her already-tousled hair, trailing his fingers down the side of her face and neck, across her shoulders. He felt her tremble slightly, but she did not move away. Wrapping his arms about her waist, he placed a kiss on her forehead, her nose, her cheek – tentatively at first, then with increasing fervor. When the trail of his kisses reached the column of her throat, she gasped and this time did step back from him, easily breaking his hold.

Nathaniel drew a deep breath as he struggled to rein in the longing that he had nearly allowed to overcome him. Warily, he watched her face for any signs of fear; he was relieved to detect none. What he did see was confusion, reticence, perhaps a touch of alarm, and (triumphant discovery!) lurking behind all was certainly some longing of her own.

"Do you see now that I must wait?" he asked huskily.

Violet's voice was not unaffected either. "I-I believe perhaps I do." She paused, catching her utterly kissable lower lip between her teeth. "Even so, I do not see how I shall ever manage—"

"You will find the determination you need."

Smiling shyly up at him, she said, "I certainly hope so."

He grinned at her, winked, and then assisted her in patting her hair into some semblance of order. She smoothed her gown while he straightened his cravat and tugged at the sleeves of his coat. Offering his arm, he opened the door of the shed and the couple stepped out into the bright sunlight.

As they made progress toward the house, Nathaniel suddenly remembered why he had sought out his wife in the first place.

"I have some news regarding Mr. Faintree," he began.

"Oh, you do?" Violet's eyes connected with his for a moment before again looking at the stone path upon which they walked.

"Yes. It appears that he was given no choice in aiding John. In fact, his wife was suffering a sickly constitution and he did not wish to jeopardize her health further by refusing to cooperate. It seems that John began to raise the rent shortly after hiring the man. Mr. Faintree gave the extra monies to John without receiving a cut, though John certainly offered it to him. He told me that he did not feel right to keep 'what weren't rightly' his. But he could not oppose my brother, under threat of termination. His wife, called Lolly, needs healthful food and they even pay a girl from the village to sit with her while he is occupied here."

"Oh, I know Lolly," put in Violet. "Knowing all this, we must increase what we send them, to ease their discomfort. Bread we send weekly, but I'll ask Peche to add some meat, and apples once they've been gathered. Lolly endures her sufferings with such good cheer."

"I am glad you have made her acquaintance, my love; you are sure to be a blessing to her." Nathaniel smiled down at his wife, thinking how very much he meant the endearment. *Not very original, I grant, but certainly nothing could be more accurate.* "He is very much attached to her. Almost, I should imagine, as attached as I am to you."

The glow in her eyes evidenced the joy she had in hearing and receiving the declaration.

"Mr. Faintree told me that he expects John at Christmastide, to receive more money from him. It is my hope to trap John and deal with all at that time." He removed her hand from his arm and wrapped said arm about her shoulders. "Would you prefer to go visit a friend during that time? Perhaps the Doberlys or even your brother?"

"Oh no, Nathaniel!" Violet stopped walking just before they reached the stairs that led to the solarium and turned to face him. "It has been pressing at me of late that I ought to forgive John, if I am to love you wholly and without reservation."

Nathaniel opened his mouth to exclaim, *Whatever for? I certainly would not.* But the words never passed his lips. The realization of the bitterness he had allowed to overtake his soul struck him with force. He had thought that merely changing the way he viewed his dealings with John would eradicate all fault on his side, but he had not accounted for the fingers of anger and even hatred which had clutched with a vice-like grip at his heart. *Help me to forgive.*

"You are right, of course." Still, Nathaniel could not discount the fact that the last time he had seen his brother, the man had threatened his wife. "Are you certain, though, that you would not prefer to stay away until I have settled this matter?"

Violet did not answer immediately, but spent more than several seconds in reflection. "I do not pretend to have no fear in this situation. I do, however, trust in the Lord to be with me and to see me through whatever may transpire. And I also trust you, Nathaniel, to protect me as best you can."

Her confidence in his providing for her safety, as well as in the Lord's providing for her every need, warmed Nathaniel's heart. "I shall certainly do my best, but I am glad that you put more faith in Christ than in me."

"Is that not as it should be?" Violet smiled up at him. "The Lord is the only One who is unchanging, who loves us entirely without selfishness, who is able to save us and overcome every weakness and indeed even turn those weaknesses into strength in Him."

"What beautiful truth you speak." Nathaniel tightened his embrace. With a sigh, he began to lead her up the steps. "Very well, you shall remain here. But I will not have you wandering about the countryside as you normally do, even with a footman. Travel only by carriage, and with no less than two footmen in attendance, in addition to the coachman. They will be instructed to carry weapons. I know it is usual procedure for them to do so, but I sincerely doubt whether a one of them has put a weapon to use in all the days of his service, so I shall remind them."

"Heaven and earth!" cried Violet. "Is it really so dire as all that?"

"I fear it is." Nathaniel placed a kiss on the crown of her head. "It appears that John has sunk quite low; we must pray fervently for his salvation."

Violet rode in a carriage that evening to the Tessel house, with Nathaniel and the children. It was surprising to her with what ease her thoughts of her husband shifted from Lord Nathaniel to the more intimate address of *Nathaniel* once she perceived the love which had grown for him, and likewise learned of his for her. The visit passed pleasantly for all present. As would be expected, the children were overjoyed to see their mama and papa. Mrs. Tessel was looking better already in the short period of time dedicated to her convalescence; it was amazing to her, as well as to Violet, what a night of sound sleep and a day spent in repose could do to begin the restoration of one's strength. Violet rejoiced to see her friend so far recovered, but knew that it was much too early to expect her to be prepared to resume the whole of her previous activities. Nathaniel was glad to visit with one of his best tenants, and Mr. Tessel was overjoyed at the honor paid his family with their visit and their kindness. Mrs. Tessel delighted in her two eldest children for the hour they were with her.

Mary was the only person in the room who seemed to notice that anything was not in the ordinary way with Lord Reymes and his wife. Nothing was amiss, but there was none of the usual reserve between them, the uncertainty on Lady Reymes' part in regard to her husband. She had confided nothing to her friend, but Mary was of an observant nature and recognized the uncertainty in her friend when the girl's husband was present, as opposed to when he was not. She wished for a nice quiet chat with her friend in order to question the young countess.

She was not so fortunate at that time, however, to have her curiosity satisfied in its entirety. After one hour had passed, Lady Reymes rose from the settee where she sat beside Mary.

"My dear Mrs. Tessel, I fear I must take the children now. It is quite their bed-time, and they have not yet had their supper. I am sorry," she apologized.

"No, no, m'lady, you have the right of it," said Mary. "Dearies, come kiss your mama good-night. Sure'n we'll meet again soon!" She clasped them to her bosom and dropped kisses on their fair heads. "Be sure to mind Lady Reymes!"

"Oh, but she's given us leave to call her Lady Violet!" said young Abraham, in quite a jolly voice.

"Has she now?" Mary smiled up at her friend. "A most kind lady indeed."

Lady Reymes pressed Mary's hand as she took her leave of her, as the men shook hands. "Do try to rest, dear, and make certain you drink the tonic the physician left for your strength."

"Oh, to be sure, m'lady." Mary searched her brain for a way to confirm her suspicion. "You're lookin' well tonight. Has Jane found a new beauty treatment?"

Lady Reymes laughed lightly as she bent down to kiss Mary's cheek. "Oh, no." In a considerably hushed voice, she confided, "I can claim nothing but the felicity of a happy marriage."

Mary's heart rejoiced for her friend. "Oh dearie, that is surely the best aid to beauty."

The countess' blushing smile was her answer.

The children were conducted in the carriage back to Bainscroft, along with Lord and Lady Reymes. The couple tucked the children into their beds after their supper, and then spent the evening enjoying a discussion of how each came to realize his or her love for the other. Their evening concluded with their nightly devotional reading, followed by heart-felt prayers of thanks for the wonderful blessing of love.

Over the next fortnight, the Earl and his Countess visited the Tessel family frequently. Usually, Violet and the children called on Mary, but Lord Reymes would accompany them at least once each week. The children continued their stay at Bainscroft, being entertained during the day by Miss Stokes and by Lady Violet in turn, and occasionally visited by Lord Reymes when his numerous obligations permitted. In a visit between all concerned parties, Lord and Lady Reymes even solicited permission from the Tessels to convey the children to London for a brief time the last two weeks of October. In addition to a plan of ordering new dresses for Violet and several things for the children, their visit would coincide with the upcoming wedding of Violet's sister Rose to Mr. Langley.

Part III

Thirteen

London, England
Late October 1808

THE REYMES PARTY settled easily into the London Town-house. The children enjoyed the change of scenery and watching different people that they had never seen before. On occasion, Lord and Lady Reymes would take them to the marketplace, simply to allow them to see all the wares the different hawkers had on display, to smell exotic spices, feel silken scarves, and taste various fruits brought from far-off lands. As the family intended to stay in London for several weeks, Mr. Garand, Mrs. Baker, and several others of the staff had gone ahead of them to prepare the house and also to see to their needs while the family was in residence. Waiting on the salver in the afternoon following their first excursion into the market was a note from Mr. Ashbridge Wyndham, inviting the Reymes party to dine with them the following evening.

The morning that they were to dine with the Wyndham family, Nathaniel called Ezekiel Harris into his office. The young man entered the room promptly, wearing full livery as the occasion to watch John had passed with his apparent withdrawal from London.

"Ezekiel. How do you do?" asked Nathaniel, standing near the fireplace hearth.

"Very well, my lord. Have you need of my services again?" The man kept his voice and face expressionless, but Nathaniel could sense an excitement behind his question.

"Not precisely."

Nathaniel had learned to admire his wife's care for those around her that he had decided to offer to sponsor Ezekiel in attending university, and without prelude, Nathaniel made the offer.

"My lord, please receive my thanks, but I cannot accept."

Nathaniel was rather surprised at Ezekiel's refusal, but bore no ill-will toward the man. "Very well. May I inquire as to why?"

"I can't hang on your sleeve, my lord." Ezekiel's words were uttered quietly and in a small amount of embarrassment.

"You would not; I am offering to be a patron of sorts, Ezekiel. I see potential in you, young man," said Nathaniel. "I would, of course, require loyalty in return and—"

"Beg pardon for interrupting, my lord, but 'twouldn't work." He grinned ruefully. "My loyalty's not a problem; you have it, sure's I stand here. I would greatly enjoy expanding my education; I'd even considered enlisting in the militia, what with all that's happenin' on the Continent. But you see, sir, I am responsible for my sister. If I went off to school, or even enlist in the militia, she'd be left alone. I do *not* approve her working, m'lord, though the sweat-shops do take girls even younger than her."

"I see," said Nathaniel. He stood for a moment, considering. "Pray, what is your age? And your sister's?"

"I am three and twenty. She is ten."

"And would you object to her working, if she was securely settled in a respectable position? Or perhaps attending a school for girls?"

"I'm a bit thin in the pockets, m'lord, to send her to school."

"What if I were to bring you – and your sister – to Bainscroft?" asked Nathaniel. "There is a small school for girls in the village."

"I couldn't accept so much, m'lord."

"Then pay me for her board, or allow her to work in the house a few hours each week, if it would ease your conscience. Nothing strenuous, but perhaps it would be of help to her, learning about the running of a household. Would that suit you?"

"I—er, yes, m'lord." The young man seemed at a loss. "But, if it don't offend, m'lord...why?"

Nathaniel looked carefully at the footman. He was about to reiterate that he saw potential in the young man and felt that he ought not to allow that potential to be wasted. But should he not be entirely truthful?

"Ezekiel, it is true that I see a keenness in you which is being unused in your current post. Certainly, you have performed admirably as a footman, and that is but one reason for you to rise to your potential." Nathaniel left his post by the mantle and took a couple of steps toward the younger man as he considered how much to divulge. "I have lately obsesrved my wife's excellent example of care and concern for others – and not simply the people, but also their undertakings, their struggles, their triumphs. I find myself wishing to emulate that example. But even more, I've recently been reminded how very much graciousness God has forborne to show me; He saw fit to bless me, so how can I refuse to be the means He would use to bless others?"

The young man seemed mildly perplexed at the reason, but expressed his gratitude prodigiously and returned to his duties after being asked to have himself and his sister ready to remove to Bainscroft in a fortnight, when the family would return from Town. For himself, Nathaniel called for his valet with instructions to prepare his coat for going out. It was high time his wife ordered some new gowns.

Penelope rose quickly the moment Violet entered the room. The last time they met was well before Violet's wedding. And to an earl, of all men! Penelope could scarcely believe that after all her teasing during Violet's Season that she did in fact marry an earl. Both of their guests warmly greeted the family, Violet doting on little Andrew. Penelope saw easily the adoration and wistfulness in Lord Reymes' face as he watched his wife holding the baby. The children Violet and Lord Reymes were keeping also adored the baby, and Penelope's heart swelled at the knowledge that her baby was cherished by others. Soon, though, the Wyndham's nurse arrived to take the children off to the nursery for their supper before the party of four proceeded into the dining room. The conversation remained light and enjoyable throughout the meal, reminding Penelope of their time together before Violet decided she must return to her childhood home in order to allow the couple privacy in their newlywed years.

In the drawing room after dinner, their intimate family party eschewed the usual practice of the gentlemen and ladies separating for a time, and instead they stayed together. It seemed an age since they last saw Violet, and Penelope knew Ash missed his sister. The gentlemen partook of port wine while standing near the mantelpiece and the ladies sipped on Madeira on a settee near the fire.

"It is excellent to finally make your acquaintance, Lord Reymes," began Penelope with the purpose of deepening the conversation from what it had been at dinner. She was determined to see for herself that her husband's positive impression of the man was correct. She had come a long way from the girl who believed few, if any, gentlemen were truly of a gentle and good nature, but there was still a streak of suspicion in her that would not rest until she had made her own assessment.

"Thank you, but please call me Reymes. We are family, are we not?"

"Indeed. And while it may be somewhat untoward, I would prefer that you call me Penelope or Penny. Every time I hear *Mrs. Wyndham*, I think of the elder Mrs. Wyndham and do not care for it one bit."

Reymes nodded his understanding almost too quickly, and Penelope could not hide her smirk.

"And how are you recovering, Penny?" asked Violet, changing the subject.

"Quite well, thank you." She reached to clasp the dear girl's hand and feeling the solid band of her wedding ring. Penelope's heart gave a painful lurch as she realized that Violet was no longer a girl, but a woman – married and with a house of her own to look after. "Dearest, we have greatly missed your company."

"I know, Penny; I've missed you as well," said Violet, squeezing her hand in return. Her eyes shone with the unspoken words between the ladies, their affection as strong as it had ever been. Penelope was unbelievably happy to see her friend again – even numerous letters were a poor substitute – but knew that their husbands would easily find the visit a bore if they were to allow their joy at seeing one another to monopolize the conversation.

"It really was terribly unkind of you to marry at a time that I could not attend," Penelope teased her friend. "I believe I cried for an entire quarter-hour when I discovered that I would not be present."

"Are you certain it was true sadness?" Violet asked archly. "Or perhaps the extreme emotionalism which Ash mentioned more than once when he came for the wedding?"

"You exposed me!" cried Penelope, feigning indignation while she was secretly delighted. Never before had she seen Violet with such lively conversation.

"Indeed not, Penny; you can thank your husband for that!" teased Violet.

"Violet! How could you possibly betray my confidence so blatantly?" Ash chimed in with a broad grin. "You will quickly learn, Reymes, that my wife has strong opinions and will assert them with little provocation."

"Indeed? So she and Violet must complement one another quite well," he quipped. "I could scarcely induce *my* wife to make a single decision at the dressmaker's this morning, or the draper's, even. She will assert an opinion on very little."

Violet offered, "That may be true, but you must allow that when I *am* compelled to assert myself, I am nearly always correct."

"Indeed," said Reymes, a smile turning the corners of his lips.

Penelope, thoughts racing, looked back and forth between the couple, whose eyes were locked, small smiles quirking their lips. A moment passed before Ash voiced what Penelope had been thinking, a warm smile upon his face. "Reymes, I must thank you. Never have I seen my sister so very open and cheerful. She's not been inclined to fits or spells of moroseness, but I've seen only glimpses of the woman here today. Thank you for freeing her."

Penelope's amusement grew when the man's face took on a rosy glow. When he did not speak, she spoke up.

"You've embarrassed the poor man, Mr. Wyndham." Ash's return smile assured Penelope that he understood the gentle nature of her scold. "And of course Violet is coloring up quite brilliantly, as well. Let them alone."

"Ash," said Violet, again redirecting the conversation, "I have discovered a strength and boldness within myself which I had never supposed existed."

"Yes, now that you are free from that dreadful woman," grumbled Ash.

"Impossible to have said it better," interjected Reymes from behind his glass.

"Ashbridge! Nathaniel!" Violet's voice was strong. "Shame on you two. She may not be the most caring or charitable woman, but she is still my mother. *Our* mother, Ash."

"If you say so," grumbled he.

Penelope, seeing that the conversation was deteriorating into a bitter place – and knowing personally the devastating effects of allowing bitterness to fester – she said, "Let us not dwell on these unhappy thoughts. We have such a short time together. Shall we play cards?"

Her smile was genuine as she moved to the card-table with the rest of the party.

Nathaniel had the distinct sensation that he was being evaluated. Mrs. Wyndham – or Penelope, as she bade him call her – watched him closely and he imagined her observing his interactions with

Violet, as well as with the other couple with a scrutinizing eye. After a time, though, he supposed that he had passed muster when she relaxed the intensity of her observation. The evening progressed with pleasant conversation and several card games. All too soon, though, the time came for the Reymes party to depart. Nathaniel watched as Penelope and his wife embraced fondly, glad of her loving family members.

As they awaited their hats, gloves, and outer-garments, Wyndham invited Nathaniel to join him at his fencing school in three days for some friendly sparring. He happily agreed. Good-byes were cheerfully exchanged before the Reymes party went out to their waiting carriage. Nathaniel held a scarcely-awake Abraham and Violet cuddled with the slumbering Miriam on their way to the house on Hanover Square.

Later that evening, after the children were settled into bed, Nathaniel and Violet retired to their private sitting room. It was considerably smaller than the one they had at Bainscroft, but it certainly was sufficient. He poured two glasses of water, for himself and his wife. While she had not approached him for more than an occasional light kiss, he still held hope that she would soon be ready to enjoy with him every aspect of a felicitous marriage. Purposely allowing her more space than he would have preferred, Nathaniel seated himself in a chair near the settee upon which she was perched.

"It was a lovely dinner, was it not, Nathaniel?" she asked.

"Quite," agreed Nathaniel. "Your brother is an admirable man."

"I am truly gratified to hear you speak of him in such a manner," said Violet with a sweet smile. "He was not always so."

"Oh?" Nathaniel envisioned the man treating his beloved Violet as shabbily as had her mama and sister and felt his ire rise.

"Nothing like I am sure you conjecture. He has always had a

fondness for me, so he behaved well where I was concerned. Indeed, he offered to let me to come and live with him and Penny after they were married. I tried, for a time, but I could not intrude upon their lives in that way."

"He seems perfectly amiable; I cannot imagine him comporting himself with anything less than dignity."

"Oh! To be sure, he never behaved with depravity, but he was for a time quite wary of others, especially others who were female."

"And was it his good wife who warmed his cold heart?" Nathaniel asked dryly.

"Not at all," protested Violet. "Neither of them desired a marriage at the outset of their acquaintance! Ash was sure that he could simply wait until he was nearly in his dotage, take a wife, and produce an heir. Penelope planned never to marry; promise that you will not tell anyone, but do you recall the Silent Painter who had become quite popular some two or so years ago?"

"I do. I considered having a portrait done, but could not bring myself to. Now he is retired."

"*She* is retired, you mean. It is Penelope!"

"You jest."

"Not at all. She planned to support herself and her aunt; I am sure you will meet her later, as well as her husband Mr. Pelter. They are dear people."

"How ever did she and your brother marry, then? Surely not in a situation like our own."

"Oh no," smiled she. "As they spent more time with one another, thrown together by a mutually beneficial arrangement – I shall tell you more at a later date, for I am much too sleepy to do justice to their story at present – both found their hearts softening."

"I see," said Nathaniel. "I have similarly observed of late another instance of the beneficial influence which an excellent woman may exert upon a man who loves her, so I suppose that it may work upon both a man and a woman."

"Is that so? Pray, who is the object of this observation? Mr. Tessel? Or perhaps Mr. Faintree."

Nathaniel grinned, foreseeing the protestations which his reply would elicit. "I am."

"Oh how can you say that?" chided his wife.

"Do you not think me admirably improved?" he asked, feigning a stricken countenance.

"Certainly not." Violet realized her blunder and flushed. "That is, you had naught to improve."

"Oh, but we all have things upon which to improve," he returned promptly.

"Even so..."

"Yes?"

"Oh, neveryoumind," she murmured.

As Nathaniel rose and walked over to her, he said, "Come now, my dear. Finish that last swallow of your water and let us retire for the evening. I am feeling worn down and you look positively exhausted. See? I ya-a-awn," he said as one overtook him.

Violet laughed before doing as he bade her. She allowed him to lead her to their chamber, and soon they both fell fast asleep.

The following two days were spent in revisiting the milliners' and *modistes'* and mantua-makers' shops. The brief visits the other day did not allow Violet sufficient time to decide what she would like to order. Madame Belanger received Violet joyfully, asking where she had been keeping herself these past two years. Violet happily filled in the kind dressmaker on the events of her life since she'd last visited the shop, skimming over the less pleasant years.

"Do you see?" asked Madame Bèlanger. "Deed I not say that you weer disteened for greater tings?"

Violet smiled at the memory of the exuberant seamstress telling her two years ago that she believed Violet would have a greater purpose than being overshadowed by her family, and that she would find joy and a new beginning somewhere far from what she had known. Still, she had not changed so entirely that she suddenly enjoyed speaking only of herself; Violet quickly asked Madame how business was progressing, effectively changing the subject. Madame Bèlanger immediately set about making notes on what sort of fabric would best suit Violet as a Society Matron as opposed to a new debutante while eloquently explaining how many more clients had been frequenting her shop since the newest Mrs. Wyndham began spreading it about that she *adored* Madame Bèlanger's gowns. Nathaniel, for his part, simply stood off to the side, offering his opinion when asked, but always directing Violet to consider her own impression of the fabrics and styles.

She was glad to have, for the first time in her life, someone who took her concerns to heart regarding her clothing. Not a single gown which would be ordered would have too-plunging of a neckline for her comfort, none of the fabric would be unbecoming on her, nothing would be embellished in a manner she did not approve. In addition to the garments ordered for herself, the Tessel children were brought along the morning of the second day, that several suits might be made for young Abraham and dresses for Miriam. Stockings, gloves, and coats were also ordered for the children, along with some shoes at the cobbler's and some hats and bonnets at the mantua-maker's. When they left the shop, the proprietress promised to send one set of clothing each for the children the very next day, and two of Violet's gowns. Violet had never enjoyed shopping so much. For her part, the dressmaker was quite excited to be clothing someone of such high station; her clientele consisted of respectable ladies, and some of the *bon* ton, but no-one so high-ranking as a countess.

After this days-long spurt of shopping, Violet was glad to rest for a few hours while Nathaniel went to Ash's fencing club to spar with her brother the next morning. After she had been settled in a comfortable chair with a new book she had purchased just yesterday, Mr. Garand announced a visitor. When she set aside her book, Mrs. Wyndham strode through the door.

"Mama!" gasped Violet. She knew that her mother and sister were to arrive in Town for Rose's wedding, but had not realized it would be so soon.

"Violet, child, I am glad to find you at home, that we might have a few moments to talk." The woman's smile, while a bit cold, appeared sincere. Indeed, her smiles were always cold, so Violet was quite pleased that her mama had come to visit her. "How are you faring at Bainscroft? We have had your letters, but I do not put much stock in letters. A perfectly amiable letter can be contrived whilst the author is weeping with depressed spirits or seething with anger."

"I am well, Mama." Violet was about to disclose the happy fact that she and her husband had come to love one another, but Mrs. Wyndham continued.

"I see that Lord Reymes has outfitted you in the latest fashion. Your clothing suits you quite well. And a good thing, too, for it would not do for a countess to look as dowdy as you often did prior to your marriage. You will not be wearing anything *too* becoming at the wedding, will you? It would be most unfair to Rose were you to attempt to upstage her. I daresay, though, it could never be done. Her gown is exquisite, and her complexion has been lovely – glowing! – of late."

"Oh no, Mama! I shall wear a simple—"

"Ah, no matter," said Mrs. Wyndham. "I suppose you have been making many visits in the neighborhood surrounding Bainscroft and most especially since coming to Town?"

"Indeed, Mama. I have even befriended one of the tenant farmer's wives. You see, she was not—"

But again Mrs. Wyndham interrupted. "A tenant farmer's wife!" Her face had taken on a reddish hue. "Really, Violet, you *must* do better than that!"

"Mama?" Violet was bewildered and could not at all account for her mother's incomprehensible words.

"Connections! How am I to be entertained when my last child is married? How shall I pass my days?"

"Mama, you once said that if only you could but see your daughters comfortably settled, you should be happy to sit at home, at your leisure—"

"Oh, Violet, how *can* you be so tiresome, even now that you are married?" Mrs. Wyndham's exasperation was evident. "You must strengthen the connections which Lord Reymes has. Then, when the Season begins, I may come to visit you, and will of course attend any functions which you do. Of course, after your connections come to know me, I will receive invitations by my own right and will no longer have to hang on your arm."

"But Mama, surely you cannot expect me to—"

"Of course I do!"

"But—"

"Oh, none of your missishness, child! I'd have thought being married to a man such as Lord Reymes these several months would have cured you of that by now."

"But this is our first trip to Town since our wedding," Violet rushed to say, before Mrs. Wyndham could once again prevent her from speaking. "While we have called upon several people since our arrival, I cannot suppose that it would be appropriate for me to call first without being introduced."

"Violet, really, you must do more to recommend yourself to people, then. Lord Reymes cannot be expected to desire to take you about in public if you are so ill-suited to a position such as his."

"I do apologize, Mama, but people are rather scarce, due to the Season not yet having begun. I daresay we shall return in Spring, when the Season is in full swing, but for now–."

"That is of little consequence to me," interrupted the woman. "I am sure there are plenty who remain in Town."

"But Mama!"

"I scarce can believe, Violet, that you would treat your poor mama with such contempt!" Mrs. Wyndham burst into unexpected tears and Violet's head spun as she attempted to keep abreast of her mama's many moods.

"I-I do not, Mama!" Violet's voice trembled. "I do not enjoy making you cross with me."

"Then do as I ask! Make up to your husband! Ask him to set up house in Town." The woman's tears ceased and her eyes brightened. "*Hold a ball!*"

"Mama! That is a great expense, I am sure you are aware—"

"Oh, with a man of Lord Reymes' fortune, that surely cannot signify." All traces of tears were gone from Mrs. Wyndham's countenance. In their place, a steely coldness descended on the woman's face and Violet felt the chill in her bones. "You are an ungrateful chit! After I have contrived to secure this marriage for you!"

"Contrived?"

"Of course I knew Mr. Peyton was lying. Indeed, his reputation preceded him. But to have you married to an Earl! To have no more worry of Rose being unable to marry Mr. Langley!"

"I cannot believe it of you." Violet's voice was scarcely above a whisper.

"Oh, such a miss! Really, girl, you ought to be grateful to me!" Mrs. Wyndham's scowl deepened. "There is certainly no possibility that you might have captured Lord Reymes' attention without my help. You really come most ill-recommended to anyone of Society worthy of notice. The Lord knows how I have been plagued with you; and now that I have properly disposed of you, you cannot even think of repaying me in this simple manner!"

Violet could hold her countenance no longer; she burst into tears. "How can you speak so?" she sobbed. "I know I shall never say such a thing to my own child."

"Oh, has that husband of yours already got you in the family way?" Mrs. Wyndham said. "Not that it's a bad thing – does naught but secure the match – but I can scarce believe he was pleased enough with you to desire *that* so soon."

Violet felt her face flame as she fought a desire to run from the room. "Mama, I am not carrying a child, so please take that thought from your head; I merely meant *once I have a child*. Lord Reymes and I have learned to appreciate one another's company, even love one another."

Agitated, Violet rose from her chair and moved to the window.

Below, ladies and gentlemen strolled sedately, servants scurried on errands, and in the street, carriages and horses crawled slowly along the crowded road.

"Oh do sit down, Violet, your nervous fidgeting tries me so!"

Violet did not sit, but she turned as calmly as she could to face the elder woman, carefully holding her hands still. "Is there nothing which I may do to please you?" she asked, despair flooding her chest, pressing hard and suffocating her at her innermost heart.

"What a silly question to ask!" Mrs. Wyndham scowled, shifting her eyes to the fringe of her shawl, where her hands fidgeted.

Emboldened by her mother's show of avoidance, Violet pressed, "Will you not answer it?"

She could see her mother's face growing more and more red. Fire blazed from the woman's eyes as she spat, "Impertinent child!"

"But – I am not a child!" Violet cried. "I am married! I have learned *so much* of myself. I have learned that I am indeed stronger than I thought I ever could be, that I am worthy of a good man's affection, even his love..." Violet looked back out the window. The injury caused by her mother's words cut quite deep. With a strength she had never before experienced, Violet turned again to face the older woman. "I *must* know why you hold such contempt for me. How have I offended you so greatly?"

For the briefest of moments, Mrs. Wyndham's eyes were wide as her face went from flushed to pale. Finally, she stood quickly as her words burst forth in a torrent of high emotion. "From the time I married your father, I cared for you and that spoiled brother of yours – and for no reward! – until my own dear child was born. Rose is *all* I have in this world. I should have discouraged her from her silly notion of marrying that fool Langley, but I could not deny her when she had already been deprived of so very much."

Violet felt that the room was spinning about her, and suddenly everything was too bright and too cold. "W-what?"

"A dowry!" the woman hissed. "Your mama settled a considerable sum on you before she passed, and so I should have foisted *you* on that fool Langley. But Rose had to go and fall in love with him."

"N-no. Not that. You...you said about my...my mother?"

Nathaniel greatly enjoyed his outing to the fencing club. Indeed, he and Wyndham had a most invigorating time, furthering their acquaintance without the pleasant but decidedly polite presence of their wives; despite the great love each had for his spouse, they agreed that time spent with only men was necessary from time to time. His enjoyment of the day was cut short, however, upon his return home.

He had not intended to eavesdrop, but when he was about to enter the sitting room, Nathaniel heard his name, mentioned by Mrs. Wyndham, regarding Violet's clothing. He did not wish to embarrass either woman with the thought that he might have heard their discussion of him. So he waited and had been, again, upon the point of entering, when Mrs. Wyndham raised her voice regarding Violet's friendship with Mrs. Tessel. Unfortunately, the conversation had careened in a downward direction from that point. He could not make out all that was said, indeed their voices dropped considerably in volume at one point, and he heard nothing but murmurings, something about the family and Violet's dowry. Nathaniel desired greatly to enter the room, but also hoped and prayed that his wife would learn to defend herself. With difficulty, he held his peace.

But only just.

With every disparaging remark from the other woman, he felt the rage surge through his blood and was sorely tempted to enter the room. Undecided, he began to pace in the small hallway outside that room, whenever he neared the doorway hearing snippets of Mrs. Wyndham's ranting and Violet's valiant attempts to control her sobs...*surprised he did not cry off...yet banished you to the cottage?...deplorable lack of grace...calls you his love? It is laughable!* His heart aching for his wife, he determined to enter the room and stop this abuse.

As Nathaniel started for the door, however, it swung open and Violet crashed into him at a run. Certainly, he was surprised, but years of being brought up to behave as a gentleman served him well. At present, his only aim was to remove Violet from the presence of Mrs. Wyndham.

Tucking her hand into his arm, he said, "Ah, there you are my love! I have been looking this age for you. Come, let us go into the garden." With a discreet glance over his shoulder, he saw that Mrs. Wyndham was unabashedly staring, listening to his words. He added, for her benefit, "I should enjoy wandering about with you, perhaps becoming lost...Oh! Is your mother here? You were just leaving, ma'am? Good day!" He nodded coolly in her direction before leading Violet away.

Once they were ensconced behind the walls of the narrow garden, Nathaniel slipped an arm about her waist. He offered his handkerchief, which Violet accepted with a silent nod of thanks. Her tears subsided about the time that they reached the back of the garden. Nathaniel stopped. Drawing his wife into his arms, he rested his chin gently upon her head for a moment. Her arms were caught between them, her fingers lightly tracing the embroidery on his waistcoat, which peeked out from his overcoat.

"Your cravat!" cried Violet after a moment, gingerly fingering the intricate folds of fabric into which her face had been tucked while he held her close.

"To the devil with my cravat," was his reply.

"Nathaniel! Your language makes me blush."

"I am sorry, sweet, but I am most deplorably out of countenance with your mother."

Violet drew back a bit from him, peering up into his face. "What did you hear?" she asked in a low voice.

"Enough," he murmured while unfolding his arms from around her, only to immediately claim her hands in his own. Looking down into her face, flushed from her sobs, eyelashes and cheeks dampened with tears, Nathaniel was unable to comprehend how any person could aim those barbed insults at such a kind woman. *Especially when that woman is her daughter!* He quickly kissed her cheek, tasting the salt as he stood straight again.

Violet's face crumpled. "I-I do apologize, Nathaniel. Indeed, I cannot imagine your – mortification." She attempted to turn away from him, but he held her hands fast. Still, she would not meet his gaze as she mumbled, "Should you wish to return at once to Bainscroft, I can feel nothing but sympathy. Of course, I would be unable to join you until after the nuptials, but—"

At this Nathaniel could stand silent no more. "Indeed I can think of no *better* place to be at present than with you. I will not leave you to *that woman's* mercy, if indeed she has any."

"What a thing to say about my –" But she stopped suddenly, pulling her lips between her teeth. Nathaniel was in rather high dudgeons and spoke quickly.

"What a thing to say about *you* in your *own house*! She may be your mother, dearest, but I cannot abide her unfeeling manner toward you. Do you *believe* what she said, Violet?" He felt his face flush with the force of his ire.

"I hardly know, Nathaniel. I feel so very confused and anxious at present, and unsure of everything."

"Of *everything*, Violet?" he repeated in a low voice, rough with emotion.

"I...I am certain of your love." Violet averted her misery-filled eyes. "And I am certain of God's love. Beyond that, I truly cannot say."

"While I am most gratified to know that you do not doubt my affection, and that you do not doubt God's love for you, I must insist that you understand how beloved you are by our staff, by so many of our acquaintance. Your quiet concern, caring disposition, and your sweet shyness, which you strive every day to overcome – all these recommend you *most* highly to anyone fortunate enough to make your acquaintance – and do not protest! Yes, I heard those words which were so designed to inflict pain, and yes, I am repeating them, but with quite the opposite intent. Do not suppose, dear heart, that my words are untrue or exaggerated simply because I borrow the phrase. I've not heard of a single unkind word being circulated about you, even here in Town. And you know what a gossipy gabster Stally can be!"

Violet was silent for a time, unmoving as she stared at her hands, enfolded as they were in his own. At length, her words came, pensively and quietly. "My head immediately wants to discount all that you have said," she began. Nathaniel made to protest, but she silenced him when she raised her eyes, directing at him a gently reprimanding look. "My heart, however, aches to believe that what you say is true. I cannot say presently whether or not I truly believe, in my heart of hearts. Not that I believe you lie to me; I know that *you* believe what you say, but I fear that you might be mistaken. I am not at my ease with strangers, and I know that what my – *mother* – said has at least a grain of truth to it."

"Most lies do," said Nathaniel.

"I do believe, however, that I shall endeavor to give credence to *your* words, and not *hers*." Nathaniel was immensely gladdened to hear her words, and even more so when her eyes took on a light-hearted twinkle as she said airily. "Besides which, I daresay the wife of an Earl ought to think rather highly of herself, or at the least, to believe what her excellent husband declares to be the truth of it."

"While I am gratified to hear such a sentiment from you, my love," grinned Nathaniel while placing a feather-light kiss upon her cheek, "please do not attempt to distract me from my purpose."

"Which is?"

"Aside from getting lost amongst the hedges, as I mentioned before we left the company of your mama, it is to compliment you until you color up quite thoroughly. I have not seen such an occurrence for this age, and I fear it has put me quite out of sorts."

"I do apologize, my lord Reymes, most profusely." There was a slight jest to her voice, which warmed his heart to hear. He hoped sincerely that whatever had upset her so was already leaving her mind. He could not hide his grin as she continued speaking. "However, it may be that you no longer *can* elicit a blush from me. I am, after all, an esteemed countess now, and no longer a mere gentleman's daughter, too timid to speak more than a few halting words to the likes of you."

"Do you think so?" he asked, rising to her challenge. He quickly pulled her into his arms, lowering his face until his lips were a breath away from the skin just below her ear. After a pause, he whispered, "Just a moment ago, you chastised me for my language, claiming that it made you blush, and yet there was none. Perhaps you are correct, but let us see." Ever so slowly, Nathaniel pressed his lips against the skin below her ear, feeling a shiver run through his wife's body even as his heart picked up its pace.. When he drew back, he saw that Violet's face was quite overcome with a deep blush.

"It may be that you still make me blush," she whispered.

With a slight grin, he drew her once again close to his heart. "My darling, lovely wife. My heart, my joy, my desire, my *love*—"

Pushing back from him to look at him with a skeptical lift of her brow, Violet said drily, "Oh, you are doing it over-dramatic, indeed, Nathaniel!"

"Am I?" he asked with a quirk of his lips.

Nathaniel lowered his head and claimed her lips with his own. The kiss started as a gently teasing caress, for he did not intend to lose himself in such an open place, secluded though they may be in the garden. When Violet sighed and leaned into his embrace, though, he found himself deepening the kiss, pouring into it the emotions which he had held so strongly in hand until this moment. Breathing heavily, he dragged his lips from her own, kissing her cheek and forehead, until he rested his chin on her head once again.

"I love you, my sweet Violet."

"And I you, Nathaniel."

The following day, Violet and Nathaniel decided the children needed some time away from the walls of the comparatively smaller room of the Townhouse nursery. While Miss Stokes took them out to the small garden twice each day, Violet knew they were used to being out of doors a great deal more than they had been since their arrival in town – indeed, even since their arrival at Bainscroft, as they often went into the garden or fields with their parents.

Knowing how Violet enjoyed being in gardens and among plant life, Nathaniel suggested an outing at Vauxhall; while it certainly was not at its peak during the cooler months, the structures would still be there, and there would be no great crowds during this time. He hoped that the time spent in the open air might restore his wife's spirits, as well. Miss Stokes was given the day off to visit some family in Town, and Nathaniel and Violet bundled the children into their brand-new coats and hats and loaded them into the carriage. Her husband explained to Violet, as they rode in the carriage to the famed gardens, that the evening they had met, several of his acquaintance had been discussing the same gardens and it made him realize that he had not seen them in quite some time.

Once there, the driver was given instructions to fetch them at an appointed time, and the foursome ventured forth. After paying the entrance fee for all of them, Nathaniel offered his arm to his lady, his hand to young Mr. Tessel, and Violet took little Miriam's hand.

They walked along the Grand Walk for a time, the children running ahead to see various things. Few people were there, and fewer blooms could be seen, due to the chilly weather. Violet was glad of her warm, fur-lined pelisse and muff, and was even more gratified to see that the children were quite snuggly wrapped in their small coats and accouterments. The cobbler had proven a miracle-worker and delivered smart little boots the day after the order had been placed. Miriam was adorable in her small bonnet.

"You have proven yourself once again, my love," spoke Nathaniel as they followed after the giggling children, "in dressing these two. I am impressed that you have so cleverly balanced fashion with sensible usefulness."

"What elegant words!" she laughed. "The truth is, I merely hoped to ensure that their clothing would prevent them from being looked down upon in Town, and yet not appear ostentatious once they return to their home with it. I do hope that Mrs. Tessel is taking the rest she needs."

Nathaniel chuckled lightly, nudging her with his shoulder. "Are you still very much worried about Mrs. Tessel?"

"I am not worried." Violet smiled up at her husband. "I must admit to being *concerned* still, but I am doing my best to both trust that my friend will obey the doctor's orders to refrain from unnecessarily strenuous activities, and that the Lord will continue to heal her."

"You are wise beyond your years." Violet merely laughed, and Nathaniel changed the subject. "Where else ought we take these two young adventurers while in Town?"

"Perhaps the Serpentine?" suggested Violet. "I think they should enjoy seeing such a long body of water."

"Indeed," agreed Nathaniel. "We might also take them driving in Hyde Park; bundled up well, taking the barouche would be enjoyable, would it not?"

"I thought the purpose of driving in Hyde Park was to demonstrate one's excellent driving abilities. Should we not take a curricle, that you may drive your own animals?"

"Will the children fit?" asked her husband.

"I can easily carry Miriam upon my lap, and young Abraham is small enough to fit between the two of us."

"True," grinned Nathaniel. "Perhaps, if we go early enough and there are few other carriages about, I can let the boy have a try at the reins."

"I daresay he would love that above all else!"

"Then it is settled," Nathaniel said, smiling softly down at her. Violet found that her breath was quite stayed, and her heart racing. Her husband's smile grew, crinkles appearing at the corners of his eyes. His head slowly lowered, nearer and nearer to hers.

Suddenly, a squeal from little Miriam broke the spell which had come over the pair, and they stepped a bit farther apart. Violet made a valiant attempt at ignoring the heat which suffused her cheeks as she directed her attention toward the children once again.

The brother and sister were skipping ahead of them, talking excitedly and pointing at the piazza around which the supper-boxes were located. Once Nathaniel and Violet gave their permission, the children began running about the area, ducking into the boxes occasionally, attempting to hide from one another.

"Will they be reprimanded?" asked Violet, glancing about. "I do not wish to offend anyone."

"Who is here to offend?" asked Reymes. "As you can see, the boxes are empty of anything which might break, and there are few people about. The chill in the air today must have kept away the few folks looking for entertainment."

Violet smiled at her husband, glad of his reassurance. "I enjoy seeing the children have such a splendid time. This place is rather eerie to me, empty as it is; the last time I was here, it was crowded with people."

"You visited during your Season?" he asked.

"Yes."

"And you partook in the supper here?"

"We did," smiled Violet. "Initially, we had only planned to hear the orchestra, and see the equestrians. After my brother was contacted by Lord Ashbridge and given an allowance from the estate, we were freed to do a great deal more. I fear Rose and her Mr.

Langley might have gotten lost in the Dark Paths; I am uncertain whether my mama would have so easily accepted their engagement had that not occurred, though she did not learn of it for some time. Rose let slip that they had been there, though, some time after."

"Is that so?" asked Nathaniel.

"Indeed. Ash and his friend, Mr. MacDougal searched for them; he would not allow me to enter them, for which I was grateful."

"I should say so."

"Yes, though I sat with my mama and Penelope and her aunt, Miss Breckenridge. Though she is now Mrs. Pelter. Even the presence of company did not serve to stem her expression of her disappointment with me."

"Even though your sister was the one to sneak away?"

"She has never been rational in her dealings with me. She blamed me for not keeping Rose in hand. Despite the unpleasantness, I had much rather endure that than the Dark Paths. They seem absolutely dreadful!"

"Dreadful due to your previous distaste for small paths in enclosed hedges, or did this experience increase your distaste?"

Violet answered contemplatively, "Perhaps a bit of both."

"I see." Nathaniel tightened his arm against his side, causing her own arm to be tucked quite snugly between them. "Rest assured, my dear, that should you find yourself upon a small path in enclosed hedges, it will be with me and I am certain that in time, you will grow to love them."

"Oh, indeed?" Violet's voice was lightly sardonic and her eyes amused. "You are quite confident in your charm, to speak such words."

"Oh, no; not at all," rejoined he. "I am merely confident that my wife will never find my presence in such a situation distasteful."

"Ah," nodded Violet. "Then you are quite right in saying so."

The couple continued to follow the children through the Gardens – wisely, though, avoiding the Dark Paths.

The wedding took place as planned. Mr. Langley's dress for the occasion nearly out-shone his bride's. What had previously been a tendency toward foppishness, now turned into a whole-hearted embrace of it. He wore a suit of bright white, embroidered with red and gold thread, cinched in at the waist, the shoulders stuffed to make them appear fuller than they were. Beneath his coat he wore a waistcoat of bright red embroidered with the same gold thread as the suit. His shirt-points came so high as to obscure half of his face and were exceeded only by his hair, which was teased to such an extreme that Violet blushed for her sister as she stood beside her ridiculous-looking bridegroom. Rose wore a lovely gown made of a washed silk over-lain by a sheer gauze with white ribbon and lace for embellishment. It suited her young, lithe figure quite well. She was quite oblivious to the extreme fashion which her groom wore, counting it to his being a leader of fashion, which suited her quite well; Fashion and Society were quite strong contenders with Love as being the central objective in her marriage. And so in this manner, Rose gained a husband.

Violet was touched by the attentiveness of her own husband. For the remainder of their time in Town, he did not fawn over her or crowd her, but he was ever at her side. His stern gaze, directed at Mrs. Wyndham, curtailed any critical remarks whenever they were all in company together, and his well-practiced hauteur continued to keep at bay those so-called "toad-eaters" who would make up to the couple for the sole purpose of raising their own social standing. She found that she grew ever more comfortable with his presence and appreciated his kindness and gentleness more than she could express.

Nathaniel, for his part, kept close to Violet's side for fear that if he left her alone with her mother for too long a time, she might retreat back into the quiet, reticent wisp of a girl she had been when they met. He remained unaware of a rather important development in the life of his wife – namely, the intelligence regarding her parentage; she rather feared that if he knew of the devastating news she had received, he would whisk her away to Bainscroft before she could convince him otherwise. She did not wish for her mama – *Is it appropriate for me to still think of her in that manner?* – to think that she left Town as a direct result of her cutting words. Neither did Violet wish to miss the celebration of her sister's marriage, in spite of the difficult relationship shared with her sister.

During the course of their stay in Town, Nathaniel also introduced Violet to some of his school-day cronies, with whom he had associated a great deal when residing in London before their marriage.

One, a Mr. Hugo Merriweather, dined with them the day following Rose's wedding. To offer variety to the party, Violet's cousin Charlotte was invited, with her parents, and another couple with whom Nathaniel was acquainted. Violet commented rather sardonically, as they comprised the guest list, that her mama should be beyond pleased with Violet's entertaining three new acquaintances. It gladdened Nathaniel's heart to hear his wife make light of that fateful visit. He was concerned, however, that Violet still mentioned the event. He had rather hoped that she would have forgotten by this time. However, as none of her words were self-deprecating, and the tone in which she spoke was never overly melancholy, he felt rather unjustified in his worrying. So it was that he chuckled along with her, claimed her hand for a gentle and loving kiss, and proceeded with making plans for the evening.

Nathaniel was content with his choice of friend to invite. Stallingsworth was in town, and a much closer acquaintance, but he was lacking one quality of import from which Nathaniel hoped dearly to benefit. Hugo was a noted Corinthian. He excelled at hunting, riding, and boxing. It was the later of these which interested Nathaniel so very much.

According to plan, the other couple was required to leave soon after the dinner in order to attend the opera. Cousin Charlotte was to pass the entire night at the house, and so the Doberlys also retired to their Town-house quite soon after the meal had been completed. Violet confessed to him that she was quite eager for a nice long visit with her cousin, and so Nathaniel was left to entertain his friend alone after dinner. As they had retired to the billiard-room, Hugo was fairly bursting with questions for his friend.

"I say, Reymes, I can scarce believe you are riveted! Was the wedding really surrounded with such scandal as was rumored?" Hugo sipped his drink while Nathaniel set up his shot at the billiards table.

"More than those gossip-mongers knew. Your turn, friend."

Hugo took his shot before saying, "Is that so? She don't seem to be in the family way."

"I will ask you just this once to refrain from speaking of my *wife* in such a crude manner. She is no barque of frailty, like so much of the female company it is your custom to keep." Nathaniel lined up and executed a perfect shot.

"I beg your pardon," intoned Hugo with an officious bow that did not hide the amused question in his voice and upon his face.

Nathaniel waited for Hugo to take his turn before continuing. "As I cannot assume anything but that your words stemmed from an as-yet brief acquaintance with the Lady Reymes, as well as a misapprehension born from my not fully detailing the events to which my words referred, of course there is nothing to forgive." He paused, taking his own shot. "It was the fault of my brother that we came into any more contact than simply being introduced at her arrival to the ball. He was attempting...well, suffice it to say that he thought he could deal with her in the manner in which you supposed she had acted. I stopped him, and soon after, she and I were espied by her meddling mama, alone and in a position which was, admittedly, rather questionable to a person who did not take the time to discover what we were truly about."

"Your turn, my friend, and what *was* it that you were about?" asked Hugo with a chuckle.

Nathaniel flinched as he took his shot, missing terribly and nearly tearing the fabric on his billiard table. "We were not about anything! I stayed with her after giving John a sound thrashing, to ensure that she suffered no lasting ill after her ordeal. Once I was assured that she would be able to return to the ballroom – all this took place on a balcony, mind you – we planned to return separately, but as she moved to the door, she tripped and would have fallen had I not caught her."

"Ah, playing the hero, were you?" teased Hugo as he made a perfect shot.

"I was not playing at anything! She would have fallen. I reacted instinctually."

"Instinct, you say? Something we in polite society seem to do all we can to suppress. We think ourselves above such base motivations."

"And now you are a philosopher?"

Hugo laughed raucously before motioning for Nathaniel to take his shot. Just as he did, Hugo spoke. "So the great Earl of Bainscroft has finally been leg-shackled. Ha! Who'd have thought?"

"While I'd not planned to take a wife until I had settled several things, I was not so against marriage as you always seemed to think, Hugo."

"No? P'haps I confused you with someone else." Hugo ended the game, beating Nathaniel handsomely.

"Perhaps." Nathaniel offered to refill his friend's glass before he continued. "Hugo. I must ask whether you would be willing to help me with something. My brother has made threats, and while the situation appears to be temporarily resolved at present, I have come to realize that my wife has no means of defending herself. If John should suddenly develop a distaste of laying low, or if another rake should—"

"Now Reymes, I ain't a man-for-hire!" warned Hugo as he settled himself into a chair near the fire.

"Of course not!" protested Nathaniel, choosing a chair adjacent him.

"And I won't incite him to call me out so's I can shoot him for you."

"I certainly do not want that."

"Then what are you getting at, man?"

"I know it may be rather irregular, but is there a way to allow Violet to know how to ward off an attacker?"

"Teach a woman to defend herself? *Highly* irregular, that!"

"Even so, the first time, he managed to corner her alone amongst a crowded ballroom. And you are the most noted Corinthian with whom I claim an intimate acquaintance – likely even among those with whom I do not claim an intimate acquaintance. Will you help me? Help my wife?"

Hugo did not speak, the slight puckering of his brow the only indication that he was doing more than simply sitting and staring.

Nathaniel knew what he asked was impossibly presumptuous. A more proper course of action would be to involve the local magistrate, and to keep Violet by his side every minute of every day. However, given the tender newness of their deepening intimacy, he was reluctant to force his presence upon her to that extent. He feared his heart may break if she rejected him, and being near her as much as he had been while in London was wearing his patience thin. He might break his resolve to follow her leading if he continued to attach himself to her for such long hours. Additionally, he also hoped that some of the anxiety which had been growing concerning her safety and well-being would abate if she were given some manner of defense.

In a somewhat desperate tone, he said, "As a dear friend?"

Hugo grunted and replied, "When you throw *that* in my face, man, I have no choice."

Nathaniel grinned sheepishly. "I shall throw whatever is necessary in your face, so long as it is for the best interest of my wife."

"You really are besotted," chuckled Hugo. "And before you say anything – yes, I see you were about to interrupt me! Close your mouth and hear me out. Understand me when I say that I mean no harm by my words. I only hope that I may find such a love someday, and I wish you happy in the sincerest manner I know how."

"Thank you, Hugo," said Nathaniel, truly touched by his friend's sincere words. Clearing his throat rather purposefully, he said, "I admit that I was not even thinking of love at the time, but now I see what an excellent match we are for one another."

Hugo nodded, smiling at his friend. "I am glad to see that the reports of your being trapped by a scheming female are quite false. Since your arrival in Town, all the gossiping biddies – though there are admittedly only a fraction of those that would have been here had the Season not already ended – have had little else to speak of, but that you are quite bewitched by your bride. The rumors which started at the announcement of your engagement centered on what means she employed to trap you."

"The boot is quite on the other leg, Hugo – I believe she would rather not have married *me* at the outset, but for the insistence of her mama."

"This is the second time you've mentioned the mother, and in none too fond a manner. I rather cannot wait to meet her. Is she as dreadful as all that?"

"May I trust you for your confidence?" asked Nathaniel, leaning forward in his chair earnestly.

Hugo nodded solemnly. "Of course, old friend."

"Mrs. Wyndham has been cruel and unfeeling to her eldest daughter for all her life. I first noticed the extraordinary effect of the lack of her presence with Violet when we had known one another for less than a day. My bride's tongue was loosed, and her spirit came alive when only the two of us were touring the estate, but the moment her mama returned to the room, she seemed to shrivel into a shell of the vibrant woman she had been."

"Wyndham, you say?" Hugo asked.

"What?" said Nathaniel, rather distracted, lost as he was in his memories of those first few visits with his bride. "Er, yes. Her maiden name was Wyndham."

"Does it happen that her father was Mr. Wyndham of Wyndmere?"

"Yes, that is her family's home. Her brother Ashbridge has since inherited the estate, though he lives in Town and allows his mother to retain the house." said Reymes, "Are you familiar with the family?"

Hugo shook his head and said, "No, no. At least, not well. My father was a schoolmate of the late Mr. Wyndham. I ask because I had been under the impression that he was a widower before he passed."

"Oh?" Nathaniel stared intently at the man, waiting as Hugo creased his brow and his eyes took on a vacant look as he searched his memory for some vague, uncertain fact.

"I really cannot say with any amount of confidence, but I do seem to recall meeting the man when I was a boy, together with his wife and a small child – a boy, I believe. His wife was quite kind, a brown-haired beauty, though I believe she may have been ill. I remember being allowed to hear a story from her – she was an excellent story-teller – but then my sisters and I were sent away to the nursery. Her child remained with her; he was quiet and somewhat sullen, I suppose, a fair-haired shadow of his mother. Her voice was very soft and I believe weak, but she was full of emotion and life." Hugo shook his head and chuckled. "Sounds odd, I know."

"Mmm. Darker hair, you say? Not at all fair-haired?"

"Yes. Of *that* I am quite certain," affirmed Hugo.

"The Mrs. Wyndham of today is decidedly fair."

"Is she?" Hugo sat quietly for a moment before speaking, "That is what I was trying to recall. I believe that less than a year after that visit, we received word that Mrs. Wyndham had been delivered of this life just as she gave birth to a girl-baby. Mr. Wyndham mourned deeply for his wife, but after a year, remarried and spoke no more of her. Indeed, I believe that my family was made privy to this information only because my father was close with him; the rest of Society may or may not have known his first wife."

"Had she no connections? No one besides her husband to mourn her death?"

"I do not know. Perhaps she was an American? Or an orphan?" mused Hugo.

"Perhaps. Rather odd for a gentleman to marry an orphan."

"Although not entirely unheard of. I daresay many of the female variety would find their tale terribly romantic."

Nathaniel did not speak, but sat quietly contemplating.

"Do you plan to investigate this further?" asked Hugo at length.

"Perhaps. But then, perhaps we shall never know," answered Nathaniel. "I would ask, Hugo, that you keep this to yourself. I would not care to distress my wife with half-constructed tales from the past – not meaning to offend, friend."

"Oh, no offense perceived, Reymes. I know a young boy's memory is nothing near to reliable. And you have my word that I shall not divulge what I've said to anyone."

"Thank you," said Reymes. "Now then, shall we go to the drawing-room and join the ladies? Miss Doberly is in Town for Violet's sister's wedding, which occurred yesterday. The bridegroom, I might add – do you happen to know him? Langley? – is a veritable coxcomb." Distaste colored his voice.

"No, I've not that misfortune," returned Hugo in a jolly voice as he stood.

They reached the drawing-room and entered to find Violet and Charlotte sitting close on the settee and talking happily. Once they had greeted the ladies, Nathaniel revealed the purpose of their joining them at this time. Charlotte was somewhat jokingly adjured to keep a secret of what they would do, to which she readily agreed.

Learning something of the art of boxing, a world forbidden to females, seemed a great lark to her.

So the evening proceeded, with the gentlemen coaching the ladies in purely defensive movements. The four of them knew that it would not be discussed after this evening, but while they were assembled in the drawing-room, a sense of secretive freedom filled the air. Violet expressed an uncertainty that she would ever be able to actually use any of the knowledge she received, but she seemed to enjoy the coaching regardless.

While her husband bade his friend farewell, Violet accompanied Charlotte to the room in which she would spend the night. Once there, Violet spoke.

"I've something dreadful that I must share with someone."

"And you cannot tell your husband?" asked Charlotte, alarm evident on her face.

"I can. And I shall. But there has not been time, and likely will not be until we return to Bainscroft, and I feel I shall burst if I do not tell someone!"

"By all means, then, tell me now!" chuckled Charlotte.

"I learned several days ago that my mama – Mrs. Wyndham, that is – is not in actuality my mother. My own mother passed away mere months after my birth, and my papa remarried a year later. Rose was born of that marriage."

"Indeed?" asked Charlotte. She was quiet for a moment, eyes wide. After several moments, she said, "I had no idea, but I honestly cannot say that I am shocked at this news. She has always been dreadfully unkind toward you."

"That is a thing of the past. I feel as though her power over me has vanished."

"Good for you, Violet!" cheered Charlotte.

"Do you suppose that your parents knew?" asked Violet hesitantly.

"I cannot say for certain, but several years ago, they did tell me that they only renewed their closeness with your family after I came along. Rose was born several years before I was, so they must not have known your mother well, if at all."

"For so many years, her voice has echoed in my head, scolding me for being too shy and dull, but now it is merely a whisper." Violet smiled slightly before asking, "Do you suppose that it shall leave me altogether some day?"

Charlotte embraced her cousin, saying, "I certainly hope so, Violet. You deserve to be free of her."

"I feel as though a veil has been lifted from my eyes, that I can see things clearly for the first time in my life."

Several days later, the Reymes party returned to Bainscroft. The carriage was heavy with their luggage, together with the purchases made for Violet and for the Tessel children. Soon, the young ones were dozing upon Violet's lap, and Nathaniel aided Violet in settling them together upon the bench. He tugged her gently over to his seat, and finally pulled her into the crook of his arm, resting his head against the cushion behind him.

Both seemed disinclined to speak and fell into a comfortable silence, looking at the children, out the windows, or closing their eyes in turn. As they went along, Violet contemplated their visit in

London. She had met several of her husband's friends and even made a couple of new acquaintances, in addition to the shopping and the wedding. *Mama would be so pleased,* she thought wryly. Somehow, the thought did not sadden or distress her as it might have done previously.

Violet's realization that her mama had truly been acting in self-interest as she had maneuvered her daughters into Society had struck her forcefully. The pain of learning that the woman whom she had believed to be her mother was not – that pain cut deep. After that knowledge had settled, though, it had also suddenly and unexpectedly released her. When she had believed her mama – *it feels odd to still think of her as my mama, but then she is the only one I've ever known* – wanted the best for her, she had felt compelled to do her utmost to follow the woman's advice, to believe there *was* something wrong with her. Indeed, the knowledge that it was not her own mother, but a woman who had been consumed by bitterness and resentment brought about feelings of pity in Violet's heart. Knowing that Nathaniel loved her and she loved him – that God had blessed her with a happy marriage despite what the woman may or may not have intended – Violet experienced a peace and contentment that she had never before known.

Truly, I tried my best never to be discontented *with my life – after all, I was sure of my salvation, knew that I was provided a home and clothing and food. But my life now so far exceeds all that I had expected ever to have.* She swiped a stray tear from her cheek.

"Whatever is the matter, my dear?" came her husband's sleep-roughened voice.

"Oh, nothing really," replied Violet. She thought it was too soon to tell Nathaniel, but then could not think of a good reason. "Do you recall when my mother visited shortly before Rose's wedding?"

"I do," he replied, his voice now entirely awake and having taken on a hard edge.

"Please do not be cross," said she, boldly turning to press a gentle kiss to his jawline. "And do wait until I've finished before you speak. Yes, I know your propensity to rush ahead the moment you believe some offense has been made to me. The other day, when she visited, she let slip a rather large and startling secret. She is not my mother, but step-mother. My own mother died shortly after I was born, and Papa married another woman a year later."

"Does this news injure you?" he asked when she had finished. Violet could feel the restrained emotion in the tension of his muscles beside and around her body.

"Not as one would have thought. I am disappointed in my father, that he did not see fit to honor my mother's memory by even telling me of her. And it hurt a great deal to learn that I had believed a woman loved me and desired the best for me who in fact never did." When she felt her husband grow tenser beside her, Violet hastened to add, "But as for hurting me in a lasting way, it is quite the opposite. I feel freer than I ever have, knowing that her words were not intended for my good."

Nathaniel raised his hands to untie the bow holding her bonnet in place and removed it from her head. She felt warm pressure on the top of her head before she felt his breath in her hair as he spoke. "You are so strong."

"No, you think too much of–"

"I do not. You've survived so much: marriage to a stranger under terribly undesirable circumstances and before that, a life of being told you are not what you should be. And more than survived, you now thrive, helping and blessing and befriending so many people, and in so many ways." He turned her to face him and lowered his head until their noses brushed. "I am so very honored to be your husband, to be loved by you."

The couple shared several gentle kisses before settling against the cushions once again, smiles playing about their mouths. Soon sleep claimed them, and they both rested until the post-chaise stopped to change horses. The remainder of the journey progressed without incident, and soon they were all settling back into life at Bainscroft.

Two days after the return from London, Violet sat upon the bed beside her husband, feet tucked beneath her to ward off a chill. Nathaniel read from the book of Proverbs – the same verses that she had read the first evening of their marriage. As his voice, rich in its masculinity, spoke the words, Violet found her heart quickened in a familiar but still unsettling way.

There is no cause to be uncertain, she tried to reason with herself, but to no avail. *Our love grows every day. I have even been able, on occasion, to kiss him before he kisses me. Why, O Lord, do I feel so unsettled?* As the prayer was silently spoken, however, Violet knew the answer.

She wished to have a marriage in every sense of the word, to truly be one with her husband. Almost ruefully, she realized just how correct Nathaniel had been. She *was* the one who must lead them on the embarkation of this journey. How could he possibly know otherwise that she truly desired it?

Forcing her thoughts back to the words he was speaking, Violet listened until the Bible was closed and the prayers were read, and finally they tucked themselves into their bed. Nathaniel must have been more tired than usual. Many evenings, he would gently stroke her hair as she drifted off to sleep, or hold her hand, or occasionally hold and kiss her for a short time. Tonight, however, he slept almost immediately.

Violet lay beside him. Drawing a fortifying breath and whispering a prayer for courage, she resolutely turned to her side and placed her hand lightly on her husband's chest. It rose and fell in time with his breathing. When she moved to snuggle up against him, he did not awaken immediately and Violet's determination nearly left her. But as he was just recently asleep, the pressure from her body brought him from his light slumber.

Nathaniel turned sleep-heavy eyes to her. When he focused on her face, seeing how close it was to his own, the sleep almost instantly morphed into something that Violet could not describe. He slowly snaked his arms around her, as though afraid to frighten her away. Violet's courage was bolstered by the yearning she saw in his eyes and she placed a small kiss on his chin.

This was all the encouragement he needed. He then hauled her to himself, smothering her face with sweet, tender kisses. Later that night, they both fell asleep in one another's arms and remained that way until well after the sun's rays were shining through the windows the next morning.

Bessie, one of the under-servants, entered the bedchamber the following morning to coax a fire from the smoldering embers in the fireplace. When she hazarded a glance toward the bed, she saw the master and the mistress with their arms entwined, both asleep with most contented looks on their faces. She hurriedly finished her task before scurrying off to find Mrs. Baker.

"It does seem that we shall have little ones in this house again, after all. Oh! I cannot tell you, Bessie, what wonderful information this is."

The news spread, as it often does amongst the staff of any great house; although if questioned, each would have summarily denied knowledge of the circulating intelligence. They all dearly loved their master, for his kind heart and the honor which governed his daily actions. Their mistress had worked her way into their hearts as well. It would be a grand day indeed when their offspring graced the home and bore evidence of the couple's love.

Fourteen

NEAR THE END of November, Dr. Curteys pronounced Mrs. Tessel well enough to resume her usual activities. Miss Stokes, no longer needed to care for the children, was asked to stay on as an aid to Mrs. Baker, at least until the busy Christmas season had passed. Violet was extremely gratified that her friend was recovered from her weakness and that the children would be with their parents again. The young boy and girl had become more and more comfortable with the household each day of their stay, and they had been conveyed to visit with their parents frequently, but there was still a perpetual sadness lurking in their eyes.

While she was happy for the sake of the Tessel family, Violet felt the loss of the children quite deeply. Her days seemed bereft of both employment and enjoyment. She was certain that she had occupied herself easily enough before the two young ones came to stay with them, but she could not remember in what manner. Although she did her best to put on a cheerful face, Nathaniel saw how his wife missed them, in her sighs and in the faraway look in her eyes when she came across some thing or another that either Abraham or Miriam had particularly favored.

Nathaniel did his best to console his wife, but saw no real change in her moods until he asked her to plan a Christmas party, to which would be invited the Dowager Countess, the Doberlys, and also Violet's family, if she wished to include them. He also asked her to plan a less formal party for the tenants and townsfolk who lived nearby. Violet, while nervous at the daunting prospect of so much to do, found that the task of planning her first entertainment excited her. She threw herself into the preparations whole-heartedly.

At breakfast one morning, as November was drawing to a close, she informed her husband that she had finalized the menu of the dinner-party with Peche.

"Have you now?" Nathaniel lowered the paper he had been perusing and grinned at her. "On what will we be dining? Or would you rather surprise me?"

"Oh, no, it is no difference to me if you should know." Violet offered a small smile. "On second thought, it is quite a difference; I should very much like your opinion!"

"I am happy to give it, though perhaps my mother would be a better person to consult." Nathaniel reached across the corner of the table which separated them and took her hand in his, lightly caressing the backs of her fingers.

"Oh, I did that already!" answered Violet brightly, pulling her hand from his to sip her chocolate. "For the first course, we will have both pea soup and pheasant soup, followed by a partridge pie and roast pheasant. I should like to have some sort of fish, but have yet to decide which. Oh, that's not all, I plan to have six courses. We shall have roast of venison for the fourth, as well, and I believe there are potatoes still in the pantry which may be used."

"Are you not forgetting something?"

"What is that?" Violet had a sinking sensation in her gut.

"The Christmas goose!"

Violet's relief was palpable. "Oh, it is to be assumed that there will be a goose. Do you really think *me* such a goose as to forget that? And the pudding, too, of course."

"But of course. In that case, the dinner should be delightful." Nathaniel leaned across the corner of the table and kissed her lips.

"Nathaniel!" Violet pushed at his shoulder with the hand not holding her cup of chocolate. "Signore Peche or Mrs. Baker or Mr. Garand or—or *anyone* may walk through that door at *any* moment!" Suddenly, her face paled again and she swallowed with effort. Violet closed her eyes against the wave of nausea that suddenly assailed her. After a moment, she finally managed to say, "I beg your pardon, I-I do not seem to be feeling quite the thing this morning."

"Are you ill? Shall I call Dr. Curteys?"

"Oh, no, I shall be quite well in a moment or two, I daresay." Violet forced her trembling lips into a smile. "I must, however, stop taking chocolate at breakfast. Too rich by far!"

Nathaniel did not seem quite satisfied, but to Violet's immense relief, he did not pursue the topic.

Having consumed only a few bites of toast, she excused herself from the table, begging her husband's indulgence.

"I really must see Mrs. Baker about the linens for the party."

"At this moment?" he questioned as he rose with her. "It is not yet December."

"Oh, but if there is any imperfection or blemish on the linens, I must ensure there will be time to order new ones." Violet began to move slowly toward the door, toward her escape, offering a smile to reassure him.

"But you've scarcely eaten a thing!"

Violet glanced back at the crust of her toast and felt another surge of sickness threaten. "I rarely eat a great deal at breakfast, you know that." She attempted a light-hearted laugh and succeeded only in tittering nervously.

"Yes, but this is a bird's fare, even for you." Nathaniel was clearly not fooled and moved purposefully toward her, grasping her hands in his own. "I usually can see at least two blushes steal across your face at breakfast alone, but you have been pale and colorless all the morning. Violet, please do not keep it from me if you are feeling poorly."

Violet was touched at his attentive manner, and turned stoically to face him. Regardless, she was unable to keep from chattering nervously in an attempt to turn her husband's concerned, *discerning* eyes from her. "Nathaniel, dearest, I *do* appreciate your concern. Truly. But I believe I am simply strained and fatigued. I did not wish to admit to you the nerves I have suffered in regard to these parties – I do enjoy planning them! – but it seems that I must allow myself to slow down a bit and not attempt so much every day." The anxiety on her husband's face relaxed a bit and she quickly pressed further, hoping to convince him quickly as she felt another wave of nausea, stronger than the others, beginning to overtake her. "Pray do not worry over me! What a goose I have been not to allow myself proper rest and pacing in such an immense task as this. If you will but excuse me, I shall go at once to lie down. Mrs. Baker can likely meet with me this afternoon regarding the linens. I am sure I shall feel more the thing with an hour or so of rest."

"Very well," he acceded, "but if this continues for more than a couple of days, I insist that you allow me to bring Dr. Curteys to see you."

"Of course, Nathaniel," murmured Violet. *I do not suppose it would be wise to divulge to him at this time that I have been feeling poorly for upwards of a fortnight.* She took herself off to their chamber to rest.

Nathaniel stooped to kiss his mother's cheek which was indulgently proffered him. "Mother, what a lovely surprise! Regrettably, Violet cannot receive you; she is feeling poorly."

"Oh dear, I do hope it is nothing serious," replied the dowager.

"She would not have you believe it was, but I am none so certain." Nathaniel handed his mother into a comfortable wing-chair before returning to his occupation of pacing the room. He had been going on remarkably well before Mr. Garand announced her – so well, in fact, that he was mildly surprised when he paused to glance at the ornate rug upon which he tread and saw no furrow in its plush fibers.

He had allowed Violet to brush him off that morning because he truly believed that she needed the rest she had promised to take, but he did not for a moment believe that the only thing ailing her was the strain of the upcoming parties. He had witnessed the organization of her mind see her through more complicated and strenuous planning than that of two Christmas parties. *Why, only three weeks ago, she wrote up a schedule of people to help care for Lolly Faintree while the girl they had hired was called to her home to bury her grandfather. In addition to that, she wrote out the menu upon which the Faintrees would dine, as well as her regular duties at Bainscroft and keeping an eye upon the Tessels and several other tenants whom she has been helping. She showed no sign of strain then, and it seemed much more involved than these parties and without any aid from household staff.*

"Natty, my child, you have drifted off somewhere without me," came his mother's gently reproving voice.

"I do beg pardon, Mama." Nathaniel smiled ruefully at her. "I was simply thinking that I cannot believe her explanation entirely. I do hope it is nothing serious that plagues her."

"What discomforts does she suffer?" asked the elder woman, her kind eyes soft in their brown depths as well as in the gently wrinkled skin about the edges. "If I may be so bold."

"She has been pale all the morning and with no appetite to speak of. Come to think of it, her complexion for at least a week – perhaps more – had not its usual rosiness. And she seemed almost ill in her stomach at least once this morning, if not more. And she fatigues so easily!" Glancing at his mother, Reymes felt dismay sink into his heart. "You do not think she is developing a sickly disposition, do you? Mind, it would not alter my affection for her one jot, but what if she were to become an invalid within a few years? Or what if she is incapable of bearing children? I cannot bear to think of her sunny self becoming—"

"Nathaniel! There is no need for theatrics, my boy!" The dowager smiled at her son. "I am glad to hear that your love would not diminish under a trying circumstance. One, however, that I do not believe you shall be required to endure."

"How can you know that?"

"A young woman in the bloom of youth, happily married to the man she loves does not suffer a decline into valetudinarianism as you have suggested." Nathaniel was rather surprised at the mild severity in his mother's tone. Upon seeing his raised eyebrows and a softening around his eyes which hinted at vulnerability, however, the kind-hearted woman lessened the intensity with which she spoke. "I suggest, Natty, that you heed your wife's explanation. Fatigue and an unsettled stomach are no reason to 'fly up into the boughs,' as your generation is wont to say."

"Yes, ma'am," replied Nathaniel meekly, with a tiny smile relaxing his handsome features.

The Dowager Lady Reymes returned his impish grin with a secretive smile of her own. Nathaniel had no earthly idea what the significance of that smile might be, but he suspected that his mother had a better idea of what was happening to his wife than did he. *I suppose I have no choice besides to take Violet at her word. And I do not doubt that she believes it to be what she has told me; there was no deceit in her mannerisms as she spoke to me. I do suspect, though, that she has been suffering longer than she let on.*

"The purpose of my visit, Natty," said his mother, breaking into his thoughts as she withdrew something from her reticule, "is to deliver these into your hands."

"Oh?"

"Yes. Your father purchased them for me, years ago, but I never decided on a setting I liked for them." She smiled as she pressed a soft velvet bag into his hand. "When I found them the other day, in the back of my jewelry box, I thought immediately of Violet."

Nathaniel upended the bag and several small but weighty objects landed in his palm. Looking down at the cool, hard stones in his palm, he had the uncanny feeling that he was looking into his wife's eyes. In the morning sunlight streaming through the windows, their smooth surfaces gleamed with a peculiar grey-green color. Their resemblance to the eyes of his wife was remarkable.

"Thank you, but are you certain that you wish to part with such a memento?"

"Nathaniel, dear, I miss your father terribly, but keeping things which he gave me will not bring him back to me."

"I am sorry," he said, tension in his words and a headache forming. "If I–"

"We are all sorry, Natty," said his mother gently. "So many things *might* have happened to change the outcome of that night. But the fact is that he is now gone, and we must strive to cherish his memory. Even so, know that he is now at rest with the Lord, and he would not wish for us to languish over him to such an extent."

Nathaniel did not wish to ask it, to pursue what she had already put to rest, but the question was nearly bursting from his mouth. "And...you do not suffer regrets from...that time?"

His mother shook her head sadly. "Natty, my boy, any regrets which might assail me are not the reality of *today*. We cannot move forward with tomorrow when we live in yesterday."

Nathaniel made no reply, but her words sat in his mind, refusing to leave, even as he held up his end of the conversation rather admirably, all things considered. The discussion which followed seemed rather benign and even paltry, and soon Nathaniel was seeing his mother to her carriage. The dowager turned to face him just before she stepped into the equipage, her aged brown eyes still as bright and perceptive as ever they were.

"Nathaniel, I feel I must inform you that John and Frances are to come to me for the Christmas holiday. No, do not presume to speak until I am finished," she commanded in her most severe matron's voice with the purpose of dispelling the exclamation which had risen to Nathaniel's lips. In a gentler tone, she continued, "I know there is no love lost between you two at the moment, and I must confess that I can scarcely blame you. His behavior has been shameful."

You know not above half, ma'am, thought Nathaniel, but aloud he said nothing.

"I wish you would, at least for this most blessed of holy days, set aside your quarrel and invite the both of them to your Christmas dinner party."

Nathaniel felt an unyielding refusal rise within his breast. But then the remembrance of his wife saying that she ought to forgive him – she, the offended party! – gave him pause. *Lord, this trouble from the past has certainly followed me into the present, and yet I have been praying for these weeks – ever since our discussion about this very matter – that You would work forgiveness in my heart. Allow me, O Lord, to be open to this opportunity.*

Therefore, it was with no small effort that he said, "Of course, Mama. If Violet consents, they will be added to the guest list."

Smiling at her eldest son, the dowager allowed him to hand her into her carriage. As her driver directed the horses back to her cottage, she smiled to herself, quite interested to discover what the future might hold.

Violet awakened to a warm hand gently caressing her back. She had fallen asleep curled upon her side; it seemed to be the only position in which her stomach allowed her any semblance of peace.

"Violet my love," whispered Nathaniel's voice close to her ear. "Would you care to partake of a light meal? The day is already half-spent."

She groggily sat up, rubbing her eyes. Sleep fogged her mind, causing her to ask him to please repeat what he had said.

"Would you care to eat?"

Violet's stomach roiled, causing her to shake her head slowly.

"Some mild tea, perhaps?" coaxed her husband. Concern for her was written in his eyes. She was unable to resist the pleading she saw there.

"Very well, I shall do my best to take some tea." Violet could not help but to return his triumphant smile with a small one of her own.

Once they were settled in the family sitting room, Nathaniel asked Mrs. Baker to please pour the tea as Lady Reymes was feeling poorly. The woman's mild surprise was evident for a brief moment, but quickly hidden, and she complied without comment. Violet managed to drink most of her tea, as well as to eat half of a bland cake, before she found herself in need of fresh air.

Upon her sudden announcement, her concerned husband asked if she was certain she wished to go out of doors. "The air has been rather chilled of late."

"I know, but the air is positively stifling in here. Please, Nathaniel."

"Very well." He rang the bell, and when Mr. Garand immediately answered the summons, he asked him to send a footman with their outerwear. In short order, he had donned his driving coat and beaver hat and she her pelisse, bonnet, and muff, and they exited the house and moved toward the orchard.

The trees there were now barren and stood in stark contrast to the iron-grey sky. Only a few birds flitted from tree to tree, searching for food and singing their songs. The rich aroma of the earth mixing with leaves and the pungent sweetness of fallen, over-ripe apples permeated the air.

Violet slipped her arm through her husband's before tucking her hand back into her muff. It forced her to walk closely with him, but as the air was as chilly as he had warned, she was glad of their shared warmth. "This is lovely," she murmured.

"*You* are lovely," he returned. "The cold brings delightful color to your cheeks."

"Oh dear, no doubt to my nose and ears, as well. There is nothing lovely in *that*." But as she spoke, she could not hold back her smile.

"Are you feeling better, then?" he queried.

"I am, thank you." Violet paused, wondering how much she ought to tell him. After several moments she continued.

"The truth, Nathaniel, is that I have been feeling poorly for more than a few days' time." She looked up into his face and what she saw in it caused her to rush on to say, "I do not believe it to be anything serious, but just now it has occurred to me that I was feeling poorly *before* I began to plan the parties. It seems that perhaps it is not entirely plausible that it is caused by the strain associated with that."

"Hm, I wonder," he said thoughtfully. "My mother seemed to think—"

"The dowager was here?" cried Violet. "Oh dear, I had quite forgotten all about our appointment! We were to discuss entertainment for the evening. It is unlike me to be so forgetful; she must indeed think me ill-equipped to manage an affair of this magnitude!" As the words poured from her mouth, Violet felt her heart beat increase its pace.

"Darling, of course she thinks no such thing," soothed Nathaniel. "When I presented my concerns to her about your health—"

"You did not tell her, did you?" Violet worried, distress coloring her voice. "She will think—"

"She will think nothing that she does not think already: that you are a delightful woman, who brings great joy to her son's life, and who would never issue a complaint of health without warrant. In fact, she expressed the opinion that *I* was the one guilty of reacting with – er, undue concern."

Violet could not help but smile at that. "Indeed?"

"Yes! Infuriating creature." Nathaniel feigned a scowl and said, "She recommended that I listen to my wife and not worry."

"I daresay your mother is a very wise woman," offered Violet, feeling the anxiety of a moment before slowly drain from her.

"Yes, I suppose she is." This was admitted by her husband with a show of great reluctance.

The couple wandered quietly for some way, until they reached the other side of the orchard. They came upon a low stone wall and Nathaniel asked Violet if she would prefer to stop for a time. After looking askance at the wall, she conceded that a rest would be nice. Nathaniel removed his driving coat and laid it across the wall. Lifting Violet by her waist, he seated her on the wall before joining her. Encircling her with one arm, he drew her near for warmth.

They sat together in a tranquil silence, enjoying the time alone together, before he spoke. "I fear I have some rather unpleasant news." She said nothing, but turned attentively to him. "During the course of my visit with her, my mother told me that John and Frances plan to be with her for Christmas. Have you any objection to including them in our invitation to Christmas dinner?"

A knot of fear clenched in Violet's stomach, causing her to need a few deep breaths before she could speak. *Lord, please let me not be captive to fear. I am weary of it. First, fear of Mama, now fear of John. I know I speak of forgiving him, but it is difficult to be unaffected by the thought of his presence here.*

"I would not mind."

"But?" Nathaniel could apparently sense the hesitancy in her voice.

"I harbor no feelings of anger toward him; it is not my place to be vengeful. But I must admit that – I-I...I am afraid of him."

Nathaniel struggled against the familiar rage that swelled against his brother. *Lord, help me remember that vengeance is Yours; if You see fit to use me to deliver justice, I am willing. More than that, though, make me mindful that the best end result would be John's repentance, not merely his punishment.*

"I will not leave you alone unless I am assured that you are in absolutely no danger. I plan to confront John together with Faintree, as well as the magistrate, should his assistance be necessary. John's offense is not only against me, but against the people of our estate."

His wife nodded, but her face still showed some anxiety.

"Shall we pray together? Ask for God's protection and guidance?"

Her face instantly softened, losing some of its tension. "I should like that very much."

Nathaniel took Violet's hands in both of his. Bowing his head, he prayed. "Lord, we ask that You would place Your protection over us and especially over Violet. Guard her, and guide our words and actions. Let Your hand also be upon John that he may see and acknowledge his sin; that he may be brought to the knowledge of salvation."

After their prayer, he felt a strong urge, for the first time in their marriage, to share with her the particulars of *that* time. But fear of distressing his wife stilled his tongue, and he instead assisted her in descending from her perch. They continued their walk, moving from the gardens to the field beyond.

"Are you certain that you wish to continue?" He could not help but worry. "Had you better rest more?"

"Nathaniel, please! I am not ill. Aside from the fatigue and upset in my stomach, I feel quite well. Better than well, even." Violet smiled at him. There was no brilliance to her smile, but then he recalled that her smile had in his experience been characterized by a quiet sincerity rather than a bright cheerfulness. Her tranquility had its usual effect upon him and he capitulated easily.

The couple, arms entwined, meandered through the field, finding a path which Violet had followed during the days that she could roam freely through the countryside. Nathaniel felt a slight twinge of anger again, that she no longer could enjoy her long rambles, but found that it did not grow beyond a twinge.

After a time of friendly silence during which each was lost in thought, Violet spoke. "I must admit to missing the children terribly."

"Do you?" He felt ridiculous answering her with such a mindless reply, but could think of nothing else to say. *I know my darling. Someday I pray that we might fill that void with our own.*

"Oh, ever so much! My days were quite filled with sunshine while the sweet little ones stayed with us."

"And I am a raincloud?" he asked.

Violet's eyes began to sparkle as she considered the thought. "Perhaps."

"Oh?" Nathaniel was intrigued by this teasing side of his wife, as he was every time it emerged. "Are you not concerned that I might rain on you?"

Although her voice carried utmost solemnity when she answered, Violet's still-sparkling eyes betrayed her when she said, "Only a very little."

Laughing, Nathaniel repeated, "Is that all? Am I so benign a presence that you can dismiss me with such ease?"

Violet smiled but would not deign to answer him.

Nathaniel decided to push a bit further. "So I am a raincloud, threatening my poor violet."

At this, his wife looked sideways at him. "*Threatening*, Nathaniel?"

"No, I suppose you would not say that. What, then?" He watched as she paused in their walk to examine some ivy climbing the trunk of a tree beside their path.

"All is dependent upon your perspective." She glanced up at the sky. "It may rain soon."

"Yes," Nathaniel agreed. "What of it?"

"Well, does the rain threaten the fields when it waters the grain? Or the trees when it delivers water to the roots?"

"No, but it might crush a weak or small plant."

"Mm, yes. It might. But if a flower's bloom fell, must it follow that the plant dies?"

"Not necessarily, but even if the plant lives, it still has suffered damage."

"Yes, but it *lives*."

Nathaniel saw that she was trying to make a point, but what that point was escaped him entirely. His inability to comprehend might or might not have been affected by her lovely eyes gazing sidelong at him. "Speak plainly, my love."

"Well, it occurs to me that when rainclouds, if you will, or misfortune finds us—"

"Are you calling me a misfortune?"

"Gracious, no! But the manner in which we became engaged was rather unfortunate."

"True. You'll receive no argument from me on *that* quarter. Please continue, and do pardon my interruption." He offered his most winsome grin, hoping that it affected her in a manner similar to that which her smiling eyes affected him.

Violet smiled back at him. "As I was saying, when misfortune comes, as it must at times because of the state of the world—"

"The state of the world?"

"Fallen. In sin. You know that Scripture says that all have sinned. We read that together just the other week. And that the earth groans as a woman in childbirth, waiting for the time that it is restored."

"Yes, please do continue," he encouraged.

"I am trying." Her slightly sardonic grin caused his heart to pound for a few breaths. "When difficulties strike, we can learn from them, grow from them, if we dare to rise again from the force of the misfortune." She glanced at him. "As an example, I believed, when we married, that it was the greatest trial of my life."

"Is that so?" Nathaniel grinned at her, in spite of the words she spoke. His confidence in her love was now as great as in his own.

"But God has turned it into the greatest blessing of my life. Well, aside from my salvation." His wife smiled happily up at him and he could not resist, after a quick glance around ensuring that they were indeed alone, to steal a kiss. Her blushing smile was good reward for his impulsive action.

Suddenly, the wind picked up and a cold drizzle began to fall from the sky. After looking heavenward in disbelief, the couple hurried along the lane, finding themselves at the door of the Tessel cottage. By the time they sought refuge under the eaves, the rain had increased to a downpour. Nathaniel pounded on the door, which was opened after several moments by Mrs. Tessel.

Violet spoke first. "Mrs. Tessel! You look wonderful today!"

Nathaniel was caught off-guard by his wife's exclamation, but he observed that Mrs. Tessel's face had filled back out to its previous proportions, the hair peeking out from beneath her cap was not limp any longer, and her eyes seemed much livelier than they had of late.

"Oh! Lord Reymes, Lady – Violet! How d'ye do?" Mrs. Tessel responded almost by rote and stepped back, ushering them into the sitting room. Suddenly her eyes flashed with indignation and a bit of humor. "What a thing to say, Lady Violet, drippin' as ye are with rainwater. But I do thank ye."

"I will not impose upon you for long, Mrs. Tessel," said Nathaniel. "Perhaps Lady Reymes could stay with you, though, while I borrow Mr. Tessel's horse and ride back to fetch a carriage for my wife? She has been suffering from fatigue lately and an upset stomach; I would not wish her to come down with an ague in addition to everything else; fever and sneezing and headaches would certainly not aid in her recovery. That is, if it would not be an imposition for her to remain beneath your roof for a short time."

"But of course you won't be imposin', Lord Reymes. Sure'n you're welcome to any of Hezekiah's clothes, though I s'pect my husband's things would never do for ye – 'twould fit poorly indeed! But Hezekiah's in the barn, if you still have a mind to take the horse." The smile she offered him was sincere but brief, and also had the same knowing gleam which he had seen in his mother's eyes upon mentioning Violet's infirmity. He could not question Mrs. Tessel, however, as the woman quickly turned her attention to his wife. "Come along, m'lady. Let's find you somethin' dry to wear."

Nathaniel smiled at the hen-like manner in which Mrs. Tessel put her arm about Violet's shoulders and guided her farther back into the house. Leaving the warmth of the building, he went in search of Mr. Tessel.

"Dear Mrs. Tessel, how good it is to see you," said Violet for the third time since they had entered the back room of the cottage. She was currently attempting to fasten the buttons on the back of the grey dress the other woman had procured for her. Warm, dry chemise, stays, and a petticoat had already been donned and Violet's wet things were drying by the fireplace in the kitchen.

Mrs. Tessel moved to help her friend. "Tis right good to see *you*, an' with a chance at a visit!" she countered. "I've scarce had ye t' m'self for five minutes since the wee ones returned. Every time ye come callin', they claim ye an' I scarce get a word in."

"How are they?" asked Violet. "I know we visit often, but I do miss them so."

"They are right as – as rain!" She chuckled at her words. "They're napping for now, which I'm right grateful for, so you an' I might visit some. Well, this dress doesn't become you as well as the lilac one Lord Reymes bought for you, but I daresay it'll do in a pinch."

"Thank you; this is just fine."

"Ye've been unwell, then?" asked Mrs. Tessel, glancing sidelong at her friend as they settled themselves before the fire in the small parlor. She began to pour out some tea, which she had set on while Violet shed her damp clothing.

"No, no. I feel fine, most of the time." Violet blushed. "Lord Reymes oughtn't have mentioned it to you; he was quite concerned for me, but I assured him it was nothing serious."

Mrs. Tessel handed Violet a cup of tea before asking, "And how are you, m'lady, besides the – er, discomfort?"

"Oh, I've been so happy! Nathaniel – er, Lord Reymes is a most attentive husband. Even when we were in London and he renewed his acquaintances with old friends, he never left me feeling unwanted or alone. Time and again, he has shown such devotion as I had never expected to receive." Violet felt her throat swell with emotion and her heart squeeze. "I am so – so *very* blessed."

"Indeed ye are, dear. And are ye to be blessed again in a rather short time?"

"In what way?" Violet was perplexed.

"Are ye not expecting to hold a child in your arms before long?" her friend asked with a meaningful glance at her. Violet stared back.

"Little Ruth?"

She chuckled a bit. "Violet, what I mean is that ye shall have your *own* child to hold."

"My...my own?" Violet did not know what to say.

"I-I assumed..." Her eyes sought Violet's face and her brows met above them in distress. "You said ye were tired an' feelin' sickly an' – oh, m'lady, I am sorry."

"Oh! No, please don't be," Violet was quick to assure her friend. "I suppose it had not crossed my mind. We have not er, that is, it has not been long since—"

As though reading her thoughts by the blush that stole across her cheeks, Mrs. Tessel understood Violet's meaning immediately. "Yes, dearie, but that don't signify. I was with child nigh unto the night after Hezekiah and I were married."

Violet felt her face flush even more. She was silent for several long moments, sipping at her tea, pondering what her friend had said. At length, she spoke. "Do you really believe I could be?"

"Oh dearie, I canna' say for certain. Ye're havin' the symptoms, though. Time will surely tell." She smiled at her friend. "Try not to fret; enjoy your time now, with your husband."

Violet's smile took on a wistful quality as she said, "Oh, I do!"

Suddenly, the women heard the sound of the front door opening. Two pairs of heavy feet stamped their way toward the room. Violet looked up to see Nathaniel enter the room, followed by Mr. Tessel. The sight of her husband, beaver top hat in hand and his clothing all darkened with the rain, warmed her heart. Only his head, which had been protected by the hat, was dry.

"Nathaniel! You are positively soaked!" she cried, rising and going to him.

"Yes, well, I did not care to take the time to change before fetching you." He smiled ruefully.

"Would you care for some tea, Lord Reymes?" asked Mrs. Tessel.

"No, but I thank you, Mrs. Tessel." Nathaniel glanced back at Violet. "Shall we?"

"Yes, of course," she replied.

"Allow me t' fetch your things," said Mrs. Tessel. She returned quickly, carrying a bundle of Violet's partially-dried clothing.

"Mrs. Tessel, it was delightful to visit with you." Violet smiled at her friend.

"And you too, dearie. Come and visit again soon, if you please." She pressed the bundle into Violet's hands. "I should like to hear of any *news* you might have."

Violet blushed at the woman's words, but had little time to dwell on them. Nathaniel hurried her to the waiting carriage. Once inside the carriage, he quickly shed his cloak and tucked her between his arm and his side.

"I see your cloak has accomplished its purpose and kept your clothing dry," Violet said. He merely nodded in response, something seeming to occupy his thoughts.

"What did Mrs. Tessel mean about news?" he asked after a time, then added teasingly, "I was not aware she – or you – were such gossip-mongers."

"Oh! Nothing." Violet grasped for a suitable answer. "We had discussed some – er, events – which are forthcoming and she merely wished to be appraised of the outcome."

"Ah," said her husband, apparently content with her answer.

Oh, why did I not tell him? Violet felt distress grow within her heart. *He should be very glad of the news, if it is indeed true. Perhaps, though, it would be better to wait until I am certain before I say anything. He may be disappointed if I am not. And indeed, I have no evidence that I am besides Mrs. Tessel's speculation. How does one know for certain? It must be—*

"We shall have a warm bath, then take an early dinner." His words interrupted Violet's thoughts. "Do you realize that it is well into the afternoon already? We were walking far longer than I had supposed."

"Oh," was all Violet managed. Sleepiness had crept upon her, tucked as she was into the shelter of her husband's arm. As she sat snuggled against him, with hot bricks thoughtfully provided by Mrs. Baker now tucked beneath her feet, Violet felt herself drifting off to sleep.

She was awakened by her husband gently lifting her from her seat and carrying her up the steps to the front door.

"Nathaniel! Please put me down; I am quite capable of walking."

He paused as they reached the door, sheltered from the rain, and looked into her eyes. She tried to meet his gaze unfalteringly, but found it was so searching that she had to drop her eyes. He chuckled, set her upon her feet, and placed a kiss on her forehead.

"Come, dearest," he said as he opened the door. "Mrs. Baker has been good enough to have baths prepared for us and our dress laid out." He grasped her hand and led her up the stairs to their chamber.

Over an hour later, the couple emerged, feeling clean, refreshed, and much more comfortable in warm, dry clothing. Just as they were about to enter the dining room, Mr. Garand intercepted them and spoke quietly into Nathaniel's ear. Violet saw his countenance change, growing tense and so far removed from the nearly jovial state in which he was as they descended the stairs. Alarm skittered through her.

Fifteen

NATHANIEL NODDED TO his butler, indicating his thanks and dismissing the man in one gesture. Turning to Violet, he saw that she was at the least mildly distressed. *Did my face betray so much?* He thought for a moment of sending her on to the dining room but knew that would solve nothing. Attempting to school his face into a more relaxed expression, he gave her a smile.

"It seems that we have visitors." He paused, praying briefly but sincerely in that time, then said, "John and Frances are here, waiting in the sitting room."

"Oh!" She did not appear to be alarmed, as he had feared she would be, though there certainly was apprehension in her features. "Shall we go to receive them now?"

"Do you mind?"

"I do not."

Amazed once again at the strength and grace of his wife, Nathaniel quickly raised her hand to his lips for a brief moment before leading her to the parlor door.

Upon entering the room, they found John and Frances sitting in two chairs on opposite sides of the large room from one another. John came indolently to his feet, offering a rather sloppy bow. To Nathaniel, it seemed he was mocking. Frances remained in her seat, nodding politely when Violet greeted her. He watched in amazement as his wife moved immediately to the other woman, asking quietly if she might sit beside her upon the settee. When Frances made room for her, Violet seated herself gracefully.

"What a pleasant surprise!" said Violet cheerfully. "We were just about to sit down to an early dinner. Would you care to join us?"

Her question, clearly directed at both John and Frances, surprised Nathaniel. He had been concerned that his wife might experience some recurrence of the fear which had held her captive, but he saw no sign of unease in his wife as she rang for a servant and asked for two extra covers to be set. After that detail had been attended, she again seated herself, speaking politely to Frances. He moved to where his brother had reseated himself and chose an adjacent chair.

"How do you get on, John?" asked Nathaniel, attempting conversation.

"Eh, we scrape by," John uttered while studying his fingernails languidly. Under his breath he muttered, "As if you care a groat," but not quietly enough to prevent Nathaniel from hearing.

Deciding not to take objection, Nathaniel said, "I understand that you are staying at the dower house. Are you comfortable there?"

John took the gentle hint and the gentlemen's conversation continued, innocuous and bland, though the younger brother's contributions were marked with decided insolence. Nathaniel found himself wondering what the ladies were saying but saw no way to enter into their conversation without also including his brother. He greatly desired to keep the man as far from Violet as was possible.

Finally, Mr. Garand entered and announced that dinner was served. Nathaniel quickly offered Violet his escort and John followed with Frances on his arm.

As they sat down to a meal of roasted chicken, quail with a spiced glazing, boiled potatoes, and venison meat pie, among other delicious offerings, the conversation was polite but quite forced for Nathaniel. In his opinion, it was not a moment too soon that the party rose and the ladies moved to the drawing room and the gentlemen to the study.

Nathaniel poured a glass of sherry for himself and one for his brother, thinking as he handed the glass to John that he would keep a close eye on how much the man consumed. *It won't do to allow the man to sink in his cups; last time he did in this house, he was—well, he was rather unpleasant.*

John sipped his drink, keeping suspicious eyes on Nathaniel.

Lord, why does he despise me so? Nathaniel struggled to calm himself. *Ought I ask him outright? Or am I coming it too strong to suppose that he despises me?*

"You, my brother," said John at length, "have a decided advantage over me. Your bride is infinitely superior to mine."

"How so?" Nathaniel could not help but ask, although pursuing the topic was clearly against his better judgment.

"Such a cheery creature. Offered such accommodating hospitality." John took another swallow of his drink before continuing. "Is she so accommodating in private matters?"

Nathaniel felt his face burn, with some aggravating combination of anger and embarrassment. "I do not pretend to be ignorant of the meaning of your crude question, but neither will I dignify it with a response. Tread carefully, brother, for if you so much as *look* cross-ways at my bride, I will not be responsible for my actions."

John laughed at this, albeit with a touch of nervous energy. He had never before seen such passion in his brother's being and found it more than mildly disconcerting. "Easy, Reymes, you rather frighten me."

Nathaniel stood, sherry in hand, considering his brother. *I cannot believe he is truly afraid; the man acts too recklessly to feel fear. And I wonder if he forgets the threats he made when last I saw him.* Aloud, he merely said, "Very good, then; we understand one another." After a sip of his sherry, Nathaniel asked, "How long will you be staying with our dear mama?"

"Until the New Year. I have made arrangements for Mrs. Peyton to go and stay with her aunt for a month, that I may visit unimpeded with my *chère-amie*. We have—"

"So you have not given up that practice, now you are married?"

"Why ever should I? Even the Regent—"

"John, take your vows seriously."

"I never take anything *too* seriously, Reymes," said John with a mocking grin. "Surely you know that."

"Nothing at all?"

"Oh, I take my pleasure quite seriously."

Nathaniel stared at the man, slouched indolently in his chair, feet sprawled lazily before him, nursing his drink and by all accounts, his grudge.

"You ought to also consider your salvation seriously."

"I am quite beyond that," said John with a sneer on his lips, "Indeed, I am all astonishment that you pretend I am not. I distinctly recall your saying as much at one point or another." He drained his glass and set it forcefully upon the side-table to his right, sitting up straight. He leaned forward menacingly, his voice losing its lazy quality and developing a sharp edge. "And while I am being frank, *brother*, I am amazed that you have not yet managed to frighten your little wife away. She was quite a little rabbit cornered by a hound when I found her on the balcony all those months ago. I'd not imagined her to be strong enough to survive a marriage to one as severe as you."

"Think what you choose of me, John, but understand this. Violet is my wife. Whether I knew her or loved or even liked her at the time of our engagement is immaterial." Nathaniel knew that what he was about to say might reveal a point of weakness, but John must know that if he chose to ill-use Violet, he would be answerable to a man who was passionately driven – not only by duty but by love – to protect her. "I love her now, as I never knew I could love anyone. Believe me when I tell you, if you lay so much as a *finger* upon her, you will receive a consequence such as you never believed me capable of exacting."

John's face paled slightly at this, but he curled his lip into a slight sneer. Before he could speak, Nathaniel set his glass on the tray beside the decanter. "I am going to join the ladies. You may join us or not; it does not signify. If you choose to remain here, however, have no thought of lifting anything from my house; I am done with your stealing from me, be it monies or possessions. Ezekiel, one of my footmen, will attend you, should you choose to remain here."

As things played out, Ezekiel's services were not required. John joined Nathaniel and the women in the drawing room, seating himself slightly apart from the group until the time came that their carriage was called and he returned with his wife to the dower house. Nathaniel was relieved at John's apparent retreat, but by no means did he suppose that the trouble with him was at an end.

Violet readied for bed with the help of her maid, taking time to think over the events of the evening as Jane brushed her hair.

She easily recognized the shock and even a curl of fear that ran through her at the news that Mr. and Mrs. Peyton awaited them upon returning from the Tessel's home. But a prayer for courage and a reassuring squeeze of the hand by her husband did wonders in strengthening her. Violet was able to face the couple with equanimity.

Mrs. Peyton had appeared to her to have a great deal of poise and town polish. The dress that she wore to dinner, a silk-satin skirt with a velvet bodice, appeared to be of a very good cut and at the cutting edge of the fashion trends. Her hair had been coifed to perfection, curled becomingly about her face. Violet might have felt intimidated by the woman had Frances not offered a friendly smile upon greeting her – a far cry friendlier than the time they met at the wedding.

The ladies chatted of inconsequential nothings before dinner, while the men sat on the other side of the parlor. Violet was gratified to discover that during the few months they had resided at Bainscroft prior to moving to Fairfield, Frances found great delight in the gardens. She was particularly glad that although Frances' appearance marked her as the cream of Society, her spirit was generally gentle and kind.

Violet discovered during their time alone in the drawing room after dinner, though, that there was the proverbial exception to the rule that Frances possessed a gentle and kind spirit. While the ladies' conversation remained light and only marginally more personal than their conversation prior to dinner, the mention of John's name by Violet, in an innocent question as to how they first became acquainted, caused Frances' eyes to become so hardened that it was only with a concerted effort that Violet kept from recoiling. The other woman answered her in a calm voice which belied the hardness in her face that she had met him the first evening of her arrival in London, and they were engaged within the week. She artfully steered the conversation in another direction after this, and they began to discuss the latest trends in fashion, the trim which was popular on ladies' dresses, and whether they should make a game of Silhouettes at the Christmas party.

Jane, finishing with her mistress' hair, startled Violet from her reverie. She watched quietly as the maid tidied the recently-redecorated dressing room before curtsying herself out the door which went directly into the hall. Violet thanked her and locked the door behind her and went in search of her husband in his dressing room.

Griffin had just finished tending to Nathaniel, so it was as the valet exited that she entered after a hesitant knock upon the open door. Her husband looked up, wearing his night-clothes and a smile upon his handsome face.

"My dear," he said, holding out a hand to her. She went to him, taking his hand and tentatively perching herself upon his lap. "You were a picture of graciousness this evening. I am once again in awe of you."

Violet blushed in spite of herself and demurred, saying, "Oh no, I did nothing extraordinary. And I was glad to have time to become acquainted with Frances."

Nathaniel had been holding her hands, but at this released them and drew his arms about her waist. Pulling her toward him until her forehead rested against his, he kissed her gently before releasing a sigh.

"Whatever is the matter, dearest?" she asked.

"John was a menace after dinner." She felt mild alarm at this news, but kept her face impartial as she met his gaze, her fingers only gently worrying the fabric of his night-shirt which covered his shoulders. Violet renewed her resolve to trust in God and also in her husband to preserve peace in the house. "I nearly lost my ability to be civil." He chuckled suddenly, seemingly at odds with the theme of their conversation.

"Why do you laugh?" asked Violet. She trailed her fingertips absently through the hair at the back of his head.

He smiled at her, rubbing his nose against hers as he said, "I *so* delight in hearing endearments cross your lips." This was followed by a tender kiss, after which he commented, "Is it not amusing that I was driven to marry you by a dispassionate sense of duty, and yet in this marriage, I have been awakened to passions such as I never knew existed?"

"Yes, I suppose it is rather ironic, my good husband." Violet tried another endearment, wondering whether it would please him as well as the simple one she had spoken a moment ago.

"I do not know that 'good' is an appropriate word to describe me, dear wife, though 'husband' certainly fits the bill." He nuzzled her neck as he murmured, "And so very glad am I to be that."

"But how did his behavior bring to mind the state of your passion?" she sat back and asked, lost as to the connection between the two.

He considered her for a moment before answering. "All my life, I have been driven by honor – dispassionate honor; it compelled me to do what I believed to be my duty."

She felt she was beginning to understand better. "Such as providing for the repairs to the tenant farmers?"

"Yes, among other things."

He was watching her with an expression she could not decipher. It was certainly fond, but perhaps there was some melancholy present, as well.

"Nathaniel, I know something weighs on your heart." Wishing to comfort him, she rested one of her hands along his jaw, her fingertips gently caressing the hair at his temple. "Will you not share your burden with me?"

Suddenly his lips were at her own jaw, mirroring where her hand lay on his. He feathered kisses up to her ear, into which he whispered, "I should much rather do this."

She used her other hand to gently push at his shoulder, smiling softly at him when he leaned back a bit and looked at her face. "I know, and I would enjoy that as well, but I believe it would be more enjoyable by far if you first relieved yourself of your burden." When he began to protest, she smiled kindly and hastened to add, "Or, at the least, shared it with me. I've come to discover firsthand that shared burdens are lighter."

"And if you think less of me?"

"What a question to ask!" Violet was very nearly indignant until she saw the vulnerable tilt to her husband's brows. "Dearest, I love you. Whatever it is, we shall face it together."

With a defeated sigh, her husband drew her into his arms, resting his chin upon her head. "It is something from the past, not something to be faced."

"Even the past must be faced at times," she whispered. "Some things will not release us until we have faced them."

"Mm." She felt what must be his lips pressing against her hair before she heard him speak, his voice somewhat muffled. "All my life, I have acted with honor, to fulfill my duty. All my life, with the exception of one night several years past." His arms tightened about her and his voice was husky as he murmured, "Never before, and never since, have I regretted my choices so greatly."

Violet remained quiet, waiting for him to continue. His voice was faraway, as though he was no longer in the room with her, but in a different place and time.

The whole family was in Oxford; we had just finished a rather lengthy examination and the Earl and Countess of the time – my parents – came to stay one night before accompanying us back to Bainscroft. I knew that most of the other families did not do so, but we were close. Close, and John was just beginning to show a propensity for seeking out trouble. I was finishing my time at Oxford and John was in his second year. The Earl and Countess' presence assured his good behavior. Or so we believed.

Mama, Papa and I were dining at the inn. Night had long since fallen, and while the tables were all full, we had a private room. A timid maid – perhaps even more timid than you, Violet – entered the room after a muffled knock, to deliver an express just arrived from John. He wrote of some trouble he'd found himself in, having been challenged by some son of a Baron who was attempting to defend his sister's honor. John asked that I be his second. For the first time in my life, I denied what duty urged me do: I refused to go.

"How can you refuse your brother?" my father asked heatedly. "We stand behind family despite their failings."

"Even when standing by them condones such behavior?"

"Even then. Can you truly say that you love your brother when you will not support him in this?"

"I refuse to be his second and be despised by all good and decent

people for approving such despicable behavior – carousing with lightskirts – forgive me, Mama, for speaking of such things! – and sullying the reputation of good young ladies!" I stood, trembling with the raw anger coursing through me. Heart pounding, blood roaring in my ears. I cannot recall if he replied, as I could hear nothing beyond my heart and my breath. "I'll have no part of it, and if 'tis so dashed important to you, then you go!"

At that, both of my parents sat staring at me, and as I caught my breath and came down from the high emotion, I could see my mother's tears and my father's anger growing.

"You are wrong," he said in a low voice that was infinitely more frightening than had he railed and shouted. "Turning your back on your brother is worse than his indiscretions." He rose from the table and left.

Unable to speak to my mother, I took my leave and returned to my rooms at Oxford. I slept little, worrying about the argument. All I could think of were the words exchanged, and how exhausting it was to continually cover for John, to pretend that his behavior did not disgust me. It never occurred to me to I worry over what might happen that night. John had a way of landing on his feet, no matter the circumstances.

The next morning, I returned to the inn, expecting a very tired and perhaps winged brother to be nursing a dreadful head-ache. John never fought a duel when he was not slightly foxed. He said that it calmed him enough to focus on winging but not harming his opponent. I had seconded him previously, and usually it consisted of convincing him to offer the apology so that the whole business might be settled quickly and without injury to either party, followed by accompanying him while he fell deep into his cups at the club. But John was not there, and neither was my father. I could not believe it. When I arrived that morning, Mama had never looked so haggard. I fear she passed a restless night alone. I am not proud of my behavior toward her, but I fear that is not the worst of it. She ushered me into the rented rooms to inquire if I had seen either man. When I told her I had not, she fainted. I carried her to the bed and called for a maid to tend her before setting out to find them.

As miserable as I felt with the discovery that all had not gone as I'd expected, it could not have been as terrible as it was for my poor mama. To this day, I still have difficulty facing her.

I was able to find John quite easily, in one of his usual haunts. I shall spare you the details of that. But when I asked John where our father was, the libertine was not even aware that our father had attempted to seek him out. I discerned from my brother's incoherent mutterings where the duel had taken place and made a careful search. A long last, I found my father lying half-covered by some shrubbery. I took him immediately to the inn, called for a physician, and he was tended to. Of course, the events of the previous evening became clear later, once my father regained his senses and my brother had sobered. I also interviewed the challenger to clarify some of the foggier points, as John had little recollection of the evening.

The Baron, actually a friend of John's, had merely challenged him to keep up appearances; his sister was not an unwilling participant in the events which were the catalyst for the duel. When the gentlemen assembled, with their seconds, all were slightly foxed and the entire event merely a bit of sport.

Only one shot was fired. Purposely high and wide, its aim was to satisfy the terms of the duel while allowing both to remain unharmed. That shot, however, struck my father. He'd been delayed in finding them, and was still some hundred or so paces from the green. As the jolly duelers left together for the club and deep glasses, my father *crawled to some nearby shrubbery to avoid being put upon by a footpad or some other miscreant. As the drink flowed freely into their cups, blood flowed freely from his leg. After a time, he managed to remove his cravat and somewhat slow the flow of blood, but by the time I found him, he was terribly weak and barely conscious.*

"My father and I spoke after he was recovered. I apologized for my part in his injuries and he forgave–"

"Your part?" Violet could not help but cry indignantly, pulling back so she might look into her husband's eyes.

"Yes," he said lowly. "Had I gone for my brother, my father would not have been hurt. He would not have died at such a young age. His health began to decline while he recovered from the shot, and he was never again able to walk without the aid of a cane. One ailment led to another, and before two years had passed, he was gone. I know that he forgave me, as has my mother, but I cannot forgive myself."

"What is there to forgive?" cried Violet hotly, surprising even herself. "You acted in a manner which bowed to the dictates of your conscience. If you had gone, perhaps you would have been the one injured – or even killed on the spot! Your father made his own choices, as did your brother!"

Violet suddenly found herself set on her feet while her husband paced in the small space afforded by his dressing room; several seconds passed before she understood how she came to be there. After a tension-filled silence, save his quiet footfalls, Nathaniel spoke.

"Violet, have you ever lived with regret?"

"Every day, Nathaniel, until I married you." He opened his mouth to speak, so Violet forged on bravely, knowing that he needed to hear her words. "I feared, before I knew you, that this marriage would simply be another shadow under which I must live; it is not, and our engagement is one of the few things from my life before our marriage that I do not regret."

He had stopped pacing and now seemed about to speak, but Violet raised her palm to him, saying gently, "Allow me to speak. Please. Remember when I told you of my mama, and how she was not the woman who gave birth to me? She has lived a life of regrets, never being loved quite as much as my own mother was. She allowed herself to grow bitter with it. That is why she has been so demanding of me, so demeaning. She does not love me as she loves Rose because I am not her natural child. While my papa was alive, she practiced more equanimity in her treatment of all of us, but after he died, and Ashbridge was no longer with us after he married Penelope, she lost all pretended kindness for me.

"I regretted every day that I did not stand up to her, assert my opinion in my wardrobe or activities, that I did not tell her I was uncomfortable when she threw me in the way of this man or that, and I could go on and on. My regret turned me into a shell of who I ought to have been, who I have become now that I've let go of it all. I tell you this not to seek your pity or sympathy, but to show that I speak from experience." She ventured to step closer to him, looking earnestly into his eyes as she spoke one more time. "Regret has a dangerous way of eating at a person, and robbing him of the joy of life in the present."

Her husband had stilled his feet, standing and gazing down at her. "That is precisely how I have felt these past years, Violet: that nothing could penetrate the cloud of gloom which had surrounded me since I found my father suffering from his injury. It increased thousandfold when he died."

Almost as quickly as she had been set apart from him, Violet was suddenly back in her husband's arms, his face buried in the space between her neck and her shoulder, his body trembling every now and then. Violet could feel his warm breath moistening her neck and his lips moving ever so slightly, but she heard no sound. By and by, though, he raised his head and Violet saw that his eyes were wet with tears.

"I cannot say if I shall ever believe that I made the right decision that night, but I daresay for the first time, I do not feel the weight of it upon my chest." His smile was wide, unhindered, and seeing it sent a jolt straight to Violet's heart. "When my mother visited with me earlier today, she also spoke of not allowing past regrets to shadow us for the rest of our lives. I could not quite embrace her words then, but she is quite right, is she not?"

Violet smiled at him. "She is a wise woman."

"I've pleaded with the Lord that He would see fit to aid me in forgiving my brother, and in learning to trust the words of Scripture, to trust Him. It seems God has brought me to a place of beginning to forgive myself. I feel quite free." He let out a quiet laugh and pulled her into his lap again as he sat upon his stool. Violet enjoyed the embrace as he gently brushed his hands through her hair. A gentle smile graced her lips. "Violet, have you noticed that you have improved me a great deal?"

"Improved you!" she cried, leaning back so that she might see his face. Her first thought was to deny such an outrageous claim. But after a brief reflection, she said, "We have discussed this previously, and again I say that I shall not deny that you are changed, but neither can I claim credit."

"You must own that you are the one *God* used, then."

"Oh, very well." She smiled and offered her lips for his kiss.

"And may I be so bold as to say that you have changed, as well?"

"You may, but I do hope that it is for the better." Violet felt her heart swell with gratitude for the things the Lord had done in her life through her husband. *Am I truly the same girl that married the formidable Lord Reymes, Earl of Bainscroft? I scarcely recognize her.*

"Oh, very much so. It has been a delight to see you slowly unfold, opening yourself to the world." He leaned close again and said just before kissing her soundly, "Opening yourself to me."

"I must admit, Nathaniel," said she after he had released her lips, "that a part of me feels as though I have only recently awakened, that I've been asleep my whole life, stalked by darkness and too afraid to awaken and face the daybreak. But now that I have, I never want to go back into the shadows."

"And you oughtn't. You've been an instrument of the Lord's, blessing so many people – myself, the Tessels...and I daresay that He is not finished with you. I delight in the compassionate heart you have, and your care for those around you – even those who have wronged you."

His arms tightened about her, drawing her close to his heart, as he showered her face with light kisses before finally settling at her lips. The couple sat together, sharing kisses and caresses for a short time before Violet said, "Nathaniel, ought we retire to our chamber for our devotional reading?"

He acquiesced, a bit reluctantly Violet thought, and led her by the hand to their bed, where he seated her close by his side before they began their reading of Scripture and prayers. After this, he blew out the candle and drew her beneath the coverlet with him, pulling her into his arms.

The following evening, waiting in his study for Faintree to arrive, Nathaniel thought again of the discussion he and Violet had shared that morning, shortly after rising from their bed. She had asked whether he thought it would be imprudent of her to call upon his mother while John was present at the dower house. She did want very much to visit with Frances, as well, but did not wish to give John opportunity for mischief. He had agreed with her and suggested that she appeal to Frances for assistance with preparations for the Christmas parties at the main house. She brightened at the suggestion and went immediately to the escritoire in their chamber so that she might compose a brief missive to that effect.

A short rap upon the study door followed by Mr. Garand entering and announcing Mr. Faintree's arrival brought Nathaniel from his reverie.

"Please, Mr. Faintree, come in," he greeted the man.

"G'day, me lor'." Mr. Faintree bowed.

Nathaniel offered him a chair before the fireplace, then took his own across from him. "How is Mrs. Faintree faring?"

His eyes mildly troubled, the bailiff answered, "Ah, me lor', she does fair to middlin'."

"I see." Nathaniel steepled his hands before him. "Dr. Curteys, I understand, has been to see her?"

"Yes, me lor'." Mr. Faintree grew more animated as he described what appeared to be the invaluable help the good doctor had offered his dear wife. "'e gave 'er a new tonic for 'er pains an' says she's one what would do well drinkin' the mineral water in Bath or some other such place."

"Is that so?"

"Yes, me lor'. Only thing is, we 'aven't the – er, inclination to travel t' Bath." The man's face flushed and Nathaniel suspected that the hesitation had more to do with financial restraints than any inclination.

Nathaniel smiled. "In that case, Mr. Faintree, may I mention a thought I happened to have regarding a house of mine located in that very city?"

"What's that, me lor'?"

"The man who manages the house is taking another position with a family who resides in Bath most of the year. As our house is used scarcely more than a fortnight, he did not enjoy existing on only board wages. I understand that your inclination is not to be in Bath, but would you be able to oblige me by managing that house for me and having it readied whenever I have need of it?"

Nathaniel was mildly amused when Mr. Faintree sat rather straighter in his chair and looked with scarcely-guarded eagerness at him. "Well, me lor' I canna' say as it'd be a simple matter what to move me missus, but I daresay she'd be glad of the difficulties, were she to be in Bath. Y'see, me lor', our daugh'er lives nigh unto Bath an' we'd surely be pleasured to be nigh unto her."

After this eloquent speech, Nathaniel found he needed to clear his throat of laughter before answering the man. "Very good, then, Mr. Faintree. I should like very much to have you installed shortly after Twelfth Night, if that suits you."

"Ah, sure an' it do, me lor'" was the gratefully smiling man's reply. Nathaniel rose and Faintree followed suit. He grasped the Earl's hand and shook it heartily.

Suddenly Nathaniel remembered one other thing he had wished to ask the man. "Oh, and would you be willing to help my new bailiff become acclimated to his duties? Your maintenance of the estate is admirable – barring, of course, the restraints placed upon you by my brother's malfeasance – and I believe he would learn a great deal from you."

"Ah, right an' I'd be honored with such a task. Thank ye, me lor', for this. Me Lolly would thankee too, were she 'ere." The man pumped Nathaniel's hand with a handshake which left the earl's arm rather sore.

After enduring several more similarly hearty handshakes accompanied by sincere and effusive gratitude, Nathaniel saw the elder man to the door and allowed himself the relief of a chuckle. *He certainly shall be able to manage the house with ease. He has managed Bainscroft well for several years, with the exception of his caviling to John's demands. The estate itself is in top form; only the relationship with the tenants has suffered any ill. As Faintree enters his dotage, he shall be glad of a smaller responsibility.*

Full of anxious energy, Nathaniel did not wish to sit quietly while Mr. Garand called for Ezekiel, so he decided to go in search of the footman himself. The young man had been able to fit himself into the society of Marquises and Viscounts, as well as unobtrusively inspired the confidence of much of the less stellar occupants of London. *He managed to get information from the Duke of Devonshire as well as Arnie McGraw, the ugliest customer amongst the cent-per-cents.* Nathaniel knew without a doubt that such qualities would serve him well as a bailiff. He would in all likelihood inspire the confidence of the tenants and his quick mind would certainly be a benefit as he learned from Faintree all the tasks which would fall to him. *If he chooses to accept the offer.*

Ezekiel was standing in the foyer, at attention in his livery. Nathaniel gestured to him and the young man followed him through the house and into his study. After eschewing the chair Mr.

Faintree had occupied moments ago, Ezekiel assumed a military-like posture and looked expectantly at the Earl.

"Is your sister settling in well?"

"She is, my lord." Ezekiel raised a hand and scratched at his head at the edge of the powdered wig he wore as a part of his livery, breaking for a brief moment the image he presented as a faceless uniform.

After looking at him thoughtfully for a moment, Nathaniel asked, "Do you enjoy wearing that wig?"

"My lord?" Ezekiel seemed confused by the question and Nathaniel had all he could do not to laugh outright. *No wonder Violet is so often offering assistance to people. This light-heartedness and elation is most – excellent!*

"Would you prefer to wear a more fashionable suit?"

"I am a footman, my lord. Livery is the expectation." But Ezekiel's eyes were curious beneath the white-powdered wig.

"My current bailiff will soon be installed at my house in Bath." Nathaniel met the younger man's eyes directly. "Would you care to be placed in his position here?"

Ezekiel seemed unable to speak, so Nathaniel continued with a scarcely-contained grin. "There is a small cottage which he and his wife currently occupy. You may move into it with your sister after he and his wife have left, should you choose. You may wish to have your sister work here as we had discussed previously while attending Mrs. Matterly's school in the village, or you may simply have her keep your house. Should you wish to take a wife—" Something changed in the young man's face which made Nathaniel pause in his speech. "Do you already have a young woman in mind?"

"Well, you see, my lord," Ezekiel began, then paused. Flushing red, he continued in a rush, "Miss Stokes and I have become acquainted since my sister's and my arrival here, and I have a good mind that she would be just the girl for me." His bashful grin spoke volumes that his words did not.

"Indeed?" Nathaniel felt that he could imagine some of the younger man's feelings. *Elation in finding a woman who inspires such feeling, fear that she will not return that feeling, joy, confidence and uncertainty*— but Ezekiel was speaking again.

"Yes. She would surely like to stay here, if you might have use of her." He kept his eyes focused downward, as though afraid that he might be asking too much.

"I actually thought to keep her on staff indefinitely, if it was agreeable to her. I suppose from what you have told me that she would be amenable to that?"

"Oh yes, my lord!" Relief flooded Ezekiel's features and Nathaniel again was fighting laughter.

He recovered quickly to ask, "And you? Would you be willing to be trained in the time from now until Twelfth Night to fill the position of bailiff?"

Like Mr. Faintree, Ezekiel also seemed to be overcome for a moment. "I most certainly would be, my lord!" The young man's face was wreathed in smiles.

"Very good, Ezekiel. Or should I say now, Mr. Harris?" Nathaniel stood and offered his hand. "I am pleased to welcome you to your new position. I'll ask Mr. Faintree to be prepared to receive you in his office tomorrow morning."

Once again, Nathaniel's hand was shaken heartily. After assuring the younger man that he was eager to have him begin his work as the bailiff, he dismissed Mr. Harris to go tell his sister the news and took himself to his dressing room to ready for dinner.

Violet had spent the day making lists of tasks to be completed, approving final menus, and beginning to order items for boxes which would be given to the tenants on Boxing Day, the day after Christmas. At her parent's home, the boxes consisted of a loaf of bread, a handful of dried fruit, and instead of the clothing which many landlords included, a few handkerchiefs were all her mama could see fit to give to the three families who lived on their land. Violet had spoken with Nathaniel about the content of the boxes and he had agreed that more generosity was in order.

So it was decided that they would include one complete suit for each male and one dress for each female, as well as a hen and a pork haunch, a basket of vegetables, and some sweet breads as well. Violet was so pleased to have such a charitable husband; she thanked the Lord daily that Nathaniel was so generous to her and to others, especially of late.

As Violet dressed for dinner, she felt the effects of her work that day sweep over her. She nearly succumbed to sleep while Jane brushed out her hair, twisting the back of it into a chignon and fashioning the front portion into soft curls about her face. Jane had just finished fastening the buttons on the back of her evening dress when Violet heard sounds coming from the direction of her husband's dressing room. After slipping her feet into the satin slippers which Jane had set out for her and thanking her maid, she moved toward his dressing room.

Nathaniel was shrugging into his waistcoat when she peeked around the edge of the doorway and he glanced up at her while fastening the cloth-covered buttons on the front. She was pleased to see that he was wearing the shirt she had made for him.

"Good evening, Wife." His smile was fond. "Did you have a pleasant day?"

"Yes, Nathaniel." She smiled back at him, wondering as she did whether now would be the appropriate time to tell him that she might be carrying his heir. Griffin cleared his throat tactfully as he held out Nathaniel's evening coat, recalling Violet to his presence. *Now is most certainly not the time.* Instead, she said as he was helped into his coat, "Mrs. Baker has assured me that all of the hens and haunches will be ready by Boxing Day, and that she has started this very day to gather the needed clothing."

"Very good." He looked down as he buttoned the front of the coat. He dismissed Griffin with a smile of gratitude for his assistance and then turned toward Violet and possessed himself of her hands. "I am glad of your generous heart, my love."

"I was but a few moments ago thinking the same thing about you!" She laughed merrily as he drew her into his embrace. The words were on her lips to share the possibility of their child when he kissed her, chasing away all coherent thought. Once he had finished, he drew back his head and regarded her lovingly.

"Really, Nathaniel, I wish you'd give me some warning," she scolded lightly.

"But that would spoil the fun!" He chuckled as he planted a sound kiss upon her lips, then deftly slipped her hand through his arm. "Peche will be sore with us if we are late to dinner. Come."

Their dinner was accompanied by comfortable conversation, but with the presence of the footmen serving and Peche coming to inquire as to whether they liked this sauce or that dressing of the hen, Violet had no time during which to speak privately with her husband. She ate heartily, however, feeling hunger for the first time in well over a month.

After the covers had been cleared, Violet was led by Nathaniel into the drawing room. He offered her some Madeira, which she declined. She had not experienced any overpowering feelings of sickness all day, but the thought of the sweet wine caused her stomach to turn.

Her husband settled into his chair as she took up her sewing. The Tessel's little Ruth had already out-grown nearly all of her clothing, so Violet intended to include several gowns for the baby in the box being prepared for the family.

"Oh, Violet, I'd intended to tell you at dinner but forgot: Mr. Faintree and his wife will be moving to Bath, to look after our house there."

"We have a house in Bath?" Violet was mildly surprised.

"Oh yes, did I forget to mention that?"

"Perhaps you did." Violet found herself amused with the information that her husband had forgotten to mention the possession of an entire *house*.

Nathaniel grinned at her. "Well, we have a house in Bath, my love, so should you ever care to visit that city, please just give me the word. I shall send notice to Faintree of our arrival date and you shall have command of the entire city for your personal amusement."

She laughed at this and said, "I have no desire at present to go to Bath, but perhaps some day. I have never been there, you know."

"Never? Mama makes use of the house for a fortnight every year, and I have business there for a few days in the year, but I find it somewhat dull after living in London for several years."

"Do you? I wonder that you do not seem to find Bainscroft to be a dead bore, then, as well."

"Oh, but Bainscroft is not at all comparable to a house in Bath, or even London. It is the home of my childhood and holds so many fond memories. It is also the center of my business, so there is much here to occupy me. And finally, it is now the place where my love dwells and that alone gives it greater appeal than it has ever before held for me."

Although he remained in his chair, merely looking at her with penetrating warmth in his eyes, Violet felt that warmth suffuse her face before wrapping around her like a blanket. Suddenly she felt very happy and very sleepy.

Setting aside her sewing, Violet rested her head against the back of her chair, closed her eyes, and did her best to attend what her husband was saying.

"I also offered to Mr. Harris – the footman who was assisting me in gathering information about John's activities in London – the position of bailiff here. I believe he has a great deal of potential which would remain unrealized should he remain a footman, regardless of the perfect shape of his calves."

Violet chuckled at this, for footmen were often chosen for their height and the shape of their calves. She murmured sleepily, "He should be glad of the better ability to support a wife. Mrs. Baker tells me that her cousin seems to have captured his eyes, and he hers, nearly upon their first meeting."

"How is it that I am the last to know of this? He told me while we were discussing the particulars of the arrangement that he was inclined to offer for Miss Stokes. Does she have any family besides Mrs. Baker?"

Opening her eyes, Violet drew a deep breath to revive her senses before saying, "Both of her parents succumbed to scarlet fever several years past, and she has no brothers or sisters. As to other family, I do not know for certain, though she does have someone in London." Her eyes drifted closed again.

"I see," came her husband's voice. *It seems farther away than it was,* she mused. "It would be an excellent opportunity for her. She could either continue to work here if she wished or set up house for Mr. Harris in the cottage Faintree and his wife are currently in."

Dreamily, Violet replied, "Yes, that would be nice. She is such a sweet girl, I should be glad to see her raising her own children and...and..."

Nathaniel observed with amusement as his wife drifted off to sleep mid-sentence. He rose from his chair, placed his glass of half-consumed port on the nearest table, and walked over to her chair. Stooping down, he lifted her in his arms and carried her to their room. He called for Jane, who helped him dress Violet for bed, and finally he gently placed the coverlet upon her. Before calling for Griffin to assist him, he tenderly stroked her soft brown hair for a few moments. Bending down, he pressed a tender kiss to her cheek.

Sixteen

ADVENT, THE TIME of preparing for the coming of the Savior, had long since arrived. Upon the commencement of this blessed season, Peche had made up the pudding which would stay in its bag until it was served at Christmas dinner. Mrs. Baker had implemented a plan of cleaning the house in which every room would be scrubbed and polished by Christmas Eve. The gardener worked to ensure there would be mistletoe enough for the house and anyone else who wished to gather a sprig. Lord and Lady Reymes continued with their preparations of boxes and bonuses. Decorations began popping up about the house – branches of evergreens, sprigs of holly, and the like – and everyone was glad of the delicious smells coming from the kitchen. The gaiety of the season had descended upon the entire household.

It was into this jovial atmosphere that Mr. Ashbridge Wyndham's family arrived the first week of December. The morning after their arrival, Nathaniel had risen early to attend to a matter on the eastern side of the estate. Violet broke her fast with him, but he departed from her in the breakfast room. She was sipping a cup of mild tea and contemplating another serving of dried fruits – her appetite had increased considerably of late – when her brother joined her.

"Good morning, Ash," she immediately said with a happy grin.

"Good morning, sister," said he, approaching to drop a kiss on her cheek. "You are looking quite well this morning."

Violet found herself blushing, for she wore one of the old gowns she herself had made prior to her marriage. "I thank you, but you must recognize this as one of the dresses I'd refashioned from one of Mama's old gowns."

"Is that so?" said he. "I admit, I was rather distracted that Season and likely did not notice much about your dresses."

"Oh yes, you were too busy pretending not to be in love with a certain raven-haired beauty," she teased.

"So I was." The twinkle in his eye did Violet's heart good. "And you, my dear sister. How are you finding the married state? We have had no opportunity for a private interview since you've become a wife. And we both know that letters are not the same."

Violet blushed at this, but bravely answered her brother. "I enjoy quite a felicitous marriage. Nathaniel is a kind and generous husband, and I find that I have come to greatly enjoy being mistress of such an estate. We have great opportunity to assist others and I have even come to count several of the tenants as friends."

"And the rest of the neighborhood?" asked Ash. "Are the other members of the gentry to your liking?"

"It should be most difficult for them not to be," laughed Violet, "for they are only Aunt and Uncle Doberly. The Stanhope house is on the other side of our aunt and uncle, so our association with them is somewhat limited. The community here is rather small, and I suppose it is well that it is I, and not some Society belle who received the honor of Lord Reymes' hand – she should likely find this place dreadfully dull. It does quite well for me, though."

"Is that so?" he said, smiling at her. "I must again admit my astonishment at the changes I have seen in you since your marriage. Even since our last visit in Town."

"Since you mention that, Ash, there is something which has occurred. I should very much like to discuss it with you."

"Are you well?" he asked, leaving his food as he peered at her with furrowed brow.

"Oh indeed!" Violet chuckled lightly. "I do apologize for having alarmed you. I am well. Quite well. What I wish to ask has to do with the past, and has in actuality been rather freeing, now that I have had time to adjust to the knowledge. Only, it is of a rather delicate nature and I should prefer to discuss it elsewhere."

"Well, sister," said Ash as he rose from the table, "shall we take a brief stroll in the gardens? I should enjoy seeing how the plants here have been prepared for the winter. I shall take control of Wyndmere soon and that is one aspect of the place in which I failed to take interest when we were younger."

"Of course. I should be pleased to show you all the particulars," Violet said as she rose. "Only allow me to call for our things."

The two exited the breakfast room and Violet asked Peter, the nearest footman, to please fetch her pelisse, muff, bonnet, and gloves, as well as whichever items her brother wore on his journey the previous day. Moments later, brother and sister were strolling through the gardens arm in arm, their feet crunching on the frozen ground and their breath creating puffs of white before their faces. Violet pointed out how the gardener had cut away all dead plant matter, spread dry leaves over the soil, and placed protective cloth over some of the more delicate specimens in the gardens. Ash listened attentively, but Violet saw how often he glanced at her with questions in his eyes.

Finally, they reached the back of the gardens, and Violet stopped and turned to him. "What do you know about the early years of our parents' marriage?" she asked him.

His face took on a guarded look, reminiscent of his expressions before he had married Penny. "Why do you ask?" he said.

"Perhaps I should tell you what I know?" she offered.

At his nod, she drew a fortifying breath and said, "A part of me believes you must already know, but I fear that you do not and might therefore be injured. However, I suppose if that is the case, you shall bear the injury with dignity, and as I mean to inflict no harm beyond what is necessary, shall accordingly heal quickly. Therefore, I shall say it quickly: Mama is not our natural mother."

Ash's face relaxed for a moment before taking on a concerned expression. "When did you learn of this?" he asked.

"So you knew? What a relief!" He nodded as she continued. "Mama – er, Mrs. Wyndham – I still have not quite resolved with myself how I ought to think of her – told me several days before Rose's wedding. It was after we dined at your home, or I should have asked for a private audience then, to discuss it with you."

"However did she tell you? Our father told me that they had determined to keep it a secret, inasmuch as they were able. The new Mrs. Wyndham feared she should not have our respect if we'd known she was not our mother."

"It was not pleasant," Violet said, her face flushing with heat in spite of the cold air. "Let us simply leave it at that."

"Did she injure you?" asked Ash, protectively stepping closer to his sister.

Violet smiled serenely at him. "Not in a lasting manner. In fact, as I mentioned earlier, it has been quite freeing. To know there was a reason for her disdain which was outside of my control – I cannot tell you how very comforting that has been. But tell me, if you please, how you came to know?"

Ash chuckled darkly before beginning. "I was fifteen at the time; 'twas nearly a month before my birthday, if memory serves me correctly. I was home on holiday from school, and Papa had taken it upon himself to acquaint me, during that hiatus from my studies, with the running of the land and house. He sent me to his chambers to fetch a document which he had left on the escritoire there, and it had fallen to the floor. I did not know this at the time, of course, and began a careful search. Upon opening one of the small drawers – I see by your smile that you recall those drawers! What a mystery they always seemed! We were always severely admonished not to open them, were we not?"

"We were," she admitted. A small gust of wind swept through the open area where they stood and she shivered.

"Should we go indoors?" asked Ashbridge.

"Oh no, unless you are too cold. I should prefer to keep this between us. I have told Nathaniel, of course – he is my husband, and I can think of nothing I would purposefully keep from him – but perhaps it would be best if no-one else knew for the time being."

"Of course. I also have told Penny, which I am sure is no surprise to you." Violet nodded even as another small shiver raced through her and he added, "Perhaps we could move back into the garden? Some of the trees or shrubs might block the wind a bit."

As they walked, he continued his story. "Upon opening one of the drawers, I found a miniature of our father with a woman I did not recognize. She was brown-haired and had your eyes. Indeed, if you were to look at it now, I believe that with the exception of her darker hair, you should think you peered into a looking-glass, rather than a miniature portrait."

"Is that so?" asked Violet, her soft voice filled with awe.

"Yes. I took it, along with the document I eventually found, to the office to ask our father about it. He closed the door and was very angry at first, but then seemed almost relieved to tell me. It is the only time I ever witnessed him weep. He said that they had been deeply in love, even though their marriage necessitated a break with her past."

"How dreadful," Violet murmured. "Poor woman. Poor Papa."

"Indeed. He said that she delighted in children and was overjoyed to learn she was to be a mother. Her time of confinement was difficult, though, and weakened her considerably. She managed, though, to give birth. Unfortunately, she never quite recovered her health and in the following years, lost several children before they ever were born."

Violet felt her heart twist at this information. She hurt for her mother, a woman she had never known, at the losses she suffered – first of her family, and then of her children. *I should be so very broken were I to lose this child,* she thought as she resisted placing a hand upon her abdomen.

"Several years passed," Ash continued, "with her rarely leaving the house or receiving visitors. She was either sick with a child growing inside her, or mourning its loss. On the rare occasions that she felt well enough to be up from her bed, she spent time in the gardens, sitting and reading, or walking a little with the aid of our father or her companion. Finally, she was successfully delivered of a baby girl, whom she named Violet. Papa said that she told him how she loved all of the flowers, but especially the tiny violets. He remembered how her face shone with a gentle light when she spoke of how they hid in the most interesting places, blooming where it seemed no other flower could grow or even flourish."

Violet felt her throat constrict with emotion, and saw that her brother's eyes shone with unshed tears as he gave her hand an affectionate squeeze.

"When she died, our father could not bear to be in Society or really even to see either of the children she had born. Our mother's companion and ladies' maid, though, offered to care for us. He was grateful, and eventually they reached an understanding. After the proper time of mourning, he married her; she bore him a daughter quite soon after their marriage, but then no other children. I suspect that our father, while he admitted no such thing, wanted a woman to serve as mother, to raise the children; and he tried to be the husband he knew he ought to be, but found that his grief was too great. He likely never visited her chamber again, and stopped all pretense of loving her, of being whole. He was quite broken, I am convinced, based upon the few times we spoke candidly."

"How dreadful for him," whispered Violet. "I wonder, then, that he could born my presence at all. He seldom left his library when it was not necessary, and much of the time when I entered a room, he would leave immediately. I had always feared that he disliked me, but it must have hurt him immensely to see me."

"Even so," Ash said, his discomfort clear in his voice, "he should not have treated you so, nor should he have allowed Mrs. Wyndham to treat you as she did."

Violet paused, thinking of what her life would have been had she known the truth, if her father had faced his grief and not allowed it to consume him. But she had learned that dwelling upon what might have been is no manner in which to have a happy life.

"Did you know, the day that I was lost in the labyrinth, he came to see me after I recovered."

"Did he?" Ash's astonishment was obvious.

"Yes. He entered my room, attempted to say that he was glad that I was well, but took one look at me, muttered something about my similarity to a *Marianna*, and left, looking as though he had seen a ghost."

"I suppose that in some manner, he had."

"It is odd, now knowing why our mama – Mrs. Wyndham, that is – has treated us with such disdain."

"Treated you, dear. She has always known not to cross me, especially after she learned that I knew the truth, for she feared I would not see to her living in the manner to which she is accustomed after our father's demise."

"Which you would never do!" cried Violet.

Ash chuckled as he shook his head. "While I am often tempted to cast her off, my conscience prevents it. While she did not fill it with love, she did make a home in which we lived for our formative years. Besides which, it would be rather unchristian of me to cast her off, would it not?"

"It would," agreed Violet.

Ash grunted before saying, "So I shall continue to tolerate her."

Violet laughed even as she chastised her brother for his unkind speech.

"Well, that has been a good conversation to have, but your lips are near to turning blue, Violet, and I believe your husband should have my head were I to keep you out in these temperatures any longer." Ash began leading them toward the house.

"But we are here at my behest," scoffed Violet. "Surely he will not fault you for my choices."

Ash stopped his steps, turning to gape at his sister. "He most certainly would. You *are* acquainted with your husband, are you not, *Lady Reymes*?" Violet laughed, and they continued toward the house. "At any rate, I daresay he may be cross with me, regardless. Dreadful awkward situation, his being our host and all."

Violet giggled again and acquiesced, "Very well. I shall call for tea and sit sedately by the fire until I am quite thawed, and there shall be no difficulty."

Ash looked askance at her, but said nothing.

As it was, there was no difficulty, as Violet had predicted. She had a truly amazing ability of smoothing things over with her husband, which caused even the staff to marvel on occasion.

Things proceeded nicely, Ash's family fitting quite well into the household. Penelope offered her lively company and assistance as Violet prepared boxes, sewed clothing, and went about her various tasks. Ash accompanied Nathaniel on hunting excursions and on rides through the estate before the snow started in earnest that year.

One mid-December morning, Violet and Penelope worked on some sewing in the family sitting room. Violet was adding a ruffle to a gown for little baby Ruth while Penelope stitched a hem into a dress.

"How does little Andrew get on, Penny?" asked Violet, digging in her work-bag for larger scissors. The ones on the chatelaine pinned to her bodice were too small for trimming the extra fabric from the ruffle. "He is such a darling little boy! Oh dear, now I've gone and spilled my bag; I suppose it can wait to be picked up, though. Oh, but I can scarce credit how very big Andrew has grown!"

With a gentle laugh, Penelope said, "Oh yes, I daresay he grows out of his clothing almost as soon as he is in it! He is certainly eats quite well."

It was into this scene which Mr. Garand entered, announcing a visitor.

"Mrs. Frances Peyton, my lady." He bowed himself out of the room.

The woman entered and curtsied elegantly. Violet moved aside the small pile of fabric beside her, and Frances came to sit near the other two ladies who nodded their welcome of her.

"Frances, may I present my brother's wife, Mrs. Wyndham. Penny, Mrs. Peyton." Violet made the introduction and smiled warmly at the newcomer. "I am so glad you're here."

Soon formalities were dispensed with and they were simply Violet, Penny, and Fran. Violet began to put away her work, but Frances stopped her with a hand on her arm.

"Oh, do continue! I would have brought some thing or other to occupy myself had I known you were sewing." Her smile expanded as she said eagerly, "I could help! What might I do?"

Immediately, a sensation of warmth and gratitude flowed through Violet. The strain of preparing for the arrival of so many guests (Mrs. Wyndham was expected to arrive with Mr. and Mrs. Langley in two days' time) had sapped a great deal of Violet's strength. It was with relief that she pulled the last gown for Ruth from the pile of jumbled fabric on her lap.

"This needs only a simple pattern stitched along the hem, Fran. It is for the new baby of one of our tenants. If you could add the decorative edge, I would be so grateful."

"Certainly, Violet. Shall I use that thread?" she asked, indicating pink and green floss wound about a card on Violet's lap.

Violet felt her cheeks flush mildly. "How silly of me to have forgotten you'd need thread. Yes." She quickly pressed the floss into Frances' upturned palm.

"And a needle? And scissors?" Frances' face was amused.

"Oh, I must say, I haven't the faintest idea where my mind has gone begging."

Frances and Penelope both smiled gently at this. Penelope commented with a laugh, "Violet, you sound just as I did shortly before I began to increase with Andrew."

The two other ladies chuckled and although Violet attempted a brief laugh, it fell flat. Fortunately, though, neither of the other two ladies seemed to take notice. They all continued with their work and the conversation moved on.

"I fear," Penny was saying, "that a simple hem is all I can manage. My talents tend more toward painting and drawing."

"Is that so?" asked Frances. "I embroider fairly well, and draw decently. In fact, I have fair talent in most of the accomplishments, but truly excel in little."

After soft chuckles all around, the three quieted and their needles settled into steady motion. Violet sat staring intently at the row of neat, even stitches that appeared beneath her hands. The satisfaction of working for someone else's good permeated Violet's soul. After several moments she glanced up to find two pairs of eyes watching her discreetly as the sewing continued.

Penelope finally spoke, gently and perhaps a bit hesitantly. "Violet, I do not wish to pry..."

Violet felt her face flush again, knowing what her brother's wife was about to say. "I do not know, Penny. I have been feeling terribly fatigued of late, and I've been rather ill for a good deal of the time, but that seems to be nearing an end."

"And your mind seems to be leaving you much of the time?" asked Penelope, fingers still working clumsily with her needle. "I could not believe how forgetful I was!"

"But I do not know it with certainty," cautioned Violet in a whisper as she took in the two beaming faces, her hands stilling over the small gown.

"But of course, Violet," said Frances. "We shan't breathe a word to anyone."

Violet grinned at them. "Though I must confess, I am beginning to believe that perhaps Mrs. Tessel was right."

"Mrs. Tessel?"

"One of the tenant farmers' wives; these gowns are for her youngest." Violet began sewing again as she mentioned the gown. "She guessed that I might be."

"How delightful that would be for you, Violet," said Frances with a bright smile. "I am happy indeed that things have turned out so very well. I must say that when I heard that you were marrying Nathaniel without knowing him in the least, I was rather concerned for you." Her face took on a pensive, rather regretful expression. "I did not know Mr. Peyton terribly well when we were wed...but never you mind that. It is excellent that your marriage has turned out so very well."

Violet was uncertain how to respond to Frances' mention of her own husband. *After all, does she know John's part in Nathaniel's and my marriage? And that it seems he was stealing money?* Rather than attempt a response to that portion of her words, Violet elected to answer what Frances said last.

"It *is* quite wonderful that we are so happy in our marriage, Frances. I am so very blessed."

"Are you enjoying this house?" asked Penny. "It is quite impressive. I think that I should become lost without someone to show me where I am going."

Frances laughed lightly at this. "Mr. Peyton and I lived here for several months after we were married. I still cannot find most of the rooms here."

"After I had recovered from the ague I contracted while on our honeymoon tour, Nathaniel showed me everything, and then Mrs. Baker took me over the house again on several occasions, as she explained how the household was run. She was very patient with me. I daresay I'm quite near to being familiar with it all."

"I am glad to see you so happy, Violet," said Penny, smiling widely.

Frances commented, "It is certainly a good piece of luck that everything turned out so very well."

"Yes; it could have very easily have been the opposite. It is truly a blessing that Nathaniel is so good and kind a husband, and that he chose to make the best of the situation. I do not believe, though, that I can credit 'luck' with having anything to do with it; surely it is God's guiding that has brought us to where we are. I must say that it is far better than I had ever hoped when we became engaged; we have grown to love one another rather more quickly than I had ever imagined we would."

Violet, having grown uncomfortable with the attention centered on her for so long a time, changed the subject. "Are you enjoying your stay with Lady Eunice, Fran?"

"Yes, she is a gracious hostess."

"I have never met her," admitted Penelope. "Pray, what is she like? I know that rumors rarely tell the whole truth."

Violet smiled at her sister-in-law and said, "She is apt to speak her mind, but she also is a kind and loving matron."

"Does she often visit you, Violet?" questioned Frances.

"We visit at least once a week, whether it be here or at the dower house."

Penelope's appraising eyes glanced out of the window as she said, "The grounds here are really quite lovely, even during the winter months. Perhaps one of these days, I shall bundle myself up and strike out with my sketching pad." She turned back to share a secretive smile with Violet, while Frances was inspecting her embroidery.

Their talk turned to the estate, the gardens, and the coming preparations for Christmas. Before Frances took her leave, she promised her assistance in decking the rooms with holly and rosemary and mistletoe. Violet was glad to have discovered an unexpected friend in this woman. She hoped that the difficulty with Frances' husband would not prove to hinder their deepening friendship.

Two days later, Nathaniel raced down the steps to the front door as quickly as he could. The tapping of his highly polished black Hessians on the marble steps echoed in the large hall. His feet hit the landing and with a few long strides, he reached Violet, who stood before the closed door, wringing her hands.

"Mr. Garand told me that your mother and sister have arrived."

"Yes, just. I believe they shall be—" she started to say, but was cut off by the sound of a bell ringing.

Motioning for the footman to wait a moment before opening the door, he grasped her arms at the elbows gently and brought her to stand before him. Looking into her eyes, trying to read what he saw there, Nathaniel asked, "Are you ready?"

His lovely wife seemed to understand what he was not saying.

"Nathaniel, darling," she whispered as she reached up to rest her palm along his temple, "I cannot pretend that I am not a little bit concerned, but I know that with God's grace and strength, and with the strength that *you* give me, I will be fine."

Nathaniel experienced no small amount of aggravation that he could not spare his wife from the ordeal of having these particular family members visit. He knew that Violet trusted the Lord to guide her through their time, but he struggled with the overpowering desire to protect her from all unpleasantness and pain. Knowing, though, that his own power to protect had its limits, he asked God for patience and the mindfulness of God's ability to work good in anything.

Mustering as bright a smile as he could, Nathaniel placed a kiss on his wife's forehead, feeling as he did so that he was relinquishing control over their lives. He knew that it was God who held all of her in His hand, and that knowledge alone made it possible for him to release the need to protect her. He nodded to the footman, who opened the door.

Seventeen

WITH THE ENTRANCE of the party came a gust of cold air. Nathaniel saw his wife shiver and drew her hand through his arm to offer some warmth as he stood close by her side.

"I declare, Violet, 'twas quite shabby of you to keep us standing out of doors for so long!" cried Mrs. Wyndham as soon as she was inside the foyer.

Nathaniel was about to answer her, claiming fault for the delay, when Violet spoke. "I do apologize, Mama, but it could not be helped. I was called upon to assure one of my household regarding a delicate matter. I do hope you did not take a chill?"

He felt pride swell in his chest. Mrs. Wyndham's wide eyes and slightly parted lips spoke the surprise her voice did not. He discretely pressed Violet's hand where it rested on his forearm.

"I shall have you shown to your rooms immediately. The fires are lit, so you ought to be warmed in no time. Shall I have tea sent up, as well, or would you prefer to take your tea with us? Unfortunately, Ashbridge and Penny have already left with little Andrew; they are spending the day with Uncle and Aunt Doberly."

Mrs. Langley had stood this entire time, with a confused expression on her face. Nathaniel imagined with an unholy glee that she could not reconcile the gracious yet commanding mistress before her with the bashful and retiring miss with whom she had spend much of her life.

Mrs. Wyndham opened and shut her mouth twice before finally answering in a prim voice, "We shall take tea with you. Where, pray, will that be?"

Violet's smile appeared genuine as she said, "Oh, just ring your bell and someone will come to show you to the room." She then turned and asked the two footmen still standing beside the doors to bring in their trunks before ringing for Mrs. Baker.

When the housekeeper arrived, Violet asked her to send tea to the Green Parlor after showing their guests to their rooms. As he watched the Mrs. Wyndham, followed by Mr. and Mrs. Langley, be led by Mrs. Baker toward the stairs, Nathaniel drew Violet along the few steps into his study and closed the door behind them.

"Nathaniel! What do you mean by—"

He cut off her words with a kiss pressed to her sweet lips. "Violet, my love, I could not be more proud of you—"

"But I did nothing—"

"You were the picture of graciousness—"

"Oh, Nathaniel—"

He pressed his fingertips to her lips, still parted in speech. "Dearest, as we are each determined not to allow the other to speak, allow me to propose a solution." With a grin that he saw caused Violet's eyes to widen with enchanting surprise, he pulled her into a tight embrace, only keeping his face back far enough to see her face. "I shall kiss you heartily, you shall return my kiss, and we may then proceed to the parlor for tea with the understanding that I am terribly proud of you, regardless of your own opinion of your actions."

With a small giggle, Violet nodded her acquiescence. As he bent his head toward her, the thought flitted through his mind, *Much as I want to see her grow in confidence and the ability to make her own wishes known, I shall not regret if she remains as compliant as ever in regards to my affection.*

Mrs. Wyndham entered the parlor mere moments after Nathaniel and Violet did. When asked if her accommodations were adequate, Mrs. Wyndham grudgingly admitted that she had no cause for complaint. Bessy arrived with tea and Violet sent the girl to inquire whether Mr. and Mrs. Langley were prepared to join them.

Nathaniel attempted to draw Mrs. Wyndham into conversation while they awaited the arrival of the newlyweds, but when he asked whether their travel to Bainscroft had been comfortable, the woman began to soliloquize on the effects of a hired post-chaise upon her newly-diagnosed gout. Why could not the earl have sent his personal carriage to fetch them? Surely it would have been more well-sprung than the rattle-trap they were forced to endure. Violet set about preparing the tea while Mrs. Wyndham seamlessly transitioned from complaining of the journey to Bainscroft to evaluating the changes Violet had made to the room. The elder woman sat on the edge of her chair, looking about the room with a critical eye. It was with relief that Nathaniel observed the door open to admit the rest of their party. *Perhaps with the company a bit more varied, the conversation will not be nearly so stagnant.*

"I say, Reymes," lisped Mr. Langley with a familiarity that chagrined the earl, "this is a bang-up place you have here! The very *epitome* of a fashionable country home."

Nathaniel seldom took notice of the attire of other gentlemen, and only slightly more often that of ladies. However, he could not help but marvel at the bright green coat Mr. Langley wore. In an effort to distract himself, he asked, "I take it you found your room satisfactory?"

"How could I not? Indeed, it stands to reason that I would. Steeped in family history and whatnot as it is, most charming! Most charming indeed." The man sent a toothy grin in Nathaniel's direction, almost making him want to laugh. *My interaction with him at their wedding was minimal,* he mused silently. *I suppose I took little notice of his foppish mannerisms due to my distraction with Violet.*

Here his gaze returned to his wife. She poured tea with a steady hand, not once spilling a drop, while listening to Mrs. Langley give an extensive account of their abbreviated honeymoon tour. It seemed that while they had been able to travel for longer than the twelve hours that Violet and Nathaniel managed, the Langleys' voyage was also cut short by one of their pair taking an ague. Mr. Langley was particularly susceptible to the chilly, damp air they found during their trip. Despite the early termination of their travels, Mrs. Langley seemed to have plenty to describe.

After a moment of assuring himself that Violet was comfortable in her conversation, and enduring an excruciating account of each of her gowns and his coats worn at each day of their travels, Nathaniel turned his attention to his mother-in-law. Mrs. Wyndham was listening to the conversation between her two daughters. Nathaniel guessed that she was comparing the two and attempting to understand what had happened to her eldest girl. *She has become a woman.* But he had no opportunity to dwell on the thought, for Mr. Langley again claimed his attention.

The remainder of their time was spent in polite conversation. Mrs. Wyndham remained quietly observant while her youngest daughter could not be constrained to hear anyone else speak for more than several seconds, and Mr. Langley continued to make outrageously exuberant exclamations. During the entirety of the time, Violet's gentle temperament made her an ideal hostess to this gathering of people.

Kneeling down upon the plush carpet in the drawing room, Violet placed a brown dress, a suit of grey, and three smaller dresses in the box before her. Only one week remained until Christmas and she knew that she must work diligently in order to complete the boxes for the tenants. The door opened and Nathaniel entered.

"How is everything coming along, dearest?" he asked, indicating the boxes strewn about the floor. "Will they be ready by Boxing Day?"

"I certainly hope so!" she laughed. "After all the time I have been working on them, it would be dreadful to not be able to give them to the tenants on time!"

He stooped to kiss the pile of curls on the top of her head and asked, "Can any of the staff help you?"

Violet had considered this, but was reluctant to ask any of them to help, as their hands were full with their guests. None of their guests had brought their own staff to attend them, so poor Jane was required to help not only Violet dress, but to assist Bessie in waiting on Rose and both Mrs. Wyndhams as well. Griffin was Nathaniel's valet and Violet did not feel that she could ask him to divide his attention from her husband, so she had enlisted the aid of the first footman, Jarvis, to attend Mr. Wyndham and Mr. Langley. Violet felt she could ask no more of Mrs. Baker, with all she was doing already to prepare for the party which was coming in two days, and Mrs. Wyndham's demanding nature was occupying all of the other members of the staff who might have reasonably been called upon to help.

"I do not wish to trouble them, Nathaniel." Violet smiled to assure her husband that she was perfectly capable of doing what must be done; his face had begun to take on a stubborn hardness which she noticed whenever he was about to argue about her well-being. "Besides, all of the preparations are finished. All I must do is assemble the items for the boxes."

"If you are certain." He seated himself upon a chair beside the place that she knelt.

"Quite. I have made a list of what must go into each box, so that I do not neglect to include anything. We have twenty-two tenants living on our land. For the ones who are not farmers and therefore have no land for a vegetable garden, I have included extra dried vegetables and fruits. To the farmers, that they might not feel slighted, I am including some small trinket that they would enjoy."

"You know each of them well enough to know what they would enjoy?" He made no attempt to hide the surprise in his voice.

"Well, yes, Nathaniel. It is really quite simple." Violet was nonplussed. "All I did was listen to them. Mr. Barnes enjoys reading books of history, Mr. and Mrs. Potts collect miniatures of the kings and queens of England, and—"

"They do?"

"Indeed." She began to see that her husband, while a good landlord and master, really did not know those under his care. "You see, dear, it is merely a matter of observing and of listening."

"Which you seem to do well, except when I ask you to rest." He fondly ran a finger down the bridge of her nose, causing her heart to flip inside of her chest. When she closed her eyes momentarily in an attempt to calm her heart, he asked, "Are you feeling ill?"

Her answer was a whisper. "No." After a composing breath, she continued, "No, I am not ill. I seem to have been quite well for the past week or so." She looked into his eyes, unaware that her steady gaze did far more to assure Nathaniel than any words might have.

The smile which dispersed the cloud of concern on his face caused her heart to start to tripping all over again. "Excellent," he said. "I must confess that I have been worrying about you, though my mother did caution me against undue concern."

"Not terribly much, I hope?"

"Only once in a while."

"Actually, Nathaniel, I have wanted to speak with you—"

"You are not seriously ill, are you?"

"No, I am not, but I do wish to—" At that moment, Rose wandered into the room, causing Violet to fall silent. Frustrated at her sister's timing, she did her best to appear nonchalant when she said to her husband, "Oh, never mind. I shall speak with you later."

She continued with placing items in the boxes while Nathaniel stood. He possessed himself of her hand briefly to place a light kiss on it, whispered "I shall see you before dinner, my love," and then took his leave of the room.

After Nathaniel had left, Violet looked up to find Rose watching with an inscrutable expression upon her lovely face. Rose ambled over to the pianoforte and Violet continued working on the boxes and listened in silence as the notes of the lively piece filled the room. After the piece ended, Rose replaced the cover on the pianoforte and looked expectantly at Violet.

"You still play beautifully, Rose." Violet smiled wistfully at her sister, suddenly regretting that they were not closer. She could not help but wonder, *Does Rose know the truth of my parentage? Of Ash's?*

"Well, yes. Thank you." The younger woman pressed her lips into a thin line and narrowed her eyes, as though trying to see Violet better, though the rays from the setting sun provided ample light in the westward-facing room. Finally, she said with some disapproval, "You have changed, Vi."

"Have I?" asked Violet, striving to not allow her sister's tone to touch the peace which had occupied her heart for some time now.

"Yes. But I cannot for the life of me understand what it is." Rose said petulantly as she stood from the bench and walked to the chair Nathaniel had vacated moments ago. "Mama gave me an earful after we came, about how ungrateful you were, and how she couldn't seem to make you feel anything for your poor mama."

Violet began, unconsciously, to gnaw on her lower lip, but said nothing.

"I think she cannot bear that you no longer cower before her."

Violet's thoughts began to run quickly at these words. *Can it be that she doesn't approve of Mama's harshness anymore than I do? Or perhaps Rose might even know that she is not my natural mother!* But Violet was careful to reveal in her face none of these thoughts; she did not wish to endorse speaking ill of anyone.

"I daresay," continued Rose, "she certainly would *not* have thrown you at Reymes as she did, had she known the effect marriage would have had on you." Rose giggled at her clever speech.

"I cannot say that it was *marriage* which has changed me, but my husband. Or rather, God's working through him." At her sister's uncomprehending stare, Violet attempted to explain, her voice quiet but strong. "He has encouraged me in becoming mistress of this home, not merely his wife, and the Lord has slowly been teaching me to be free of the fear that for so long shadowed my words and actions."

Rose looked a bit perplexed at this initially, but eventually her smile chased away any trace of confusion. "Whatever has changed you, it seems for the best." She paused, looking down at her slender, soft hands for a moment before saying, "Violet, however I might have behaved in the past, I am glad that you seem to be so happily settled now."

Violet, moved by her sister's tender words, felt heat pricking at her eyes and smiled tremulously up at her sister from her place on the floor. "Thank you, Rose," she whispered. "I am truly blessed."

Rose, clearly uncomfortable with the tender moment which had occurred between the two, suddenly blurted, "Would that I was so blessed."

Violet's shock was considerable. *It is not possible that Rose could be unhappy, is it? Did she not marry her heart's desire?* Thinking of the changes which had occurred in Mr. Langley since the beginning of their acquaintance with him, she wondered if the changes were seen as favorable to her sister. *I have never stopped to consider whether Rose might be happy in her marriage. As she was nothing less than rapturous about it during the time I lived with my family, I simply assumed that she still was.* Violet felt her heart go out to her sister, something which had never occurred to that point.

"Have you a nice house?" she ventured. "I remember that Mr. Langley was renting a house in London."

"Oh!" Rose seemed to blush, but Violet was not certain she was seeing correctly. "We are living in his brother's house, while he and his family are at their country seat."

"I see." Violet was uncertain from this answer whether Rose saw this as good or not. "London seems to have a great deal of amusement to offer. Are you able to go see much of the city?"

"We do see some of it, but I must admit that I wish that we went more often about Town." Rose studied the ring on her finger as though some great mystery could be discovered in it. "My hope is that once the Season begins, we will have many more entertainments."

"Yes, there is always a great deal happening during that time." Violet remembered her one Season, wondering briefly whether she would enjoy another more now that she was rather assured of herself and more easily able to speak with new acquaintances.

The rest of their conversation stayed in the realm of the weather, the upcoming Christmas festivities, and new fabric that Rose purchased recently.

Later that evening, Violet was undressing after their guests had retired for the night; Jane was indisposed with her sister at the moment. Nathaniel entered her dressing room, dressed for bed and looking comfortable and relaxed. Violet was struggling with a tangle she had caused in her hair when trying to remove several pins. Nathaniel grinned and gently removed the brush from her hands.

"May I?" he asked.

"Yes, I would certainly appreciate the help." Violet smiled briefly at him before turning and settling onto the newly-arrived, low-backed chair perfect for this task. After a moment of sitting without feeling the brush in her hair, she turned once again to face him. Nathaniel stood there, regarding her thoughtfully.

"While I am sure that this chair is ideal for someone of Jane's stature in brushing your hair, I am rather too tall for it to be of use to me. Would you mind terribly sitting on the bed?"

"No, Nathaniel, I would not mind," she said, "but I must warn you that I am liable to fall asleep before you finish."

"Are you?" he asked as he took her hand and led her to the bed. "Then I shall have to make it my task to ensure that you do not." The grin on his face spoke more truly to his intent than did his words.

Violet smiled demurely and allowed him to assist her onto the bed, settling among the soft covers as he began to draw the brush through her hair. Violet luxuriated in the soothing motion of the brush moving softly though her hair.

"Now, my darling love, what is it you wished to tell me before we were interrupted by your sister earlier this evening?" her husband murmured close to her ear once the brushing stopped. He carefully climbed from the bed, returned the brush to her dressing room, and came to sit before her on the bed, taking her hands in his own.

Violet paused momentarily, wondering whether she ought to tell him, after all. *What if there is no child? What if something happens to the baby if there is one? I would spare him any pain, whether it be from losing a child or not having one at all.* Still uncertain, she decided that there would be time later to tell him.

"Oh! I – I er, think that it is nothing of – that is, nothing that cannot wait until a later time." Drawing a silent and deep breath, she put on her sweetest smile and moved to kiss her husband. *He really is most easily distracted,* was her last coherent thought as he deepened the kiss.

Eighteen

Two days before Christmas, Mr. Faintree, Mr. Harris, and the local magistrate, Mr. Lopton, were gathered in the library, awaiting the word of Lord Reymes. That word would call them to action or dismiss them were their services not required.

Nathaniel had reviewed his information with those three men, asking them to be available while he confronted his brother with the evidence against him. After ensuring they would be comfortable waiting in the library, Nathaniel removed himself to his study. He sent a man to the dower house to fetch his brother; after that was accomplished, Reymes started to pace.

As he waited, he prayed. *Oh Holy Lord, I thank You for creating this opportunity to speak to John.* Indeed, he should never have attempted to confront his brother in such a manner were the Wyndhams and Langleys not already engaged to spend the day with the Doberly family. It truly seemed to be the hand of Providence that Mr. Lopton was available and the other two men whose aid he had enlisted were also willing to be of assistance.

Despite this indication of God's hand being upon this, Nathaniel still felt unsettled; nerves were beginning to get the better of him. As he turned at one end of the room, he felt his stomach clench, his palms begin to sweat, his heart beat faster and faster. Seeing a decanter of wine sitting on the table, he was tempted to swallow a glass in an attempt to calm his nerves, but quickly decided that he wanted to be in possession of his full faculties for this interview. *Please, Lord, guide me and guide my words. May Your Spirit work in John's heart, that he may see what he is doing is wrong – both in regards to the money and the manner in which he is living his life! May he see his need for You.*

At that moment, the door swung open, hitting the wall with a bang which reverberated to Nathaniel's very soul. *It is time, Lord. Guide me!* John sauntered into the room, an insolent sneer marring his fine features. He was closely followed by a harried-looking Mr. Garand, whose eyes spoke of his regret at not being able to restrain Mr. Peyton long enough to announce him properly. Nathaniel assured and dismissed his faithful butler, and the older man exited with a bow, closing the door behind him.

"Fine weather we're having, eh Reymes?" asked John as he sauntered across the room. He poured himself a glass of wine and settled comfortably into a chair.

"Reasonably so, I daresay." Nathaniel walked to the fireplace and rested his arm along the mantle. Leveling his gaze on his brother, he prayed that his face revealed none of the turmoil inside. He knew that it would be easy to exact justice; but more than justice, he wished for reconciliation. "John, you must know why I have called you here."

"On second thought," muttered John just loudly enough for Nathaniel to hear him, "seems a storm is brewing."

"I have the testimony of several people affirming that you have been pilfering monies from the tenants, as well as from the estate here." Nathaniel was careful to keep his words neutral in regards to himself. He sensed on an instinctual level that if John believed him to have been offended personally, he would be less likely to cooperate.

"If I have – and I admit to nothing! – it was a small loss to you," John returned flippantly from his seat.

"It is of no consequence to my own well-being, but I assure you the loss was acutely felt by the tenants from whom you stole." Nathaniel strove to maintain a purposefully calm cadence.

John examined his wine through the cut glass goblet before answering. When he did speak, his tone was light and conversational, sitting at odds with what he said. "You have the title, the estate, everything – do not begrudge me what little I might or might not have taken from some inconsequential farmers."

Nathaniel felt his mild annoyance grow into a scarcely-containable, burning anger. His voice rumbled low and tense as he carefully enunciated, "They *work* for their food, for all they have."

"As do I," chuckled John with a sardonic lift of his brow. "It is terribly tiresome, making the necessary threats to persuade others to comply with my plans, to make the arrangements for collecting the funds your tenants have so *kindly* donated to my cause."

"Your words mock them," Nathaniel admonished. "Not all are born to titles or even the life of a gentleman. While it is generally held that the mark of a gentleman is that he does not work, neither does one steal!"

"So you would prefer to keep company with your *tenants*" – he spoke the word with a sneer, evincing his view that individuals of such a distinction as quite beneath his touch – "than with me?"

"If those tenants are honest folk, doing their utmost to live peaceably and honestly, and if you have not changed your dishonest ways, then yes, John, I would."

"What a charmingly put sentiment. Positively flooded with a heartfelt attempt to make the prodigal brother see the error of his ways, and in the same breath, exonerates you entirely."

"What do you mean to say, John?"

"You refuse to acknowledge your own part in my misdeeds."

"Which is?"

John stood abruptly, face burning red and brows furrowed darkly. "Surely you must know!"

"I declare I do not."

Nathaniel thought he heard a muttered, "That is *just* like you," before John began angrily pacing. "That night."

He knew what his brother referenced. There was only one night – early morning, if one wished to quibble over specifics – which served him and his brother as both a source of commonality and yet which simultaneously expanded the already-growing chasm between them.

"I know you blame me," muttered John. "Do you not think that I also blame myself? That not a day passes in which I despise myself and my choices that night?"

Nathaniel could not speak. His recent conversation with Violet regarding that night had begun a slow process of healing from the guilt he had carried, but it was still quite fresh. The wounds in his heart had been cleared of infection, but still had a great deal of healing to do. He could not yet comprehend the words which presently issued from his brother's mouth. In the time that Nathaniel stood silent, his brother stayed still, standing with feet planted, shoulders sagging, hands slightly extended in a manner that could only be seen as pleading. John's face was overcome by an array of passing emotions, each taking its turn, but the last one, the one to remain, was indecipherable. His hands slowly closed into fists, his eyes narrowed, and his jaw tightened.

With a tightly controlled voice – a rarity for him – John said, "There will be no more – how did you so righteously term it? – *pilfering* of the tenant's money or of your own. So you need not fuss. Good day, brother."

With that, John rose from his chair, placed his now-empty glass on the table, and bowed formally to his brother before leaving the room. At this, Nathaniel turned from his brother, bracing himself with his hands upon the fireplace mantle and hanging his head, feeling very much as though he had just now been trampled by a coach-and-four.

Violet closed her eyes, allowing the dulcet sounds of the sonata she played to seep into her very soul. The preparations for Christmas and her family's presence had so occupied her time of late that she had not practiced for some weeks. The music was a balm to her weary spirit; she did not even practice her scales as she usually did before taking up the piece of music. The sun began to sink in the sky, casting the room into shadows. Those shadows no longer bothered her as they might have. She delighted in the fading light, the altered appearance of the room – all was a sign of the night of rest which the Creator had supplied for His creation.

So engrossed was she in her playing that she failed to notice the darkness descend to the point of completion or to hear the parlor door open, followed by footfalls. Suddenly, reality crashed upon her as she was grabbed roughly from behind and pulled from her perch on the bench, toppling it over as her feet caught. As Violet struggled against her assailant, her hands struck several discordant notes on the pianoforte; their dissonance echoed the fear within her heart.

Violet was being dragged into a forceful embrace and her lips roughly assaulted by a harsh mouth before she realized who was attacking her.

"Mr. Peyton!" she cried, trying to turn her head away from him. "Unhand me this instant!"

His laugh had a desperate edge to it that frightened Violet more than their first encounter on the balcony, all those months ago. He crushed her beneath his mouth again. She struggled, trying in vain to free her wrists from his grasp.

When John released one of her arms and began to let his hand roam over her body, Violet took advantage of her free hand and managed to "land him a facer" as Nathaniel's friend Mr. Merriweather would have termed it. *Thank You, Lord, for what Nathaniel and Mr. Merriweather taught me.*

"You little she-devil!" squawked John as he held his nose, from which a small trickle of blood dripped. He staggered backward and fell into a chair. Violet tugged one of her new lace-trimmed handkerchiefs from her sleeve and passed it to the man who a moment ago had been attacking her.

Smoothing her rumpled gown, she said in a surprisingly steady voice, "Mr. Peyton, I greatly resent that epithet."

"Hmph," he grunted, trying to curb the blood-flow.

"What can you possibly mean," began she, moving toward the door, "by attempting such a thing – again? I am *married* to your brother! Are you so depraved that even this fact has no bearing upon your conscience? Or your actions?" Violet had nearly reached the door and was still cautiously moving toward it, fearful even as she spoke so boldly that John might suddenly recover and – detain her.

"That fact is the very cause of my actions!" he spat, removing the handkerchief from his face. The smear of blood made Violet's stomach turn. "Nathaniel, my parent's favorite. Nathaniel, the first-born and heir. Nathaniel, who has been favored in *everything*!"

"But I know with certainty that your mama loves you dearly," offered Violet, her hand on the doorknob. It was cold and hard within her grasp. "She is greatly grieved by your indiscretions."

"Ah! That is the key. She may love me, but her hatred for my actions is stronger than that love." A flash of pain revealed itself in his face before anger and malice surged once again to hide it. It was the sight of that pain, which put her so strongly in mind of a miserable young boy, which caused Violet to pause in her flight. She drew a steadying breath as she made the decision not to leave just yet.

Violet knew the words on her tongue would not be kind, but must be said, nonetheless. *Besides,* she thought, *I can certainly run out the door and scream if he starts for me.* "I daresay I can find no fault in her for that. A sin is a sin, regardless of the great love one may have for the sinner."

"Am I so very despicable?" he sneered.

"I would not say that." Violet's heart ached for the pain she suspected the scornful question hid. There was a vulnerability in his eyes that she had never seen in any previous encounter with the man. When she continued, her words were spoken haltingly and a bit uncertainly – not due to doubt of their accuracy; rather, she wanted desperately to express herself clearly. "I would, however, say that this is also the way in which God views sin, is it not? He loves all people, but His hatred of sin is such that an unrepentant heart is damned, regardless of His love. He cannot abide sin."

John sat silently, broodingly. Violet felt her heart sink a bit, but tried again nevertheless. "God loves us and calls us to repent. He is the One who gives us all we need – more, even."

These words did elicit a response, albeit an angry, bitter one. "Then why did He not allow *me* to have enough?"

"Not enough?" cried Violet. "You have an excellent, lovely wife, a good estate, a generous living. This is indeed more than many second sons are entitled to, to speak nothing of the countless people of lower classes, who were not born to such privilege as you were. You are *truly* blessed!"

But as she finished the last sentence, John was already speaking. "Ah, but I am still a second son! God could have made me the first! If Nathaniel would have been just as pleased with a smaller living, which I suspect he would have even preferred, why was he not born second?"

Violet felt her patience begin to wear thin. *Indeed, why am I even remaining here in this room, discussing this with him? I ought immediately to go and find Nathaniel and report to him John's shocking behavior.*

Instead of leaving the parlor, she found herself saying, almost reluctantly, against her will, "God owes you no explanation." But once she had started, she was committed. "Indeed, I might ask why Rose was given to marry a man whom she adores whilst I was pressed to marry a stranger? Why does a good, kind family like the Tessels have so very little?" Violet paused, shaking her head. "But what right have we, the creation, to question our Creator?" She scowled at John, her face betraying more disdain and incredulity than she realized. "You are wrong, John, as I am certain you must know. You deserve no good thing – oh, don't fly up into the boughs! – neither do I. Nor do any of us. But God's grace is such that he gives to both the righteous and the unrighteous. And Mr. Peyton, you *know* that you are among the unrighteous."

The man's countenance changed at this. Before flushed with rage, his face now blanched, drained of all color. His eyes, which had previously been scowling, widened now with something akin to fear. His mouth released its tension and dropped slightly open.

His words, uttered quietly and fearfully, rang with the tone of a first prayer in a very long time. "I...I do know that."

"You do?" Violet was a bit baffled at this sudden change; she did not know what she expected, but certainly not this.

"I..." He paused, laying his head against the high back of the chair in which he sat. His eyes were closed, and Violet would have been certain that she saw a tear escape his closed lids had it not been so dim in the room. When he spoke, his voice was low and pained and so transformed that Violet would not have known it was he that spoke had she not seen it with her own eyes. "Did Nathaniel ever tell you about our father's passing?"

Violet felt her heart constrict with a painful jolt of pity and sorrow. "Only recently," she admitted.

"Then you must know that if it had not been for me, our father would still be alive."

Violet's voice shook slightly, but she forced the words, "It was his choice to go after you."

Mr. Peyton chuckled mirthlessly, shaking his head. "I suppose, but he would not have needed to make such a choice had I not attempted such a folly. Not only have I been overcome with greed and malice and anger, but I've the blood of my own father on my hands."

Violet quietly opened the door beside her, then left it – her escape – and moved to the fireplace. After lighting several candles to brighten the room, she came to sit on a chair near his. Closer to the door than his, but still near his. "None of that is unforgivable. Indeed, it is very dreadful, but *all* sin condemns. I myself would be lost were it not for Christ's sacrifice on the cross."

"You? Perhaps the only blameless one in this whole mess."

"Even if I have not erred in relation to – to *this* matter of you and Nathaniel and myself, I am by no means sinless." John's smirk and quirked eyebrow told her that he gave no credence to her words. "I lack trust, I allow others to push me into doing what I do not wish to do, I am fearful a great deal too much of the time. Those sins, while not affecting anyone else as directly or as immediately as those you have mentioned, are still damning." Violet drew in a deep breath, to calm her heart, which was beating with abandon after what she said. *I have never made so pointed a confession in my life,* she admitted. "I am, however, also covered by His blood, marked with His cross. My sins can no longer accuse me."

John was silent for several moments, merely staring into the coal-fire. The smudge of blood beneath his nose had dried, sitting in dark contrast with the pale skin above his upper lip. His hair was disheveled, his clothes rumpled. His face, however, was what caught Violet's particular attention. The hard glint she had heretofore observed in the man's eyes was no longer present. Instead, a depressed hollowness had taken up residence, which seemed to be reflected from the man's very soul. Perhaps it had been there all along.

Violet leaned forward to place her hand on his own. He flinched at her touch, but did not pull away from her. "John," she said in a whisper, "you can have that same covering, that same forgiveness and wiping clean of your sins. Stop resisting the promptings of the Holy Spirit. Allow Him to remake you."

John stared at her for some moments, his eyes hopeful yet fearful. Finally, he spoke in a voice ragged with emotion. "But how?"

Violet stood and said, "Why not start with apologizing to Nathaniel? I am sure that he would be pleased to speak to you about these things."

"Are you trying to dismiss me?" asked John, petulance creeping into his voice.

"Certainly not! To be sure, I am happy to speak with you, but I believe you would begin to feel better were you right with your brother." She smiled gently at him. "Besides, I have no Bible in this room. It would be helpful in discussing all of these things with you."

"Very well. I left Reymes in his study." John offered his arm and they left the room together, in search of Nathaniel.

Nathaniel still could scarcely believe what had happened since John had left his presence. He had thought the matter was settled. John had not been forced to make restitution for what he had taken, but neither could he steal more from the tenants or from the estate, for his channels of doing so had been blocked. He appeared to no longer be a threat.

Then he had attacked Violet.

Nathaniel was tempted sorely to exact some revenge on his brother, or at the least to let his fist fly into the man's face. But more than that, he was astounded by his own blindness. All these months, he had suspected John might retaliate, but never imagined it would be in their home. When he thought that harm could have come to his wife, he felt ill. But here were Violet and John, sitting in his study with him, Violet seeming to be quite well and John, broken.

Violet had entered the room about an hour ago, alone, and informed Nathaniel of her encounter with John. Much more concerned with his soul than her safety, she explained that he seemed to be on the precipice of – what, she was unsure. Her thought was that he was about to either repent or to fall into an abyss of self-loathing. Her hope was for the former. Nathaniel, much as it might chagrin him, hoped for the same.

Will I never be done warring with myself? Nathaniel wanted to welcome his brother's apparent change of heart, but he found it difficult not to believe it a fraudulent change on John's part. On the other hand, never before had the younger man even *acted* remorseful, let alone offered a spoken apology; and before Nathaniel's eyes, John had done both. He had said aloud that he regretted his actions, as well as prayed both aloud and silently, begging God's forgiveness. For all appearances, John was truly repentant. *As I cannot read his heart, I must take him at his word. If he is sincere, it would certainly be pleasant to have a brother again.*

Nathaniel was answering questions of John's with as much honesty as he could, regarding faith and life in Christ when the door opened suddenly and Mr. Garand entered, saying as he did, "Mrs. Frances Peyton is in the parlor. Shall I bring her here?"

Violet spoke up quickly, saying, "No, thank you, Mr. Garand; I will meet her there." To the brothers, she said, "You two may finish your interview; I will entertain Frances until you are through."

Nathaniel watched as she rose and left the room, admiring her feminine form and the manner in which wispy tendrils curled about the nape of her neck. He smiled to himself, but when he looked back to John, the man's face was stricken once again. "Whatever is the matter, John? Only moments ago, it appeared that the very peace of Christ was upon your face."

"It was, Nathaniel. But the thought has just occurred to me – not only have I been a terrible brother to you and Violet, but a dreadful husband to Frances."

Nathaniel did not care to lie and it appeared that John already knew the truth, so he said nothing.

"I am ashamed of myself; I have used her most ill, shamelessly taking what I wanted from her and offering nothing close to the love or care with which I see you treat your wife." John hung his head. "Will she ever be able to forgive me?"

Nathaniel felt the last of his resistance to his brother fade at his question. *I was once at the same place – oh, not in hoping that Violet would ever forgive me. But wanting a loving and mutually beneficial marriage.* "I cannot answer that, John, but I certainly can and will pray for you, for healing in your relationship with her."

"Thank you, Nathaniel."

"You are, of course, most welcome, brother." Nathaniel's voice caught on the last word.

John smiled ruefully at him, then said with a resigned tone, "I will, of course, surrender the entirety of my living until such a time as my debts to you and anyone else can be paid. I fear I have not kept account of what I owe, but I am certain you have, fastidious as you are in your bookkeeping. I shall put myself upon your mercy for the total. My wife has her own allowance, provided generously by her dowry – I suppose her father saw more of my true character at the time than she did – but if you would be so kind, I certainly should appreciate a small amount so as to provide food and shelter." Nathaniel nodded his consent and John continued. "As long as I am making a clean breast of it—" Nathaniel's heart sped up its beatings. "I might as well confess that I had believed you to have convinced our father to add that stipulation to his will."

"What stipulation?" Nathaniel knew of no such thing.

"The continuance of my living was contingent upon my marriage within a year of his death."

For a moment, Reymes was silent with shock. "It was?" he asked stupidly. *I'd no idea our father was such an eccentric.*

"Indeed. I suppose he had hoped it would grant me some much-needed stability." John laughed self-derisively. "But all it managed was to destroy a young woman's innocence. What shall I do about my wife? I could live with my own consequences, but she deserves none of this."

"I do not know." Nathaniel realized that, more than anything else, John was unable to come to terms with the manner in which his indiscretions had harmed his wife. *He may not love her, but at least now he is concerned with her well-being. Even, it seems, above his own.* "John, our situations are not the same, but when Violet and I became engaged, I determined to love her. At first, it was truly only a duty, and my love was no deeper than what anyone might have for a fellow human." John nodded thoughtfully.

Nathaniel continued, striving to explain clearly how he came to love his wife. "It may have never grown beyond that, and I should have made the best of our lives together. We had several similar interests, we enjoyed one another's company. I found that in time, my affections deepened, that my love was growing into what a man would wish to feel for his wife."

"I am glad for you, Nathaniel, but I still do not see what bearing this has on my situation with Frances." John's exasperation was thinly veiled.

I suppose that patience is something he has not had to use much in his manner of living, thought Nathaniel wryly. "As I said, it is not precisely the same, but you can choose to love your wife." John's blank look showed that he did not comprehend what Nathaniel was trying to tell him. "Apologize to her, treat her with kindness and love. She may not be ready to trust you immediately, but in time, with prayer and patience, you may win her yet."

John looked thoughtful for a time, then said, "Well, I shall certainly try my best. And thank you, for your prayers."

With a grin, Nathaniel said, "Of course."

"Frances! How delightful to see you!" said Violet. "I was not expecting you today; I do hope that you will still be available tomorrow to assist me in the hanging of the greenery?"

"Certainly!" said Frances, taking Violet's proffered hands and placing a light kiss on her cheek.

"John is visiting Nathaniel in his study. Are you both able to stay for dinner, do you think? Mrs. Baker told me on my way to you that it would be served at eight, in thirty minutes."

"I suppose that would be fine; I cannot speak for Mr. Peyton, however." A shadow passed over Frances' face, causing Violet's heart to ache for the woman. *She cannot have been content with her marriage up to this point. Indeed, what woman would? Wedlock with an ungodly man... I do not believe that I could have been content or even happy if Nathaniel was anything like John has been up to this point in time.*

"Frances, I must share with you some excellent news!"

"You are to have a child?"

"What? Oh, not that; I still have not found the appropriate time to tell Nathaniel, so do not say anything to him, if you please." Violet smiled shyly before recalling herself and continuing exuberantly. "John has been speaking with Nathaniel and with myself about God and repentance and faith. I believe that his eyes have been opened to see how his behavior poses such a severe danger to his soul."

Violet was prepared for the woman's face to light up like the chandelier in the ballroom while she cried out that nothing could have made her happier. She was not, therefore, prepared for Frances' face to grow cold and hard, her lips to form into a thin, taut line, her nostrils to flare, her eyes to narrow slightly as she stared vacantly at a spot on the wall that Violet could not see. The words which came from her mouth were spoken quietly, deliberately, and made Violet's heart ache even more.

"Well, I declare! He has never tried this tactic previously." When she glanced over and saw Violet's surprised face, her expression softened slightly and she said, "Violet, you must understand, any love I might have felt for the man – and that is questionable, as we knew one another only a week before we were engaged – has long been dead."

"But I was fond of Nathaniel only a week into our marriage; I am be the first to admit that I was terribly shy of him at the outset."

"Oh, but your husband has never ill-used you, disregarding the love you offered." Frances laughed bitterly. "There was a time that I might have been overjoyed to hear that he had repented of his ways. But no more; I cannot believe it."

"Surely you do not think I would lie to you!"

"Oh of course not, dear," Frances said with an odd mix of affection and pity in her voice. "I know *you* would never do me a false turn. But I cannot so easily dismiss what I have learned of Mr. Peyton in almost a year of marriage. These few months have taught me to be skeptical. I cannot trust him."

Violet worried her lower lip for the space of several seconds before asking, "Can you trust God?"

"Trust God?" Frances' voice was cold again, alien to Violet's ears. "Where was He when I was fooled into marrying that cad?" She softened her voice again when she looked at Violet's face. "Oh my dear, pray do not look so very shocked. My husband has never been cruel, but neither has he been loving or even particularly kind. We simply exist together, tolerating one another as best we can. Even you cannot be ignorant that some marriages are not love-matches. Or that they lose love eventually."

Violet saw that Frances was unable to hear of any possible good resulting from her marriage, so she decided to be silent on the matter for the time being. After a moment, she asked, "And I suppose you cannot find any comfort in prayer?"

"Gracious, no! Not at all," said Frances firmly. "I have tried, mind you, but to no avail."

But apparently God did answer, for John has repented. Hasn't he? Yes, I am convinced of it. And it stands to reason that if he has repented, he will also be kinder to his wife. Aloud, she said, "May I pray for you?"

"If you wish to waste your time in performing so ineffectual a ritual, please do not allow me to deter you."

"Ineffectual?" Violet's heart sank a small bit as she began to understand Frances' opinion of God.

"Indeed! Prayers do very well in solemn settings like services at the church, but have no effect whatsoever on daily life." Frances no longer had the harsh set to her face, but her words were spoken with a caustic humor that did not fit their content.

"Oh, Frances," Violet murmured as her heart sank further, "I am so very sorry to hear you say this, but I will pray, nonetheless."

"Yes, well..." Frances studied her fingernails for a moment, and then changed the topic of conversation. Violet decided to forgo dressing for dinner, knowing that while her day-gown was not correct eveningwear, such an intimate dinner party would not look down on her clothing. She and Frances discussed the latest whitework patterns published by Ackermann's and the current trend of shorter sleeves on ballgowns until dinner was announced.

Later that evening, after a delicious meal of ham and partridges and boiled carrots, John and Frances departed for the dower house. Violet retired to the drawing room to check once again that each of the boxes were complete. She had only three left when the door opened and her husband entered the room.

"Good evening, my love." He stooped to place a kiss on her cheek before joining her on the settee.

Violet was seated upon the floor, bent over a box so that she might ensure that her list and the items in the box matched. When she saw that everything which ought to be was in the box, she looked up at her husband and smiled.

"Good evening, Nathaniel. Pray, do forgive my delay in greeting you. I had nearly finished and knew that if I stopped, I should have lost my place and been required to start over again."

"How sorry are you?" asked her husband with a mischievous glint in his eyes.

"Beg your pardon?"

Nathaniel smiled and, shaking his head, lowered his head toward her. Violet allowed only a brief kiss before she scooted away and reached for another box.

"Are you intentionally avoiding me?"

"Gracious, no!" cried Violet. She then asked, "How was your conversation with John?"

He was silent for a moment before answering and when Violet had finished with the box, she looked up into his face. A cloud that she did not understand seemed to dim his features. His eyes stared, unseeing, into the darkness on the other side of the windows. She wanted desperately to ask him whatever was the matter, but with much prayer managed to keep her peace.

"Knowing my own faults gave me much-needed humility when speaking with him. I believe...I hope...that he is turned onto a good path, now."

"I am glad," said Violet before going on to tease him. "Though I cannot for the world think of what faults you might be referencing."

"You know that I take too much responsibility on myself; we have discussed this previously." Violet recalled again the words they exchanged. *Will I never be finished with feeling badly about that?* "Violet, my darling, please never regret what you said. I dearly needed to hear it."

"I do not regret having said it, but having caused you pain." Violet's smile was sincere but tremulous when Nathaniel moved to sit beside her upon the floor and took her hands in his, compelling her to slide closer to him on the floor.

"I know, love, but it truly has been such a great help to me. Your words began to open my eyes to how strong the need for control was in my life." Gently placing a kiss on her mouth, he smiled and said, "I married you in order to control a situation, but it turned out that God was in actuality guiding me, even if I was attempting to avoid just that."

"Is that so?" asked Violet. With a small chuckle, she confessed, "I had no idea what you were asking me at the time. The entire evening was all too much and somehow I did not hear a word of your proposal. I assumed you were asking me to dance."

"Truly? I took you into a private room to ask you to *dance*?"

"I supposed you had apologized for what happened, then asked for my hand in the next set."

Nathaniel threw back his head and laughed heartily. Still chuckling, he drew her into his embrace, rested his forehead against hers and said, "I was asking for your hand, but with a much more permanent intent. Would you have accepted, had you known?"

Violet smiled broadly, wrapped her arms about his neck, and said plainly, "No, I would not have. But I am glad I did." His answering smile drew her attention to his lips, firm and inviting. She stretched her neck and tightened her arms about his neck until her own lips met his briefly.

Nathaniel grinned and moved back toward her for another kiss, but Violet dodged out of his reach and cried, "Nathaniel! I *must* finish these boxes."

Reaching out to gently grasp her arm and draw her back to him, Nathaniel murmured into her ear, "You're feeding me faradiddles, as my dear mama would say!"

"Indeed I am not! Only the Tessel's box remains."

Nathaniel considered her for a moment before finally releasing her. "Very well, Violet. But once we retire, you are mine."

Smiling demurely, Violet attempted to calm her skipping heart and concentrate on her task, ignoring as best she could her husband's steadfast gaze. A quick assessment of the contents of the box revealed several new items that she had not included.

"I daresay Peche has sneaked some sweets into this box, no doubt for the children," she commented. "And Miss Stokes, I imagine, has left these books."

"Is that so?" She glanced up to find his eyes roving over her face, her hair, her neck, evincing the little attention he paid her words.

Suppressing an urge to roll her eyes, Violet smiled and said, "Of course. You must have noticed how enamored with the children the whole household was."

At her words, Nathaniel sat back a bit and arrested her gaze with his. "They'll spoil our own children even more."

Violet hoped he could not read her thoughts. *Ought I tell him now? He would be so happy.* The memory of her sister Rose's sad eyes when last they spoke, and of Frances' bitterness just this evening popped up and refused to be pushed aside, and Violet could not bring herself to voice the words of her joy.

"Why so glum, my love?" Nathaniel had scooted back a bit and was studying her face intently.

Violet thought to deny any feelings besides bliss, but knew that she could not fool her husband. "I cannot help but remember conversations I had with Rose and then with Frances. I fear that they are not so blessed in marriage as we."

"Rose? I thought she was rapturously in love with Mr. Langley."

"As did I, but I fear that she may be awakening to an unpleasant reality in regards to her marriage."

"And that being?"

"I do not know. But there is sadness in her eyes." Violet shook her head.

"I am sorry to hear that. We will pray for her during our devotional time."

"Thank you, Nathaniel."

"And we can pray for John and Frances, as well. I know that it will take time for him to overcome his past actions in his wife's eyes, but John is sincere about the reformation of his life." Nathaniel reached up to tuck a stray tendril of her hair back into its place. "God's Spirit has truly touched his heart."

"Yes, Nathaniel, and I rejoice that it is so. But Frances is very bitter. She harbors no affection or even kind sentiments for your brother."

The gravity of the couple's broken relationship seemed to impress itself upon Nathaniel then. His dark brows drew together as he considered her words. Finally, he spoke slowly. "Then when John said that he did not know how he would be able to make amends with Frances, he spoke the truth." His lips pressed into a thin line for a moment before he spoke again. "We shall, of course, pray that God will heal their relationship."

"Yes, dear. God answered our prayers for John. Praying for Frances and for Rose and Mr. Langley would not be wasted time."

"Your heart is so beautiful, my love."

"My heart?" Violet's bemused expression elicited a smile from her husband.

"Yes. You show such care and love for people. I can see God's love shining out through you."

Violet felt mild discomfort at this praise and attempted to tease her husband back into the less serious mood in which he had been moments before. "What a kind thing to say, Lord Reymes. Now, I find that I am quite fatigued; I believe that I shall retire for the evening."

"So soon? Are you certain that your boxes can wait?" His voice contained the same teasing note as it had previously.

"Oh, but I have finished."

"Have you now?" Nathaniel asked as he stood.

"Indeed."

"In that case, my Lady Reymes, might I escort you to your chamber?" He bowed formally before offering his arm.

After she rose and took his arm, Violet's brows arched and she said, "How can you be so very...so very—"

"Charming?"

"Arrogant."

"Assured."

"Assured? Of what?"

"Assured that I am a man deeply, irrevocably, *unabashedly* in love." He paused, looking at her meaningfully. "And that you, dearest, feel the same."

Violet's features relaxed into an intimate smile. "I know that you are, Nathaniel. And yes, I do."

He leaned toward her, slowly, deliberately. His lips merely a breath from her own, he whispered, "Say it."

"Beg your pardon?"

"Say it." She felt the warmth of his lips, so near her own. "Say that you love me."

"I love you."

His lips feathered over her own, eliciting a lovely feeling of warmth blossoming in her heart and spreading throughout her body. She smiled, unable to hide her happiness.

"On second thought," he said as he scooped her up into his arms, "I have a better idea."

With a soft shriek, Violet cried, "Nathaniel! Put me down! What will the servants think?"

"There are very few about, Violet. It is late."

After a pause in which she considered his words, and also how very lovely it felt to be snuggled into her husband's arms, her own draped loosely about his shoulders, she said, "Oh very well. Please do set me down, though, if carrying me should be too burdensome."

"No, it shall not happen." Nathaniel grinned and started walking. Violet's heart raced, joy and happiness coursing through her veins. They had passed through so very much, both as individuals and together, and Violet knew she could expect more hardship to be a future companion for periods of time. At the present, though, she rejoiced in the lovely knowledge of mutual affection, love, and respect shared with her husband, and in the beautiful grace showered upon them by God.

Epilogue

CHRISTMAS EVE DAY dawned bright and cold. Nathaniel awoke early to the sound of the Yule-log being dragged around to the door through which it would be brought to the large fireplace in the ballroom. Violet, still sleeping soundly, sighed softly as he carefully slid an arm from beneath her head and withdrew from the bed. She stirred, but then rolled over to her other side and continued in sleep. Nathaniel drew the coverlet up over her shoulders with the intention of keeping the chill of the room out of the bedclothes. Standing and shivering for a moment, he enjoyed the sight of his lovely wife, her hair splayed across her pillow and her face peaceful in slumber. He closed the bed curtains with a grin.

After dressing with Griffin's assistance, he retrieved the gift he had procured for her from a locked drawer in the chest within his dressing room. Holding the piece of jewelry delicately, he smiled softly to himself as he gazed at it. Lovely stones, those his mother gave him all those weeks ago, were set in a delicately scrolling silver brooch.

"It is uncanny, is it not?" he mused presently, studying the stones against the bright morning light from the window, looking for all the world like his wife's eyes staring up at him.

"What is uncanny?" came a sleepy voice from the doorway to his dressing room. He turned to see his wife, hair in disarray about her shoulders, eyes drowsy, and mouth smiling.

"I had meant to give this to you tomorrow," said he, "but I suppose now is as good a time as any." He gently took her hand, pressing the brooch into it.

"Nathaniel!" she breathed, face wreathed in smiles. "It is lovely."

"Then in that regard, you and it bear the same likeness," he said, drawing her near.

"Wait!" she cried, backing up abruptly. "I shall return momentarily."

Violet ran from the door, leaving Nathaniel rather perplexed. He smiled when she returned almost immediately, holding something behind her back. "Happy Christmas, Nathaniel."

He received the gift from her hand, the smile freezing on his face upon seeing the tiny framed painting. Or, that is what it appeared to be upon first glance. In the painting itself, there was a background washed softly in, with what appeared to be a blanket and even a small baby rattle on the edge. But the center was empty. *What is it?* Looking to Violet for a clue, her excited smile, tinged with a bit of nervousness about her eyes, told him nothing. When she did not say anything immediately, he raised his brows in question.

After taking a deep breath, Violet stepped close to him and said, "It is a miniature, or rather, it will be once Penny paints it, of our first child."

Nathaniel felt an odd sensation in the pit of his stomach, which he could not identify. The entirety of the room seemed to fall away as he stood staring at his wife. "Violet, do you mean to say—"

He moved to clasp her hands, the small gift held awkwardly between them, in both their hands.

Her words were a whisper. "I believe so. I was uncertain whether to say anything initially, because I did not want you to be disappointed if I am not, or if something were to happen—"

"Why did you change your mind?"

"I realized that you would rather share in the joys and the sorrows, whatever they may be."

"How right you are." Nathaniel drew his arms about Violet, pressing her close to his chest. She felt his heart beating steady and true, her own overflowing with peace and joy. She looked forward to the years to come.

Discussion Questions

1. Class and position in Society were deeply engrained in people living during the Regency Era, as you may have noticed in some of the interactions between characters in the *Violet's Daybreak*. Do you see any of this today? How do you feel about this?

2. Motherhood during the Regency era had great disparity between the classes. Mothers of the peerage and the gentry were often expected to hire nurses, governesses, and tutors to help with rearing their children, while mothers of the lower classes had a great deal of work to do, but also kept their children close to them. Which do you think you would prefer? How is motherhood today similar? Different?

3. What do you think of Violet's relationship with Mary Tessel? Are there any other relationships in the novel that you found interesting?

4. Have you ever faced a time of uncertainty like Violet's, where you couldn't quite see where you were going or why? Are you able to identify any growth that happened as a result?

5. It was out of Nathaniel's character to not help his brother when asked to be his second for the duel. Why do you think he refused? What unintended consequences did you see?

6. Has there ever been a time that a choice of yours had unintended consequences? How did (or do) you deal with that?

7. Nathaniel and Violet at one point discuss the problems of letting regret fester. Have you ever harbored a regret or do you still? Why are these so powerful in our lives?

8. Nathaniel has a moment of clarity when he realizes that he cannot save his brother. Sometimes we make the same mistake he did, in placing too much of the responsibility (or credit) of salvation on ourselves. Do we ever do this with salvation – ours or others'?

9. Do you think that *Violet's Daybreak* was aptly named? Why or why not?

10. Psalm 18:27-28 is part of a prayer expressing faith in God's strength and guidance in the psalmist's life, and ultimately in His salvation. Why do you think it is that imagery using light is so often used in Scripture? What might that mean for your life?

Sarah grew up in Ohio and currently lives in Texas with her husband and their four children. Besides writing, she enjoys volunteering at church, sewing historic clothing, and spending time with her family.

Having written stories almost since picking up her first pencil as a child, Sarah's hope is that her writing will uplift and encourage her readers in their walks of faith.

Sarah enjoys connecting with her readers and would love for you to visit her blog at www.sarahebaughman.blogspot.com.

www.ingramcontent.com/pod-product-compliance
Lightning Source LLC
Chambersburg PA
CBHW051511250626
47156CB00001B/53